From Laughter, to Longing, to Love . . .

"Do you always talk this much?" Tom's chuckle rippled the still, warm air, and he pulled away from Lillie and smiled.

"I do when I'm nervous," she admitted. "When I'm nervous I start chattering like a magpie. I can't seem to help myself. All these words fill up my head, you see, and before I know it they start falling out of my mouth, and I—"

Tom's hearty laugh cut her short. "And are you nervous now?"

"Are you?"

He raised his eyebrows and regarded Lillie with a quizzical look.

"Yes. I suppose I am," he confessed.

There was something about the bewildered look on Tom's face that set Lillie laughing and something about her laughter that brightened Tom's expression. She smiled up at him.

"Perhaps we'd both be a little less nervous if you'd just kiss me and get it over with," she suggested.

Like swimmers testing the waters, their lips touched and parted. Convinced it was neither too hot nor too cold, they met again, and drank deep. . . .

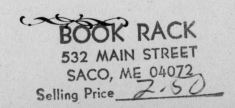

BRIGHT PROMISE

CONNIE DEKA

DIAMOND BOOKS, NEW YORK

This book is a Diamond original edition,
and has never been previously published.

BRIGHT PROMISE

A Diamond Book / published by arrangement with
the author

PRINTING HISTORY
Diamond edition/June 1993

ISBN: 1-55773-901-3

Diamond Books are published by The Berkley Publishing Group,
200 Madison Avenue, New York, NY 10016.
The name "DIAMOND" and its logo
are trademarks belonging to Charter Communications, Inc.

PRINTED IN THE UNITED STATES OF AMERICA

10 9 8 7 6 5 4 3 2 1

For Mary McGuinness,
a good critique partner,
a wonderful writer,
and a great friend.

Without her encouragement and support,
this book would not have been written.

Thanks, Mary!

My special thanks to Tim Simonson of Wellington, Ohio, who has a special gift for making history come alive.

Author's Note

While "baseball" has been treated as one word since the 1930's, it is being treated as two words in this book, in keeping with the early traditions of the game.

BRIGHT PROMISE

Wellington, Ohio
May 1876

THE BOY HAD large brown eyes set in a face so like the hundreds of others Lillie Valentine had photographed in the past five years—pale, wide-eyed, pinched by emotions years older, and wiser and wearier than any child should be expected to endure, much less understand.

Lillie shifted uncomfortably behind her camera, trying to dismiss the potent effects of the child's liquid gaze. It was no use.

Try as she might, she could no more overlook the boy than she could disregard the steady drip of rain that trickled inside her high collar and dribbled down her back.

When she came to Wellington two weeks ago, she had not imagined she'd find the haunting specter of child labor in this small, picture-perfect town. Yet here it was, staring back at her, unmistakably, from the other side of her camera.

Lillie fought to check the shiver that snaked through her at the thought, as chilling and as unexpected as the shower that had sprinkled them all on their way to Greenwood Cemetery.

How many times before had she seen just such a face? A hundred? A thousand? Her workroom walls were lined with the images, constant reminders of life's harsh realities in shades of gray, black, and white.

Even for all its melancholy, this boy's face was remarkable; a face of such classic beauty, it could have been sculpted by a Renaissance master.

The boy's lashes were long and luxurious, his cheeks, high and perfectly formed. His hair was black, like the newly turned ground at his feet, and it struggled against the macassar oil that had been applied with more regard for convention than appearance.

His chin was rigid and squared, so like that of the man at his side. For a moment Lillie shifted her gaze to the thickset, dark man who stood closest to the coffin.

It was obvious the boy got his looks from his mother rather than his father. There was none of Vincent Palusso's sullenness in his son's face, none of the distrust that narrowed the older man's eyes when he shot a look at Lillie. He had hired her at considerable expense, his stern expression seemed to remind her, to record the final minutes of his wife's funeral.

"You take the picture now, yes?" Palusso's voice cut through the stillness.

"Yes. Now." Lillie smiled briefly, apologetically, and motioned to the friends and relatives standing behind the casket to line up so she could get them all into the picture.

Again, she bent to peer through the lens.

The coffin was perfectly centered, the two surviving next of kin placed strategically to one side of it. Holding up her left hand, Lillie motioned to the mourners to remain perfectly still for the exposure.

He was just another little boy, she reminded herself, checking the pose one last time, her gaze traveling to the child in spite of her efforts to stop it. Just another child.

Her own advice did little to brake the stream of remembrance, and Lillie's head filled with thoughts of another little boy. He was taller than Vincent Palusso's son and not nearly as handsome. But his hair was just as dark, his eyes as large, and wide, and brown.

Swallowing the lump of emotion that rose to her throat, Lillie promised herself she'd allow the small comfort of remembrance later, when she was home. There, she could again examine her photographs. There, in private, she could remember.

Lillie scanned the crowd one last time. The effort of anticipation adding to the strain of his mother's funeral was obviously too much for the Palusso boy. Sometime while Lillie had been lost in her own thoughts, his fragile mask of courage had slipped. His chin was quivering. It shook like the leaves of the tulip tree at Lillie's back, and his thin lips trembled.

About to open the shutter, Lillie paused to give the boy time to compose himself. Her moment's hesitation was enough to warn Vincent Palusso that something was wrong. He glanced down at his son. His response to the boy's distress was obviously spontaneous and all the more frightening for it. Palusso's eyes signaled his displeasure; his right arm flexed and tensed, as if to strike a blow.

Behind her camera Lillie bolted upright, strangling on a word of protest.

It must have been her movement that reminded Vincent Palusso where he was. He stopped and pulled his arm back to his side, indicating with a mumbled curse and a quick, venomous look at Lillie that she should get on with her work.

Lillie nodded. If the boy had not been there, she might have been tempted to prolong the ordeal. She'd been known to make more than one difficult customer wait interminably while she fussed and fidgeted with her camera. But she could not make the child suffer any more than he already had. With one last glance at the crowd to make sure everyone's eyes were open, she took her picture.

After the exposure Lillie removed the glass-plate negative from her camera and tucked it neatly into its carrier. She folded the camera and hauled it up over her shoulder, carrying it here as she had been accustomed to carrying it through the crowded streets of Cleveland where she had learned her trade.

By the time she was ready to leave, the crowd had dispersed. Vincent Palusso was already on his way out of the cemetery gates, his son walking, head down, ten paces behind.

Lillie sighed. Her first assignment as Wellington's new town photographer was over. It was not an auspicious beginning.

1

"ANTHONY! YOU GET it. You get the ball, Anthony!"

Tom Reilly raised his voice and waved toward Anthony Palusso. The child was standing in the far corner of right field, watching as the older boys practiced, his expression as wistful as any Tom had ever seen.

The thought brought a brief, unexpected smile to Tom's face. He imagined he'd looked as moony-eyed back in the days when he'd watched the older boys play base ball outside his Boston home.

As quickly as the memory came, he banished it, wondering, briefly, how he could even begin to feel nostalgic about Boston.

"Anthony!" Irritated with himself, Tom yelled for Anthony again and gestured toward the tattered base ball that had rolled into the outfield.

Anthony looked up, his attention finally drawn away from the boys who were practicing their throwing. But before he could respond, Nathan Hatcher had already come up with the ball. Anthony looked over at Tom and shrugged, his gesture a pathetic mixture of disappointment and pessimism. He went back to watching the game of catch.

When Nathan ran the ball back to the pitcher's point, Tom

nodded his grudging thanks. "You could have let him get it, Nate." He rubbed the ball between his palms, the familiar feel of its leather covering somehow reassuring. "The kid's dying to play."

"Aw, he's just an Eye-talian." Nathan waved away Tom's objection. "He don't know nothin' about base ball. He don't even speak English good so he can understand what we're doin'. And even if he did, he's too small to play with us."

"He won't be small for long." Tom glanced over his shoulder to where Anthony stood scuffing the toes of his boots in the grass. At nine years old, Anthony was as scrawny as most little boys. But for all his spareness, his legs were long for a boy his age and his shoulders already showed the promise of filling out, wide and broad like his father's.

"He'll be bigger than you in a year or two, Nate," Tom said. "Bigger than most of the boys. Wouldn't surprise me if he turns into one of the best ball players we've seen in these parts."

"Nah." Nate pulled his cap off his head and fanned a bee away from his face with it. "He ain't never goin' to learn the game. His old man won't let him. He don't even want Anthony comin' down here watchin' us, from what I've heard. Wants him workin' all day up there at the foundry, sweepin' the floors so he can help pay the old man's bar bills."

Tom gave the boy a firm look, but somehow, all the words he knew he should say refused to come. There was no use lecturing Nate for giving voice to what everyone in town knew to be true.

"How is Anthony ever going to learn to play base ball if you older fellows won't give him the chance?" he asked, overlooking Nate's remark and going right to the heart of the matter. "How about calling him over here? We'll toss the ball around, the three of us, and the kid will be thrilled."

"Aw, Mr. Reilly." Nate made one last, plaintive effort, his face screwed into the same painful expression Tom had seen him use when Nate's father, the town blacksmith, asked the boy's help at the forge. "Do I gotta listen to you? It's not like you're our teacher or nothin'. Just our team manager.

Besides, the other boys, they'll tease me for certain if they see me practicin' with some Eye-talian."

Pushing one hand through his dark hair, Tom looked up at the cloudless sky as if searching for patience. He sighed and looked back down at Nate.

"What did you have for dinner last night?"

"Huh? Dinner?" Nate rubbed one dirt-smudged finger under his nose and looked at Tom as if he'd grown two heads.

"Dinner. That's right. What did you have for dinner?"

Nate's eyes narrowed with the effort of concentration. "Ma made taters. I do remember that. And chicken." His eyes flew open and he gave Tom a smile that said he was very pleased, both with the memory and with himself. "Fried chicken. And there was peas from the garden, a'course, and an apple pie later on, but the apples weren't as good as they should'a been seein' it's the end of the storage season and sometimes they get a little mushy and—"

"What do you think Anthony had for dinner last night?"

This question was completely unexpected, and it stopped Nate cold. "How should I know?" He lifted his shoulders in a gesture that clearly said he also did not care.

"I'd venture to guess Anthony didn't have half what you did," Tom said. "Maybe potatoes. Maybe something Anthony was able to snatch from someone else's garden. That's probably all." He pinned Nate with a look he hoped was more eloquent than his words.

"I'm not telling you to be best friends with Anthony. Just remember, he doesn't have the things any of you other boys do. Not much of a home, no friends. He doesn't go to school because he doesn't speak English well, and even if he could, I don't think that son of a—"

Tom stopped just in time and cleared his throat, though he suspected what he was about to say would hardly have brought scandal to fourteen-year-old Nathan Hatcher's ears. The boy had pricked up at the slightest suggestion of hearing a genuine cuss word, and now his face fell.

"I don't think Vincent Palusso would let Anthony go to school," Tom finished pointedly. "You're right about that.

They need every penny Anthony brings in since Vincent was hurt in that foundry accident. And now, since Anthony's mother died—"

"You know what they're saying about that, don't you, Mr. Reilly?" As suddenly as Nate's hopes had been dashed, his face brightened again, beaming with the delectable light of gossip. He lowered his voice and leaned closer. "They're saying he killed her. Vincent Palusso. They're saying he killed his wife by workin' her too hard and beatin' her when he didn't like the way she did things."

"You'd be better off practicing your hitting than standing around in back of your father's outbuildings gossiping." Tom shook his head. "Go on." He nudged Nate toward the outfield. "Go call Anthony over here."

Nate conceded defeat. He turned to trot across the park and stopped in his tracks. Tom followed Nate's dumbfounded gaze. To his surprise, Anthony was no longer standing in right field. He was walking toward the road, side-by-side with a woman.

Tom squinted, trying for a better look. Even with the late afternoon sun shining full on her, he could tell the woman was dark-haired, dark enough to be one of Anthony's Italian relatives. But even from this distance, he knew she was not. If she was, he would have seen her around town. And he was certain he had never seen this woman before.

If he had, he would remember the gentle curve of her hips, swaying slightly beneath her long, dark skirt as she and Anthony left the park and stepped onto Main Street. If he had, he was sure he would recall the smooth movements of her arms in her white blouse as she gestured toward something in the distance, the graceful slope of her neck, the high, bubbling laugh that floated to him on the May breeze.

If he had met her before, he wouldn't be nearly as curious as he was now.

"Nate? Who's that?" Tom thrust his chin in the lady's direction. "Who's that with Anthony Palusso?"

Nate gave the woman one last look, and his face reddened all the way from his chin to the roots of his sandy-colored hair. "Don't you know, Mr. Reilly? Honest? Ain't you heard?"

8

"Heard what?" Anthony and the woman were nearly out of sight, and Tom strained to catch a last glimpse of them.

"That's Lillie Valentine." Nate gave Tom a meaningful wink, trying with all his might to look worldly. "The photographer. You know, the one who inherited old man Graham's business."

"You mean the one who—"

"That's right. That's the one. The one who was the old man's mis—" Nate caught himself. His eyes widened and his voice cracked. "That is his . . . uh . . . his lady friend."

Lady friend? Those weren't the words Tom had heard used to describe Miss Lillie Valentine.

"Hank Graham left his Wellington business to her when he died a month or so ago, didn't he?" As if Nate were reading Tom's mind, he took up with the exact story Tom had heard the night before when he'd stopped into the Morning Star Saloon for a beer and a quick bite of dinner.

"Well, everybody knows what old man Graham was like." Nate's eyebrows rose as he spoke until they were nearly in line with the shock of hair that flopped over his forehead. "He'd come waltzin' in here every four months or so, back from that fancy photography studio of his in Cleveland. And every time he'd have a different woman on his arm. My ma, she says some of 'em even wore paint on their cheeks."

That much of the story was true. Though Tom had lived in Wellington a little less than a year, he'd seen Hank Graham himself a time or two. He was as much a gadabout as any man Tom had ever met, a handsome man of more than sixty years who most times was accompanied by a woman young enough to be his daughter.

The thought sent Tom's temper soaring. It wasn't that he gave a damn what any man did in private. Hank Graham could bed the entire female population of Cleveland for all he cared. What concerned him was that one of Graham's women had taken an interest in Anthony.

"What's she doing with Anthony?"

Tom hadn't realized he'd voiced the question until Nate answered it.

"I seen them together a time or two before." Nate shrugged. "Ever since Anthony's mother died. Criminy! I'd be the one dead for certain if my ma ever saw me with a woman like that. She drinks wine, you know. That Valentine woman. Drinks it right there in her own house when she thinks no one's lookin'."

Tom crossed his arms over his chest. "And how would you know that?"

Nate flushed redder than before. "Promise you won't tell my pa?" He looked up at Tom and apparently found the reassurance he needed in the older man's face. "We went 'round there three nights ago," he said, his expression so eager, it seemed he was about to burst. "Me, and Hiram Wahl, and Ben Stock, and Barney Greer. We waited until after it was dark and we went 'round to her house and we peeked in the parlor window. Only we didn't see much of anything."

Nate's lips curved into a disappointed frown. "Only her sittin' there all by herself, drinkin' a glass of wine. But that's enough to prove what kind of woman she is, ain't it? I mean, what kind of lady would take a drink of alcohol unless it were for medicinal purposes?" Nate's blue eyes glazed with remembrance, and suddenly his face took on a bemused, dreamy look, a look that clearly said his thoughts were on something other than the therapeutic use of spirits. He sighed. "She sure don't look sick."

As appealing as the glimpse of Lillie Valentine had been, Tom found himself not caring how the woman looked. He was more concerned about her intentions toward Anthony than he was about either her looks or her habits. He glanced at Main Street one last time. There was no sign of Anthony or Lillie Valentine.

"Where does she live?"

Nate's lips widened into a grin. "Me and the boys, we figured you'd be askin' about her sooner or later. Only seems fittin', don't it? A woman as pretty as that and—"

"Hell and damnation!" No sooner was the curse out of Tom's mouth than he regretted it. It was one thing for Nate to hear him label Vincent Palusso with the crude appellation he so rightly deserved; another all together to make Nate the brunt of his anger.

Nate had meant no harm, he was certain of that. His prattlings were no more than flights of fancy, wishful thinking common to every fourteen-year-old. It wasn't Nate's fault that Tom was sensitive to any mention of romance.

It wasn't Nate's fault it still hurt.

Tom turned away, momentarily flustered and not about to let Nate know it. He tried to pretend Nate's innocent reference to women and love was nothing more than a minor irritant, but Tom had to admit, the thought hurt like hell.

He shook his head, baffled by the absurdity of it all. He'd thought he'd put all that behind him, thought he'd conquered the feelings of betrayal, the wrenching in his gut that twisted his insides each time he remembered Boston, and base ball, and Rebecca.

He'd thought the pain long gone, packed away with the other disturbing memories. He'd been wrong. Nate's simple statement had ripped open wounds he'd hoped were long healed.

It was not a comforting thought, and it did little to improve Tom's mood.

He clamped his mouth into a hard line and offered Nate a thin-lipped smile by way of apology. "You'd best be glad you said that in front of me rather than your father. He'd have you behind the woodshed if he knew you were making plans for me and Miss Valentine. And I'll come after you with a switch myself if I hear you've been near that woman's house again. Now, where did you say she lived?"

"It is magic, *sì* signorina?" Anthony looked up from his examination of Lillie's camera and grinned, unconcerned that he had just finished his third oatmeal cookie. His smile was a blend of dazzling white teeth and cookie crumbs.

Lillie crossed the garden, a pitcher of lemonade in her hands. "No," she said, returning his smile with one of her own. "It isn't magic." She refilled Anthony's glass. After depositing the pitcher beside a teapot on a nearby table, she sat on the ground next to where the boy was studying her folding camera mounted on its tripod. "It's photography."

Raising herself on her knees, Lillie pointed to the back of the camera. "This is where I put the glass plates. They're very special. I coat them with silver and chemicals." She pointed again, this time to the front of the camera. "And when I open the shutter, here, the light paints a picture on them. White in the places where the light is bright, dark in the places where there is less light."

Anthony nodded solemnly. "*Sì.* Yes. This I understand. But the rest, it is magic, is it not?"

Lillie sat back on her heels and laughed. She was still laughing when she heard the garden gate swing open. Anthony heard the scrape of the bolt, too, and his smile faded. His face paled. Gulping down a small, startled noise, he squared his bony shoulders and turned to face the intruder. A look of utter relief swept over his face.

"Ah, Signóre Tom! *Mólto bène!* This is very good, I—"

"Anthony, go home!"

Lillie was not as surprised by the man's sudden appearance as she was by the vehemence of his words. The voice was not one she recognized. Neither was the man.

Her mouth open in wordless anger, she stared across her garden at the man Anthony had called Tom. He was a tall man, made to look all that much larger from her vantage point in the short-cropped grass. Brown-eyed, his hair nearly as dark as her own, he stood against the white picket fence, his shoulders back, his arms stiff at his sides as if he were holding some powerful emotion in check.

Wherever he had come from, he had come at a run. He breathed in great drafts that caused his shirt to strain against his broad chest, and there was a thin sheen of perspiration on his forehead and another along the firm line of his top lip. He flicked it away with one finger, his gaze traveling from Anthony to Lillie, his eyes sparking with the reflected fire of the setting sun.

They were good eyes, for all their anger, earnest and attractive. There could be as much happiness contained there as there

12

was hostility now, Lillie suspected, though it seemed from the stony set of his face that he did not let the happiness surface as often as he should.

Although it was not fashionable, the man was clean shaven, his face just darkening with evening stubble that accentuated his square jaw and gave him an aloof, almost foreign look. His face was tanned, the tiny network of lines around his eyes reminding Lillie of other men she'd seen and photographed, some of whom worked outdoors, others of whom smiled a great deal.

This man was not smiling.

He shot one quick look at Lillie before he leveled another frown at Anthony.

"I said home, Anthony. Now."

Anthony looked from Tom to Lillie, his eyes filled with tears, his face mirroring his confusion.

"That's all right, Anthony." Struggling to force her words past the painful knot of anger in her throat, Lillie reached for a handful of cookies and tucked them into the boy's pocket. "You go home. It's nearly dinnertime, and I'm sure your father is anxious to see you."

"*Sì.*" Anthony whispered the word. Whether he was trying to convince himself or Lillie, she did not know. He scooped his black cloth cap from the nearest chair and jammed it on his head. Before he could leave, the man stopped him, one hand on Anthony's shoulder.

"We'll talk tomorrow, Anthony."

"*Sì.*" The boy nodded halfheartedly and disappeared through the garden gate.

Lillie bounded to her feet. Her hands instinctively curling into tight fists, she stared at the stranger in disbelief. "Do I know you?"

One corner of the man's lips twisted with annoyance. "You don't know me." He stabbed a finger in her direction. "But I know you. That's all that matters. And I'll tell you right here and now, I don't want you near Anthony again. Not ever."

Lillie took one step forward. "You have no right to tell

that boy who he can and cannot socialize with. You are not Anthony's father."

Tom gave her a withering smile, his voice heavy with sarcasm. "It's seven o'clock. Vincent Palusso's probably asleep on one of the tables down at the Morning Star, drunk as usual. And as long as he's not capable of protecting Anthony—"

"Protecting him?" Lillie's voice rose, echoing back at her from the freshly painted eaves of the house and startling a pair of mourning doves that had been resting there into a frenzied flight around the yard. She paid them no mind when they flapped over her head. Pulling herself up to her full height, she took another few steps toward the bold stranger. "Protecting him from what? Or is it dangerous to give a child lemonade and cookies?"

"Damned woman!" Tom mumbled the curse beneath his breath. He spun away and paced to the end of the garden. "Damned, unreasonable woman!"

He tossed a look over his shoulder toward Lillie.

She was younger than he expected her to be. Perhaps that's what bothered him the most. She was far younger and far more attractive than any of Hank Graham's other women.

She wore her hair pulled away from her face, wound into a thick coil at the nape of her neck. It was a style he had seen other, less impressive women, wear, a style that made most of them look not only dowdy, but downright puritanical. Lillie Valentine looked anything but.

Her severe hairstyle served to emphasize the smooth sweep of her forehead, her small, well-proportioned nose, the clear rose color of her cheeks and lips.

Her chin was still raised in a gesture that showed her defiance as undoubtedly as the small arc of electricity that flared in her hazel eyes. It was a toughness he found as unexpected as her youth, a courage far beyond her years, and Tom wondered, briefly, where any woman learned that sort of boldness. This one would face a den of lions if they stood in the way of something she wanted or believed in. He was certain of that. This one had courage.

The thought did little to dissolve his anger. Boldness was

a fine thing in a woman of character. It was something else altogether in a kept woman, a vice rather than a virtue, a sure sign of self-indulgence.

Again thoughts of Rebecca flickered through Tom's mind, and he cursed himself, concealing his discomfort the only way he knew how, beneath a layer of anger.

"I'd hoped we'd make this quick and civilized." Tom came to stand in front of Lillie, glowering at her from beneath his dark brows, his words clipped and terse. "But if you insist on being stubborn—"

Lillie threw up her hands in mock surrender. "It's difficult to be civilized with a man who isn't civil," she said. "And I can't possibly be stubborn because I don't know what I'm being stubborn about. Perhaps if you'd explain yourself, tell me what it is I'm said to have done—"

"Anthony already has three strikes against him, don't you see that?" Ignoring her protest, Tom hurried on. "He's too strange, too uneducated, too different. This is a small town—people aren't used to outsiders. The Italians who live on the other side of the railroad tracks are looked on as something of a race apart. It's a damned shame when that kind of prejudice hurts boys like Anthony and ruins their chances."

"But I—"

"People are already talking about seeing the two of you together around town. The last thing Anthony needs is the reputation he's bound to get fraternizing with a loose woman."

Tom had not meant to speak so bluntly. He had hoped to phrase things more delicately, explain them more sensibly. The words had slipped. In his anger he had let them slip. He stopped, obviously as surprised by his own candor as Lillie was.

He watched the color drain from her face. Then, instantly, it was back again in a rush of heat that raced up her neck and stained her cheeks as vivid as the setting sun. Her expression hardened and she aimed a devastating look at Tom, sizing up everything from his rough-spun white shirt to his dark work trousers, from the scuffed toes of his boots to the smear of field dirt across his cheek and along one side of his nose.

"And how on earth would you recognize a loose woman if you saw one?"

Tom rose to the challenge in her voice, facing her with a look as crushing as her own. "You don't need to recognize them, only know their background. And when a girl as young and pretty as you inherits a home and business from an old goat like Hank Graham—"

"Don't you ever! Don't you ever talk that way about Hank Graham." Lillie's voice sank to a whisper, and her eyes blazed her resentment. To steady herself, she reached for the nearest object. She laid her hands on her silver teapot, grasping it until her knuckles were white, one hand on the still-warm handle, the other on its shiny lid.

She met Tom's scathing look head-on. "If you want to believe what the town gossips are saying about me, you do that, mister. But don't you ever say anything bad about Hank. He was a better man than most, and if he had faults—"

"His faults are no more a concern to me than yours." Tom strode to the gate and punched it open with one hand. "The only thing I'm concerned about is Anthony. And the only thing I want from you is your promise to stay away from him."

"And the only thing you'll get from me is this." Where the notion came from, Lillie never knew, but somehow the gesture seemed both fitting and justifiable. With one swift movement, she pitched the teapot at Tom's head.

It missed by no more than an inch or two, the dregs of the pot splattering out as the lid came off its hinges.

It was not often she surrendered her self-control. In this case, Lillie decided, it was worth it. The fact that Tom never moved when the pot came whizzing by his head said a great deal about him, both as a man and an adversary, and Lillie made a mental note to remember it.

Aside from that, whatever it cost to repair her favorite teapot was certainly worth the moment of surprise that froze Tom in place, worth his look of absolute astonishment when he eyed her as if she were a madwoman, worth it, especially when he backed away and through the garden gate, and Lillie considered how delightfully difficult it would be for this impertinent and tactless man to get the tea stains out of his shirt.

2

DAMNATION!

Tom tossed his hammer onto his workbench and eyed the small steam-powered engine he'd been working on with distaste.

Wiping the stream of perspiration from his forehead with the sleeve of his shirt, he sat back against the nearest table and shook his head. It was as if the entire day had been cursed from the beginning. First he'd dropped Mrs. Tucker's favorite lamp and shattered it to pieces, then he'd tripped on the loose floorboard in his workroom and banged his knee into the sharp corner of the table, and now this.

At least he could pay to replace the lamp. And his knee would heal. But this engine, this was something else. He'd hoped he could salvage what was left of the old machine and use its guts for another project, but it looked as if that was a pipe dream.

The damned engine was as stubborn as that damned Valentine woman.

Tom caught himself nearly before the thought had fully formed, but it was too late to stop it. Funny how the truth could sneak up on you when you least expected it.

As it had so many times in the last few days, a hazy picture

19

of Lillie Valentine formed in his mind. When he'd barged into her garden last week, he'd been far too angry to notice much more about Lillie than her youth and her stubbornness. Now he found himself wondering again exactly what she looked like.

He had a vague memory of hazel eyes, a dim recollection of lips that were fuller than was fashionable and all the more attractive for it, an indistinct remembrance of lilac scent, starched white frills around her face and throat, and hands that were capable, and work-worn, and strong enough to heave a teapot twenty feet.

Not that it mattered what the woman looked like. Tom shook off the thought. But it would be helpful to recall a little more about her before he had to visit her. It would be comforting to remember a bit more before he had to face her and eat crow.

Tom swore softly to himself and studied the dapple of tea stains on the front of his shirt, stains he had struggled, unsuccessfully, to scrub out. He would wear it when he went to call on her, he decided, like a hair shirt. He would wear it, and say his piece, and put the woman from his thoughts once and for all. And he would do it tonight.

His mind made up, Tom went back to his workbench. There was nothing like the hefty weight of a hammer in his hands to bring his thoughts back to what was practical, nothing like a little good, aggressive pounding to take his mind off the fact that he'd been an utter and complete ass.

The brass bell inside the repair shop door jingled to announce Lillie's presence. It didn't seem to matter. The musical sound of the bell was nearly lost beneath the earsplitting noises of pounding coming from the back room.

Lillie walked as far as the long, freshly scrubbed wooden counter that separated the front of the shop from the back.

"Hello!" She raised her voice, hoping to attract attention, but as long as the pounding continued, the repairman would never know she was here.

A portion of the counter was cut and hinged to serve as a pass-through to the back of the store. Setting her broken teapot down, Lillie lifted the heavy section of oak. She walked behind the counter and passed the shelves of neatly arranged articles; those needing service lined up meticulously, like waiting soldiers, those repaired and ready to be picked up, tied in brown paper and tagged. She stuck her head into the back room.

"Hell—" The word died on her lips, and the sound of the pounding stopped.

Hell.

She had no idea how appropriate a word it was.

With a disgruntled exclamation, Tom tossed down his hammer, grimacing at the sound it made when it banged into the piles of nuts and bolts that had been carefully sorted and stacked on his workbench.

He shook his head, regretting Lillie's bad timing as much as he regretted his own bad luck. Having just convinced himself he would go around to talk to her this evening, he was not prepared to see her in his shop now. But here she was, standing just inside the door of his workroom. And here he was, surprisingly, incredibly, tongue-tied.

He was not usually at a loss for words. He supposed it had something to do with his Irish ancestry. Some called it the gift of blarney. Some called it, bluntly and, he suspected, quite correctly, something else altogether. Whatever it was, right now it was failing him, and Tom felt as mortified as a boy just caught doing something as particularly appalling as filching a pie from where it stood cooling on a widow's windowsill.

Lillie had no such problem. Her hazel eyes clouded with resentment, she aimed a level look at Tom and pointed in the general direction of the front of the store and the sign that hung above the door. "If I'd known you were the Reilly of Reilly's Repair Shop," she said, "I would have gone somewhere else."

"You can't." Now that Tom had found his voice, he realized he didn't have nearly the courage to say the things he should. "You can't," he said again, starting anew and hoping for the best. "There isn't any place else. Ever since Zeke Cash died and I bought his business, I'm the only fix-it man in town."

"Then perhaps I don't really need a fix-it man." Lillie gathered her skirts in one hand and retreated to the front of the shop, snatching her teapot from the counter as she went by and wrapping her arms around it so Tom could not see it. It was bad enough unexpectedly facing the man she'd nearly decapitated with the thing. It was worse still that she had come to him to have it repaired.

"Miss Valentine. Don't leave."

Tom spoke hesitantly as if he could not trust himself to finish, but his words stopped her just as she was about to open the door.

"I was coming by to see you this evening."

This was too preposterous, and Lillie swung around to face him. Tom had followed her through the opening in the counter, and he stood not four paces from her, his hands out in a gesture that was both staying and apologetic.

Now that he had her attention, he seemed at a loss for what to say. He started to speak, the sound of it nothing more than a small noise somewhere between a grunt and a groan. He swallowed hard and started again. "I was coming by to tell you how sorry I am for the way I spoke to you the other day."

Lillie did not answer. Though her mind raced to form a stinging comment to hurl back at him, the words would not come. There was a spark of honesty in Tom's dark eyes, a softening of his lips that told her he was sincere.

He took another step toward her. "I talked to Anthony about you," he explained. "He told me how kind you've been. Of course, I was in too much of a temper to listen." He laughed, but there was not as much good humor in the sound as there was self-contempt. "That's not what made me change my mind. But then I happened to meet Andrew Wallace—"

"My attorney?"

"That's right. He's my lawyer, too. We weren't talking about you," Tom added quickly, as if to excuse the breach of etiquette. "At least, not at first. But then Andrew happened to mention how awful it is that people in town have taken such a dislike to you. I told him it was only natural, and he—"

"He said it was none of your business?"

"No." Tom smiled. It was the first time Lillie had seen the

rigid expression on his face ease up, and she responded to it instinctively. The tightness in her shoulders slackened, her grip on the teapot loosened.

"He would have been justified," Tom continued, watching Lillie relax and taking it as a good sign. "No. Andrew said he didn't figure people knew the real story. They knew Hank Graham and they knew he left you his business. They automatically assumed two things: One, you're no photographer, and two, you were one of Hank's women. Andrew respects your confidentiality, don't worry about that. Though he didn't explain, he did say the relationship was really quite different."

"Quite."

She owed Tom no further explanation, and Lillie found she could not speak the words even if she did.

With a small shake of her shoulders she tried to rid herself of the memories. It didn't work. The picture was indelible, as real as if it had been taken with one of her cameras, etched on glass by a miraculous combination of chemicals and light, printed, and matted, and framed, so that it hung in front of her eyes, even when she did not want to see it there.

It was as hard to forget as the acrid smell of burning chemicals that had stung her nose and seared her lungs. As difficult to dismiss as the sounds of splintered glass that had crunched beneath her feet like old, dried bones. As terrifying as the memory of Hank Graham's charred body and the undeniable, indelible awareness that his death was all her fault.

As it always did, the thought brought tears to her eyes, and Lillie turned from Tom to hide her distress. Walking to the counter, she set down her teapot and rummaged through her handbag for a handkerchief.

"Now if only I could convince the good people of Wellington that I'm worthy of their business." She dabbed at her eyes, fighting to keep her voice as light and level as possible. "So far I haven't done much more than take two sets of mourning pictures, one at Anthony's mother's funeral, the other for a farmer in Blue Goose Corners. I think they hired me because they had no choice. They needed pictures before their loved ones got put into the ground, and even if I'm not a genuine photographer, I am the only one in town." She laughed, a sad, small sound that was more cynical than merry.

"I won't be able to keep Hank's business going much longer if I have to depend on someone's dying to get work. It seems I've been labeled the local outcast."

Tom did not answer, but Lillie did not have to turn around to know that he had come nearer. As if a fog had settled around her, cutting off both her oxygen and her access to the outside world, suddenly the air seemed hot and close, the temperature far too blistering for a beautiful May morning.

"I'm sorry. I'm as guilty as the rest of them." Tom's words, spoken close behind her, ruffled the feathery wisps of hair along her neck, the silky tones of his whisper flowing through and around her, filling the empty places inside her with warmth.

It may have been his words, as soft as a murmur, but Lillie could have sworn she felt actual contact as well, a delicate, nearly imperceptible touch, as if he had grazed the tips of his fingers along the skin at the back of her neck.

She liked to think it was not panic that made her shy away. She told herself, rather, that it was prudence; prudence and the innate ability she had to see trouble coming and run from it as quickly as she could.

Tom Reilly, she suspected, could be trouble.

She didn't need to prove it. She need only remember how appealing his dark eyes looked when he asked her to stay, how soft and round and mellow his New England accent sounded when he told her he was sorry, how easily he could have avoided an apology altogether and how he had apologized all the same.

Tom Reilly could be trouble, indeed, and trouble was the one thing she didn't need any more of.

Shaking off the mesmerizing power of his voice, Lillie crossed the room and stood at the front window, her gaze fastened to the procession of milk carts and delivery wagons outside.

"Thank you for your concern." She glanced at Tom over her shoulder before she returned her attention to the buzz of activity out on Mechanics Street.

Disgusted with himself, Tom ran one hand through his hair and leaned back against the counter, his long legs stuck out in front of him. What had possessed him? How had he had the nerve to approach her so boldly, to speak to her so impertinently, to touch her so intimately?

It was a madness, surely, the kind of insanity his father always warned him could be caused by the lethal combination of a beautiful spring morning and an attractive woman. A madness that had to stop.

And yet he could not help himself. Annoyed or not, Tom could not help but notice the superb silhouette Lillie made against the light streaming in through the front window.

Unlike the last time he had seen her, when she was dressed casually in a skirt and white blouse, today Lillie was dressed for business. Her gown was dark green, cut tight at the waist and close over her bosom, the back not caught up in one of those ridiculous, stylish bustles, but loose, flowing naturally, soft over her hips and back end.

Her hair was styled the same as it had been the last time he saw her, away from her face and in a heavy knot at her neck. Tom imagined she thought it quite a sophisticated look, and he had to admit, the first time he'd seen her, he'd thought the same. But today, with the sun pouring through the window like melted butter, its rays adding coppery highlights to her dark hair, the look was rather more artless than sophisticated, as unaffected and straightforward as the lady herself.

With a whispered curse, Tom pulled his gaze away from Lillie. He spun to the counter and stopped, his attention caught by the broken teapot.

"Is this why you came to see me?" He might be a madman, but his sense of the ludicrous was as keen as ever. Tom held up the pot in one hand, the broken lid in the other, and, laughing, turned to Lillie.

"I thought . . ." Lillie felt a rush of blood in her cheeks and looked away. "I thought . . ." she began again and dared a look at Tom.

His smile was infectious, his laugh, contagious. Before she could stop herself, Lillie was laughing, too.

"I thought I'd have it fixed," she said. "It took rather a nasty whack against a rather hard fence."

"And came close to knocking some sense into the head of someone who sorely needed it." As quickly as it began, the laughter in Tom's eyes stilled, and he caught Lillie's gaze with his own and held it, his eyes telling her his sentiments were serious though his tone was not.

The moment turned into two, then three, each of them unwilling to break the fragile bond of kinship that had been forged by his sincerity and shaped by her forgiveness.

Lillie was the first to look away. She cleared her throat and stared at the tips of her boots while Tom collected himself and set down the teapot. He rocked back on his heels and regarded the woman in front of him with nothing short of open curiosity.

She was as much of a mystery today as she had been one week ago. More so, really. Last week he had decided quite definitely who and what Lillie Valentine was. Today he knew no more about her than that she had been wronged.

He knew better than most exactly how that felt, and Tom shifted uncomfortably, his irritation all the more absolute for the thought. He was as guilty as the rest of the narrow-minded folk of Wellington. Guiltier. He had been the only one bold enough and fool enough to actually confront her with the charges. He was the one who owed her restitution.

A voice inside Tom's head told him what he was about to do was unwise. He wasn't sure why. Three or four years ago it would have seemed the most natural thing in the world. She was a pretty girl, and now that they'd made their peace and she wouldn't be flinging teapots at him, he supposed she could be quite civilized. He was obligated to her for at least this small kindness. What harm could there be in asking her to step out with him?

He cursed himself silently when a picture of Rebecca flashed through his mind. She was a pretty girl, too, and she had done more than break his heart.

Rebecca had betrayed him. Rebecca had abandoned him. She had taken everything he thought was good and whole and real in the world and turned it into a parody of itself, a warped reflection in a mirror where every image mocked him and made a sham of all he believed.

The thought should have made Tom hesitate, and he did, but only for a moment.

"Perhaps the folks in town would come to accept you if they got to know you better." Tom ventured into his invitation, eyeing Lillie for any sign that she would refuse him.

So far so good. At least she was still smiling. Perhaps she did not see what was coming, though Tom feared he was about as subtle as the four o'clock express train from Cleveland.

"Decoration Day is coming up." He dangled the words like bait on the end of a fisherman's hook. "With it being the Centennial year, I expect they're planning quite a celebration. There'll be the usual speechmaking in the morning. But in the evening there's a social. You know, punch and pie and maybe some dancing if we can persuade the cornet band to play. Perhaps if you went. Perhaps if I . . . if I introduced you around, people would come to realize their ideas about you are wrong."

"Perhaps." Lillie had seen the invitation coming for a mile, and she was as nervous about it as Tom apparently was. Grateful to have it over with, she released the breath she'd been holding, her words more relieved than enthusiastic. "Yes. Perhaps that would work." It was not the most gracious acceptance she had ever made, and appalled by her own bad manners, she pulled a face and looked away.

Tom was being kind, nothing more. She calmed herself with the thought, telling herself again that the warmth she'd heard in his voice, the heat she'd felt from his touch, were nothing more than the overworkings of her imagination. Tom was being kind. He was appeasing a guilty conscience, silencing the pesky voices of remorse the only way he knew how, by doing penance. It was rude of her not to accept.

"It's very kind of you." She offered Tom a smile. "If you come collect me around—"

The rest of her sentence was cut off by the jangle of the front bell.

27

The middle-aged gentleman just entering the shop was by far the most elegant person Lillie had seen in the entire time she'd been in Wellington. Most of the town's three thousand or so residents were sturdy, hardworking folk, clean, and honest, and simple. This man was obviously a cut above and not about to let anyone forget it.

His boots shone like mirrors, reflecting the glittering pools of light thrown from the gold pocket watch that hung from a chain on his vest. His suit was perfectly tailored. It fit like a second skin over shoulders that were a bit too bowed, a stomach that was a bit too round, and legs that were too stout, and too short, and too stubby.

Lillie laughed to herself, thinking of the old expression about the pig in the poke. This poke was nothing short of exquisite. The pig, she was afraid, was still very much a pig.

Tom shoved himself away from the counter and gave the newcomer a quick, formal nod. "Good morning, Montgomery. What can I do for you?"

"Just happened to be in the area." The man examined the cuffs of his trousers, checking to see if they'd been soiled out on the dusty street. "I don't usually do this sort of thing myself, you know, but my man dropped a clock off to be repaired a few days ago, and I wondered—"

Montgomery looked up and his eyes lit at the sight of Lillie. With an expansive motion he swept his bowler hat from his head. The gesture wreaked havoc with his thinning, mouse-brown hair, causing it to stand straight up in well-oiled spikes around his fleshy face.

"Good morning, miss." Montgomery made Lillie a showy bow. "I'm sure we have not had the pleasure of meeting." He stepped forward, his hand extended. "Elmore Montgomery, at your service. And you are . . . ?"

"Lillie." She expected his hand to feel like a cold, dead fish, and she was not wrong. "Lillie Valentine."

"Miss Valentine has taken over the photography business here in Wellington." Tom supplied the information, though he suspected Montgomery was hardly listening. His eyes glowing, Montgomery slid his gaze from Lillie's face to her shoes and back again, obviously enjoying the sight.

It was a vulgar display of familiarity, and had it been any other woman, Tom might have been tempted to remind Montgomery of as much. He suspected he didn't need to step in here. Lillie had the situation well under control. She lifted her head a fraction of an inch and pinned Montgomery with a look that made the little man squirm.

Montgomery recovered as graciously as he could and had the good sense to look embarrassed even if he did not feel it. "You must forgive me," he said. "It isn't often we have new people come to town. And it is seldom, if ever, that they are quite so beautiful. Am I right, Reilly?" He tossed a look at Tom, but didn't wait for an answer.

"Not that I know everyone here, mind you." Montgomery gave a small smirk and a disparaging glance toward the front window, as if disassociating himself from the town and its people. "I keep my main residence in Cleveland. We're here for the summer, of course. Mother and I. We're only forty-five miles from the city, but we may as well be five hundred. It's so much quieter here, and the dear girl's nerves are not what they used to be. I—"

"Cleveland?" Lillie's head came up and a spark ignited in her eyes. "Elmore Montgomery of Cleveland? The one who owns Montgomery Woolen Mills?"

Montgomery preened like a rooster. His stocky shoulders came back, his face lit with a grin. "One and the same." He bowed again, his cheeks immensely red. "I am pleased to see you know the name."

"Who doesn't?" Lillie spun away and paced to the other side of the store, casually fingering the repaired and never-claimed household items and farm tools Tom had for sale near the far windows. She prayed her face did not betray either her excitement or her trepidation.

Elmore Montgomery. The Elmore Montgomery.

He either had not recognized Lillie's name or was a far more accomplished actor than he looked to be.

Lillie reminded herself that the latter was just as possible as the former, and far more probable. A man like Montgomery didn't get to be as powerful as he was by being either stupid or careless. No. There was nothing about Elmore Montgomery that could be taken lightly. Not his money, or the influential friends it bought, or his reputation as a monstrous employer who made his fortune on the bent and broken backs of the children who slaved in his woolen mills.

The thought sent a bolt of anger coursing through Lillie, an anger that threatened to give her away. She controlled it carefully, tucking it deep inside with all the other emotions she had learned to hide: the bitter loneliness, the fear, and the fierce, biting hatred, a hatred so tangible she felt she could hold out her hand and touch it. Her hatred was the phantom that dogged her steps and haunted all her dreams, and the only way to exorcise the demon was to face it. To face it and conquer it, and she decided this chance meeting with Elmore Montgomery was the perfect opportunity to begin.

Pasting a smile on her face, Lillie turned and strolled over to where Montgomery and Tom were examining an onyx mantel clock.

"It looks fine." Montgomery approved the repair work with a quick, disinterested wave of one hand, and while Tom went to wrap the clock, he turned his attention back to Lillie.

"So, you're new in town." Montgomery's watery blue eyes lit with renewed interest. "I was just thinking, Miss Valentine, that you might stop by the house this Sunday. Mother and I have tea at four, and I'm positive she would be delighted to meet you." He leaned nearer and lowered his voice, though it was more than evident that Tom could hear every word he was saying.

"She is sorely lacking in refined companionship here, and it grieves her so, but what can I do?" Montgomery raised his shoulders in a gesture of despair. "I know she would be as delighted with your wit and manners as I have been."

Wit and manners. Tom ripped a sheet of brown paper from its roll with far more force than was necessary. A man like Montgomery wouldn't know wit and manners if they snuck up behind him and bit him on the buttocks.

The corner of Tom's mouth twisted with annoyance. The

worst thing was, Lillie seemed to be falling for the hogwash. He heard her now, giggling like a lovestruck farm girl over some comment made to her by her swain.

He had not taken Lillie for the type whose head would be turned by a man of money. The thought irritated Tom more than he cared to admit, and he flipped the wrapped clock over and tugged the string around it with a grunt of disgust.

Why the realization hurt, he wasn't sure. He knew only one thing: Lillie was just like Rebecca.

Driving the thought from his mind at the same time he banished all emotion from his face, Tom wheeled around and pushed the clock toward Montgomery. "That'll be thirty-five cents."

"Thirty-five . . ." Montgomery patted his pockets. He came up empty. "Put it on my bill, will you, Reilly?" He dismissed Tom with a nod and perched his hat back on his head. "Good day, Reilly. Miss Valentine, I shall look forward to seeing you this Sunday. Four o'clock. Don't be late. Mother hates tardiness." With that, Montgomery hoisted his clock into his arms and swept out of the store.

Lillie watched him go, relieved to see the last of him. There was more behind Elmore Montgomery's vacuous smile than friendship. She was as certain of that as she was of her own name.

"I'll get the teapot repaired in a week or two."

Tom's comment snapped Lillie out of her thoughts, and she turned to him, struck by the timbre of his words more than what he said.

The friendliness was gone from his voice and from his face. Tom stood behind the counter, his hands flat against the wood, his arms straight so that his muscles stood out like corded ropes. He stared at Lillie as if she were a stranger.

"That will be fine." Lillie attempted a smile, but it faltered beneath the sudden and unexplained chill in Tom's eyes. "And as far as Decoration Day, I know I'll be busy during the day taking photographs, but if you'd like to stop by for me around six—"

"I don't think I'll be going to the Decoration Day social."

31

Without another word, Tom stalked into the back room.

He left Lillie standing at the counter, her mouth open in wonder, her heart throbbing in perfect, painful rhythm to the pounding that had begun anew in the back room. Not ten minutes ago she would have sworn Tom had invited her to accompany him to the social. Was she losing her mind, or was it just her hearing that was faulty?

Lillie shook her head. She honestly didn't know. She only knew that at first she had accepted Tom's invitation out of a sense of propriety. But if she accepted only to be polite, now that the invitation had been taken away, why did she feel so dreadfully disappointed?

3

"THERE'S NO USE asking again, Jonah." In spite of his best efforts to contain it, Tom's annoyance was more than evident. He slashed one hand through the air, hoping to temper his exasperation by channeling it to his gestures rather than his words. "I've told you a hundred times. I won't play on Wellington's base ball team."

Jonah Hatcher stepped back and rubbed one finger under his nose. He was one of the few men in town taller than Tom, and he looked down at him with an expression remarkably like the one his son, Nathan, used when he wanted a favor. The resemblance was so strong, had they been discussing anything else, Tom would have been tempted to laugh.

But as the conversation had turned from machinery to base ball, Tom's spirits went from merely dismal to downright grim. Laughing was the last thing he felt like doing. It was bad enough he'd been talked into accompanying Jonah and his family to the Decoration Day festivities; worse still that his friend had taken advantage of the situation to bring up a subject he knew to be prohibited.

"It's only a local team, I know," Jonah said. "No glamour in it. But we need a hurler, Tom. Need one bad. Ever since Jimmy Mathews left for the army and—"

"And you've got three thousand people in this township. You can't tell me out of all those folks, there aren't at least a dozen far more talented than me."

"Now, that much isn't true." Jonah either did not recognize the signs of Tom's irritation or he steadfastly refused to acknowledge them. He pressed on, poking one meaty finger at Tom good-naturedly.

"I've watched you practicin' with the boys, and you're as fine a hurler as any I've ever seen. A good striker, too. You can hit the ball a mile. Makes me wonder why you waste your time tinkerin' with those machines of yours. If I had your kind of talent, I'd head straight for Cleveland and try for a job with the Forest Cities. Base ball's a full-time job now for some of those boys. They even pay them real salaries. I hear you can make as much as two thousand dollars a year in cities like Cleveland, and Philadelphia, and Boston."

Boston.

Tom looked away, the thought embittering him more than ever toward the idea of playing ball for the Wellington club nine.

"I'm not the only one who thinks so," Jonah said, luring Tom back into the conversation with the small note of mystery in his voice.

Conceding defeat, Tom sighed and turned to Jonah. The blacksmith was rocked back on his heels, his burly arms crossed over his massive chest. "Just the other day Alex Campbell said as how you'd make a fine ball player."

Automatically, Tom's gaze searched the park for Alex Campbell, the editor of the weekly *Enterprise*. There was no sign of the man, but just the mention of his name sent a tiny prickle of warning through Tom.

"What does Campbell know about base ball?" Tom tried to laugh when he spoke, but even to his own ears, his words sounded too strained, his laugh too forced.

Jonah scratched one hand through his hair. "He knows enough that he's interested in watchin' you when you coach the boys," he said. "And he knows something about the professional teams. Funny thing, he said there was a player for some team out East, Tom Reilly by name. Same as yours."

If Jonah was fishing for information, he was too shrewd a man to be conspicuous and too good a friend to force the issue. He underscored the information with one pointed look, then breezed on with his story as if it were nothing more than idle gossip.

"Said that Tom Reilly was quite a famous athlete before—"

"Before?" Despite his best intentions, Tom barely squeezed the word past the sudden dryness in his throat.

"Before . . ." Jonah rolled the word over his tongue as if it were a good cigar. "Can't remember!" As quickly as the moment of pensiveness came, Jonah dismissed it with a laugh. "Somethin' about a scandal. But you know how my mind is when it comes to things like that. Ask me about a horse I shod six months ago or six years ago, and I'll tell you and tell you true. Ask me about some town rumor and I'm lost. That's the kind of thing best left to women. The missus and her lady friends, they're the ones in charge of keeping up to date on such as that. Just look at 'em now."

Jonah tipped his head in the direction of the park benches situated beneath a bank of flaming torches just across from the town hall.

The night was warm with little breeze, the light steady and true. In the glow of the flames Tom saw that Sarah Hatcher and her friends were deep in conversation with none other than Lillie Valentine.

"She's been seen around town with Elmore Montgomery, you know," Jonah said, following Tom's questioning look and filling in the answers before he could ask. "Had dinner with him at the American House Hotel just this past Tuesday, and tea at his home the Sunday before."

Tom discarded the information with a grunt. "For a man who isn't interested in rumors, you're remarkably well informed."

"Not informed." Jonah waved away the word. "Just interested. As is everyone else around here, from what I've seen. Ever since Elmore Montgomery's been squirin' her around town, the good ladies of Wellington have changed their tune about Miss Lillie Valentine."

Jonah snickered, whether with amusement or disgust, Tom did not know. "All it takes is money. Montgomery's support has given that girl all the respectability she's ever likely to need." He shook his head, watching the circle of chattering ladies. "I wouldn't be surprised if they're not schedulin' their portrait sittings with her right now." Lifting his chin in Lillie's direction, Jonah changed the subject as deftly as if they'd been discussing nothing more unusual than the weather.

"Nice-looking woman, ain't she?" His comment was neither impertinent nor vulgar, but a simple statement of fact.

"Hmph." Tom could think of nothing more intelligent to say. The realization was nearly as annoying as his inexplicable fascination with Lillie.

"You met the lady?" Jonah's expression was as innocent as a babe's, though his eyes gleamed with a spark of mischief.

"Yes."

"Like her?"

"I did." The answer was so automatic, it stunned even Tom. He reconsidered. "I thought I did," he amended the comment. "But when I realized she'd rather be seen with a man like Montgomery, well, I . . . I suppose most women would."

"Think so?" Jonah sucked in his lower lip and chewed on it thoughtfully. "Can't say I know any woman who would, he's such a high and mighty little man. And not very friendly. Course, I don't know many fancy ladies, just the good, honest ones around here. I suppose a lady who comes from a big city such as Cleveland . . ." He let the implications of the remark trail away into the warm night air.

"She don't seem real fancy, does she?" Jonah continued, his gaze again on Lillie. "Works real hard, from what I've seen. Seems to know what she's doing with that camera contraption of hers."

"Seems to me she's latched on to the first money she found." Tom's words were more abrupt than he'd intended, but he did not stop to revise them this time. "Wait until the season really starts and the rest of the wealthy Clevelanders come down to their summer homes. She won't know which way to turn."

Jonah clicked his tongue, his eyes sparkling with delight and the certain knowledge that he had caught Tom in his own lie. "You're mighty emotional for someone who don't like the lady."

"Like her?" Tom snorted. "About as much as I like playing base ball."

"Which brings us back to . . ."

Tom groaned. He was about to say more when a weight flew against the backs of his knees, nearly knocking his legs out from under him. He balanced himself and spun around.

"*Scusi!*" Anthony Palusso lifted himself off the ground from where he'd slid to a stop at Tom's feet. He brushed the dirt and grass from the legs of his trousers. *"Mi dispiace tanto. How you say, I am sorry. I was not looking where I was going."*

No. Tom saw that much was true. Anthony had not been looking where he was going because he was too busy looking back over his shoulder—toward the general direction of the pie tables.

Tom stepped back for a better look at the boy. In his everyday work clothes, Anthony was not nearly as presentable as the other children at tonight's function, children who had been scrubbed and groomed and dressed for the occasion in their finest summer clothes.

Anthony's trousers were rough-brown homespun, worn at the knees and almost too short. His shirt was the same one Tom had seen him wear the day before and the day before that. Two of the white buttons at the front had apparently been lost, and Tom had no doubt Anthony had decided to replace them himself. There were two big, black buttons there now, sewn on with a thread of such hideous green color, Tom wondered who would use it in the first place. But it was neither Anthony's clothing nor the excessively angelic expression on his face that caught Tom's attention. It was the lumpy bulge beneath Anthony's shirt.

Fighting to control a smile, he pinned Anthony with a look.

"Cherry or apple?" Tom asked.

Anthony flushed all the way from his neck to his forehead. For a moment it looked as if he might try to talk himself out of his predicament. He apparently thought better of the plan. *"Ciliège,"* he said, "they are too messy."

"Then it's apple." Tom didn't need to confirm his suspicion further. A heavy syrup was already soaked through the front of Anthony's shirt, marking it with a sticky-looking brown stain. "Apple pie is five cents a piece."

Anthony looked at the ground. *"Sì,* Signóre Tom."

"And I," Tom said, "have a taste for some. Will you come with me?"

Anthony's head flew up, and his eyes widened until they looked as if they'd pop out of his head. "No. No." He shook his head and waved his hands to emphasize his point. "I am not so hungry now. I—"

"My treat." Without waiting to hear any more of Anthony's protests, Tom said his goodbyes to Jonah and, wrapping one arm firmly around the boy's shoulders, led him to where the minister's wife and five daughters were selling pies in front of the Methodist church.

"One piece of cherry pie for me." He dropped a ten-cent piece into the minister's wife's hand and winked at her. "Nothing for my friend, Anthony. He says he's not very hungry this evening."

Though she looked nearly as formidable as her husband, who was known throughout the county for his plain-speaking approach to his flock, Emily Johnson was neither mean-spirited nor lacking in humor. She glanced from the dime in her hand to the front of Anthony's shirt and nodded knowingly.

"One piece of pie," she said. "Coming up."

Suzannah, the oldest of the Johnson daughters, gave Tom his plate and batted her eyelashes. Mary handed him his napkin and blushed. It was either Annabelle or Deborah who gave him his fork—he never could keep them straight—and

Margaret who finally dished up his piece of pie along with an embarrassed giggle. His regards and best wishes given to all the Johnson girls, Tom led Anthony to an empty park bench across the street and sat down to eat his pie.

"You may as well finish yours before it's too mashed to eat." He handed Anthony the napkin and watched as the boy extracted the nearly flat piece of pie from beneath his shirt and wrapped the square of cloth around it. Moving the napkin down as he nibbled, Anthony finished the pie and wiped his mouth on the sleeve of his shirt.

"*Grazie.*" He smiled up at Tom, his mouth gleaming with syrup. "But they would not have caught me, I don't think. You did not have to pay."

The biteful of pie in Tom's mouth soured. He forced himself to finish it, and set the half-eaten pastry on the bench next to him.

"Even if they didn't catch you, you still had to pay for the pie." Tom had not meant to sound quite as righteous as he feared he did, and he cleared his throat and looked away, troubled by the uncomfortable thoughts Anthony's petty theft had aroused. It was difficult to define the concepts of honesty and integrity for a boy like Anthony, who knew only the brutal realities of life. Harder still to explain the importance of honor when you had none of your own.

The thought flashed through Tom's mind like wildfire, blinding him to all but the inescapable pain of remembrance. He pushed it to the back of his mind, hiding it away as he had all this past year, hoping to forget, but knowing he could not.

With a mumbled curse Tom shook off the thought and offered the rest of his pie to Anthony.

The boy did not hesitate. Perfectly pleased with himself, Anthony swung his legs back and forth and wolfed down the pie. When it was gone, he burped loud and long, laughing heartily at his own impoliteness and stopping only when he saw Tom was not laughing, too.

Too lost in his own thoughts to bother with Anthony's decided lack of manners, Tom tilted his head back and studied the dome of stars over their heads. "Honor is important to a man." His voice was no louder than a whisper, and he could imagine his words streaming up into the night sky and scattering there, floating endlessly among the stars, as irrevocable as all he had lost. "A man's honor is like his name. You can't see it, but he wears it every place he goes. It's the way people recognize him. The way they know what kind of man he is."

"Honor?" Even though Anthony pronounced the word with difficulty, Tom could tell from the tone of his voice he knew full well what it meant. He pulled his gaze from the tranquil sky and looked down at Anthony.

"If you steal, you lose your honor," he said. "People will say Anthony Palusso is a wicked boy."

"You know this is not true." Anthony hopped off the park bench, his lower lip thrust out in defiance. "I . . . I do not care what they think. But you, Signóre Tom, you know this is not true. I am a good boy." Anthony swung around and studied the bustle of people in the park across the way.

He must have seen something that pleased him. His dark eyes lit with inspiration and he grabbed Tom's hand and hauled him across Main Street. "I will prove it, yes?" Anthony said. "I will do something special for you, Signóre Tom."

"Charming. Absolutely charming." Elmore Montgomery tipped his hat and eyed Lillie up and down, not unlike she imagined he'd examine a horse he was planning on buying or a bale of uncarded wool that had just been shipped into his mill.

She shifted slightly beneath the open admiration in his eyes and lifted her chin, meeting his fawning look with one that was equally unwavering.

"And how are you this evening, Mr. Montgomery? Mrs. Montgomery?" She offered her compliments to the elderly lady on Elmore Montgomery's arm.

Valencia Montgomery dipped her elegant head in something more like a dismissal than a greeting and turned her attention to the dancers swirling by on the makeshift floor that had been constructed outside the American House Hotel.

His mother's attention occupied, Montgomery took the opportunity to disengage himself from her. He sidled closer to Lillie. "Those photographs we talked about . . ." His gaze slid from Lillie's face to the low-cut bodice of her gown, and his lips spread into an expression that was not quite a smile. "I'm ready to have them taken," he said, shifting his gaze to beam his approval at her. "I'm ready any time you are."

This was no place to show her anger. The thought jolted Lillie back to reality just as she was about to tell Montgomery what he could do with the aforementioned photographs. She curled her fingers tight against her palms and wrapped her thumbs around them, as if at least the pretense of preparing for a fight would help contain the indignation that raced through her like molten lava.

If he saw her set her jaw, if he saw the quick, harsh flash of outrage in her eyes, Montgomery made no indication. "Perhaps you could stop at the house this week," he said, lowering his voice. "Mother needs to be in Cleveland for a rather important appointment, and we will have the place to ourselves. It might be more . . . convenient"—he emphasized the word—"for both of us."

Dear Lord in heaven! What had she gotten herself into?

Lillie squeezed her eyes shut, trying to affect a show of calm she did not feel. When she opened them again, Montgomery was still watching her. She tried to smile, but her lips refused to move into anything more than a stiff grin. She recovered as quickly as she could and forced a silvery laugh.

"Oh, no, Mr. Montgomery." She wagged one finger in reproach. "You will not hide your mother's beauty all that easily. I would not dream of coming until I can photograph both of you."

Lillie raised her voice to attract Valencia Montgomery's attention, insinuating herself on the old woman's presence whether she would have it or not. "Since you will be gone this week, I look forward to seeing you for the photographs next week, Mrs. Montgomery," she said. She smiled at them both, a genuine response to the cold reception she was receiving from Valencia and the look of absolute despondency on Elmore Montgomery's face.

"If you'll excuse me—" Before Lillie could say more, she felt a tug at her skirt.

"Hello, Anthony!" She looked down at Anthony Palusso and smiled. It was all she had time to do. Without a second's warning Anthony grabbed her hand. It wasn't until he thrust it into another hand that she had the chance to look up.

Tom Reilly was standing not two feet from Lillie, looking as stunned as she was.

Anthony patted their hands where they were twined together. "You dance," he ordered, his voice rising above the noises of the crowd, causing heads to turn.

Tom and Lillie blinked at each other in an embarrassed silence. The stillness was punctuated only by the delighted twitters coming from the people around them who had taken an interest in the little drama and had paused in their conversations to watch its denouement.

As if it were a priceless piece of porcelain that had been entrusted to him, or perhaps a hot potato, Tom bobbled Lillie's hand in his own for a few uncomfortable seconds.

"I . . ." They spoke in unison, each of them grappling for the words that would explain away their mortification.

The realization that they were standing in the center of a crowd of curious onlookers struck Lillie and Tom at the same moment. They dropped their hands to their sides, both of them turning stern looks on Anthony.

"If this is what you dragged me across the park for—" Tom glared at Anthony at the same time Lillie admonished him, "Anthony! It's hardly polite to—"

Anthony's voice cut across them both. "You dance." He grabbed Tom's hand again, but Lillie saw what was coming and tucked hers behind her back.

Anthony would not be deterred. He stomped one foot. "You must dance. I promise you I show you what a good boy I am. I show you how I help." He looked from Tom to

Lillie. "I promise Signóre Tom I do him the favor. You must dance. Go."

Wellington was a small town, and like most small towns, there was nothing quite as diverting to its inhabitants as arranging the romantic lives of the unattached men and women who lived there. Tom knew as much, even as he looked around and saw the amused faces of the people who were watching.

He ignored Jonah Hatcher, who was standing at the outer edge of the circle, egging him on with a few hearty words of encouragement. He ignored Nathan, standing at his father's side, so eager to see Tom's response, he looked as if his eyes would pop from his head. He was even ready to ignore Anthony's continued pleading. What he could not ignore was the look on Elmore Montgomery's face.

The little man's neck reddened as if his starched collar was far too tight. The color raced from there to his fleshy cheeks and from his cheeks to his receding hairline. Montgomery's eyes bulged, his lips puckered as if he were not only watching something he found considerably disagreeable, but tasting it as well.

Tom's mouth pulled into a thin-lipped smile, and a rumble of something that was almost laughter vibrated through his chest. He tossed Montgomery a look and turned his attention back to Lillie. "Miss Valentine?" Bowing slightly at the waist, he offered Lillie his arm.

Because she did not know what else to do, Lillie accepted it and let herself be led out onto the dance floor.

The members of the cornet band had been as interested as all the other onlookers and had stopped playing. Now that the matter of the dance was finally settled, they joined in the smattering of applause that welcomed the couple onto the dance floor and launched into the strains of a waltz.

Tom was an accomplished dancer, and Lillie followed his lead, falling into the rhythm easily. Absorbed by the gentle tempo of the dance, she took a few moments to collect herself before she dared a look at Tom.

He was not looking at her at all. His gaze was fastened over her head, his dark eyes on the blur of faces crowding around the dance floor. His jaw was nearly as rigid as the arm he held around her, his expression distant.

After his abrupt dismissal of her in his repair shop last week, Lillie did not know why she expected anything more from him than indifference. Indifference? She turned the word over in her mind, not liking any side of it. She could have accepted his indifference. But this? The emotion she saw just behind the stony mask of detachment Tom wore was something more like dislike. It was unfair, unfair and unexplainable, and it sent Lillie's temper flaming.

She stared at Tom and refused to back down until he was unnerved enough to look at her. "You didn't have to do this."

"Do what?"

"Dance with me. You didn't have to ask me to dance just to save me from embarrassment. I've been humiliated in public before. You should know that. It wouldn't have bothered me."

"I didn't do it for you."

Tom's gaze flickered over her face briefly before it returned to the scene in back of her.

Lillie pressed her lips shut and considered the situation. She could stop dancing, here and now, she told herself. She should stop. There was no use staying out on the floor with anyone as rude as Tom Reilly. But as they swung around and into the pools of light thrown by the windows of the American House Hotel, she saw Anthony watching them. His face was nearly as bright as the hotel windows, lit with an enormous and very satisfied grin. He waved a sticky-looking hand in greeting.

Lillie smiled back, convinced she had discovered the secret behind Tom's invitation to dance. "You're only dancing with me because Anthony asked you to." She didn't expect much more of an answer to this observation than she had gotten from the others, but she ventured into it, anyway. "He probably thought I was bored or lonely, silly little darling. He didn't know—"

"He didn't know you were here with Elmore Montgomery."

Lillie sucked in a sharp breath. "Elmore Montgomery?" She studied Tom's face, looking for some clue to his feelings in the dark eyes that darted her a look as if measuring her reaction to the name.

He was as good at hiding his emotions as any man she'd ever met simply because he had the kind of face and manner most people found too formidable to question. He was a fine-looking man, that much was undeniable, but to someone like Lillie, who had been trained to look for and capture emotions in her camera, Tom's manner was suddenly as transparent as Anthony's. As if the pieces of a particularly difficult jigsaw puzzle were falling into place, Lillie saw the logic of Tom's actions.

"That's why you asked me to dance!" Struck by the absurdity of the situation, Lillie threw her head back and laughed. "You're jealous! You asked me to dance because you thought . . . You thought I . . . You thought Elmore Montgomery and I . . . !"

As quickly as her laughter came, it stilled, and another far more appalling thought entered Lillie's mind. She stiffened, the muscles in her arms and back tightening until she could feel them straining against each other. Her back as straight as a poker, her head high, she looked into Tom's eyes.

"You think I'm cultivating Elmore Montgomery for his social connections. You think I'm using him to further my position in town. To build my business and—"

"Aren't you?" Tom looked at her hard this time, his gaze neither superficial nor transitory, but so intense and insistent it caused her to miss a step in the dance.

It wasn't the tone of his voice that sent her heart pounding inside her ribs and caused her blood to boil. It wasn't the set of his mouth, thin, and hard, and unrelenting. It was the censure in his eyes.

Lillie skidded to a stop and traded him reproachful look for reproachful look. She owed Tom nothing. The thought blazed through her mind at the same time she decided on a course of action. She owed him no excuses, or explanations, or apologies. But she owed herself the chance to be heard. And there was only one way to make Tom Reilly listen.

"Come on." Without waiting for him to agree or disagree, Lillie took Tom by the hand and pulled him off the dance floor and on through the park, ignoring his spluttered protests at the same time she ignored the startled looks on the faces of the people around them.

She dragged him onto Main Street, glaring at him over her shoulder when he dared to slow down. "Come on," she said again. "It's time we had a talk."

4

TOM LET HIMSELF be dragged down Main Street, not because he fancied being led across town by a woman half his size and with twice his daring, but because he was, quite simply, curious.

From the direction they were taking, he could guess they were headed to Lillie's house on Grove Street. But as to why, he was as baffled as he had been when she'd hauled him from the dance floor, as interested in their destination as he was in the mysterious woman who thought nothing of dragging him off in front of hundreds of quizzical spectators.

Lillie's own expression left little room for interpretation. Her head was high, her shoulders rigid. Her mouth, when she turned around to make sure he was keeping up, was pulled into a tight-lipped scowl.

She was angry. Dodging a horse cart out in the street, Tom wondered at his own use of understatement. Lillie was more than angry. She was outraged, the color rising in her cheeks like the heavy, round dots on the ends of stout exclamation marks.

She didn't slow down once, not even to light a lamp when they entered her house. She merely marched on through the

47

darkness, her footsteps muted by the carpets on the floor, her white summer gown shimmering just ahead of Tom until she seemed more incorporeal than substantive, more like a fabrication of mist and moonlight than a real woman.

She must have had eyesight like an owl's.

The thought amused Tom and he nearly chuckled out loud. She may have been able to see in the dark, but he bounced into furniture, tripped over the tasseled ends of rugs, stepped and misstepped. It was as if the darkness and the reckless feeling of letting himself be led into the unknown by the touch of Lillie's hand had robbed him of all sense of spatial relationships as well as his common sense.

They came to an abrupt stop and Lillie released Tom's hand. Because her back was to him, he couldn't quite see what she was doing, but he could well imagine. Tom heard a drawer slide open, and he listened to the distinct sounds of matches ruffling in their box.

Lillie struck a match. A tiny halo of yellow light illuminated her face, and when she glanced at Tom, her eyes glittered like small, round mirrors. Without a word she bent to touch the match to a lamp waiting on the table. She adjusted the wick, the sudden, bright light throwing their shadows against the far wall, where they twined and danced for a few mad seconds.

Tom took the moment to look around. They were standing in front of a closed door in what must have been the back of the house. From what he could see, the kitchen was behind them, the door to the back porch just to their right.

Lillie handed him the lamp, and while Tom held it above her head, she bent and unlocked the door. She pushed it open and, taking the lamp from Tom, waved him into the room.

All the wildness was gone from her expression. She gave him a look as firm as it was level, her breathing steady and even, her cheeks drained of their high color, whether from the peculiar effects of the lighting or the quieting of her own reckless energy, he did not know.

Tom squinted into the darkness beyond the open doorway.

It was impossible to see anything more than a few indistinct shapes in the room, squares of ambiguous color against the ebony shadows behind them.

Lillie poked the lamp farther into the room, not speaking, but making it perfectly clear that she expected him to enter.

A thousand questions crowded into Tom's mind. Why were they here? What did she want him to see? Or do? Or know? One look at Lillie told him all his questions would be answered, but only after he'd entered the room.

Tom stepped over the threshold and waited while Lillie came in behind him and closed the door. She moved into the center of the room and swung to her left, then her right, the lamp held out in front of her.

For a few moments the effects of the light arcing dizzyingly across the walls sent Tom's head into a queer, giddy spin. He reached out one hand, steadying himself against the heavy stillness of the air, and looked around.

Tom peered past Lillie into the deeper shadows over her shoulder. The room was no bigger and no more remarkable than the workroom of his repair shop, he decided. Except for the photographs.

The sweeping lamplight flickered and winked over photographs, hundreds of photographs, all of them edged in dark, unassuming wood frames like the black borders used to accent newspaper death notices.

The lamp still held out at arm's length, Lillie glanced over her shoulder at Tom and breathed a sigh of relief. He had finally seen the pictures. She could tell as much from the dazed, blank look on his face as from the interested spark that had suddenly kindled in his eyes. He had seen the photographs. He would understand.

Tom took a step closer to the wall directly in front of them and studied the pictures there, his gaze wandering along the orderly rows, examining each photograph in turn.

Lillie held her breath. It would take a few more minutes for him to realize what he was looking at.

The understanding came sooner.

With a quick, distinct breath Tom moved back a step, his shoulders automatically straightening, his jaw tightening as if he'd been punched. His dark brows dipped over his eyes.

"They're all children." Tom turned to Lillie, his voice husky. "Photographs of children."

"Yes." Lillie's own response stuck in her throat. With one finger she traced the frame of the photograph nearest to her. The picture showed three girls, none of them older than nine or ten. Their clothes were dirty and ragged, their hair wild around their faces, not as if it had been tousled by the tender hand of a loving parent, but rather as if combs, and bows, and ribbons had simply been forgotten, deemed as pointless as all the other useless trappings of childhood.

Remembering the day only a year earlier that she had taken the photograph, Lillie sighed. Each of the girls was so different, and she was grateful that she had captured their differences, whether by skill or luck, pleased that their characters and temperaments had transferred so naturally from life to glass-plate negative and from negative to paper.

The brown-haired girl on the left seemed far more somber than any child should. The little blonde in the middle looked lost and frightened in front of the camera. The tall, plain girl on the right stared at Lillie, stared at her still through time and space as she had that cloudy afternoon, grim, and defiant, and angry.

"Did you take these?" Tom's question snapped Lillie out of her thoughts, and she turned to him.

"Most of them." She cleared her throat and directed the light toward the wall opposite them where a series of older, more primitive-looking pictures hung. "Hank took those. Hank Graham. He spent some time traveling in West Virginia ten or twelve years ago taking pictures of the workers in coal mines."

"Coal mines? Surely those aren't pictures of children? Children don't work in coal mines." Tom heard the denial in his own voice echo back at him from the picture-lined walls. He didn't need to wait for Lillie's answer. He knew her answer. Knew it from the tight line of her shoulders, the solemn, determined set of her chin, the tiny, nearly undetectable flutter that trembled over her lower lip. She bit back the evidence of her emotion and set her lamp on the nearest table. Then, tipping her head, she directed Tom toward the far wall.

Somehow, even before he crossed the room, Tom knew he was walking into something it would be impossible to walk out of. His feet felt heavy, as if they'd been weighed down with lead, his eyes, though they longed to look away, seemed riveted on the pictures that stared back at him, unwinking, from across the room.

"Breaker boys." Lillie pointed to a picture hanging at her eye level. It showed a group of thirty or so young boys staring at the camera through what seemed a nearly impenetrable gloom. They were clothed in black, their cheeks and hands, from what Tom could see, nearly as dark with soot and grime as their clothing.

"They pick out pieces of slate and other waste from the coal as it rushes past to the washers." Lillie ran one finger gently over the rows of grimy faces. "They sit in this building, called the breaker," she explained, her hand absently outlining the blurred structure in back of the boys. "They sit in there from six in the morning until six at night, every day of the week except Sunday, bent over the coal chutes, picking through the coal."

Tom's gaze followed Lillie's finger as it drifted over the photograph, stopping at each small, dirty face before it moved on to the next.

"Their little fingers get scraped and cut," she said, her voice dropping until Tom had to strain to hear it. "Sometimes . . . sometimes there's a worse accident. Their hands can get mangled and torn by the machinery. They can be dragged into the chute. Dragged in and smothered to death." A small noise of grief bubbled up from Lillie's throat.

"Hank used to tell a story. He told the story of the day he went to one of the mines and asked a boy of eleven or twelve if he knew who God was.

" 'God?' the boy answered. 'No, I don't know God. He

51

doesn't work here. He must work in some other mine.' "

Lillie's hand froze over the lines of small, forlorn faces. She caught her lower lip in her teeth, her eyes still fixed on the photograph, conveying both her absolute horror and her infinite sorrow.

She didn't move when Tom stepped closer, and he wondered if she'd forgotten his presence. Her face was as sad and serene as that of the Madonna in a Pietà, her hand, though it was steady where it rested above the picture, was as white as marble, each bone and vein outlined by the blending of lamplight and shadow.

What possessed him, Tom never knew. He laid his hand over Lillie's, and when she did not flinch or pull away, he tightened his hold and moved her hand from the picture. Closing his fingers over hers, he drew her nearer.

His touch was warm, and so comforting, Lillie did not think to take her hand from his. She looked into Tom's eyes, her own eyes shiny with unshed tears.

"It's frightening. Don't you think?" A single tear spilled from Lillie's eye and rolled down her cheek. She did not move to wipe it away. "Frightening and very sad." She shook her head and her gaze traveled around the room. "It's all very sad."

Tom could think of nothing to say. Lillie was still watching him, still waiting to gauge his reaction to the terrible things she'd told him. He shifted uncomfortably and looked away.

It wasn't that the things Lillie spoke of had put him off. Certainly, he was disturbed. Any right-thinking man would be. It wasn't that he was either naive or blind. It was just that other thoughts had crowded into his mind. Thoughts that had no place here in this little room. Not here. Not now.

Whatever understanding they had achieved in their time together was delicate. Tom reminded himself of the fact over and over. He could not risk shattering it any more than he could risk destroying Lillie's trust.

Dropping her hand, Tom stuffed his own hands deep into his pockets and spun away. He paced to the other side of the room and planted himself there, far enough, he hoped, from the disturbing effects of Lillie's nearness, the maddening sight of her trembling lips, and the nearly overpowering temptation to touch them with his own.

He drove the notion from his mind and struggled to find something, anything, to say that would keep it at bay. He found his salvation, unexpectedly, in a small photograph that sat apart from the others on a low, marble-topped table, a photograph of a dark-haired boy.

The picture was familiar and he lifted it and turned it to the light. It was only then he realized it was a child he did not know.

"I thought—"

"He does look like Anthony, doesn't he?" Lillie took the photograph from Tom's hands and replaced it carefully on the table. "He's my brother, John. He died eight years ago."

Tom looked from the photograph to Lillie. "Is that why you're interested in Anthony?"

She did not deny it. "Yes," she admitted, her voice small but firm. "The first time I saw him at his mother's funeral, he reminded me of Johnny. Then I saw the other resemblance, the resemblance to all these other children." Lillie swept the room with one all-encompassing gesture. "He was one of them, wasn't he?"

"Yes." Tom nodded. "From what I've heard. Anthony and his family came here from Boston about a year ago. When they were back East . . . yes, he worked in some factory, just like these other poor youngsters you've shown me."

"And now?"

"Now? Now Anthony sweeps up at the foundry, but that isn't anything like what you've described. The people around here, they wouldn't let such an awful system exist in Wellington." Again, Tom's gaze swept the room and the hundreds of tiny faces that stared back at him.

"Why does anyone?" he asked. "Why do parents allow their children—"

"Allow?" Lillie's voice rose, and she looked at Tom in wonder. "Is that what you think?" Too agitated to stand still, she turned from him and stalked to the door and back again. She came to stand in front of Tom, her eyes blazing. "Is that what people really think?"

"People think . . ." Words failed him, and Tom looked at her and shrugged. "People think children work because they want to work. Back in Massachusetts, the children who work in the mills are said to have the best of everything. Their parents don't care for them, so the factory owners do. They provide a wholesome work area, steady wages, and some of them even give the children an education."

Lillie laughed, but there was no amusement in the sound. She propped one fist on each of her hips. "Where shall I start, Mr. Reilly? Where shall I start to tell you what a lot of humbug that is? The education? Yes, some of the employers do provide their workers with education. But not until after they've worked their shifts. How many seven-year-olds, do you think, can stay awake long enough to learn their letters and numbers when they've been on their feet for twelve hours? Then there's the steady wages.

"Yes, their wages are steady. They're also abominably low. Do you know why mines, and mills, and factories hire children? Do you, Mr. Reilly? They hire children because they can get them cheap. They hire children because if they hire their fathers, they have to pay them living wages. Instead, they give their factory jobs to the children. The fathers, they grow despondent because they aren't fit to provide for their families. And the children? You can see what happens to the children. These are the lucky ones."

Again, Lillie swept the room with a broad, restless motion. "A considerable number of them die within the first two or three years after they begin work. They die of consumption from spending their days in airless mills without food and sleep. They die of gas poisoning in the steel mills. And the ones that don't die . . ." She blinked away the memory.

"Have you ever heard of phossy jaw, Mr. Reilly? It's a disease the children who work in match factories get. The phosphorus they use to make the match heads is poisonous, you see. It eats away the bones and flesh of their jaws and leaves them hideously deformed. It eats away their bones and it eats away their flesh. It eats away their little lives until . . ." Overcome with emotion, Lillie pressed her hands over her mouth.

Though every instinct warned him to keep his distance, Tom took a step toward Lillie, his hands out to her. She waved him away with a small, convulsive gesture.

"I don't have pictures of the children with phossy jaw," she continued, her voice dropping even further until it was no more than a whisper against the darkness. "They're too self-conscious to have their photographs taken and I . . ." She squeezed her eyes shut as if the action could block the memories. "I just couldn't do it."

Lillie brushed a hand over each of her cheeks, banishing her tears. "So, as to the wholesome work environment you spoke of . . . There's no such thing as a wholesome work environment for children, Mr. Reilly."

It may have been a trick of the light, but Tom swore her face was shining, not with tears now, but with courage. She looked at him, her gaze steady, her eyes flaming with fervor and the certain righteousness of her cause. "I'm going to prove that. I swear I'll prove it, even if it's the only thing of value I do with my life. And do you know who's going to help me, Mr. Reilly?" Unexpectedly, like the sun peeking from behind a bank of thunderheads, a smile lit Lillie's face. "Elmore Montgomery."

"Montgomery?" Tom could not have been more surprised if she'd named the Queen of England. "But doesn't he own—"

"Montgomery Woolen Mills. Yes. Here." She grabbed Tom by the elbow and, twirling him around to face the other wall, pointed to another photograph.

The picture showed two young barefoot boys standing atop a monstrous-looking piece of machinery.

"Bobbin boys." Tom heard his own voice pronounce the words even before he realized he'd spoken them. "I know enough about the mills from living in Massachusetts to know they're the ones who mind the bobbins on the spinning machines. What does that have to do with Montgomery?"

"Take a closer look." Lillie pointed to the background of the picture.

"Montgomery Woolen Mills." Tom read the name emblazoned on the sign in back of the children, understanding beginning to take shape in his mind. "You mean you've actually taken pictures there? That Montgomery employs children?"

"Hundreds of them." Lillie took a deep breath and let it out with a sigh. "About eighteen months ago Montgomery's foreman hired Hank and me to take pictures of the entire work force." Lillie snickered and pointed to the picture of the bobbin boys.

"I'm sure he was thinking of something a little more formal. Rows and rows of docile and obedient employees looking as dedicated and industrious as Montgomery would like them to be. Hank was busy with his portrait work, so I started working on the project. It meant a lot of money to the studio. But after a week I couldn't do it any longer, not when those little faces were looking back at me through my camera. I walked out. But not before I slipped into the factory for the pictures I really wanted."

Lillie spun to Tom, her face alight with new intensity. "I intend to show them," she said. "As soon as I can get someone to listen, as soon as I can get someone to answer the letters I keep writing to the state capital in Columbus. I intend to present them to Governor Hayes, to show him what's really going on behind the closed gates of this nation's factories. I'm going to stop Elmore Montgomery. I'm going to stop him and every other employer who builds his profits on the lives of helpless children."

"And Montgomery . . . ?"

The outrage on Lillie's face cleared and she laughed, the sound of it as pleasant as water purling in a brook. "You still don't see, do you, Mr. Reilly? Do you think women are far too sensible to be devious? Or is it that you think we are far too simple?" She looked at him, her eyes bright, her head tipped to one side so that her dark hair dipped across the exposed skin of her shoulders.

She had no idea how enticing she looked. Tom hoped to

calm the tingling in the pit of his stomach with the thought. Had this been any other woman, he would have sworn on a stack of Bibles that she was trying to seduce him. The radiant eyes, the direct and very unnerving look, the bewitching tilt of her head. They were conspicuous signs, signs he knew enough to read correctly because he had seen them so many times before.

And yet with Lillie . . .

With Lillie things would never be so simple. With a laugh Tom conceded defeat. "I don't believe there is a diplomatic answer to either one of those questions."

"Very wise." Lillie regarded him with a sympathetic look. "That is, I think, the proper answer, and you deserve the truth for giving it. I have ingratiated myself to Elmore Montgomery enough to have him commission me for some family photographs," she explained, the smile fading from her lips but the irony of the situation still very much apparent in her eyes.

"Don't you see how valuable those pictures can be? A photograph of Elmore Montgomery playing croquet in front of his mansion should serve as a nice contrast to the pictures I have of the children toiling in his mill. Elmore Montgomery at tea hanging next to this . . . ?" She pointed to a picture of a solitary child chewing on a crust of bread. "It will help my cause, I think."

Tom watched Lillie's high spirits disappear, as ephemeral as the fire dancing in the lamp, and for a second, he could swear he saw a cloud of worry darken her expression.

He had never been a cautious man. Not for himself. But the brazen assurance that rang in Lillie's voice sounded somehow as much like a death knell as it did courage. Tom looked at her hard. "Do you think there might be some danger?"

"Perhaps." Lillie banished his concern with a shrug. "It is a chance I will have to take," she said, her voice firm. "I owe it to Hank. And I owe to all these children. Besides, I think Elmore Montgomery is too dazzled to see the method behind my madness." She wrinkled her nose. "His interest in me makes me far more nervous than presenting my photographs to the governor."

Lillie may have found the thought of Elmore Montgomery's infatuation amusing. Tom found it repulsive.

"You'd be wise to stay as clear of the man as you can," he advised her. "I don't think Montgomery's as simple as he appears. When are you scheduled to take the pictures?"

"Next week." Lillie laughed again. "It was supposed to be this week, but Mrs. Montgomery will be in Cleveland. I've been called rash and I've been called foolhardy, but I've never been called stupid. I'll wait for her to come home before I go anywhere near that house."

"And I'll wait until you do to go see that chain pump Montgomery wants me to have a look at."

Lillie's expression went blank for the briefest of seconds. As understanding dawned, her face lit with an appreciative grin. "You mean—"

"I mean Montgomery wants me to repair some things around the house. If you let me know when you'll be there, I'll be sure to stop by on the same day." Tom smiled, his eyes lighting with a certain boyish playfulness Lillie had not seen in them before. "My presence and your determination," he said, "should be enough to keep Elmore Montgomery at a safe distance."

It wasn't relief she felt sweep through her. Lillie answered Tom's smile with one of her own, all the while trying to sort through the curious jumble of sensations that filled her insides. This was surely not relief. Relief, she suspected, was more of a catharsis, a release of emotions.

This was something else altogether, not a release, but rather a buildup, a swell of warmth that began somewhere below her heart and spread through her limbs like warm honey.

Letting the emotions out would be something akin to a dam breaking. Lillie was not prepared for the resulting flood.

Her hands clutched at her waist, her fingers twisting over themselves, she stared at Tom, searching for the words that would convey her gratitude and still be neutral enough not to betray her feelings. She settled for the only thing that came to mind.

"Thank you."

"No. Don't." Tom put up one hand as if to catch her words. He closed his fingers over them. "I owe you an apology. Again." One corner of his mouth pulled into a lopsided smile. "And you . . ." With the same hand he had used to intercept her words, he stroked his knuckles down Lillie's cheek. He opened his hand before he reached her chin, giving her thanks back to her. "You don't owe me a thing."

It wasn't his touch that sent Lillie's heart thumping so wildly she swore Tom could hear it. His touch was as airy and delicate as a spring breeze whispering through blossom-laden trees. It was rather the look on his face that set her soul aflame. There was tenderness in his eyes, eyes that were warm and reassuring, eyes that reflected the skittering flame of the lamp.

It may have been the flame. It may have been their talk of Elmore Montgomery and his mill. Whatever it was, it caused a picture of Hank to form, unbidden, in Lillie's mind, and a snake of foreboding to slither up her spine.

Hoping to disguise her uneasiness, she stepped back out of Tom's reach and took the lamp from the table.

Tom had said it himself. She owed him nothing. Lillie studied her own distorted reflection in the globe of the lamp and repeated the thought over like a litany, the same thought that had presented itself as they whirled across the dance floor.

It did not help. What Tom could not possibly understand was how much she owed him. She owed him the favor of keeping her distance. She owed him the courtesy of making sure he stayed as far as possible out of her entanglement with Elmore Montgomery. She owed him the kindness of her indifference.

It was not what she wanted; not the counsel whispered by her heart, nor the unmistakable and very disturbing advice offered by her body.

Lillie drew in a breath to steady herself, suddenly more

aware than ever of Tom's physical presence: the width of his shoulders, the strength inherent in the muscles of his arms, the rich appeal of his lips, and his eyes, and the touch that had shattered her self-control.

It was not what she wanted, she told herself again and again. But it was the wise, the safe, thing to do.

Lifting the lamp and struggling to hold it steady though her hands shook with the effort of control, Lillie turned and walked to the door. Without another word she opened the door, her palm damp against the crystal knob, and led Tom through the house and to the front door.

"I'll look forward to seeing you next week, then." She chanced a look at Tom, hoping her forced courtesy was not nearly as transparent as she feared it might be.

If he noticed her reluctance, Tom did not show it. He smiled down at her, his eyes filled with warmth and affection. "Next week." Nodding, he turned and walked out the door.

On the front porch Tom took a deep breath of night air. Odd, now that he was outside with the stars winking down at him and the moon rising over the fields at the side of the house, he felt far more confined than he had inside the little room with Lillie.

It was a foolish notion. Tom knew it even as he began his walk home. It was foolish to think their time together had been anything more than a brief interlude, the type of fleeting encounter that happens only once or twice in a lifetime when some magic takes hold and acquaintances become friends, and friends become confidants. It was foolish to think the friendship might last into the light of day, as foolish as the song Tom found he was whistling.

He turned onto Main Street, his hands poked into his pockets.

It was foolish to entertain wild fancies, unwise to pretend what he had no right to imagine. Still, he could not stop himself from thinking, and there was only one thought in his mind.

He had felt the realization creeping up on him even while Lillie told her stories of the sad, laboring children. He had seen it in the sparkle of her eyes, heard it in the commitment that rang in her voice as true and sure as any bell. But it wasn't until now that Tom's vague notions formed themselves into words, their sounds reverberating through his mind, as invigorating as the cool night breeze that pushed against his back, nudging him home.

Lillie was not like Rebecca.

Lillie was nothing like Rebecca.

5

THE DOOR OF the Morning Star Saloon snapped open, sending
a stab of light streaming into the darkened street outside.

Tom tensed, his senses on the alert. From his vantage point
across the street in the shadowy entrance to the barber shop,
he watched a dark shape fill the doorway of the saloon. The
figure pitched to the right, settled itself, and emerged onto the
beaten pathway that served the town as a sidewalk.

His hands curling into fists, his eyes fixed, Tom stepped
forward. The moon was only a half toward full, the clouds
that scurried by it nearly obscuring what little light it gave.
A gust of wind sent them scattering, and the feeble light told
Tom all he needed to know. This was not the man he was
waiting for.

Tom stepped back into the doorway and hunched his shoulders against another sharp burst of wind, wind with the smell
of rain on the end of it. It rattled the canvas awning rolled and
stored over his head and sent the beaten dust of Mechanics
Street spinning in small whirlblasts that stung his eyes and
tasted dry, like ashes in his mouth.

Wiping the grime from his lips with one finger, Tom thought
of how different tonight was from last night, when he'd walked
home from Lillie's, a song on his lips.

Lillie. Tom smiled to himself. Now, there was a thought that was sure to warm even the most blustery night.

Lillie Valentine with her soft, husky voice. Lillie Valentine, with her hair pulled away from a face as unforgettable as it was exquisite. Lillie Valentine, with her hand in his, her skin as warm as the look in her eyes.

Another blast of wind interrupted Tom's musings. He firmly set aside thoughts of Lillie, reminding himself that the task at hand tonight required all his concentration. Later, when he was alone, he would permit himself the luxury of thinking of her. For now, there were more pressing issues at hand.

A raindrop landed on Tom's cheek, and he turned up his collar and wondered if it wouldn't be easier and far less uncomfortable just to walk into the Morning Star and see who was inside.

He chuckled at his own simplicity, dismissing the idea as soon as it had formed.

It would hardly be unusual for him to be seen at the Morning Star. He'd spent enough evenings sidled up to the comfortable bar, shooting the breeze with J. S. DeWolf and his friendly, efficient crew of workers.

But it would seem odd if they saw him talking to Vincent Palusso.

Just thinking about Palusso caused a stream of white-hot anger to rise in Tom. He worked his thumbs over his knuckles as if the gesture could help contain his outrage and reminded himself, not for the first time in the past year, that a rash act would do more to hurt than help his cause.

Bursting into the Morning Star would definitely be rash, Tom told himself. The last thing Palusso needed was the kind of audience he was sure to get if Tom confronted him in public. No, that kind of showdown would serve no purpose, and it would give Palusso a hell of a good reason to be uncooperative.

And what would it do to Tom?

Tom caught himself just as the question came into his mind. He twitched his shoulders to banish it, but the thought refused to be expelled so easily. It lodged there in his brain, inescapable and pestering.

Without the proof he needed to back up his claims, a public confrontation would hurt Tom far more than it could ever hurt Vincent Palusso. It would expose Tom's past here in a town where he had taken great pains to keep it a secret. It would open him up to questions he would rather not answer, feed the fires of suspicion and gossip he feared had already been started by Alex Campbell's inquiries.

Tom thought back to all Jonah Hatcher had told him about Campbell and the questions the young *Enterprise* reporter had asked. It wasn't that Tom begrudged Campbell his inquisitiveness. The man had to make a living.

Tom felt an odd, unfamiliar emotion rise in his throat. He cleared it away with an abrupt cough, as disturbed by the sensation as he was by the unexpected insight that seemed to build along with it.

It was just that he liked it here, dammit. There, he admitted it to himself. He liked it here in Wellington. But if Campbell kept asking questions, he was sure to get to the bottom of things sooner or later.

And if he did?

If Campbell found the answers he was looking for, Tom would be forced to leave Wellington, to pull up stakes and say goodbye to the town and the people who had come to mean so much to him in the past year.

This time the emotion that crowded Tom's throat and strangled his breathing was easier to identify. It tasted like disappointment and had all the bite of regret.

Tom would have to leave here just as he had left Boston, dishonored and disgraced.

He had only one choice. He had to get to Vincent Palusso before Alex Campbell did. He had to get Palusso to admit the truth.

It wasn't the shape of the figure emerging from the Morning Star that alerted Tom to the man's identity; it was the song he was humming.

Strains of a well-known Italian tavern song floated to Tom

on the night air, the off-key tune hummed in annoying counter-time to the splatter song of raindrops.

His shoulders stiff from the long wait, Tom stood and stretched. He watched Vincent Palusso step out onto the street and waited until he was a good twenty paces ahead before he started his pursuit.

Up Mechanics Street, across Railroad Street and through the train yard, Tom followed undetected. Though his footsteps were muffled by the damp ground, he suspected Palusso would not have noticed his presence even it if had not been raining.

His coat slung over his shoulder, his steps unsteady, Vincent Palusso seemed no more concerned about being trailed than he was about the time of night and the growing volume of his song.

The night watchman on duty outside the passenger depot at the station hardly seemed to think the sight unusual. He waved to Palusso and continued on his rounds. Tom pulled back into the shadows, waiting while the man passed.

Once they were outside the perimeter of the station grounds, Tom quickened his pace. By the time Palusso turned onto Union Street, Tom was right behind him.

He stopped in the shadow of Disciples Church and, planting his feet, raised his voice. "Palusso!"

Palusso might be drunk, but there was nothing wrong with his reflexes. His muscles tensed and he spun around, his shoulders pulled back, his eyes dark slits of distrust.

He darted a look back and forth among the murky shadows that lined the street. "Who is it?" Palusso leaned forward, straining to see beyond the obstacles of darkness and rain. "Who is calling me?"

Tom took a deep breath and let it out slowly, steadying himself. He stepped from the shadows. "It's me. Tom Reilly. I need to talk to you."

Palusso made a rude noise. "Talk? We have nothing to say to each other." Without another word he turned and resumed his walk toward home.

"Yes. We do." Tom took another few steps, closing the gap between them, leaving only enough space to ensure his own safety and guarantee Palusso a measure of comfort.

"Crazy American!" Palusso must have felt Tom at his back. Turning, he spat on the ground.

It was more of a reaction than Tom had hoped for, and he jumped at his chance, launching into his story quickly, while he still had Palusso's undivided attention. "I want to talk to you. About last summer. You remember. You came to see me at the ballyard. It was right before the Red Stockings were to play St. Louis."

Palusso did not respond. Tom watched him shake the rain from his shoulders. From the tilt of his head, Tom knew he was still listening.

"I can refresh your memory if it isn't clear. There were four of you who came to call. Tough lot. You said you had a message. A message from Gino Lenardi."

As soon as the words were out of his mouth, Tom cursed himself. He should have left this confrontation for day. He knew that now. He should have challenged Palusso in the daylight when he could have seen his expression. Instead, now all he saw was a shifting of the shadows around the other man's face. Palusso may have been shocked. He may have just been smiling. Whatever his reaction, he did not let on with his voice. It was as smooth as a pond in winter, and just as icy.

"Lenardi!" Palusso laughed, the sound of it cutting through the rain. "You're crazier than I thought. Lenardi is a big, important man. Everyone knows that. Why would you think I—"

"I know you worked for him." Tom took another step closer, his gaze trained on Palusso's face, searching through the shadows to meet his eyes and hold contact. "I know you placed all his bets. Horse racing, boxing, base ball. You can't think I've forgotten that you wanted me to hippodrome that game against St. Louis."

"Hippodrome!" Palusso wrapped his accent around the word and spit it back at Tom. "A funny American word for something so simple, yes?" He made a noise deep in his throat, a sound halfway between a cough and a laugh. "All right. What's the difference? Yes, I came to you. I asked you to do a small favor for Don Lenardi. But you, you fool, you would not listen to what I said. You were too good. You were the great Tom Reilly and you were too proud to—how do you say it?—to dump a game, to lose a game on purpose. Too honest to hippodrome. Too good to use your brain and make some money for yourself and for Don Lenardi."

"Yes." It wasn't the admission that tasted sour in Tom's mouth. He would have given Palusso the same answer today as he had given him then. It was the memory of all that came after that sent his heart into his throat. He schooled his rising anger and spoke, his words forced between clenched teeth. "Until you brought Danny into the picture."

Drunk or not, Palusso was as wary as a wild animal. He dropped his jacket on the muddy ground and kicked it out of the way. Pivoting around to keep as much distance as possible between himself and Tom, he circled to his right and stopped, his shoulders back and level, his lip curled with distaste. He spoke in Italian, the words unintelligible but his meaning all too clear.

Tom accepted the insult in silence. He swept a wet strand of hair from his forehead, struggling to keep his voice as unemotional as possible. "I followed you here to Wellington, Palusso. You know that, too. You've been going out of your way to avoid me all this past year. It's not that easy. I followed you and I'll continue to follow you. Until I get at the truth."

"This is why you come after me in the dark like a wolf hunting its dinner? Because you want the truth?" Palusso snorted his disbelief. "You don't need it. You already know the truth, Reilly. You know it, and you won't listen because you know what happened to Danny, it is your fault. You know it is your fault your brother is dead."

He had expected the accusation. He would have been surprised if Palusso had not voiced it. Still, nothing prepared Tom for the potent fire of the words. They slammed into him along with an avalanche of emotions that tore through his gut like claws of flame, ripping away the last vestiges of his carefully guarded self-control.

His hands tensed and clenched, his thumbs working over

his fingers, the rub of callused skin against hardened knuckles somehow both raising his confidence and feeding his courage. He stopped himself just as he was about to charge Palusso, fighting to regain some control before the Italian could see his weakness and take advantage of it.

"I traded my life for Danny's." Tom heard his own voice fall flat against the wall of rain surrounding them. "When you came to me and asked me to throw the game, I laughed at you. I ordered you away. But you came back and you told me that Danny owed Gino Lenardi a great deal of money. And if I didn't hippodrome the game, Danny would be killed. I traded away my honor and my reputation to buy Danny's life. I lost that game on purpose. And you—"

"No, no, no." Palusso raised both hands, palms out, as if warding off the ramifications of Tom's indictment. "You speak too quickly, signóre. You accuse too readily. Lenardi, he killed your brother. That is why I am here where he cannot find me. I do not wish to be involved any longer. Your brother was my *amico*." Palusso brought one hand to his heart. "My friend. I see what happen to him. And I vow this is not the kind of life I want for myself, for my family. I bring them here so they can live better. I come here to work with my cousin on the dairy farm. But he . . ." Palusso looked away and mumbled a particularly foul curse.

"After I am here, he decides he does not need Vincent's help." Palusso sighed. "He sends me away and I must work in the foundry. And there I am injured." With his right hand, he kneaded his left shoulder.

"I cannot provide for my family. My wife, she dies from the heartbreak. And my son, he must work to bring in money." Palusso shook his head, the action sending a shower of raindrops from his black, shaggy hair. "I have caused trouble for your family and mine, signóre. I am sorry for it. But I swear to God above, I did not have anything to do with your brother's death."

The die was cast. Whether he knew it or not, Palusso had decided on the game and named his stakes the minute he pretended to be but another victim of Don Lenardi's vicious crime machine. It was enough. At least Tom knew the game now. He had no choice but to play.

Forcing himself to relax, he closed the space between himself and Vincent Palusso in three quick strides and stuck out his right hand. "I believe you," he said.

It may have been his imagination, but Tom swore he heard Palusso let go the breath he'd been holding. The hand he clasped to Tom's was wet, whether with the perspiration or relief or guilt, Tom did not know.

"*Bène!*" Palusso smiled, his teeth showing white in the dark shadows. "Then all is well. All is settled between us. I will leave you now. *Buòna nòtte,* signóre. Good night."

Tom waited while Palusso bent to retrieve his coat. He slung it over his shoulder without another look at Tom and resumed his walk home, his stride long and loose like that of a man who had been relieved of a great burden.

Hoping to catch him off guard, Tom settled back and watched him go. He waited until Palusso was at least ten feet away before he cleared his throat.

The Italian did not stop.

"I do believe you had nothing to do with Danny's murder," Tom said, his voice raised, carrying on the night air so Palusso could not fail to hear and understand. "You see, I don't think Danny's dead."

He expected no reaction and he got none. After a pause so brief Tom thought it might have been nothing more than a trick of light and shadow, Palusso continued on his way. A second later, he started humming again. His song followed him down Union Street and around the corner onto Johns.

Tom allowed himself to relax the muscles in his shoulders and neck. Gulping a breath of night air, he rocked back on his heels and stared into the darkness that had closed over Vincent Palusso like a shroud.

There. He had done it. Tom congratulated himself on his boldness at the same time he wondered how foolish he'd been.

He had set the wheels in motion. Nothing could stop them now. He had either found the perfect scheme for flushing Danny out, or he had opened himself up to unspeakable danger.

6

"COMING!"

Fighting to control the oath that nearly erupted from her lips, Lillie struggled to her feet and brushed her hands against the skirt of her gown. She rolled her eyes and sighed. The last thing she needed on the day she'd decided to clean the attic was a visitor. Now here was her second caller of the day. And from the sound of the determined knocking coming from her front door, this one was getting impatient.

She swept across the attic, her skirts trailing through the dust, sending up clouds of powdery dirt that clung to her clothes and hair. Fanning away the airborne particles with one hand, Lillie stopped at the top of the stairs long enough to look out the front window. There was little she could see beyond the slanted roof of the front porch and the trees surrounding it. She leaned through the open window. "Coming," she called again, and hoisting her skirts, she hurried down the steps.

At the bottom of the stairs she pulled to a stop. There was a gilt-edged mirror hanging just to the left of the front door, and she peered into it. The sight was very much worse than she feared.

Her hair was covered with a layer of cobwebs that made her look as gray as an old woman. Her face was streaked with grime. The dust mingled with the sweat on her forehead and trickled down her face along with it, outlining her jaw with coal-black stripes.

Lillie swiped at the cobwebs, but the gesture did little more than unsettle them. Instead of sitting evenly over her hair like a frothy net, they floated into clumps around her ears. One of them dipped over her forehead and she pursed her lips and blew it away, not caring so much where it landed as she did about keeping it out of her eyes.

About to open the door, Lillie realized she'd unbuttoned the high collar of her gown when the heat in the attic had become stifling this afternoon. Relieved she'd remembered before she greeted her visitor, she pushed the tiny horn buttons into their holes and brushed a streak of dust from her shoulder.

It would have to do.

After a final check in the mirror and a rueful shake of her head, Lillie pulled open the front door.

She was not sure whom she had expected. A neighbor, perhaps, coming to call with the latest town gossip. A customer, here to schedule a portrait sitting. A door-to-door salesman peddling his wares. Whatever she had expected, whoever she had thought to see, it was not Tom Reilly.

She caught her breath, momentarily taken aback, and stared, dumbfounded, into Tom's dark eyes.

He could hardly have been surprised to see her. He was the one who had come to call. He was the one who had pounded on her door, rousing her from her work. Still, Tom looked nearly as abashed as Lillie knew she must.

His mouth opened and closed; his gaze traveled from Lillie's dirt-smudged face to the top of her head. From there he let it wander down, taking in everything from the streak of dirt across the bodice of her gown to the border of grime that hemmed her skirt.

Lillie shifted from foot to foot, not as bothered by her disheveled appearance as she was by the precise way Tom's gaze touched each piece of dusty clothing, each inch of exposed, and very dirty, skin.

It wasn't as much surprise that snatched her words as it was embarrassment. Lillie traded uncomfortable looks with Tom, neither of them able to speak.

Suddenly aware of the uneasy silence, Tom cleared his throat. All the way from his house on the other side of town, he had been practicing what he'd say to Lillie. He had it memorized, learned by heart: the casual way he would greet her. The graceful way he would pretend to be just passing. The charming way he would finagle an invitation into the house and give himself the perfect excuse, he hoped, to get to know Lillie better.

He forgot each carefully studied word, all his eloquence lost beneath his surprise, and smiled, suddenly reminded of a fairy tale his mother had told him when he was a boy.

Sleeping Beauty.

Tom allowed himself another leisurely examination of Lillie, his gaze traveling, this time, from the dirty toes of her shoes to the equally grimy tip of her nose.

She looked like Sleeping Beauty, just woken from a hundred years' slumber, all cobwebs and dust. A long spider's web trailed from Lillie's hair to her shoulder. Feeling Tom's eyes on it, she brushed it aside and it trailed out beyond her back, buoyed by a current of late afternoon air, like the gossamer wings of an angel.

The smile in Tom's eyes intensified. His gaze moved to the front of Lillie's gown, the buttons done up at cockeyed angles. It was an awkward glance, he knew, as disconcerting to Lillie as it was to him, yet he could not help himself. The day had been warm and Lillie's dress clung to her, delineating each delectable curve. Odd, he had not noticed before how round and appealing her bustline was, nor how her breasts moved against the fabric of her gown with each small breath she took.

The unmistakable flicker of fire in his gut warned Tom to move on. He forced his gaze to the streak of dirt across Lillie's skirt and from there to her shoes. They were caked with a layer of dust, her white stockings—what he could see of them peeking from beneath the hem of her dress—were nearly as gray as her hair.

"I have a feeling I've interrupted something."

Tom's words woke Lillie from the spell of his scrutiny, and she laughed self-consciously and whisked her hand across her hair.

"The attic," she explained. "I've been cleaning the attic."

Tom looked as embarrassed as Lillie felt. "We finished up base ball practice early today," he said, "and I thought . . ." That sounded as false as it did forced. Tom heaved a sigh of surrender and started again. "That is, I wondered . . ." Gathering his courage, he launched into what little he could remember of his studied speech. "You see I was just passing by and I . . ." Grimacing, he mumbled a curse beneath his breath. "I suppose I shouldn't have stopped by unannounced."

"Oh, I don't mind. Not really." Lillie rubbed her hands over themselves, whether to try and banish the layer of grime on them or to still their trembling, she was not sure. It was hard to know what to think when Tom was staring at her like this. She looked away, anxious and more than a bit nervous beneath his penetrating look, a look that seemed to trail fire wherever it touched.

Bending at the waist, Lillie made a great show of studying the path of the sun. "I suppose it's about time I was finishing up anyway," she said. "It's nearly dinner time and—"

"I brought a pie." The last thing Tom wanted was to sound conspicuous, but he could not seem to help himself. His eyes were on Lillie, his brain muddled by her surprising, and somehow very appealing, messiness. The words were out of his mouth before he could stop them.

He made a face, annoyed by his own bungling, and when Lillie gave him a surprised look, he recovered himself and indicated his left arm with a tip of his head. There in the crook of his arm, held tight against his body, sat a round plate covered with a red-checked cloth.

Lillie's surprise turned to skepticism. She looked at him, a question in her eyes.

"You were just passing and you brought a pie?"

There was something particularly gratifying in catching Tom at his own game. Lillie pinned him with a look, watching intently as his barefaced lie crumbled around him. At least he had the good sense to look contrite. Tom's mouth twisted into a one-sided smile, his cheeks reddened.

"Well, not just passing," he admitted, his voice as apologetic as his smile. He lifted his right hand from his side. "I brought—"

"My teapot!" Lillie did not even try to control her delight. The sight of her old, familiar teapot winking back at her from Tom's hand was much like that of a welcomed friend, too long gone and sorely missed. She laughed. "You fixed my teapot!"

Her smile dissolved the last of Tom's apprehension. "I'm sorry it took so long," he said, easing the tension from his shoulders. "I know I promised it to you last week, but I've been busy at the shop and I didn't have the chance until today and . . ."

Lillie was still watching him, her eyes aglow with a certain knowledge that made Tom's words falter.

"A teapot and a pie." She nodded, carefully considering the situation.

A voice inside her brain warned Lillie what she was about to do was more than imprudent. It was foolish, risky, but she had to admit, there was no fighting a man who was so determined and at the same time so utterly charming. Unwilling to admit she'd lost the war, Lillie did recognize that she'd been outmaneuvered, at least in this skirmish.

She smiled and, stepping aside, waved Tom into the house. "Mr. Reilly, it seems you've just invited yourself to dinner."

"I'll make the tea. Why don't you wait in the parlor?"

"Hm?" Tom had heard the question. She was certain he had.

Vaguely aware of the sound of Lillie's voice, he pulled his gaze and his thoughts away from the appealing sway of her hips beneath the clean, brown skirt she'd put on before dinner. She'd run a brush through her hair, too, ridding it of its cobwebs. It tumbled nearly to her waist; caught up at the nape of her neck with an ivory ribbon that matched her clean blouse.

Tom heard Lillie deposit a stack of plates and cutlery in the sink and watched as she turned back to him, drying her hands against the white linen apron tied at her waist.

"I said I'd make the tea." She smiled at him. "You can go into the parlor and wait."

"I could help." Suddenly aware that he'd been lost in thought while Lillie cleaned up, Tom bounded from his seat and tried to remove the drinking glasses from the table before she could.

"Oh, no." Lillie was too quick for him. She snatched the glasses from the table and, turning, kept them safely from his reach. "If there's one thing I loathe, it's a man who tries to help in the kitchen. More trouble than they're worth." She tossed the malediction over her shoulder along with a heart-melting smile.

"I won't be but a minute," she promised, shooing him out of the room. She poked her head toward the front of the house. "The parlor's that way."

Tom had no choice but to listen.

Making his way through the kitchen and along the narrow, picture-lined hallway that led to the parlor, he shook his head. With Lillie there never really was a choice. He had suspected that much on Decoration Day, and the time they'd spent together this evening only served to confirm his suspicions.

It wasn't that she was a forceful woman. Reminded of the pushy and ambitious social climbers he'd known in Boston, Tom shuddered.

No. Thank goodness. Lillie was more dynamic than forceful. He'd decided that even before their soup was eaten and the chicken was served. She wasn't as meddlesome as she was both strong-willed and strong-minded. She'd proven that between bites of succulent garden carrots and thick, stick-to-your-ribs potatoes, voicing her opinions, none too subtly, on everything from the country's economy to the pitiful state of the nation's poor.

It was a pleasant change from the sorts of ladies he'd known back home. The unexpected thought brought a smile to Tom's face. Pleasant, indeed, to listen to a woman discuss politics instead of fashion, world events instead of society's scandals.

His shoulders back, his hands in his pockets, Tom made his way to the parlor.

He stopped just inside the door, jolted back to reality by the unexpected and equally astounding sight that met his eyes.

The parlor was nothing like the kitchen, where they'd eaten dinner. The kitchen was plain, almost spartan, every inch of it utilitarian and pragmatic, the domain of a woman who was as organized and orderly as she was opinionated.

The parlor was something else altogether. Tom glanced around. The place looked less like the sitting room of a respectable lady than it did the salon of a high-priced whorehouse.

From every corner of the room gold gilt glittered in the light of the setting sun. It sparkled at him from picture frames, winked at him from the tassels of the draperies, flashed at the edges of brocade-covered tables, marble-topped sideboards, and plush, red-velvet sofas and chairs.

The gold and red motif was repeated in the heavy embossed paper on the walls and even on the tin ceiling, its classical design highlighted with gilding and embellished with bloodred accents.

But perhaps nothing in the room was more striking than the painting that hung on the far wall.

Tom took a step toward the massive portrait, his eyes trained, not on the magnificent golden frame, but on the figure of the young lady portrayed in the picture.

She was a beautiful creature; her skin like cream, her eyes pools of clear blue, her hair, a cascade of red-gold fire down her bare back.

Though the young lady was obviously naked, the painting was not nearly as indecent as it was provocative. It must have been the eyes, Tom decided, pulling his gaze away from the long, sloping stretch of the girl's bare arms and concentrating instead on her face. The eyes glowed with an inner flame that invited exploration, at once both as innocent and wanton as the girl's brazen smile.

It must be the eyes, Tom told himself again, for very little else of the girl was visible. She was lying on her stomach, her well-proportioned figure only hinted at, hidden both by the folds of the sumptuous couch where she lay and the potted palms that had been carefully positioned to hide the beguiling charms of her well-rounded backside.

"I see you've met Flossie."

The sound of Lillie's voice brought Tom spinning around. Feeling as guilty as a boy caught peeping in a neighbor's window, he looked over her head, hoping the chagrin he felt didn't show in his face. It was not that he was embarrassed by the sight of the girl Lillie had called Flossie, or ashamed to admit he'd been admiring her.

That would be far too simple an explanation. Even through his embarrassment, Tom knew as much.

No, his mortification came more from being caught in his own treacherous thoughts than it was from looking at Flossie. For while he'd been looking at the painting, he realized, it was not Flossie's face he saw. Not Flossie's blue eyes or her red-gold hair.

The hair he'd seen was brunette. The eyes, though they were just as alluring, were dark. The smile? The smile he'd imagined was far more genuine and sincere. The rest, he speculated for a moment, would be just about the same. And that was saying a great deal.

Caught again by his unmanageable thoughts, Tom gave Lillie a nervous half-smile.

"Flossie?" He tossed what he hoped was a disinterested look over his shoulder at the painting. "Is that her name?"

Lillie laughed and set the tea tray she was holding on the nearest table. She settled herself on one of the red-plush chairs and invited Tom to sit opposite her. "I don't know her real name," she said, carefully laying out the cups and spoons and plates of pie like a professional gambler dealing his cards. "But she looks like a Flossie, doesn't she? So that's what I call her."

Lillie looked up and regarded the painting for a few moments before she shrugged off the problem with another, airy laugh. "She was Hank's." Catching the connotation in her own words, she pressed one hand to her heart and stifled a giggle. "I mean the painting belonged to Hank. Everything did." She cast a glance around the room. "Hank was a wonderful man, but he had some rather eccentric tastes. He opened the photography studio here in Wellington because he genuinely needed the money it brought in. But the house . . ." Lillie sighed. "I'm afraid the house wasn't as much for business as it was for monkey business. It's pretty awful, isn't it?"

"It's . . ." Tom sat down. He couldn't recall ever meeting a woman who was so delightfully candid. The thought was as disarming as Lillie's open smile, and he returned it, stalling while he searched for the words that would be neither too hypocritical nor too honest. "It's different," he admitted. "I'll bet the good ladies of Wellington have never seen anything quite like it."

"That would surely ruin my reputation, wouldn't it?" Lillie's eyes sparkled with mischief. She poured the tea and, with a graceful movement of one hand, urged Tom to eat his pie.

"I've been anxious to remove Flossie from the wall, but she's just too big for me to handle by myself. I've got a space all cleared for her in the attic." Lillie took a bite of pie and pointed to Flossie idly with the tip of her fork. "It's a good thing you can't see that wall from the windows. Nathan Hatcher and his friends would—"

Tom coughed, fighting for breath when his mouthful of pie wedged in his throat. He pounded his chest. "You mean you know—"

"That they've been peeking in my windows? Of course I know it!" Lillie laughed, more so, Tom supposed, from the look of total amazement on his face than from the thought of Nathan and his friends playing Paul Pry at her window.

"It's hard to miss four sets of little round eyes staring back at you through the glass." Lillie smiled knowingly. "I'm afraid they've been sorely disappointed. They haven't seen anything even hinting of scandal, though I suppose there's enough gold gilt in here to start tongues wagging. I've finally got the kitchen the way I like it, mostly because it's the one room Hank never used. But the rest of the house . . . the rest of the house is just as bad as this." She shook her head, but there was more forbearance than condemnation in her eyes.

"Hank was a darling. Really. But he was quite a bounder. You should see my bedroom. There's more red velvet up there than in a bordello."

The words had slipped. Tom was sure they had. Lulled by the informality of the dinner they'd shared, soothed by the quiet familiarity of their surroundings and the pleasant friendship they'd begun to forge, Lillie had let a blunder of incredible proportions venture past her lips.

Her cheeks turned as red as fire at the same time she brought her hands to her mouth, as if the gesture could scoop the words out of the air and bring them back to her again. Far too abashed to hazard a look at Tom, she poured herself a cup of tea and made a great show of adding milk and stirring it.

Tom covered his laugh of unadulterated enjoyment by pretending to clear his throat. Poor Lillie! She was far too embarrassed to look at him, but he couldn't help but wish she would. He would like to see her face, to watch the color rise there, tracing her cheekbones with flame, to see her lips pull into a smile of embarrassment and, he imagined, wicked delight.

There was no way he could think to calm her ruffled nerves short of going to her, taking her hand in his, and whispering his understanding in her ear.

Tom cautioned himself even as the thought entered his mind, forcing himself to stay firmly put though every nerve and muscle, every instinct and impulse urged him to follow his heart. With her talk of bedrooms and bordellos still floating in the silence of the room, the last thing Lillie needed was a man hovering over her like a bird of prey, ready to strike.

And the first thing she needed? The first thing she needed, Tom decided, was a definite change of subject.

"The pie's delicious, isn't it?" Tom swirled the last bite of his pie over his plate and smacked his lips. There was no response. The only sound in the room was the clicking of Lillie's spoon, still tapping a nervous staccato against the sides of her cup. "Sarah Hatcher made it." He offered the additional information as a last resort.

"It is good." Lillie's words were breathless, as if her embarrassment had robbed her of her voice as well as her composure.

But at least she was talking again. Tom breathed a sigh of relief and leaned forward, hoping to capture her downturned gaze.

"You miss Hank, don't you?"

It had not been a calculated question, yet Tom realized the moment it left his lips that he'd said exactly the right thing.

Lillie's head came up, her gratitude and appreciation for his sensitivity apparent in the tiny smile that touched her mouth.

"Hank was my father's best friend." Lillie took a deep breath, and, after depositing her plate on the table, she sat back, her hands folded together on her lap. "Papa was the captain of a Lake Erie ore ship. When he was swept overboard in a storm, Hank took it upon himself to watch over our family. I think . . ." She stopped as if considering her next words carefully.

"I think," she finally said, "that he was quite in love with Mama. He didn't dare tell her. He thought he wasn't good enough for her. But he did everything he could to make sure we kept a roof over our heads and food in our cupboards. When my brother Johnny died in an accident at one of the steel mills, I was the only one left to support Mama. Hank gave me a job as his apprentice."

"And left you his business when he died."

"Yes." Lillie straightened a fold in her skirt, the red stain of her cheeks suddenly deeper against the rest of her face, which had gone quite pale. She caught her lower lip between her teeth and held it for a minute.

"The studio in Cleveland burned, you know." She looked directly at Tom, her eyes aglow with the certain memory of the blaze. "Hank was killed in the fire. This was all that was left." Lillie glanced around the room, and her voice dropped until Tom had to strain to hear it. "He left me everything."

Unable to tear his gaze away, Tom watched her, measuring the depth of her feelings, counting the small, shallow breaths she used to steel herself against the flood of emotion that clouded her eyes with unshed tears.

It was all she had in the world. For a moment he let his gaze wander the garish room. All Lillie had was contained here beneath this roof, the legacy of a man who had obviously loved her like a father. A man who had bequeathed her his livelihood, and, Tom supposed, one who had, by launching her career, guaranteed Lillie not only her place in the world but her self-respect as well.

Her memories of Hank were potent. Tom need only look at Lillie's face to know it. They were powerful memories underpinned with a sadness that was so palpable, he felt he could reach out and touch it.

It was none of his business. Reluctantly Tom stifled the questions that crowded his mind. There was more than just sadness behind her reaction to Hank's memory, but the reasons were none of his business. Still, he wanted more than ever to learn the workings of Lillie's heart, to soothe away the melancholy that creased her brow and darkened her hazel eyes, the sorrow that snatched the color from her face and silenced her sparkling laugh.

Helpless this time to heed the warnings of his heart, Tom leaned forward, and before Lillie could pull it away, he took her hand in his.

"Show it to me," he said, his voice as soft as a caress. "Show me your studio."

She did not answer him. Not in words. The flash of understanding in Lillie's eyes was the only answer Tom needed. Still holding onto her hand, he stood and, with a gentle tug, he pulled Lillie from her chair.

Standing face to face, hand in hand, there was no other place for Lillie to look than into Tom's eyes.

They were as dark as ever, yet something in their shadowy depths had lit with a glow she had not seen in them before.

Startled, she made to pull her hand away, but Tom would not allow it. He tightened his hold, his fingers folding over hers with more surety than strength, more warmth than coercion.

Too overcome by his tenderness to resist it, too grateful for the warmth of his companionship to fight it, Lillie nodded her silent agreement. She turned, and keeping her fingers wound through Tom's, she led him to her studio.

7

IT WAS A mistake.

Leading Tom to the studio, Lillie shifted her fingers inside his, hoping the uneasiness she felt wasn't nearly as apparent as she feared, struggling to keep her breathing even, certain that each sharp breath she took spoke her trepidation as shrill and loud as an alarm signal.

It was a mistake to let Tom take her hand. A mistake to agree to show him something as self-revealing as her studio. A mistake to think she could let a man like Tom Reilly into her home and her life and not expect to pay the consequences.

Briefly she chanced a glance at him from the corner of her eye.

He was watching her carefully, his expression as friendly and straightforward as it had been in the parlor, his eyes sparkling like the summer sun that sent its last streaks slanting through the windows.

It was all a mistake. Lillie was sure of it.

Yet she could not stop herself.

The realization did little to calm her nerves. Inside the studio she untangled her fingers from Tom's as quickly as she could and went to pull back the draperies.

"It isn't nearly as fancy as the gallery in Cleveland." Tying back the last of the curtains, Lillie offered the apology over her shoulder. "We had two separate studios there," she explained. "One just for formal portraits, the other for more casual pictures. This will have to do for both, at least until I can earn enough money to add another room."

It took her a moment to realize Tom had not responded in any way. Lillie turned to see what he was doing.

Tom had come as far as the center of the room and stopped there, his head tipped back, his gaze fastened on the myriad dots of reflected light that sparkled on the ceiling like stars.

"It's like a dreamland!" Tom turned around, his gaze wandering the room, his face as open and delighted as a child's at Christmas. "Like one of those fairy tales my mother told me about when I was a boy." For some reason the thought seemed to amuse him and Tom laughed openly.

It was hard not to be caught up in the magic of his laugh. Lillie responded instinctively, not sure what she was smiling about, but enjoying the sensation nonetheless.

"There isn't as much magic in it as there is sensibility," she said. "The walls and ceiling are made of glass. They give me the best light for my work, even on cloudy days."

Tom strolled across the room and peered out. Like the walls of a greenhouse, the glass studio walls granted an unobstructed though slightly indistinct view of the outside. The trees and shrubbery that lay beyond the expanse of Lillie's freshly clipped lawn were distorted; their leaves looked soft and blurred around the edges like those in the paintings of the impressionist artists Tom had seen in a Boston exhibit. Even their color seemed more a thing of art than reality. The greens in the grass and the trees looked deeper, the blue of the sky more luxurious, like the aquamarine of the ocean at sunset.

It took Tom a moment to figure out why. He ran one hand over the smooth glass wall. "It's green."

"That cuts down on harsh shadows and helps diffuse the light."

Still smiling, Tom spun around and went to examine Lillie's cameras. There were two of them: her massive studio camera and the lightweight camera she used for outdoor work. Tom took time to inspect them both, studying everything from the cranks and gears on the camera rest where the heavier camera was mounted, to the neat and compact folding tripod on the other.

His curiosity satisfied, he turned and wandered across the room to where a collection of country gates, rustic benches, and papier-mâché rocks was stacked against the wall. "And what are these?"

"They're props." Lillie came to stand opposite Tom, an assortment of odd-sized, dun-colored rocks between them.

"I use them in my photographs. There seem to be a great number of elderly ladies who fancy themselves country maidens." Lillie laughed and leaned on the nearest gate, one arm thrown over it dramatically. "They like nothing better than to pose against a vine-covered gate." She stood up straight and pointed to the rocks.

"Gentlemen, it seems, are more inclined to pretend they've been hiking through the wild and untamed frontier and they've just stopped to rest." Lillie gathered her skirts and plunked down on one of the rocks, posing as she had posed hundreds of subjects, with one elbow on her knee, her chin in her hand. She shook off the stance with a smile.

"People love this sort of rustic charm in their photographs, and it's far easier to create the effects here in the studio than it is to take all my equipment outside."

She paused and looked up at Tom. She wasn't sure what sort of response she expected. Most men she tried to discuss her work with simply nodded, dismissing her out of hand as nothing more than an obviously bored female, driven into the questionable avocation of photography by her decided and inexcusable lack of a husband and children.

But Tom . . . Tom was different. She had sensed as much when she showed him her pictures of the working children, and he did nothing to disappoint her now. He was just as interested here, at the end of her little lecture, as he had been at the outset. The combination of their familiar surroundings and the excitement of discussing her work with someone who cared, was as comforting as it was potent. Realizing she'd lost some of her uneasiness, Lillie smiled up at Tom.

She was not prepared for his reaction.

Though he didn't say a word, the expression on Tom's face softened from curiosity to interest, and from interest to admiration. Affection glimmered in his dark eyes, affection and some other, more difficult to define emotion that caused Lillie's pulse to race, the blood pounding to her head and her ears until all she could hear was its rush.

She looked away, hoping to assuage the unfamiliar riot of emotions inside her by concentrating instead on something— anything—that would quiet the tumult and cool the surge of heat that flooded through her body.

She did not need to hear the sounds of his boots or to look back to Tom to know he had taken a seat on the rock beside hers. She felt him there; there in the suddenly stifling close-ness of the air, there in the temperature of the studio which skyrocketed, abruptly and surprisingly, far beyond what was conceivable on a pleasant June evening.

Lillie stared down at her hands, clutched together on her lap. It wasn't until she heard Tom's quiet chuckle ripple the air that she dared to look up at him again.

The flash of amusement dispelled some of the intensity from Tom's expression. Drawn by his laughter, Lillie eyed him curiously.

"What is it?" she asked. "Have I said something terribly rude again?"

"No." The smile on Tom's face did not disappear; it quieted until it was nothing more than a sparkle in his eyes. "You haven't said a thing wrong. It's just . . ." He held her gaze, his mouth pulling into a lopsided grin. "It's just that you're so dif-ferent!" Tom laughed, as if the statement was more confession than compliment. "You're so honest. So direct. Your work is important to you"—he glanced around the room—"and you're not ashamed to admit it. Lillie, I've never met a woman like you before."

This time there was no escaping the look of undisguised yearning that glowed in Tom's eyes, brightening their depths with dark sparks of fire.

Lillie opened her mouth to speak and found she could not. The emotion in Tom's expression snatched her words as certainly as if he'd stolen them from her lips. She snapped her mouth shut and pulled her gaze from his.

One more minute beneath the unsettling scrutiny of Tom's brown eyes would surely cause her to lose her balance, Lillie warned herself. One more moment spent this close to him would erase all cautions from her mind and cause her to follow the dangerous dictates of her heart and the equally alarming suggestions coursing through her body with each pounding pulse. One more second and she would jeopardize all she had worked so hard to accomplish; jeopardize it happily, readily, in exchange for one taste of Tom's lips.

Already, she felt like a circus performer, caught in the middle of a precarious tightrope. Retreat was impossible, progress treacherous, and the prospect of falling into the surrounding void both possible and probable.

Gulping down her misgivings along with the tight knob of tension that nearly strangled her breathing, Lillie coughed politely.

"Would you like to see the photographs I took of Elmore Montgomery?" As casually as she could manage, she rose from her seat on the rock and hurried across the room. "I have them drying in the darkroom," she said. "Just stay there. I'll bring them out."

Lillie did not have to look at Tom to know he was offended by her hasty withdrawal. She could feel his irritation in the decided chill that suddenly filled the air, hear it in the exasperated sigh that escaped his lips.

His sigh was followed by another sound, a sound that made Lillie catch her breath. She pulled to a stop, too startled to move.

Tom's boots rapped against the hardwood floor, and he fell into step behind her.

"You didn't have to get up." Even to her own ears her voice sounded too hurried and far too jittery. Lillie expected Tom to offer some charming and altogether impossible to disregard reason why he needed to follow her to the darkroom. Eager to deny him the chance, she forced a pleasant laugh.

"I never did thank you for coming to Montgomery's house when I took his photographs last week. Did you see his face when you walked in right behind me? I was afraid the poor man was going to have an attack of apoplexy."

He wasn't the only one.

Tom checked the rejoinder that nearly escaped his lips.

He could well imagine how Elmore Montgomery felt, for Tom suspected he was feeling much the same way now.

He cringed, reluctant to admit he could have anything in common with a man as despicable as Montgomery, loath to face the truth, though it was staring him in the face.

Montgomery would have felt just as confused as Tom did now, Tom told himself. He would have wondered why Lillie was friendly and open one minute, as tight as a clam the next. He would have been baffled; upset that she had not allowed him the opportunity to tell her all the thoughts whirling through his mind, frustrated that she had cast aside his attentions, disappointed and more than a little disheartened that she had seen fit to remove herself from his presence with the flimsy excuse of looking at photographs of someone he neither cared for nor cared to see.

That was where the similarities ended. Tom comforted himself with the thought. For while Montgomery may have felt all the disappointment Tom did now, Elmore Montgomery was neither determined nor daring.

And Tom?

Tom definitely was.

He followed Lillie to the darkroom, his gaze on the fascinating twitch of her long mane of dark hair, and a slow smile came to his lips. Watching her walk into the room, he paused at the doorway and leaned against the jamb.

"No glass ceiling." Tom craned his neck to see inside the room. There were no windows, either, and the room was nearly as dark as night.

Lillie didn't seem to care, and Tom wondered for a moment if her surefooted confidence in the dark came from the familiar surroundings or the desire to get as far away from him as quickly as she could. She maneuvered her way across the pitch-dark room without hesitating, and he saw her stop near a darker shadow that must have been a table and heard the shuffle of papers.

After a moment Tom's eyes adjusted, helped along by a faint gleam of light coming from the studio. It seeped through the open doorway, illuminating the room with an otherworldly glow.

The place was not as small as Tom first supposed, but it was terribly crowded. Beside the table where Lillie stood, there were two other small wooden tables in the room and shelves along each of its walls. They were crammed with an assortment of bottles and tins, so many that the room looked like an apothecary's shop or the laboratory of a chemist.

"I never thought . . ." Tom had not realized he'd spoken aloud until he saw Lillie jump, startled by the sound of his voice. She gathered the photographs she'd been collecting into a neat pile and tapped them against the table, her eyes wide with an expression halfway between niggling worry and total panic.

Whatever he had done to displease her, Tom could not believe it had been anything to warrant such a strong reaction. He took another step into the room, studying Lillie's face in the flush of emerald light that flowed from the studio.

Her eyes were not as frightened as they were perplexed, he decided. Not as repulsed by the thought of his attentions as they were both hesitant and unsure.

"There really isn't enough light in here to see these well." Lillie's lips twitched into a nervous smile, and she took a step toward the door, the photographs in her hand. "Let's take them outside where you can see them better."

"No." With one hand on her arm Tom stopped her before she could leave the room. She raised her eyes to his for the briefest of moments, then lowered them again and stepped back, beyond his reach.

"I want to see how you do it." Hoping to soothe her, Tom sidestepped Lillie and went to stand against the largest of the tables. "This is even more mysterious than the studio," he said, looking around. "I'm convinced it's magic. Come on, Lillie. Show me how your magic works."

Seemingly relieved that he had turned the subject again to the familiar and very safe topic of photography, Lillie offered him a grateful smile. "No magic." She shrugged and went to lay her photographs on the table next to Tom.

He turned and peered at them briefly, unable to see much of anything through the gloom. "And no windows or lamps, either." He laughed. "You must be able to see in the dark. Like a bat." He bent to try and get a better look at the photographs, but it was no use. Tom shook his head. "How do you do it?"

This time the laugh that escaped Lillie was genuine. He heard her grope for a box of matches and watched her strike a match and light a single candle that sat on the table in a silver holder.

"Your eyes will adjust in a minute," she promised and blew out the match. "It's essential that the glass-plate negatives not be exposed to too much natural light," she explained, pulling the candle closer. "So I work by candlelight."

"With the door open?"

"No." Lillie's voice was as suspicious as the look she threw from Tom to the open door and back again. "When I'm developing, I keep the door closed. That isn't necessary now," she added quickly when Tom made for the door.

"Certainly it is." Tom clicked the door shut and came to stand back at the table. He glanced around the room as if seeing it for the first time. There was something about candlelight that made even the most prosaic of scenes romantic.

Even in the emerald glow of studio light, it had looked no more than a workroom. Now, with the candle flickering in the center of the table, it looked more like a cave, the secret sanctuary of an alchemist.

Or an enchantress.

The thought appealed to him, and Tom turned it over in his mind.

Standing amid her mysterious bottles, her tins and pots of chemicals, Lillie looked like a sorceress. Tom laughed to himself and amended the thought. He suspected Lillie would have looked like an enchantress no matter where she stood. With her hair tumbling down her back and her eyes picking up the flicker of the candlelight, she couldn't help but look both mysterious and beautiful.

Hers was a strange witchcraft, a powerful magic, one that made him long to possess her one minute, and the next, urged him to set her free to explore the seemingly unlimited boundaries of both her dreams and her talents.

A glimpse of the photographs on the table drew Tom's mind from his thoughts. With one hand he spread the pictures out on the surface before him, his fingers automatically sorting through them.

At the sight of one of the pictures, Tom's eyes widened with surprise, his mouth fell open, and before he could stop it, an amazed and very sincere expletive escaped his lips.

"Montgomery?" He lifted the photograph in his hands for a better look, casting only the briefest of glances at Lillie both to offer his apologies for his language and to confirm his suspicions.

He wouldn't have known it for all the world. Wouldn't have known the man in the picture was Elmore Montgomery if he hadn't been told.

The Montgomery he knew was a fussy, meticulous man. For all his irritating personality traits, Tom would give the man that. Montgomery was the wealthiest man in town, and he wasn't afraid to let everyone know it. Each hair—what he had left of them—was always in place, each button shining, each shoe burnished until it shone like the sun.

The man in the photographs was all these things. He was scrubbed and polished and dressed to the nines, seated in his conservatory and surrounded by a portion of his famous Montgomery orchid collection.

Had any other photographer taken the picture, Tom supposed there would have been little to distinguish it. But in Lillie's skillful hands, what might have been an ordinary portrait had been turned into a stinging character study. In the brief time Lillie's shutter had been opened, she had captured more than just Montgomery's face, more than just the extravagance of his surroundings.

Instead of looking merely comfortable, Montgomery looked complacent. Instead of appearing merely reserved, his expression was frozen into a look as harsh as it was inhuman. He stared back at them from the portrait, his face as devoid of emotion and warmth as if it had been carved from stone.

"It's frightening." Tom fingered the picture. "You've captured his personality perfectly. How . . . ?" He looked at Lillie. "How do you do it?"

Lillie glanced down at the picture and nodded as if she saw all she had hoped for contained in it. "It's easy with a man like Montgomery. He isn't as adept at hiding his true personality as he likes to think. These aren't the pictures I'm going to show him, of course." Carefully she retrieved the picture from Tom's hands, put it aside, and picked up another stack of photographs.

"He's going to see these." Lillie flashed him a set of technically sound and perfectly lackluster portraits. "I'm saving these others," she said, "for the meeting I hope to have with the governor."

Tom did not answer. He could not, for he realized there was nothing to say. Nothing to say to a lady who was as determined as she was beautiful. Nothing to say to a lady who had set her sights and her mind on one purpose and one purpose alone, and who would not let the fires of hell or all the money and power of the Elmore Montgomeries of the world stand in her way. Nothing to say. Nothing to do. But kiss her.

Lillie blinked back at Tom in bewildered silence. Where he had joined in the conversation earlier, even expressing what she thought was interest in her work, now he simply stared at her.

Why did he have to look at her so when she spoke, as if each word was somehow so important, as if each syllable she uttered contained some ancient wisdom he could not find anywhere else?

Frowning, Lillie busied herself moving bottles of silver salts from one side of the table to the other, wishing she could order her unstable emotions as easily as she rearranged her supplies.

Why did Tom have to throw her head into a spin? To take even the most innocent of occasions and blow it so far out of proportion that she could barely think or know how to evaluate it herself?

She knew the answer to her own questions, knew it as surely as she knew her own name. Ignoring both the panic and yearning that rose in her at the thought, Lillie carefully unpiled a batch of glass-plate negatives on the table and stacked them up again.

She stopped when Tom's hand covered hers.

For a moment she could do nothing. She was paralyzed by the touch, immobilized by the feel of his skin against hers.

Recovering, she tapped the glass plates with her fingers. "These are what I use in the camera," she explained, hoping the familiar repetition of technical facts would dull the sweet surge of longing that clouded her brain and caused her voice to quaver. "I've got hundreds of them stored in the basement. Negatives of all my photographs. I'm just getting these ready to use. I coat them with an emulsion of silver salts in a gelatin solution."

"I know." Lillie heard Tom's voice, no louder than a whisper, and felt his words ruffle the hair around her left ear.

"It's quite a radical process." Lillie's own voice sounded small and high against the whooshing noises in her head. "It wasn't even developed until five years ago, and it's far from being perfected."

"Uh-huh." Tom's voice dropped even lower, and this time Lillie felt his lips, not his words, against her ear.

"I've been experimenting on my own, seeing if it's feasible—"

"Oh, it is." One of Tom's arms stole around her waist, and he pulled her nearer. "I'd swear it is."

Lillie's eyes grew round, but her voice never lost its crispness. "Of course," she continued, "it doesn't always work the way it should. When I want to be certain of a picture, I still use the wet-collodion process."

"Wet-collodion." Tom's tongue brushed the rim of her ear.

It was a startlingly agreeable sensation. Lillie caught her breath, a response that caused a small noise to escape her lips.

Tom took the sound as a tacit expression of consent. His lips skimming a line from her ear down her neck and back again, he tightened his hold and turned Lillie to face him.

Agreeable, indeed. The words echoed in Lillie's mind along with the thunderous pounding of her heart. Agreeable, and all the more dangerous for it.

The thought froze Lillie in place. Pulling her rationality around herself like a shield, she tightened her shoulders and caught her lower lip in her teeth.

"Lillie? What is it?"

Straightening, Tom looked down at her.

She expected him to be exasperated. She almost wished he were. At least if he were angry, she could counter with an outburst of her own. A good old-fashioned argument might not be sincere on either of their parts, but it would dispel the agonizing tension between them.

Instead of anger, Tom's voice was edged with infinite tenderness. Lillie looked up, feeling her face redden at the undisguised look of desire in his eyes.

"Did I do something wrong?"

There was no way to answer him, no way to explain the tug-of-war inside her: her heart urging her to give in to his tender affections, her mind advising her not to.

"It isn't . . . isn't anything." Extricating herself from Tom's arms, Lillie turned to the table, her hands folded on its pitted surface, her gaze fastened there.

One moment stretched into two, two into three, and a deafening silence filled the air. Lillie squeezed her eyes shut, wishing she could tell him, but fearing no excuse would ever be complete enough to explain away Tom's confusion or good enough to dull the keen pain of the insult she had offered him.

Without stepping closer, Tom placed one hand on Lillie's left shoulder. She would have liked to brush it off, to cast his hand aside. She could not. The gesture was too gentle, the touch too warm.

"What are you hiding from, Lillie?" There was no suggestion of reproach in Tom's voice. His words were as tender as his touch. Reaching across her, he brought his other hand to her right shoulder and turned her in place, not so much holding her there as steadying her from the impact of his words. "Why are you fighting this?"

Lillie offered him a tremulous smile. "I'm not fighting at all. I—"

"You are." His hands still on her shoulders, Tom moved back a step and looked into her eyes, his own expression as insistent as she had ever seen it. He tipped his head toward the door. "Do you want me to leave?"

"I want . . ." Lillie hoped he would not notice the tears she felt stinging her eyes. She dashed them away with the back of her hand. "I want . . ."

"Lillie, if this is something you don't want, all you have to do is say it." Tom's dark eyes reflected his concern. "I'll admit that wouldn't please me. But you know I'd respect your wishes. Just say it, Lillie."

"Isn't that what I'm saying?" Lillie's voice rose. Frustrated, she knocked Tom's hands away and tossed him a look, daring him to oppose her. "When you try to hold me and I pull away, isn't that what I'm saying? When you try to kiss me . . ." Her courage evaporated beneath the memory of his lips against her skin. Lillie took a deep breath and began again. "When you try to kiss me and I—"

"Say it with words."

Tom's challenge reverberated through the silence of the darkroom, cutting through Lillie's feeble excuses. Stunned into silence, she looked away.

"You can't, can you?" There was no satisfaction in Tom's voice, only the ring of certainty. More abruptly this time, he grabbed for Lillie's shoulders and spun her around.

"You can't say it because it isn't true. Don't try to deny it," he added quickly when Lillie opened her mouth to speak. "You can't. I can see it there in your eyes, Lillie." Keeping one hand on her shoulder, he brought the other to her face and skimmed each eyelid in turn with one callused finger.

"I can hear it in the soft huskiness of your voice when you talk to me." Tom slid his hand from her face. His fingers cupped beneath the ivory ribbon at the back of her hair, he traced a line from her chin to the high collar of her blouse with his thumb.

"I can feel it in the air when we're in a room together." From her neck he moved his hand to the long tail of hair at her back and twining his fingers through it, tipped her face to his. "You won't send me away, Lillie. You can't. No more than I can go away."

It was too much. Unable to resist the hushed temptation in his voice, unable to endure the sweet agony of his touch, Lillie closed her eyes and tilted her head back.

When he realized she was fighting him no longer, she heard Tom take a sharp breath of air, as surprised a sound as it was pleased, and felt the scalding touch of his lips on her neck.

"Dear Lillie." Tom's lips moved against her ear before he trailed a line of small, honeyed kisses along her jaw.

"This wasn't supposed to happen." As if she had no control of them, Lillie's words flowed from her in rhythm to the clamorous cadence of her heart. "I'm supposed to be cleaning the attic. I—"

"Do you always talk this much?" Tom's chuckle rippled the still, warm air, and he pulled away from Lillie and smiled.

"I do when I'm nervous," she admitted. "When I'm nervous I start chattering like a magpie. I can't seem to help myself. All these words fill up my head, you see, and before I know it they start falling out of my mouth, and I—"

Tom's hearty laugh cut her short. "And are you nervous now?"

"Are you?"

Tom had not expected to have his question turned back on him. He raised his eyebrows and regarded Lillie with a quizzical look.

"Yes. I suppose I am," he confessed.

Lillie responded with a smile, and Tom pulled his shoulders back. "Is that funny?" he asked.

"Not as funny as it is reassuring."

There was something about the bewildered look on Tom's face that set Lillie laughing and something about her laughter that brightened Tom's expression. She smiled up at him.

"Perhaps we'd both be a little less nervous if you'd just kiss me and get it over with," she suggested.

Tom answered her with a grin.

Bit by bit, the smile faded from his face. He caught Lillie's gaze with his own and held it, his look as mesmerizing as a magical spell. His eyes still on hers, Tom tipped his head and slowly brought his mouth down to Lillie's.

Like swimmers testing the waters, their lips touched and parted. Convinced it was neither too hot nor too cold, they met again, and drank deep.

The kiss was not as long as it was satisfying. After no more than a moment Tom released Lillie's mouth and stepped back.

"That wasn't so bad, was it?"

Lillie sighed contentedly and opened her eyes to find Tom smiling.

"No." She formed the word, but no sound escaped her.

Tom's mouth twitched into a mischievous grin. "It'll be far easier the next time."

"Next time?" Her voice back, the words escaped Lillie's lips like a sigh. Maintaining her equilibrium was nearly impossible. She turned from Tom to stare at the far wall, convinced she could never find her balance when he was watching her this way, reluctant to look at him and face the hurt she feared to see in his eyes. "There shouldn't be a next time," she said.

Her words fell like lead against the sudden pall of silence between them, and for a few minutes, there was no sound in the room beside the harsh rasp of Tom's rough breathing. Finally she heard him walk to the door of the darkroom and back again.

"Why?" His voice ripped the stillness. "Why shouldn't there be a next time, Lillie?"

How could she explain?

Swallowing her misgivings, Lillie turned to Tom.

There was not as much anger as there was confusion in his dark eyes, not as much confusion as there was both disappointment and displeasure. To give herself courage, she raised her chin, refusing to back down from Tom's gaze.

"Maybe I'm off and running before I've had all the facts," she admitted. "Maybe I shouldn't listen to what other people have to say. But . . ." Lillie drew in a breath and let it out again.

"Everyone I've ever loved has left me." She offered the statement by way of explanation, not expecting sympathy or pity for it, only acceptance. "My parents, my brother, even Hank. Oh, it wasn't their fault," she added quickly when Tom began to protest. "Certainly none of them wanted to die. But, don't you see? Walking into . . . into something like this with my eyes open when I know you'll leave, too—"

"What on earth are you talking about?" Tom's face clouded with bewilderment. He took a step closer, his hands out in a gesture of appeal. "I never said anything about leaving."

"You didn't have to." This time Lillie could not endure the look in Tom's eyes. She glanced away. "Alex Campbell says—"

"Campbell?"

There was something about the inflection of Tom's voice that caused Lillie to turn back to him. It may have been a trick of the light, but she could have sworn Tom's face paled. He pinned her with a look.

"What about Alex Campbell?"

"He was here earlier today," Lillie explained, controlling her voice so that it did not betray her anxiety, praying this explanation would be enough to satisfy Tom, enough to save her from telling him the whole truth. "He stopped by to ask me some questions. Questions about you."

"Did he? And what did you tell him?"

Lillie shrugged. "I didn't tell him anything. I don't know anything about you, do I? He thought I did. He saw us leave the Decoration Day social together and . . ." She shook off the

98

rest of her explanation with a twitch of her shoulders.

"I know you're from somewhere back East," she continued. "I can tell as much from the way you talk. Alex says it's Boston."

"Alex?" Tom wrapped his tongue around the name as if saying it left a bad taste in his mouth. "And what else did Alex tell you?"

"Nothing. Not really. Not for certain." Annoyed with Tom for making her feel guilty, annoyed with herself for letting his unspoken accusations bother her, Lillie fought to regain her composure. Gathering her courage, she faced him, her dark eyes meeting his and refusing to look away.

"Alex says you left Boston without a word of warning to anyone. He says he's certain you'll do the same here if you have to. What did he mean, Tom? What did he mean, if you have to leave?"

Damnation!

Tom moved back a step, out of range of the blistering indictment in Lillie's eyes, but not out of range of her questions. Weighing his options, he rubbed one hand over his chin.

It wasn't that he wanted to lie to Lillie. Certainly, she had proved herself both too generous and too sincere to deserve that kind of treatment. But he didn't want to worry her, either.

If she knew Campbell was looking to expose Tom's sordid past and make public knowledge of the scandal that drove him from Boston, how would she feel? What would she do?

Tom glanced at Lillie, hoping to find some clue to her reaction from the look on her face.

He could read nothing there. Nothing beside a kind of desperate concentration, as if she were holding tight and steady to her emotions, waiting for Tom's response.

He didn't want to lie to her.

Tom looked away, the memory of another beautiful face, another sparkling laugh, forming itself in his mind before he could stop it.

He hadn't wanted to lie to Rebecca, either, and he didn't. He had told Rebecca the truth. The whole, despicable thing.

And Rebecca? Rebecca had sent him away without giving

him time for explanations. Sent him away, alone, to face the brutal scrutiny of the newspapers, the contempt of society, and the malice of the people of Boston.

But Lillie was not like Rebecca.

Briefly Tom glanced Lillie's way. There was no evidence of Rebecca's vanity in Lillie's plain, unadorned clothing. No evidence of Rebecca's pride in the honest, demanding way Lillie had chosen to earn her way in the world. No evidence of Rebecca's selfishness in this woman whose singular mission in life seemed to be the eradication of child labor and all the horrors it encompassed.

Even so, the memory of Rebecca and the heartbreak she'd caused him turned Tom's stomach sour and robbed him of all rational thought.

He told himself what he was about to do had nothing to do with the taste of Lillie's lips, nothing to do with the way she felt in his arms, the soft crush of her breasts against his chest, the silky feel of her hair beneath his hands. He told himself and told himself again, hoping the repetition would convince him it was true.

With both his hands he reached for one of Lillie's.

"Alex Campbell doesn't know what he's talking about. He has me mixed up with someone else." His fingers worked over hers, smoothing the tension from her. "I'm not going to leave, Lillie. I swear it."

Lillie looked from their intertwined hands to Tom.

"I believe you." She smiled, the worry gone from her brow.

It was the most he could ask of her. At least for now.

Winding his arm through hers, Tom led Lillie from the darkroom. Without a word they walked side by side through the house until they were standing at the front door.

"Good night, Lillie Valentine." Tom bent to brush the briefest of kisses against Lillie's lips.

Outside, he paused long enough to wave goodbye to her before he turned and walked toward home.

He had meant what he said. Meant every word of it.

He had no intention of leaving Wellington. Not if he could help it.

The trouble was, he had not heard a word from Vincent Palusso. Not a word about his brother, Danny. Not a word that would help erase the black mark associated with his name and leave him free to stay here in the town he'd begun to think of as home.

Tom swung from Grove Street onto Main, berating himself with each step he took. He had meant every word he said about not leaving, he told himself again and again. He had meant every word. But could he keep his promise?

8

"JUMPIN' MOSES!"

Alex Campbell hurled a handful of papers at the far wall of his office and stalked back to his desk, the cigar he had clenched between his front teeth held so tight, it nearly snapped in two. Still grumbling, he snatched up another pile of papers.

Her head poked through the open doorway, Lillie watched, fascinated. It wasn't that she had never seen a tantrum before. Hank had been famous for his. But there was something about a grown man tossing reams of paper in the air that was particularly outrageous.

Stifling a smile, she decided it was best to interrupt the newspaper editor before he could start all over again. Lillie coughed politely and raised her voice. "Mr. Campbell?"

Campbell swung toward the doorway and turned crimson from the top of his starched shirt collar to the roots of his copper-colored hair. "Miss Valentine!" He lowered his arm and stared at Lillie, his mouth open. "How long . . . ?" Campbell's Adam's apple jumped in his throat like a fishing bob. "How long have you been there?"

"Long enough to know you're upset." Lillie smiled her sympathy and, scooting through the open doorway, closed the door softly behind her. "Is something wrong?"

It was not the right question to ask.

Campbell puffed out his cheeks and his face darkened until it was nearly the color of his mahogany desk. "Wrong!" he bellowed. "My printin' press is down, Miss Valentine, and I won't be able to get the part I need to repair it for three weeks. Has to come all the way from Buffalo. Buffalo!" Campbell's bellow turned into a roar. "Holy snooks! Who ever heard of anythin' takin' three weeks to get here from Buffalo?"

Like a hurricane gaining force over water, Campbell's anger increased as he recounted his troubles. He paced a well-worn path from one side of his office to the other, his cigar twitching like a hooked fish, splattering a trail of ashes behind him.

"Besides that, let's see," Campbell grumbled. "There's the boy who's supposed to be runnin' my errands. He's down with the measles. And my only reporter has quit. Received a better offer from a newspaper in Chicago. And then there's that ding-swizzled . . ."

Catching himself, Campbell stopped and gulped down the rest of his diatribe, his face losing all traces of color, his bluster dissolving beneath his embarrassment. "I guess you get the picture." He cleared his throat and stared down at his shoes. "I hope you'll forgive me, Miss Valentine."

"Oh, that's quite all right." Lillie shrugged off the apology and eyed the office, searching for a way to get closer to Campbell's desk. If the place was carpeted, it was impossible to tell. The floor was covered with what looked to be a permanent layer of newsprint. Mountains of it were heaped around the room, some in neat piles, others in mounds so precarious, they looked as if they'd topple at any moment.

Lillie picked her way around the papers nearest the door and stopped. The place was a jumble. Finally finding a haphazard pathway, she made her way to the chair across from Campbell's desk only to find it, too, was piled with papers.

Lillie reached for the nearest batch and transferred it from the chair to the floor. Before she was finished, Campbell was at her side.

"Excuse me!" Campbell swept the rest of the papers onto the floor. He pulled a handkerchief from the pocket of his plaid suit coat and wiped the seat of the chair.

"Please." He waved Lillie toward the chair, then stopped her abruptly when a cigar ash plopped right into the middle of it. With a tight, apologetic grin Campbell brushed the ash from the chair and handed Lillie into her seat. He flittered around her like an anxious butterfly, his large square hands flapping against his sides, his feet dancing a nervous hornpipe through the stacks of old newspapers on the floor.

Hoping to eliminate some of her own uneasiness at the same time she gave Campbell time to regain his composure, Lillie settled back. Too late, she realized one leg of the chair was shorter than the others. It tipped and Lillie sat up straight and scooted to the edge to balance herself.

Not quick enough to help her, Campbell screwed up his face and offered her an uneasy smile. Because he obviously did not know what else to do, he went to the other side of the desk, picked up an earthenware mug, and poked it toward Lillie.

"You'll take coffee with me, Miss Valentine?"

Dubiously Lillie eyed the stained cup in Campbell's hand.

"Thank you. No." She smiled and traded her level look for one of Campbell's openly curious ones. "I haven't come on a social call," she said. "I have some questions I'd like to ask you."

"Questions?" Campbell took the cigar out of his mouth and rolled it through his fingers, regarding it quizzically, as if he'd lost all memory of how it got there. He set it in the center of an ashtray piled high with half-smoked butts and, plunking down in his worn leather chair, craned his neck to see Lillie over the heaps of papers on the desk between them.

That was nearly impossible.

"Dagnabbit!" Campbell mumbled and, rising from his chair, he made his way around to the front of the desk. He whisked away an inkstand and, blushing furiously, scooped up a paperweight in the shape of a well-endowed and obviously unclad nymph and stashed it beneath a copy of last week's *Enterprise*.

Satisfied at last, he smiled and parked himself on the desktop.

"I'm the one who usually asks the questions," Campbell said.

"I realize that." Lillie shifted uncomfortably, as much to try and balance her chair as to dispel her own anxiety. To stall for time while she ordered her thoughts, she pulled off her gloves and tucked them into her handbag.

She had practiced her speech to Campbell over and over last night, and it hadn't sounded the least bit peculiar. Lillie comforted herself with the thought, telling herself what had sounded so logical last night should certainly sound just as reasonable and rational in the light of day.

But would it?

For a moment Lillie replayed the scene of last night's encounter with Tom over in her mind. She pushed aside the memory of his kiss, though it struggled to overshadow all else, and concentrated instead on Tom's reaction to the news of Alex Campbell's visit.

The more she thought about Tom's response, the more puzzling it became. For a brief time last night she had convinced herself that Tom was simply jealous, jealous of Alex Campbell.

Lillie darted a glance at Campbell. He was an attractive enough man, she supposed, hardly older than herself, twenty-five perhaps, twenty-six at most. Although he was far shorter than Tom and slighter of build, there was a certain appeal in his lean figure, a certain attraction in the sparkle of eyes that were both alert and intelligent.

But Tom Reilly could no more be jealous of a man like Alex Campbell than the sun could be jealous of the moon's cold light. Lillie discarded the ridiculous notion without another moment's hesitation. There simply was nothing for Tom to be jealous about.

And yet in the small, dark hours of the morning when sleep refused to come and Lillie sat, awake, in her bed, the same haunting thoughts kept troubling her.

If Tom was not jealous, why was he so upset by Campbell's visit?

Taking a deep breath for courage, Lillie raised her eyes to Campbell's and kept them there. "Yesterday, when you stopped at my house, you asked some questions about Tom Reilly," she began.

"Reilly?" Campbell sat up, his blue eyes wide with interest. All the nervous tension was gone from him. In its place was a kind of intensity that defied description. He was more like a terrier on the scent of its prey than anything else, Lillie realized; vigilant and poised for action. "Have you thought of anything, Miss Valentine? Anything that might help with the inquiries I'm making?"

"I'm afraid not. I don't have answers for you, Mr. Campbell. I have more questions. The questions you asked yesterday, they were vague at best. I want to know . . . I want to know why you're interested in Tom Reilly."

Whatever Campbell had expected, it wasn't this. His eyebrows rose, disappearing beneath the lock of carroty hair that tumbled over his forehead, and he let out a long, soundless whistle. "I might ask you the same thing," he said, eyeing Lillie with renewed interest. "Yesterday you said there wasn't anything you could tell me about the man—"

"And I still can't. But—"

"But now you have questions of your own to ask. Why?"

Why?

It was the same question that had been pounding through Lillie's head throughout the night. Why couldn't she accept Tom at face value? Why couldn't she believe him when he said he had no intention of leaving? Why couldn't she let herself surrender to him and all the love and tenderness he offered?

The answer was as simple as it was troubling.

Weeks ago she had convinced herself to stay as far away from Tom Reilly's warm smile and simmering looks as she could. It was too late for those warnings now. Lillie knew it. She had already lost her heart to the man.

Now the best thing he could do would be to leave her. The best thing for him. The best thing for her.

The thought tore through her mind before she could stop it, and yet she knew it was true. It was the best—the safest—

thing for both of them. Lillie settled her shoulders in a straight, unyielding line and set her mouth.

If Tom left, they would both be better off.

But she was damned if she'd let him disappear from Wellington and from her life without knowing what drove him away.

Taking in a calming breath of air, Lillie fastened her gaze to Alex Campbell's.

"What do you know about Tom Reilly?"

For a moment Campbell met her eyes, and she could have sworn he was about to speak. He opened his mouth and snapped it shut again, bounding from the desk and turning from her before he could say a word.

His back to her, Campbell heaved a sigh. "In spite of what most people think of newspaper reporters, I do consider myself a gentleman." He spun back to Lillie. "I've probably ruined a reputation or two in my time, and I hope to ruin a few more before they plant me in the ground. But I'd never defame any man without the evidence to support my accusations. And I'd never want to start rumors or trouble when I don't have all the facts."

Lillie refused to back down. Keeping her head high, she rose from her chair and faced Campbell. "You've already caused trouble, simply by coming around to my house to ask me about Tom. You owe me more than just excuses, Mr. Campbell. Tell me why you're interested in Tom Reilly."

As if he were an actor waiting for the perfect cue, Campbell's face lit instantly with a grin that was at once both angelic and shrewd. "Tell me why *you're* interested in Tom Reilly."

His challenge stunned Lillie into silence. She blinked at the reporter, feeling inept and more than a little discomfited. "I . . . I . . ." Her throat suddenly dry and tight, Lillie's words were no more than croaks. Regaining her courage in the heat of the rush of anger and embarrassment that swept through her, Lillie scowled at Campbell. "You said you were a gentleman!"

"And I am!" Campbell threw back his head and laughed. "I'm sorry. I just couldn't resist. Beggin' your pardon, Miss

Valentine, but if you haven't heard the rumors flyin' around town about you and Tom Reilly, well, you're the only one who hasn't."

Lillie felt the blood drain from her face. "Rumors?"

Still smiling, Campbell rocked back on his heels. "Started back around when you kidnapped the man from the Decoration Day social. Really, Miss Valentine"—Campbell leaned closer and lowered his voice, as if sharing a confidence—"you can't go shanghaiin' a man in front of a town full of folks starved for gossip and not expect to become the object of some small talk yourself."

"Good heavens!" Lillie dropped back into her chair. "What are they saying?"

Campbell sucked on his teeth, prolonging the agony. "Not much," he finally conceded. "And some of those old hens are just dyin' because of it. There's nothing like a half-rumor to get some folks worked up. I think they'd be a lot happier if you two would just get it over with. Elope out your front window. Let him carry you into the courthouse for a marriage license—"

"Mr. Campbell!" Lillie looked at the reporter aghast. "Tom Reilly and I are friends, I will admit that much. But as to all this about courthouses and marriage licenses"—Lillie fanned the heat from her face with one hand—"it's ridiculous."

Campbell nodded sympathetically. "I know it. I know it, Miss Valentine. And I'm not sayin' half the people who are spreadin' the rumors are believin' them, either. But you don't know these folks as well as I do. It's summer and things are slow and everybody's feelin' kind of lazy. Even the half that doesn't believe what they're hearin' are itchin' for excitement. And, well, you and Tom Reilly seem to be the only ones around here likely to provide 'em with it."

"Really!" Lillie made a soft, clicking noise with her tongue. It was bad enough she had come to Campbell to unearth what she could about Tom's past; worse yet that the motives she thought so private were being aired in public like Monday's wash.

Mortified, Lillie stared at her hands folded in her lap.

As if he'd given her long enough to consider the situation, Campbell interrupted her thoughts, his voice more gentle than she had heard it before. "See what rumors can do?"

Lillie's head snapped up. "You mean—?"

"Don't get me wrong." Campbell held up one hand to stop her words. "Everything I've told you is true. You really are the object of back-fence gossip from one end of the township to the other. But maybe now you can see why I don't want to say too much to anyone about Tom Reilly. At least not until I know what I'm talkin' about."

Lillie nodded, not conceding defeat but acknowledging the undeniable logic of Campbell's position. "I appreciate your decency, Mr. Campbell. And your integrity." She stood. "If it's any consolation, I hope you're aware that anything you told me about Tom would be for my personal use and mine alone. I'm not about to start another set of rumors flying."

"I realize that." Taking Lillie's arm, Campbell smiled and led her through the maze of discarded papers and to the door. Outside, he stopped and turned to her.

"I'm sorry I can't be of more help. I can only imagine how frustratin' it is for you. Despite my reputation for bein' hard-nosed, I do have a soft spot in my heart when it comes to young lovers. If there was any way—"

Campbell's statement was interrupted by a shout from across the street.

"And don't come back unless you plan on paying your bill when you do!"

They heard John Baldwin's voice boom from his dry goods store long before they saw him.

A second later the door of Baldwin, Laudon & Co. burst open, and Vincent Palusso dashed into the street. Close at his heels was John Baldwin, a broom brandished over his head.

"And don't think I'll forget this time, Palusso." Baldwin waved the broom menacingly. "I'm past forgetting."

They heard Palusso mutter a reply in Italian. He emphasized his point with a rude, unmistakable gesture before he turned and stalked down the street.

"Great Horn Spoon! And in front of women and children."
Alex Campbell raised both his hands in front of Lillie's face
to block her view. He watched Palusso round the corner and
disappear into the doorway of the Morning Star Saloon, and
only when he was convinced that Palusso was gone did he
lower his hands. He shook his head. "No manners. And no
morals, either."

Suddenly, as if struck with an idea, Campbell's eyes brightened.

"You know, Miss Valentine, there's not a thing I can tell
you about Tom Reilly in good conscience. But I don't think
it would betray a confidence to let you know that there is
someone in town who may be able to answer your questions.
Someone who, I don't think, will be bothered by either the
ethics or the morality of the things we've discussed."

Confused, Lillie followed Campbell's gaze. "Vincent
Palusso?" She looked back to the reporter in wonder.

Still staring after Palusso, Campbell nodded. "That's where
our answers lie, or my name's not Alexander Cornelius
Campbell."

"Palusso?" Lillie was still not convinced. She shook her
head, hoping to clear the cobwebs she was sure were clouding
her reasoning. "What on earth could a man like Palusso know
about Tom?"

"That's exactly what I'm tryin' to find out." Campbell's
expression was thoughtful. "I do know Tom Reilly never
showed up here in Wellington until about a year ago, right
after Vincent Palusso and his family moved to town—"

"Coincidence." Lillie dismissed the allegation with a toss of
her head.

"And that Reilly's been seen following Palusso home a time
or two." Campbell raised his eyebrows, daring Lillie to dismiss
this second piece of evidence as cavalierly as she did the first.

"He's concerned about Anthony, of course." Even to herself,
Lillie's defense sounded feeble. The realization made her far
more uneasy than she cared to admit and far more adamant
than was either prudent or rational. She covered her apprehension with a flippant laugh. "You know how fond Tom is

of Anthony. Everyone in town does. He's always—"

"Always following Vincent Palusso in the middle of the night? Always checking with Mr. Finch, the postmaster, to see if Palusso's received any out-of-town mail? Always asking Molly Clerkwell over at the telegraph office if Palusso's sent or received any messages?"

Campbell's words, as relentless as they were penetrating, drilled into Lillie like needles. As if she could ward them off with the gesture, she folded her arms across her chest. "If that's all you have to go on, Mr. Campbell—"

"It isn't." Campbell sucked in a sharp breath and his jaw tightened. "But I won't be drawn in to tellin' you more. I told you earlier—"

"You told me earlier that there was nothing you could say about Tom. Not until you were sure. Now you're telling me—"

"That Vincent Palusso has the answers to this little mystery." As quickly as it came, the flash of anger in Campbell's pale blue eyes evaporated, and he smiled at Lillie. "The man's as surly as a blacksmith's dog. I haven't been able to get him to say a word. Perhaps you'll have better luck with him."

"Me?" It was as if Campbell were reading her mind. Lillie covered her uneasiness with pretended indignation. "You certainly don't think a lady like myself—"

Campbell's hearty laugh stopped her. "Miss Valentine!" He clapped her affectionately on the shoulder. "You are a far better photographer than you are an actress. It's only taken me this little while with you to determine you've got brains as well as looks. You may even have enough guts to make a good reporter." For a moment Campbell's face went blank, as if he were totally astounded by the wisdom of the words that had tumbled from his mouth. The next second his eyes popped open and his face split with an enormous smile. "Say! Have you ever considered—"

"No." Lillie rejected the offer before he could propose it. "I have quite enough in my life without a job as a newspaper reporter. Besides, I fear I am not as objective as a reporter is supposed to be."

"Oh, that's not what I've heard."

Campbell's voice was so self-assured, Lillie could not resist. "Whatever are you talking about?" she asked.

"Cleveland." Campbell's smile turned into an ear-to-ear grin. "You've got quite a reputation for your work in the mills and factories. A reporter's heart and soul, after all, I think."

Lillie gave Campbell a precise, even look. "I would appreciate it if you would keep that information to yourself. There are those in town—"

"Like Elmore Montgomery?"

She nodded. "I suspect he would not be pleased if he learned who I was."

"Done!" Campbell stuck out one hand and shook Lillie's with enthusiasm. "We're crusaders for justice. Both of us, in our own way. I'd consider it an honor to keep your secret, Miss Valentine. And if you find out anything from Vincent Palusso . . . ?" Campbell let his question trail off into the air.

"Don't be ridiculous." Lillie removed her gloves from her handbag and pulled them on. She tossed a look in the direction of the Morning Star Saloon. "There isn't anything Vincent Palusso's going to tell me. You said it yourself, the man is hardly forthcoming. And a woman like me—"

"A woman like you could charm the birds out of their songs." Campbell moved toward his office. "Good luck, Miss Valentine."

"Thank you." Lillie had gone no more than three steps toward the Morning Star when she stopped and turned back to the newspaperman.

"You might find some luck of your own if you knew where to look for it," she said. "I'd suggest you ask little Anthony Palusso to run your errands while your regular boy is ill. He's a conscientious child, and I know he has some free time in the evening."

Campbell nodded his gratitude. Before he could enter his office, Lillie stopped him again.

"And Mr. Campbell?" She gave the reporter a subtle, knowing smile. "You might ask Tom Reilly to have a look at that printing press of yours."

113

*   *   *

"Is there something you're needing, Miss Valentine?"

Struggling to hide his astonishment beneath his most hospitable smile, J. S. DeWolf rubbed his meaty hands against his linen apron and looked from Lillie to the rosewood clock hanging near the front door. "You're mighty early if you're here for lunch. We don't open the restaurant for two hours yet."

Lillie offered the Morning Star's proprietor a smile. "I'm not looking for a meal," she said with no more than a glance across the lobby at the closed door of the restaurant. "I'm looking for Vincent Palusso." She stood on tiptoe to see past DeWolf's bulky figure and into the saloon. "Is he—"

"Miss Valentine!" DeWolf's mustaches twitched, and he shifted himself to stand squarely in the center of the doorway. "A man's home may be his castle, but his tavern is his sanctuary. If we let women in, the poor men of this town will have no peace."

Lillie wasn't sure whether she should laugh with contempt or scream with outrage. With an effort she controlled both sentiments. She pinned DeWolf with as composed a look as she could manage. "My money's as good as Vincent Palusso's," she said. "Better. I can pay cash." Lillie reached into her handbag, drew out a one-dollar bill, and pressed it into DeWolf's hand. "Here. Payment in advance. How many of your male customers do that?"

DeWolf's amazement was complete. He stared at Lillie in wonder, his jowls quivering. The surprise was enough to rob him of his voice, at least for the moment. Before he could regain it, Lillie brushed him back with one delicate movement of her gloved hand and walked into the bar.

It didn't take her long to find Vincent Palusso.

He was slumped in a chair in the farthest corner of the Morning Star, his elbows propped on the table in front of him, his nose nearly immersed in the foam of his beer.

He didn't notice her.

Lillie thanked her lucky stars and, moving to the bar, spoke to the young bartender. "Have a bottle of your best whiskey brought to Vincent Palusso's table, will you?"

The young man had been drying a drinking glass. He stopped, the glass raised at eye level in one hand, his towel dangling from the other, and looked at Lillie as if she were speaking another language.

She forced a smile. "I said, a bottle of whiskey." She repeated the request, slower this time, just in case he really did not understand.

J. S. DeWolf had followed Lillie into the bar, and the young man looked to him for guidance. Across the room DeWolf nodded.

Lillie smiled her approval and watched the bartender put a bottle and glass on a nearby tray. One hand on the bar, the other on top of the whiskey bottle, Lillie stopped him. "And don't forget to bring two glasses."

Turning away, she congratulated herself. So far, all had gone exactly as she had planned. Her eyes on Vincent Palusso, Lillie warned herself the next part of the scheme would probably not be as successful.

She was right. She knew it the moment she approached the table.

Palusso's head came up, and he eyed her uncertainly, not as surprised to see her in the Morning Star as either its owner or the bartender had been, but simply and plainly irritated—irritated at them, for letting her disturb his leisure, irritated at her for having the audacity to do it.

Lillie doubted the Italian phrase Palusso mumbled was an invitation to sit down. She pretended it was. Depositing her handbag and gloves on the chair to her right, she seated herself opposite Palusso and waited for the bartender to bring the bottle to the table.

"One glass for Mr. Palusso," she ordered him. "The other is for me."

The young man shook his head and poured the drinks, filling Palusso's glass nearly halfway and splashing no more than a mouthful into Lillie's. She didn't protest. She directed him to leave the bottle, and when he was gone, Lillie filled Palusso's glass to the brim and poured an equal amount into her own.

115

"Alla salute!" She raised her glass in a friendly gesture, hoping the one phrase of Italian she'd learned from Anthony was not only appropriate but pronounced correctly.

Palusso did not respond. He simply watched Lillie, his dark eyes drawn into slits like a hawk's about to slaughter its prey.

Lillie fought to keep her composure beneath Palusso's ruthless look. In the hopes of goading him to some response, she took another drink.

"It's really quite good," she said. "You should have some. I've paid for the entire bottle."

Eyeing the half-full bottle, Palusso grunted and raised his glass. *"Salute."* The word was spoken neither as a toast nor a pledge. It fell from Palusso's lips like a curse. Half his glass emptied in one gulp, he swiped one hand across his mouth and settled his broad shoulders against the high back of his chair. He let his gaze wander from Lillie's face to the front of her emerald-green gown and back again. "What is it you want from me, camera lady, that you bribe me with drink?"

There was no use delaying. Lillie hauled in a deep breath and gave Palusso as level a look as she could manage. "It isn't a bribe. It's a payment."

"Payment." Palusso rolled the word over his tongue along with another mouthful of whiskey, and his face split with a grin as obscene as the look in his eyes. "Ah! I understand. I hear around town. I hear you are all alone at that big house of yours. This, it is not good for a young lady. It make her sad. It make her lonely." Palusso laughed deep in his throat and preened, sleek and satisfied. "You are here because you want a man."

He was mocking her, purposely baiting her, waiting for her composure to crack. Lillie knew it, just as she knew she would never give him the satisfaction. Keeping the stinging rejoinder she was tempted to fling back at Palusso to herself, Lillie returned his coarse look with one of utter solemnity.

"Not today. Thank you." She took another drink, more to give her trembling hands something to do than because she enjoyed the taste of the whiskey. "What I do want to discuss with you is a business proposition."

"Business?" Palusso finished the whiskey in his glass and poured himself more. "What do you offer to me in return?"

Lillie looked from Palusso to the bottle and back again. "The rest of that bottle, for one thing," she said. "Other than that . . ." She reached for her handbag and pulled a roll of dollar bills out of it. She counted the money and, sweeping her hand along the bottom of her purse, came up with a handful of coins to add to it.

"Other than that, I am willing to pay three dollars and seventeen cents," she said. She flattened the bills and set them in the center of the table, the stack of coins on top. "Can you use three dollars and seventeen cents, Mr. Palusso?"

Palusso did not answer her. With his head tilted to one side, he eyed her warily. "And for this three dollars, what is it you want?"

"Only the truth."

"The truth!" Palusso laughed and kept on laughing until he looked at the money on the table. Then his smile faded. He ran his tongue over his lips. "I am not a wise man. But I am not a stupid, either. Even I know you do not come to Vincent Palusso for the truth. There is nothing you can want to know that I can tell you. I would like to help you, signorina, I really would. I would like your money. But there is nothing—"

"You can tell me about Tom Reilly."

With all the swiftness of clouds scuttling across the sun, the confusion cleared from Palusso's face. Left in its place was an anger so overpowering, it transformed his expression. His mouth thinned, a slash of red against his swarthy skin.

Like a panther ready to spring, he raised himself in his chair, his body tense, his eyes alert, his voice low and menacing. "Who is it? Who sends a woman to ask these questions? Is it Campbell?" He grunted a sound of disdain. "He is the kind of man who would hide behind a woman's skirts. Or is it Reilly? Reilly!" Palusso spit the name at her.

"He is the one. He is the one who sends you to ask questions because he cannot find the answers for himself. He sends you to me? There." Palusso made a rude gesture of dismissal with his hands. "I send you back. You go back to him and you ask him questions for me. Ask him about Boston. Ask him why a man who has everything—money, talent"—he snickered—"women—you ask him why he risk it."

Before Lillie could reply, Palusso sprang from his chair. His hands flat against the table, his arms straining, he stared at Lillie. "Ask Tom Reilly about Danny. Ask him why his brother is dead, and he did nothing to stop it."

His words were like stones, slamming into Lillie. She braced herself against the onslaught, tightening her jaw so Palusso would not see her lips tremble.

Seeing that she would not wither beneath the rush of abuse and hatred that fell from his mouth, Palusso snorted his contempt and spun away.

It was only then Lillie allowed herself to relax, only then she closed her eyes and let go the tight, painful breath she'd been holding.

The next second she sucked it in again as a pair of hands came down on her shoulders.

"I tell you one more thing, signorina." Palusso was behind her. He bent close and purred in her ear. "You stay away from my Anthony. And you keep him away from Reilly. You do this for me, signorina." Palusso's fingers dug into Lillie's skin. "You do this for me, or I will make you sorry you did not."

With that, Palusso was gone.

Lillie propped her elbows on the table and took a few deep, calming breaths. It was only then she noticed the whiskey bottle was gone. And so was her three dollars and seventeen cents.

9

"HOTTER THAN BLAZES!" Gasping for breath, Jonah Hatcher swiped one arm across his forehead and leaned against the open doorway of Tom's workshed. He threw a look over his shoulder into the shed and the iron printing cylinder they had just hauled from the *Enterprise* office. "I don't see why you had to bring that thing here to repair it," he puffed. "Would have been a darned sight simpler to leave it where it was. Fix it right there."

"Not when all my tools are here." Tom emerged from the outbuilding, one hand up to shield his eyes from the midday sun. Squinting against its light, he undid the buttons along the front of his shirt. He stripped off the shirt and draped it over the nearest rhododendron bush.

"Besides," he said, "Campbell could talk the leg off a bird. He wouldn't give me a moment's peace the entire time I was there. At least if I work here, no one will disturb me."

"Hm." Jonah seated himself on a nearby rain barrel and pulled a pouch of chewing tobacco from his pocket. "Seems to me you're more interested in avoiding Campbell than he is in avoiding you."

"Maybe." Tom declined Jonah's offer of a chew and propped his hands on his hips, casting a glance around the

119

all-too-familiar yard while he waited for Jonah to change the subject.

"Might help to talk about it."

Tom met Jonah's offer with silence, weighing the relief of confiding in his friend against the foolishness of letting Jonah be party to a secret that could well become as dangerous as it was dishonorable. His wisdom overcame his need.

Tom scuffed the toe of his boot in the dirt. "Might not," he said.

"Suit yourself." With a grunt Jonah hauled himself off the rain barrel. He spit a stream of tobacco juice onto the ground. "But I think it might help to remember you have friends in this town. Friends who are willing to believe the word of an honest man. If you change your mind . . ." Jonah stuck out one hand, the gesture one of farewell as well as friendship.

Tom gave him a fleeting half smile. "I won't." He clasped Jonah's hand. "I appreciate your loaning me your wagon. I should be finished in a week or so. If I could use your cart again . . . ?"

With his usual good grace Jonah accepted Tom's evasiveness. "Any time," he said, and he turned to leave. He was halfway across the yard when Tom heard him mumble and saw him spin around. "By the way, I knew there was something I was supposed to mention to you. Heard it this morning from Cal up at the livery stable. He tells me that Vincent Palusso spent half the night at the American House, buying drinks for everyone in the place. Now ain't that an interesting piece of information?"

Interesting, indeed. His eyes narrowed, Tom considered the news. It wasn't for another moment or two that he realized Jonah was watching him, waiting to hear his reaction.

When he didn't respond, Jonah looked up at the sky, his mind seemingly on nothing more than the robin that flitted from the apple tree at the back of the shop to the peak of the shed. He rocked back on his heels. "I wonder where Palusso got money like that."

"Can't imagine." Tom was saved from saying any more by the sound of Jonah's horses, neighing and stomping their impatience out in the street. "You'd best get those animals home." He crossed the yard to Jonah and clapped him on the back. "I'll see you at the Fourth of July celebration?"

"Sure will." Though he was obviously disturbed that Tom was neither willing nor likely to say more, Jonah seemed to forget his disappointment in the excitement of talk of the upcoming holiday. "Gonna be the biggest thing this town has seen since President Lincoln's funeral train stopped here," he said. "You're not gonna fight us about coming the way you did at Decoration Day, are you?"

"I'll be there." Tom held up one hand. "I promise."

Jonah smiled and gave him a knowing wink. "And maybe this time you won't be leaving so early on the arm of the prettiest lady in town."

No sooner were the words out of Jonah's mouth than Lillie rounded the corner into Tom's yard. With her camera held up tight in her arms and her shoulders thrown back to support it, she looked like a soldier on sentry duty. Tom smiled to himself, pleased with the picture she presented: a neat, polished soldier in her dark blue dress.

Lillie took one look at Tom and Jonah and came to a halt. No matter how hard she tried to silence it, a voice inside her head reminded her—none too delicately—of the rumors Alex Campbell had assured her were making the rounds of the town. She was not so sure about Tom, but she could see in a glance that Jonah Hatcher had heard the gossip. At the sight of her he poked Tom in the ribs with one elbow.

It was bad enough she was here at all, the same small voice scolded her. Worse still that she had come unannounced and uninvited and found Tom in an embarrassing state of undress.

Embarrassing for her.

Lillie felt the blood rise in her cheeks at the same time a dribble of perspiration tickled its way down her neck.

It was apparently not so embarrassing for Tom.

As if he were oblivious to both the implications of greeting her half-dressed and the distress it was causing her, Tom simply smiled, seemingly as pleased to see her this afternoon as he had been when he'd stopped at her house two days ago.

Not sure if she should stand her ground or run for cover, Lillie traded looks with the men. "I didn't mean to interrupt," she stammered.

"No interruption at all, ma'am." Because he was not wearing a hat, Jonah tugged at his fringe of sandy-colored hair. "I was just on my way back home." He gave Tom a very broad smile, nodded his goodbye to Lillie, and disappeared down the alleyway that separated Tom's shop from Miss Boutwell's millinery next door.

Keeping herself at the far end of the yard, Lillie fought to ignore the ball of panic that rose, suddenly and painfully, beneath her heart.

It wasn't that she had never seen a half-naked man before.

Lillie gulped in a great draft of humid air and repeated the thought. It didn't help.

She may have seen hundreds, Lillie told herself. She may have seen thousands. But none had ever turned her legs to a substance as jellylike as the collodion she spread on her glass plates. None had ever tied her stomach in knots, or spun her head until she was not sure which way was up, and which down. None, she told herself conclusively, was as appealing as Tom Reilly.

Before she could stop herself, Lillie's gaze slid from the welcoming and pleasantly surprised smile on Tom's face to his bare chest, and from there to the play of sun and shadows that sent ripples of sultry air radiating around him like a trans-lucent halo. It undulated over him, liquid heat, accentuating the solid muscles of his neck, his long, powerful arms, the breadth of his shoulders and the smooth and intriguing slant from shoulders, to chest, to waist. Forcing her gaze upward again, Lillie studied the thatch of dark hair on Tom's chest, and the sheen of perspiration on his skin that made it look as shimmering and enticing as silk.

She had seen half-naked men before.

Lillie repeated the thought over in her mind, hoping it would slow the surge of blood that swelled through her veins at the same time it would persuade her far-too-active imagination to cool.

It did not.

The more she tried to keep her gaze from Tom's body, the more her eyes seemed drawn to it. Unable to move, she simply stared, her cheeks hotter than the noontime sun, her breathing so quick and erratic, she was sure Tom must think her as foolish as she was rude.

To her surprise, it seemed Tom thought neither.

His smile widened.

"I didn't expect to see you today." His dark, assessing gaze never leaving Lillie's face, Tom took a step nearer.

As if that one step made him able to perceive the tumult going on inside her head, Tom pulled to a stop and looked down at his chest. "I wasn't expecting a visitor," he said and made a move to retrieve his shirt. "I'll just—"

"No need." To cover the chaos of emotions inside her, Lillie made a great show of setting down her camera and adjusting the legs of the tripod. "I've seen men in various stages of undress before," she assured Tom in as even a voice as she could manage. "It's an occupational hazard. When you take photographs of workers . . ." Without completing the thought, she gave one leg of the tripod a final tug and settled it in the grass.

Tom paid her no mind. Before she was done, he had already slipped his shirt back on and was buttoning it. He came across the yard in three easy strides and stood looking down at her.

"I'm glad you stopped by," he said, his voice as soft as the look in his eyes. "Is there something I can do for you?"

"Do?" Her reply was no more than a squeak, and Lillie cursed herself for losing control of both her emotions and her voice. She gave Tom what she hoped was a steady smile. "I'd like to take your picture."

"My picture?" Tom's surprise seemed genuine. He laughed, more self-conscious than amused. "Why on earth would you want—"

"It's for a series of photos I'm completing on workers." Lillie breathed the words out along with a fervent prayer that he would not recognize her story as the lie it was. "You've seen my photographs of the working children," she continued. "I'm also interested in adult workers. I thought if I stopped by—"

"But I'm not ready."

"That's just it." Lillie giggled, more than a little relieved that, so far, he seemed to believe everything she was saying. "I don't want you to be ready. I don't want your hair combed or your face washed or your clothes brushed. Those kind of pictures are fine in the studio. But they're portraits, and I'm not looking for portraits. I'm looking for photographs that show what people really look like. Not when they're fancied up, but everyday, when they're doing good, honest work."

"But . . ." Tom ran one hand through his hair and tucked his shirttails into his trousers.

It wasn't that he didn't want to cooperate.

Another glance at Lillie—at the neat bun of hair scooped against the back of her neck, at the trim fit of her blue gown, tight across her breasts and skimming her hips, at the determined picture she made standing there with her arms at her sides, her eyes imploring yet bold—another glance told his head everything his heart already knew. He would like nothing better than to cooperate, to do anything the woman asked.

But a photograph?

Stalling for time, Tom bent to brush the dust of the street from his trousers.

He had seen enough photographs of himself in the Boston newspapers to last a lifetime, and he'd sworn he'd never allow another one to be taken. They could be used too easily to identify a man, and that could be dangerous and far too damning, especially in the wrong hands.

Straightening, he caught a glimpse of Lillie's hands where they rested against the skirt of her gown. These were not the wrong hands. He knew it instinctively, like he knew when to wake in the morning, even before the birds had begun their songs or the sun had peeked over the horizon.

It was not a new insight, yet it seemed to make his blood flow faster, to catch in his lungs and cause some painful emotion to lodge itself beneath his heart.

He made one last effort to dissuade her, and himself. "But—"

"But if you'd rather not." Sometimes her own audacity surprised even Lillie. She raised her eyes to Tom's and shamelessly batted her eyelashes, tightening her lips into what she hoped was an irresistible pout. "I suppose I could ask Mr. Ogden up at the bakery or the men at the foundry. I'd hoped—"

The sigh that interrupted her was not one of exasperation. It was one of surrender. Tom smiled. "Of course you can take my picture."

"Good." Lillie smiled back, not sure if her reaction was one of relief at having talked him into her scheme or just a natural response to his engaging smile. She told herself she'd rather believe it was the former, but the pleasant rush of warmth that surged through her body warned her it was not. Feeling her cheeks aflame again, Lillie shooed Tom toward the workshed and followed him inside. There were windows on two of the shed walls, and she nodded, approving. There would be enough light for her pictures.

Five minutes later the camera was set up just inside the door. Tom eyed it as if it were some outlandish instrument of torture. "What do you want me to do?"

"Relax, for one thing." Lillie couldn't contain the burst of laughter that escaped her in response to his anxiety. "You must have had your photograph taken before." She slipped a plate holder from its carrier and slid it into the back of the camera. Pretending to fumble with the flange, which prevented light from entering the camera and exposing the plate, she kept her voice light, her tone even. "Didn't you ever have your picture taken in Boston?"

Her question was met with stony silence.

Too careful to let Tom see how the stillness unnerved her, Lillie fiddled with the camera for a few more moments before she looked up to find him staring at her. His jaw was tight, his eyes piercing her as if he could read the motives behind her question with one searching stare.

She returned the look with one of utter bewilderment. "I'm sorry. I didn't hear your answer. I asked if you'd ever had your photograph taken in Boston."

Whatever the reason for Tom's wariness, he shrugged it off. "Of course," he answered. "But never like this." He took in the workshed, his tools, and Alex Campbell's printing cylinder with one sweep of his arm. "They were always portraits, like the ones you mentioned earlier. You know, the kind where my hair was combed, and my clothes were brushed—"

"And your face was clean." Lillie pointed to the smudge of grease along one side of Tom's nose. "No!" She shouted when he made a move to wipe it away. "I said natural pictures, and that means dirt and all."

Obediently Tom moved his hand away from his face. He picked up the mallet lying on the table and raised it, as if he were about to strike the cylinder. "How's this?"

Lillie tilted her head and studied the line of his raised arm and the effect it had on the composition of the picture. "That's fine," she assured him, "but . . ."

But it was not fine.

Bending to peer through the lens, she reviewed the composition again, looking for some clue to what was wrong.

The lighting near Tom's face was perfect, years of experience had taught Lillie that much. It was just enough to delineate his cheekbones, the strong, firm line of his chin and jaw, the slightly crooked angle of his nose that gave it both its appeal and its character.

At his back the light that seeped through the open spaces between the wallboards made the mallet and the huge printing cylinder stand out from the clutter of tools that hung along the wall. The angle of Tom's legs was just right, too. His feet apart, his weight forward on his right foot, she could see his muscles as they strained against the fabric of his dark trousers.

His arms . . . his arms were another thing altogether.

Lillie straightened and shook her head, exasperated and annoyed.

The sleeves of Tom's white shirt blended too readily with the light streaming in from the window at his side. Once the picture was taken and the glass-plate developed, he would look to be no more than a head and legs, and that, Lillie knew, would never do.

She propped her fists on her hips and considered the situation.

"Is something wrong?" Tom lowered the mallet and turned to her.

"No." Reluctant to admit she had not planned far enough ahead to anticipate problems with the light, Lillie dismissed his concern instantly. She peered through her lens once more and mumbled a very unladylike curse.

"Yes," she admitted. "The light's all wrong against that white shirt of yours. I don't suppose you could bring that thing outside?" She pointed to the printing cylinder.

Tom ran one hand over the back of his neck. "It just took us over an hour to haul it in here," he explained, his dark brows low over his eyes. "Even if I wanted it outside, I could never move it myself. And you would never be able to help."

"Well, perhaps we could try . . ." Lillie darted around the cylinder to check the composition from another angle. It was no good. Wherever she stood, the glare was just too great.

There was one solution, of course. A rather obvious one.

From the corner of her eye she chanced a quick glance at Tom. Obvious or not, he had apparently not thought of it. It was up to her to save the photograph, and this opportunity to ask Tom the questions that had been nagging her since her talks with Alex Campbell and Vincent Palusso yesterday.

Sighing again, more for effect than anything else, Lillie moved back to her camera. One hand on its bellows she swung around to face Tom. "I could come back later in the afternoon, I suppose, or . . ."

"Or?"

Lillie closed her eyes and blurted out the words. "Or you could take off your shirt again."

There was no response.

Slowly, as if she were afraid of what she might see, Lillie opened one eye. She opened the other.

Tom wasn't doing anything. He was merely standing there, gaping at her. Then, as if the request was not only startling, but pleasing as well, a slow smile lifted the corners of his lips, a smile that traveled all the way to his eyes.

He tossed the mallet down, crossed his arms over his broad chest, and leaned back against the table. "It's not every day an attractive young lady asks me to disrobe."

He was teasing her.

Lillie felt a smile twitch its way around her mouth. It was rather a delightful game, but as men were so apt to do, Tom was being a little too sure of the rules. A little too sure of himself.

She assumed she was supposed to be following the same rules. She should blush. She knew the rules would state that categorically. She should blush, and stammer, and probably look down at the ground and refuse to look up again until he apologized for acting like a cad.

Lillie wondered what Tom would do if the rules were changed. She scolded herself for the wicked plan that popped into her head at the same time she resolved to go ahead with it.

"That would be even better," she said, struggling to keep the delight from her voice. "Go ahead and undress. It will make a far more artistic picture. You know, like those statues of the old Greek gods."

Tom's face went ashen. He stood up straight. "But they didn't wear anything at all! Are you asking me to—"

It was all she could take. Lillie dissolved into laughter. Tom's eyes narrowed with suspicion, then widened with a look that could only be described as one of absolute relief. "You almost had me believing you!" He wiped the back of his hand along his forehead before he smiled and shook one finger at her in mock warning. "You'd better watch yourself, young lady. One of these days someone is going to take you up on your suggestions, and then what might happen?"

What might happen?

The prospect struck them both at the same time.

Lillie knew Tom's fading smile was a reflection of the expression on her own face, sensed that the quickening of her heartbeat was an echo of his, recognized, somewhere deep inside her where the truth could not be easily brushed aside, that what *might* happen was very much on both their minds.

For an instant she found herself wishing she could read the emotions behind Tom's fixed look. She wanted to know what thoughts caused his chest to rise and fall erratically, to learn why his dark eyes were suddenly lit with an inner fire, to understand the reason his expression softened at the same time his fingers clenched over themselves and his knuckles turned white.

As quickly as Lillie made the wish, she found herself rescinding it.

This was not teasing. Not any longer. This was serious. So serious, it was terrifying. And dangerous. And far too tempting to even dare consider.

Hoping to ease the tension that suddenly filled the air, as real and tangible as the oppressive heat that pushed in from every side, Lillie concentrated on her camera. Her fingers trembling, she rechecked the plate holder, resettled the legs of the tripod, readjusted the bellows. Bending again, she looked through the lens. "I think that will work just fine," she said, her voice quavering more than she liked. "It really will help to remove the shirt."

Tom shook himself out of whatever thoughts were holding him spellbound. In one quick movement he undid the buttons along the front of his shirt, slipped out of it, and resumed his position back at the workbench. "How's this?" Keeping himself motionless, he darted a look at Lillie, waiting for her approval.

"That," Lillie said without sounding nearly as jittery as she was, "is perfect." With an effort she pulled her gaze away from the glistening line of perspiration that made a soft rivulet in the hair on Tom's chest. "I'll need you to hold very still."

The first exposure went well. When she was done, Lillie allowed Tom a moment to relax while she removed the plate holder from the camera and inserted another.

Hoping to gauge his mood, she smiled over at Tom. He returned the smile with a heart-stopping one of his own.

It was now or never, Lillie told herself. Now, when he was relaxed, unsuspecting.

She adjusted the flange on the camera. "You know," she said, "I have a picture similar to this. It's of my brother, John. You remember, I told you about John."

Tom nodded, and when Lillie directed him, he picked up the mallet again.

She peered through the lens, then straightened, prepared to remove the cover over the shutter. "Do you have any brothers?" she asked.

Tom sucked in a sharp breath and held it for a second, as if steeling himself against the onslaught of her words. He tensed at the same time his eyes glinted at her with a look that was suddenly as wary as it was curious.

"I left Boston to get away from my family," he admitted, his voice tight and unnatural. "It's not something I like to discuss."

So much for that approach.

Lillie accepted the rebuff with a quick, apologetic smile. "I didn't mean to pry," she said. "It's just that I heard—"

"Heard what?"

Tom's question cut through her poorly disguised inquiry like a butcher's knife through suet. With a grunt he tossed down his mallet and faced her. Where only minutes before the expression on his face had been soft and appealing, now it was as hard as if it were cut from granite.

"I asked what you've heard." He took a step closer to her, his arms at his sides, his hands balled into fists. "What have you heard and who have you heard it from? You haven't been talking to Campbell again, have you?"

For one mad moment Lillie was tempted to lie.

It would be easy enough, she told herself. She'd simply shrug off Tom's apprehension and laugh her way over the nearly impenetrable wall he'd erected between them.

As quickly as the notion formed, she dismissed it.

Alex Campbell had been right. She was not a very good actress. Lillie accepted the realization along with the well-deserved look of reproach Tom directed her way.

There was something beyond the suddenly frosty look in his eyes that said her lies would get her nowhere. Something that told her this was far too important to be made into a game, even one designed to preserve her dignity.

Fighting back her apprehension, Lillie met Tom's gaze and refused to back down.

"I talked to Vincent Palusso. He says—"

"Palusso?" Tom's exclamation rattled the weathered wallboards. He took two steps toward Lillie, then swung around and paced to the far end of the shed and back again.

Damn the woman!

With each step he took, Tom repeated the curse over in his mind, expecting that the repetition would soothe his anger.

It didn't. The more he said it, the more earnest the oath became. First it was Jonah, fishing for information, and now Lillie. How much could any one man take?

Tom pulled himself to a stop alongside his workbench and swiped one hand through his hair. If she'd give him a moment, perhaps he could figure it out; determine why just thinking about Lillie discussing his private life with Vincent Palusso sent his temper soaring sky high.

It didn't take more than a moment for Tom to find the answer. He knew it, as surely as he knew the time of day by the slant of the sun or the time of night by the height of the moon.

He didn't want Lillie to know the truth.

The awareness hit Tom like a physical blow. With one hand he grabbed at the workbench to steady himself. A sudden icy chill filled his stomach, and he studied Lillie, hoping to discover how much she'd learned, praying it had not been the complete truth.

In an effort to divert the subject from his foolishness to hers, he leveled a stern look at Lillie. "It's indiscreet to be seen with Vincent Palusso," he said. "People in town will talk."

Lillie shrugged away the criticism. "We met in a public place. There's nothing anyone can say accept that we shared a bottle of whiskey at the Morning Star. Last I heard, there was no crime in that."

"No crime. No. But there's talk of Palusso being seen at the American House last night, spending money like it was water. You don't want to be involved—"

"So that's what happened to my money." Lillie's cheeks reddened, and she grasped her lower lip between her teeth. "Why, that no good snake. He took my money and he—"

"Your money?" Something in her voice struck a chord inside Tom. "Now I'm convinced you're in over your head. Why would you give Palusso money? He's a dangerous man—"

"Is he?" As if to try and gauge the truthfulness of all he said, Lillie took two short, unsteady steps toward Tom and stopped. She parried his question with one of her own. "Why? Why is he dangerous?"

"Why?" Tom grunted and discarded the question with a quick lift of one shoulder. "You know as well as I do. That man has a reputation."

"That's not why you want me to stay away from him." Lillie turned away. She snapped her camera closed and bent to loosen the legs of the tripod. With a quick reproachful glance at Tom, she slammed each leg up into itself. "You're afraid of Vincent Palusso, aren't you?" she challenged him. "Afraid of something he knows. If it's any consolation, he didn't tell me much of anything. He said I should ask you. He said I should ask you about Boston."

How any statement so simple could boil his blood so completely was beyond Tom. He didn't care why, he only knew it did. Forcing himself to keep from crossing the shed and shaking some sense into Lillie, he stood his ground and glared down at her.

"Stay out of it," he said, his voice so low it was no more than a rumble in his throat. "Stay away from Palusso and stay away from Campbell. They don't know what they're talking about."

"They know enough to recognize trouble when they see it. Why else would you follow Palusso through the town at night? Why else would you check on his mail or wait for him to receive a telegram?"

This was too much.

The closest thing at hand was his mallet and Tom picked it up and weighed it in his palm, itching to hurl it at the far wall. Instead, he banged it down on the workbench.

"What makes you think any of this is your business?" Try as he might he could no longer control his temper, and his voice boomed against the walls of the shed like cannon shot. He banged the mallet against the pitted table again. "What makes you think you can go snooping into other people's lives, poking that pretty nose of yours where it has no business?" One last time he slammed the hammer into the table.

"You are the most willful, stubborn, prying woman I've ever met. Stay out of it. Stay far out of it. It will backfire on you, Lillie. Backfire on both of us. I promised you I would stay in town, but if you keep meddling into things that don't concern you, I'll have no choice. I'll have to leave."

If he expected Lillie to be upset by the confession, he was disappointed.

Her face an impassive mask, Lillie lifted her camera, slung it over her shoulder, and turned to go. Before she stepped into the sunlight, she stopped and tossed one last look at Tom.

"That would be fine with me," she said, her voice as chilling and precise as his own. "As a matter of fact, there is nothing I would like more."

10

"I'M REALLY GLAD you're able to help me today." Bustling by, Lillie tousled Anthony Palusso's dark curls. "It's not easy making wet-plate prints," she said. "It takes a lot of equipment. And it takes a great deal of help. You're a godsend, Anthony. You really are."

Anthony was busy peering into the glass window at the front of Lillie's retouching stand. He looked up and smiled when she went by, his dark eyes bright with satisfaction and the reflected warmth of Lillie's compliment. The next second he went back to examining the stand, his thin, eager fingers playing with the hinges on the sides of the cabinet one second, poking into the drawer where Lillie kept her shadowing pencils the next.

Lillie smiled to herself and went into the darkroom. Earlier in the morning she'd packed two bottles of collodion into her big black valise. It never hurt to have another. She grabbed the bottle off the shelf and hurried back into the studio, stopping only long enough to give Anthony a quick, inquiring look. "You do have enough cookies in your pocket to last through the morning, don't you?" she asked.

His mouth already ringed with cookie crumbs, Anthony grinned and patted both pockets of his battered jacket.

"And you do know if you get thirsty anytime this afternoon, there's a jar of lemonade out in the garden, keeping nice and cool beneath the lowest branches of the lilac bush?"

Again, Anthony smiled and nodded.

"Good." As she usually did before she left for an assignment, Lillie made one final sweep of her studio to be sure she hadn't forgotten anything. Before she could finish, she pointed Anthony toward the back door, feeling fairly confident she would complete her search and make her own way there long before he stopped fiddling with the retouching stand. "We're ready," she said. "Are you sure your father won't mind?"

As if he'd been prodded to attention, Anthony stood up straight. His eyes darkened and his face paled. The transformation lasted no more than an instant. The next second he had replaced it with a cocky look, one so similar to his father's, it made the hair on the back of Lillie's neck stand on end.

With a lift of his scrawny shoulders, Anthony brushed off her question. "My father, he will not notice, I don't think, signorina. He has not been home for two, three days."

"Not home?" Lillie paused in her search and turned to face the boy. "What do you mean, not home? Surely he can't have gone far on the money he got from me!"

Anthony shook his head, the look in his eyes telling her adults were impossibly dull-witted. "No, no, signorina. That money, it was gone like this." He snapped his fingers. "He spend it at the hotel the day he got it. He has more money now. So much more money."

Curiosity was a terrible thing. Lillie reminded herself of the fact, though, even as she did, she knew she would not heed her own warning. Curiosity had caused the commotion between her and Tom last week. Curiosity had lured her into an embarrassing situation with Alex Campbell and another, more compromising one, with Vincent Palusso.

Still, she could not seem to help herself. Carefully she settled the collodion bottle into her valise, closed the bag, and lifted it with one hand. "Where did your father get this money?" she asked.

"You know, signorina, it is a funny thing." Anthony scratched one hand through his thick hair. "My father, he never have money. You know this to be true. But then, three nights ago a man, he come to visit our home. And when he leave, I see my father with a—how you say it, signorina?—a wad."

"Wad. Yes, that's correct." Barely listening, Lillie agreed mechanically. One hand at her mouth she tapped her top lip. "You said a man came to your home. Who was the man?"

Anthony squeezed his eyes shut, trying to remember. It didn't seem to help. When he opened them again, he looked no more enlightened than he had before. He screwed his face up, the look saying he was clearly confused. "A big man," he said. "Tall with black hair, wide shoulders. It was dark, only one lamp lit. I thought it was Signóre Tom."

"Tom?" The startling news caused Lillie to drop her valise. She scooped it out of the air before it could hit the ground and held on to the leather-bound handle with both hands. "Why would Tom give your father money?"

"Signorina, signorina." Obviously long-suffering and about to lose his infinite store of patience, Anthony rolled his eyes. "I said I thought it was Signóre Tom. I did not say it was Signóre Tom."

Like an actor readying himself for his entrance on stage, Anthony drew in a breath, moved back a step, and strode forward. With both hands he pretended to be parting a curtain and peering beyond it.

"I look out from the back room and watch them, and after a while the big man turns and I see it is not Signóre Tom, but a man who looks like him. I drop the curtain before they can see me." He replaced the imaginary draperies and, crouching down on his heels, bent his head. "And I try to listen, but I cannot hear good. When I lean too close"—Anthony clapped his hands together and fell onto the floor—"they see me and they kick me outside until they are finished." He stood and held both arms out at his sides, his palms up. "When I come back in, the man is gone and I see my father with the money."

"And that's the last you've seen of him? Your father, I mean. He's been gone for two days and you haven't seen him? He hasn't been there to get you your dinner or your breakfast?"

Anthony shrugged, a gesture so apathetic, it was chilling. "I am almost ten years old, signorina. I do not need a father to get my meals."

"And what do you eat?" Lillie went to stand opposite Anthony. Setting her valise on the floor, she bent to look into his eyes. "What do you eat when you're all alone?"

Anthony hoisted up Lillie's bag in both his hands and dragged it to the door. "I eat whatever I can find," he said, his voice muffled by the distance between them. "Bread. Cheese. There is usually something."

Usually something.

The words echoed inside Lillie's head and filled her mouth with a sour taste like vinegar. One hand on the back of the nearest chair to brace herself, she stood. She ignored the sick, twisted feeling in her insides and tried to keep her outrage from her voice. "You know, Anthony, you can always come here." She ventured a look at the child, hoping the statement sounded more like an invitation than an appeal. "I mean, when your father isn't home. If you're lonely or . . . or hungry and there isn't anyone around. I'm by myself and I'd appreciate the company."

It may have been a trick of the light, but she could have sworn she saw Anthony smile. He hid the expression with a respectful and very grown-up nod. "That is good of you, signorina, and I will think about it. If I am ever alone."

"*Bène.*" Lillie tried the Italian expression she'd heard Anthony use so many times and was rewarded with an appreciative smile.

"You learn good, signorina." Anthony pushed the back door open and stood against it so Lillie could pass outside. "Someday, perhaps we will speak together in Italian, you and me."

"I would like that very—"

The rest of Lillie's reply was lost when a shaggy dog of uncertain ancestry and even more dubious manners rounded the corner and jumped on her, knocking her words away along with her breath.

She staggered back and would have fallen if it hadn't been for Anthony.

"Down!" His voice low-pitched, his tone firm, Anthony commanded the dog. Instantly the animal sat back on its haunches, its long pink tongue lolling out one side of its mouth, its dark eyes lovingly trained on the boy.

Having lost little more than her breath and her dignity, Lillie recovered and studied the situation. "What's this?" she asked, looking from Anthony to the dog and back again to Anthony.

Anthony pulled his shoulders back and puffed out his chest. "This," he said, patting the dog on the top of his matted head, "is Tom."

"Tom." Lillie studied the mangy animal. In spite of her resolve to put aside the anger she felt each time she thought of Tom and the terrible argument they'd had last week, she could not control herself. She found herself whispering a silent prayer that the dog had a better disposition than his namesake.

From his appearance she had to guess the prospect was not likely. The animal was no more than a puppy; she could see as much by the proportions of its feet compared to the rest of his body. His coat was a tangled mess of black fur, thistles, and twigs; his feet were caked in the same mud she had made Anthony scrape off his shoes before he'd entered her house this morning.

"Tom." Lillie nodded and tried to contain her smile. "That's his name?"

"*Sì.*" Anthony's expression grew solemn. "When I find him by the river, I make a wish for a female dog. But this is not so. He is a male dog, so I name him Tom."

"And if he were a female, what would you have named him then?"

Anthony looked up at her, his expression as sweet as a cherub's. "Why, then, of course, I would have called him Signorina Lillie."

Red, white, and blue.

Tom stood back in the shade of an oak tree and scanned the scene in front of him.

The American House Hotel was draped in red, white, and blue bunting. So was the gazebo across from the town hall, the front of the Congregational Church, and the outside of the cabinet factory.

Even the townsfolk themselves seemed to have been caught up in the heat of red, white, and blue fever. Bow ties, gowns, parasols: Tom watched, amazed, as an odd assortment of patriotic finery made its way past him and on toward the American House.

"Mighty impressive, huh?" Jonah Hatcher breathed in deep and cast a glance around the center of town. "Nothing like the Glorious Fourth! And nothing like today's celebration. Makes you appreciate all our forebears done this past hundred years, don't it?"

Tom nodded. Though he was not usually given to sentiment, he had to admit, something about today's celebration caused his eyes to mist.

With a short, bitter laugh he imagined what some of his highfalutin Boston friends would say if they could see him now, smack in the middle of nowhere, celebrating the Fourth of July with farmers, laborers, and other assorted townspeople.

Tom laughed again, not bitterly this time, but with a sense of relief. They might be farmers and laborers—or as he knew his Boston friends would say, hayseeds and hicks—but they were the most honest and industrious people he'd ever met. And the most friendly.

He nodded good morning to the minister's wife and her line of giggling daughters, following behind her like ducklings.

"You're going to be in the picture, ain't you?" Jonah poked Tom's shoulder and pointed toward the hotel where the citizens of Wellington were assembling for a formal group portrait.

Tom eyed the scene. Although the photograph was not scheduled to be taken for another thirty minutes, the spectacle outside the American House looked to be one of utter chaos.

Farmers from the surrounding areas had arrived in town bright and early this morning. Their carts and wagons were lined up along Main Street, their wives gossiping in tight groups, their children scampering around the park. The cornet band was tuning up in front of the hotel. Adding to the confusion, the mayor, Austin Palmer, stood at the center of the gazebo, clearing his throat with all the gumption he could muster, trying his best to begin the formal festivities.

In the midst of the chaos one figure stood out, the picture of composure.

Lillie was already behind her camera, directing the crowd to line up against the facade of the American House. Like a conductor before an orchestra, she seemed to have control of the whole situation. With one wave of her hand she instructed people to move right or left, steered lost children to searching parents and lost parents to searching children, calmed even the members of the town council, most of whom could not wait for their turns both in front of the camera and behind the podium.

"You don't look too eager to get into that photograph." Either following Tom's gaze or reading his mind, Jonah lifted his eyebrows and sucked on his teeth. He scratched one meaty forefinger along his cheek. "You and the lady had a falling out?"

Tom snickered, but there was no humor in the sound. "A falling out is putting it mildly. You know, Jonah, there are some things about women I just don't understand."

"Some things?" Jonah threw back his head and roared with laughter. When Tom looked at him in wonder, Jonah clapped him on the shoulder.

"I've been married fifteen years," Jonah said. "Besides my Sarah, we got six girls of our own in that house. Some things about women you don't understand? I'll tell you, my friend, there are a lot of things about women I don't understand. If I did, I'd be the richest man on the face of God's green earth."

Still chuckling, Jonah waved to his wife and family as they rounded the corner from Mechanics Street. He said his goodbyes and went to stand with them for the group photograph.

Tom watched him go. But only for a moment.

As if she were the lodestone and he the magnet, his thoughts and his gaze returned to Lillie.

While just about everyone else in town was draped in red, white, and blue, Lillie was dressed in green, the same simple green dress he'd seen her in the day she came calling at his shop, asking him to fix her teapot. The dress without the bustle. The one that flowed along the smooth curve of her hips and the tempting roundness of her backside like . . .

Mumbling a curse, Tom turned and stalked through the park. The Morning Star was closed today. But he knew J. S. DeWolf and his staff were inside, preparing food for tonight's big picnic.

He needed a beer.

One beer was hardly enough, but Tom pushed away the second before he'd taken more than two sips and went back outside.

Looking toward the American House, he smiled approvingly. The town photograph had apparently been taken: There was no longer a lineup of people outside the hotel. Instead, the park was filled with groups of picnickers, families and friends gathered together over a holiday lunch.

At the far end of the park Tom could see the small, dark tent that had been erected just to the south of the Methodist Church. He didn't pause to look at it. He knew what it was. He'd heard talk around town. Talk of how Lillie was going to take special mammoth wet-plate photographs of today's celebration, photographs that apparently had to be developed right on the spot in what was apparently called a light tent.

Wishing he could shift the focus of his thoughts as easily, Tom walked away, concentrating instead on a line of children trying to hobble their way down Main Street on homemade stilts.

When he came to the empty lot at the corner of Magyar Street and Main, Tom paused to listen to a snake oil salesman, busy enticing people with his exotic wares.

"Of course it cures the grip." The man waved a bottle of vivid blue liquid over his head. "And the ague. Why, it's even God's gift—God's gift—to those of you sufferin' from the rheumatism."

Tom shook his head, amazed at how naive a holiday crowd could be. Any other day of the year these were the most practical people on earth. But give them a sunny blue sky, the song of summer birds in their ears, and a whole day off without the responsibilities of workshop or farmstead, and they turned as gullible as babes in the woods.

He watched a burly farmer hand the flimflam man a dollar bill and was about to walk away when something else caught his eye. Anthony was in the crowd, eagerly watching the medicine show.

For a moment Tom thought of dragging the boy away, lecturing him on the art of prudent buying and giving him a hefty dose of the one thing this salesman wasn't peddling— healthy skepticism. But the sun was shining, the birds were singing, and it was a holiday.

He tapped Anthony on the shoulder, handed the boy a fifty-cent piece, and crossed over to the park.

There were no more than a dozen or so paces between him and Lillie's light tent when he heard what sounded like an argument.

Tom tipped his head, curious, but he could make out little except the low rumbling voice of a man, apparently very upset, and the softer, muffled answers of a woman.

It took him another minute to realize the voices were coming from the tent.

" . . . betrayed me, dammit." The man's voice rose further. "You led me to think—"

"Don't be ridiculous!"

This was Lillie's voice, and Tom stopped, frozen in place by the unmistakable hostility of her words. "If you weren't so caught up in your own—"

As quickly as Lillie's reply came, it stopped, cut off by a faint, muffled cry.

It was all Tom needed to hear.

Without waiting to see if anyone else had heard the argument and decided to respond, without stopping to think what

Lillie would say or who she might be talking to, without pausing to consider his own impulsive reaction, Tom sprinted across the grass and burst into the tent.

It took a moment for his eyes to adjust to the dim light inside, but when they did he saw that Lillie was backed against one wall of the tent, a look as fierce as lightning flashing from her eyes. Standing directly in front of her was Elmore Montgomery.

Tom crossed the tent in two quick strides and, clamping his hand down on Montgomery's arm, spun him around.

Montgomery blinked, his mouth agape, his expression a mixture of outrage and complete astonishment. Even in this light Tom could see that Montgomery's cheeks were red, but it took him another moment to realize why.

Montgomery's hair was shining with something that looked to be a cross between egg whites and glue. Even as Tom watched, the viscous substance oozed its way down Montgomery's head and over his ears and plopped unceremoniously on the shoulders of his expensive suit.

Recovering with a grunt, Montgomery turned his head to look at his right shoulder. As if he could not believe the sight, his eyes widened and he shivered, the action sending even more of the sticky substance sliding down his head. Montgomery's jowls quivered, and he jerked out of Tom's grasp and directed a venomous look at Lillie.

Lillie never flinched. Clutching a dark glass bottle at her waist, she pulled her shoulders back. For no more than an instant her gaze flashed to Tom's.

He could read nothing in her eyes, nothing past an instant of surprise, a moment of astonishment, before she turned her gaze away again and trained her full attention on Elmore Montgomery.

"How dare you!" Montgomery spluttered. He looked from Lillie to Tom. "This young lady attacked me. She . . . she poured that stuff . . ." He eyed the bottle in Lillie's hand with revulsion. "She poured that sludge all over me. I'll have the shrew arrested. Arrested for assault. You're my witness, Reilly. You saw it. You can testify on my behalf."

Tom stepped back, considering the situation. "I suppose I could do that," he said.

Lillie's enraged outcry and Montgomery's self-satisfied bark of approval overlapped, the intensity of both their responses smothered by the walls of the tent. Lillie stepped forward, her eyes flashing at Tom the way he'd seen them flash at Montgomery, but before she could speak, Tom stopped her with one quick movement of his hand.

"I said I supposed I could." Tom turned his attention to Montgomery and smiled. "That is, if you want everyone to find out you attacked this woman."

"What!" Montgomery's eyes popped open. "I never—"

"Saw it with my own eyes." Tom nodded. "What an awful thing. Miss Valentine here, trying to do her work, and you sneaking up on her, coming at her like an animal—"

"I . . . I never . . ." Montgomery's protest was lost in a gurgle of outrage.

"She had to protect herself. Poor thing. Had no choice." Tom leaned toward Montgomery and lowered his voice. "It would be an awful thing for your reputation if the people of this town found out," he said. "Worse still if Alex Campbell got wind of the incident. I don't imagine it would take long for the newspapers in Cleveland to pick up on a story like this."

"So that's how it's to be." Shaking his shoulders, Montgomery gathered the shreds of his dignity. He threw his head back and, completely ignoring Tom, turned a vicious eye on Lillie.

"I won't forget." Montgomery's voice was as cool now as it had been furious before. "I never forget."

"Neither do I." Lillie stepped forward, the brown glass bottle held at her waist like a shield, her voice as steady as the look she directed at Montgomery. "I haven't forgotten the woolen mills. I haven't forgotten Hank. And I'm going to make sure you never do, either."

Montgomery accepted her challenge in silence, his malicious glare battering against Lillie's. Lillie gave no ground. She simply returned the look, her eyes as icy as Tom had ever seen them. But when Montgomery pushed past Tom, threw back the flap of the tent, and disappeared outside, Lillie let go a long, unsteady breath.

Hoping to regain her strength along with her composure, Lillie closed her eyes and willed herself to relax. Even with her eyes shut she could tell Montgomery had left. When he yanked the tent flap aside, she saw the brightness of the afternoon sunlight. As quickly as it came, the light was extinguished. Hoping to avoid another confrontation, she found herself wishing Tom would leave, too.

She knew she could never be that lucky. He was still here, not three paces away. She could hear the smooth trace of his breathing, the muffled sounds of his boots against the grass.

"It's a good thing I came along."

Tom's comment brought her to attention. Trying to control her temper and finding it inordinately difficult, Lillie shook herself into action. Kneeling, she deposited the bottle of collodion back in her valise and snapped the case shut. She stood and tossed a look at Tom.

"I don't see why," she said. "I obviously had the situation well under control." She turned toward the inner part of the tent where another flap separated the outer entryway from the small, dark area where her glass-plates were developed. "If you'll excuse me . . ."

"Lillie."

Tom's hand came down on her arm and stopped her. His touch was not as rough as it was insistent. Steeling her courage, Lillie spun to face him, not even trying to hide the outrage that still simmered in her.

Tom's dark eyes searched her face. "Is that all the thanks I get?" His expression was as exasperated as his voice. "You had the situation under control. Is that all you have to say? I thought that was a handy little rescue."

"I'm surprised you bothered." Lillie shrugged out of his grasp. "I would have thought you had better things to do than come to the rescue of the most willful, stubborn, prying woman you ever met."

"You *are* the most willful, stubborn, prying woman I ever met." Tom matched her word for word, his voice as clipped as hers. "You are also," he continued, his words softening along with his look, "the bravest and the most determined woman I've ever met." He tipped his head in the direction of the tent opening and the now-departed Montgomery. "What was that all about?"

Lillie laughed off the question. She hoped the affectation would convince Tom she was not afraid of Montgomery at the same time she prayed that by treating both Montgomery and his final warning with indifference, she could dull the sharp pang of worry that had already begun to eat its way through her self-control.

It didn't work. Montgomery's parting threat still ringing in her ears, she shivered and looked at Tom, searching his eyes for comfort. "He knows who I am," she said. "The foreman of his woolen mill is down for the holiday. He saw me at the group photograph session this morning and—"

"He knows you from Cleveland?" Tom's voice cut through hers. He understood. The intensity of his words told her as much. He understood enough to recognize the danger. "So Montgomery knows you weren't taking his picture simply for the pleasure of it."

Lillie mumbled a word of derision. "I'll never be invited to tea again."

"And now you've got Montgomery angry at you."

"It's nothing." Lillie shook off his concern, too moved by the look of admiration in Tom's eyes to let him know how much it affected her.

"And you're still angry at me."

Lillie did not respond. She looked away.

"Well, I'm just as angry at you." The note of challenge that edged Tom's voice caused a new spark of fury to flicker in Lillie. She snapped her gaze to his, ready to meet and dispute whatever criticisms he would pose.

But as soon as Tom had her attention, the anger melted from his eyes. His voice softened. "There," he said. "We're arguing again. Does that make you feel any better?"

He did not wait for Lillie to answer the question. As if to give himself courage, Tom sucked in a deep breath and scooped Lillie's hands into his.

It was not the feel of his hands against hers that caused Lillie's heart to jump into her throat. She reassured herself of the fact even as she found herself winding her fingers through Tom's.

She was upset, a rational voice inside her head reminded her. Still reeling from her showdown with Elmore Montgomery. Still tired from a long morning of exhausting work. Still dizzy from the effects of the dark tent and the sultry air.

Why else would she be standing here, paralyzed? Why else would she be too weak to move away, too helpless to fight the seemingly innocent contact of Tom's hands against hers, a contact that made her heart turn over inside her?

With an effort Lillie pulled her thoughts away from the unsettling effects of Tom's touch. She did not attempt to pull her hands away, even when Tom raised them to his lips.

"That day you came to take my picture, why did you say you wanted me to leave?" he murmured, his words no more than a whisper against her fingers.

Of all the questions he could have asked, this was the one she dreaded most. The one she could not bring herself to lie about. The one she would never dare to answer honestly.

"The truth, Lillie."

He must have been able to see inside her head. Still holding her hands close in his, Tom pinned her with a look, a look that searched beyond her excuses and lies, a look that demanded the truth.

"You don't want to know." Lillie's feeble response fell dead against the canvas walls.

"I do." Tom tightened his hold, and his eyes sparked with the intensity of his response. "I've been over and over it inside my head, and I still can't understand it, Lillie." He commanded her attention when she looked away. "Lillie, tell me. Please."

It was too much.

Unable to bear the tenderness in Tom's eyes, unable to endure the gentleness of his touch, Lillie decided on a tactical retreat. It was the coward's way out. She was certain of that. But right now the coward's way seemed the only way.

Brushing past Tom, she hurried to the entrance of the tent and was outside before he could recover from his surprise and move.

The sunlight was blinding.

Lillie blinked against the brightness, but she didn't let it stop her. She strode across the park, never bothering to look back.

"I just want to know why you want me to leave."

It was Tom's voice, raised above the hubbub of the afternoon festivities. Raised enough to carry down Main Street so that it seemed half the citizens of Wellington heard it. They stopped—all of them—and turned to stare.

Lillie, too, was frozen in her place. For one moment she entertained the thought of running home as fast as she could and hiding beneath her bed. She knew that would do her no good. They were already attracting a small crowd, a crowd so eager to see and hear all that was going on, it surrounded them, foiling all chance of escape.

There was only one thing to do.

Praying the embarrassment did not kill her before she had a chance to exact her revenge on Tom Reilly, Lillie turned to face him.

Tom stood just outside the tent, his hands on his hips, his lips clamped shut to contain the frustration and anger that had prompted him to raise his voice.

He cast a glance around the small circle of interested picnickers who had gathered to see what was going on. The sight obviously surprised him as much as it had Lillie.

His astonishment lasted no more than a moment. The next second one of Tom's dark eyebrows shot up and his face split with a slow, sly smile.

His gaze still fastened to Lillie's, he gave her a formal nod of assent, as if to say he'd accepted her challenge, accepted it and was prepared to meet it. Pulling his shoulders back, he grinned a friendly greeting at the people who were gaping at him.

"I just want to know why she wants me to leave," Tom said again, with a wide-eyed, innocent scan of the crowd. "Is that asking too much?"

Apparently not. As one, the townsfolk turned their collective gaze on Lillie.

She hesitated, too confused to know what to say, too embarrassed to say it, even if she did.

"I . . . I . . . ." Lillie looked around the circle of interested spectators, hoping for deliverance.

It never came. The townsfolk of Wellington merely stared at her, stared at her and waited.

Lillie was sure her face was getting redder by the second. It wasn't the sun. It wasn't even the heat. It was the awkward situation, the fixed looks on the faces in the crowd, the self-satisfied smile on Tom's face.

The realization did little to help her composure. "Oh, bother!" Lillie wailed. Pivoting on her heels, she pushed through the crowd, not sure where she was headed and not even caring.

She didn't need to turn around to know Tom was following her. She only needed to see the animated, excited expressions on the faces of the onlookers to know it was so. Tom caught up to her in less than a minute and, grabbing for one of her hands, spun her to face him.

"You'd better kiss her!"

The voice was Jonah Hatcher's, Lillie was sure of that, just as she was sure that the grunt punctuating the last word was the result of Sarah Hatcher's elbow strategically meeting her husband's ribs.

Tom obviously heard the suggestion, but blessedly, he ignored it. "I asked you a question, Lillie," Tom said. His voice was hushed, too quiet to be heard by any except those closest to them. The crowd moved in, straining so as not to miss a single nuance of the conversation.

Lillie looked from the host of eager faces surrounding them to Tom. "You asked me a question," she said, "but I'm not about to answer it. Not here."

"Then when will you answer it?" An elderly lady sitting on a checkered picnic blanket got Lillie's attention by tapping on the toes of her shoes. Astonished, Lillie looked down, and the woman shook a denuded chicken bone at her in admonition. "It isn't right to make a gentleman come begging, my girl. You'll see. You'll lose him. Lose him for certain, making him run after you." The old woman shook her head and mumbled under her breath. "Not the way things were done in my day."

"You see that?" Tom winked his thanks to the old lady and turned his attention back to Lillie, struggling to contain a smile. "We can't disappoint the poor old thing. She wants to know, Lillie. When will you answer my question?"

"What was the question?" The voice obviously belonged to a latecomer, and as one, the crowd heaved a sigh, reluctant to pause in the middle of the drama to bring the man up to date.

"Reilly wants to know why the photographer lady here wants him to leave," another voice explained. "Just got here myself. Don't know for sure what it's about—"

"She can't owe him money." This was a woman's voice, and with each syllable the lady spoke, Lillie felt the blood drain from her face. "Pays her bills right on time. Even at the dry goods store. Why, I know for a fact she ordered three yards of bright blue fabric not two weeks ago and—"

"Must be another reason then," Jonah Hatcher broke in. He was apparently recovered from the blow to his midsection and enjoying the show as much as anyone. "You say she wants him to leave? Lovers' spat, you can be sure of that. Tom said something to offend her. You know how he can be."

"Or it might have something to do with her going to see Alex Campbell last week." Try as she might, Lillie could not identify this voice. She stopped making the effort. Instead, she merely stood still, too stunned to do any more than listen. "She was in Campbell's office, you know. Right inside about nine o'clock in the morning—"

"And then over at the saloon." Another voice chimed in. "But that's not to be spoken of when women and children are here—"

"Except that we women know it. No. I think it more than likely has something to do with Hank Graham. You know, he left her the house and the business and . . ."

Dazed, Lillie listened to the flurry of voices all around her, discussing her life—her private life—as if it were the plot of some popular romantic novel.

Too embarrassed to look anywhere else, she brought her gaze up to meet Tom's. As talk of Lillie's private goings-on increased, so did Tom's chagrin, until he looked as mortified as Lillie felt. Their gazes locked, bewilderment and amazement mirrored on both their faces. It was too much. They both began to laugh.

Their laughter was enough to silence the townsfolk, who were sure they had missed something significant.

The sudden, uncanny silence made Lillie laugh even harder. She laughed until her sides ached, and when she saw tears welling in Tom's eyes, she laughed all the more.

It wasn't until both their laughter slowed that Lillie fished a handkerchief from her pocket, wiped her eyes, and handed the square of silk to Tom.

"Well," he said, swiping at his own eyes. "What's it to be, Lillie? Will you tell me why you want me to leave?"

"Why does she want him to leave?" The crowd took up the question, passing it from person to person until it echoed around Lillie, filling the park and the clear July air.

It was too much like the scene of some farcical play. Lillie shook her head, certain the gesture would wake her from a sound sleep, confident the preposterous dream would end.

It did not and she shrugged, surrendering to the crowd, and the day, and the look in Tom's eyes that told her there would be no respite from the badgering until his question was answered.

Two could play the game as easily as one.

The idea presented itself before she had sense enough to stop it, and Lillie succumbed to it, deciding what Tom could give, he could just as well take.

She smiled at him sweetly and, grabbing for one of his hands, held it tightly in her own. Lillie cleared her throat and raised her voice so it could be heard all the way to the back of the crowd. "I want him to leave," she said, "so I can stop thinking about him."

Tom had not expected such bluntness. She could tell as much from the look on his face. The reality of the situation dawned slowly, but when it did, his cheeks paled, his eyes grew wide with a look so akin to panic, it nearly made Lillie feel sorry for him. Nearly.

"Why don't you want to think about him?" The question was shouted from the back of the crowd.

"Yeah, Reilly's a nice enough young man. You could do worse!" This comment was met with a smattering of applause and cries of "Here! Here!"

"You're right," Lillie admitted, glancing over her shoulder to acknowledge the statement. "He is nice. Too nice. Far too nice to concern himself with a woman who's willful and stubborn and prying, don't you think?" She glanced around the crowd for acceptance and was rewarded by another sprinkling of reassuring cheers.

"That don't mean he should leave." Nathan Hatcher sounded so personally affronted by the suggestion that Lillie was tempted to stop the game.

But it was too late for that.

Nathan was standing just to the right, and Lillie directed a quick look at the boy. "Not the best thing for him or even for Wellington," she said, her voice ringing through the July air, as clear as a bell. She tightened her hold on Tom's hand and looked at him. "The best thing for me," she admitted. "Because then I could stop wondering what he's doing, and where he's going, and who he's speaking to."

Her boldness did not last as long as her discourse. Before she got any farther, her courage wavered. Her voice trembled and she finished her speech in a whisper meant for Tom's ears alone.

"I want you to leave so I can get on with my life and take back my heart and stop worrying about you."

She had never seen him at a loss for words.

Tom's lips twitched as if there was something he wanted to say. His eyes flashed to Lillie's as if there was something he needed to tell her. He couldn't. He merely stood and stared at her, too amazed to say anything.

"Now you'd better kiss her!" Jonah Hatcher's voice broke the stillness.

For a moment Lillie was afraid Tom might follow the advice. His eyes lit with a devilish spark. He smiled, first at the crowd and then at Lillie, and leaned forward.

He never had a chance to do more.

As quickly as the mischievous look brightened Tom's dark eyes, they clouded with bewilderment and he sniffed the air uncertainly and looked around him.

Lillie, too, smelled the source of his surprise long before she saw it. She didn't need to look down to know they'd been joined by Tom the Dog.

"What the—?"

Tom looked from the dog sitting squarely on his feet to Lillie.

"Tom," she said, barely controlling a smile. "That's his name. Tom. He belongs to—"

"Scusi! Scusi!" They heard Anthony's voice from the back of the crowd.

Tom nodded, understanding perfectly without further explanation. He loosened his hold on Lillie's hand and waited for Anthony to propel his way through the crowd.

"He is a good dog, Signóre Tom. Really." Anthony began his apologies before he was within three feet of Lillie and Tom. "He cannot help it that he wants to come meet you. I tell him about you. I tell him he will be lucky when he can meet Signóre Tom."

"I see." Tom's nostrils flared and he eyed the dog. "And have you told him how lucky the rest of us will be once he's been washed?"

"It is not his fault." Though Anthony could not possibly know why the crowd was gathered, he took full advantage of the audience to further his cause. He looked around, his hands out in appeal. "He see the ducks over at Signóre Wadsworth's pond and—"

"Good Gad!" The exclamation came from Lawton Wadsworth, who was standing right at the center of the circle. The old man's face turned an unattractive shade of plum, and he pushed through the crowd and hurried toward home.

Tom looked down at Anthony. "Did you ever think that maybe the dog's just hungry?"

"Hungry." Anthony considered the recommendation. "*Sì*. He is hungry, signóre." The boy looked from Tom to Lillie expectantly. "I am, too."

It was all Lillie needed to know.

"Come on," she said. The crowd parted, and Lillie wrapped one arm around Anthony's shoulders and led him to where she'd left her picnic basket. "Let's have some lunch."

Anthony tugged her to a stop. "And Tom, he will have lunch, too?"

Lillie turned to find both the man and the dog waiting for her answer, the expressions on face and muzzle so forlorn, she could ignore neither one.

"Yes," she said. "Tom will have lunch, too. Both Toms!"

11

"Do you wish you could be in Philadelphia, at the Centennial Exhibition?" Lillie sipped the last of her lemonade and looked around the park. "I hear it's quite exciting."

"Nope." Tom answered without hesitation. He brushed the crumbs of Lillie's fresh-baked buttermilk biscuits off his hands and leaned back on his elbows. "This is as exciting as I like it, and that's just fine by me. The city, the noise, the traffic . . ." He made a face. "I can do without all that."

Lillie wrapped her arms around her legs and rested her chin on her knees. "It would be nice to see Archibald Willard's painting, though, wouldn't it? I hear it's the highlight of the Exhibition. He'd already left town with it by the time I moved to Wellington, so I never saw it. Did you, Tom? I hear it's called *The Spirit of Seventy-Six.*"

"It is. And I can point out to you right here and now the men who posed for it." Tom swung around and pointed casually to a group of men and boys lounging outside the town hall. "There's the adult drummer," he said. "And the boy drummer. I hear the fife player's gone off to Philadelphia with Mr. Willard for the Exhibition."

"And you're glad you're not with them."

"That's right." Tom sighed and laid back against Lillie's

picnic blanket. "I'm happy right here," he said. "Right where I am."

It was almost too perfect. The thought nagged at Tom's mind even when he tried to put it to rest. Now that he and Lillie had called a truce—at least while they finished their lunch—he found himself feeling guilty. The day, the lunch, the company. It was all too perfect.

Tom opened one eye and watched as Lillie began to repack her picnic basket. Fascinated by each smooth, efficient move, captivated by the enchanting play of light and shadow against the silky green fabric of her gown, bewitched by the mahogany highlights the sun brought out in her dark hair, he settled back and enjoyed the view, content.

It had hardly sunk in yet, all Lillie had said when they were in the park, surrounded by curious onlookers. It had hardly sunk in at all.

Between Anthony's constant jabbering over lunch, and Tom the Dog's constant begging, they had had less than a moment between them to discuss all that had been said. And now, now when Anthony was finally gone somewhere and the dog was gone with him, what were they talking about? Art.

Tom shook his head, annoyed with himself. He rolled over onto his stomach, propped his head on his arms, and gave Lillie a searching look.

"Did you mean all those things you said?" he asked.

Lillie did not look at him. She continued her packing, wrapping the last of the blueberry pie in a square of cloth before she set it on top of the basket.

"You mean all that about wanting you to go?" She tossed the question out as if it were no more than a casual inquiry, but Tom saw the brief tightening of the muscles of her neck and jaw that betrayed her real feelings. "I had to say something, didn't I?" Finished, Lillie sat back. "I mean, you were intent on embarrassing me in front of the entire town. I had to defend myself."

Tom raised himself on his arms, his face no more than a few inches from Lillie's, his eyes probing beyond hers. "And you didn't mean any of it?"

For a moment he thought she was about to lie, to brush off his question with another one of her elegant, feathery laughs. She did not. Lillie looked away, but only for a second. Just as quickly, she brought her eyes back to his.

"I meant every word," she admitted, her brow creasing as if the admission was as much a puzzle to her as it was to him. "I suppose it's about time you knew that."

Tom felt a smile crinkle the corners of his mouth. He spun around so that he was sitting next to Lillie and took her right hand in his left.

"I'm glad." He brought her hand to his lips and placed a kiss on the center of her palm.

"Don't." Though she couldn't control a giggle, Lillie tried to pull her hand away. She looked over her shoulder to the other picnickers still relaxing in the park. "We don't want another scene."

Tom laughed. "No. We don't."

He stood and offered Lillie a hand. Pulling her to her feet, he was about to offer to take her picnic basket back to the house when Anthony ran up.

"Here it is! I got it!" Anthony waved a bottle of bilious green liquid above his head. He pulled himself to a stop in front of Tom and Lillie and presented them the bottle with a flourish.

"This," he said with a wide smile, "is for you."

He handed the bottle to Lillie, and while Tom waited for her to tell him what this was all about, he gave Anthony a look.

"Is that what you did with my fifty cents?" he asked, not as exasperated as he was interested. "What is it?" When Anthony did not answer, he turned back to Lillie. "What is it?"

"What is it?" Lillie cleared her throat. "It is," she said, reading the label, " 'Doctor Dennison's Miracle Formula. A tonic from the East. A restorative elixir made from a secret recipe of wondrous herbs and spices. Guaranteed to stimulate the interest of even the most reluctant of admirers.' I'm afraid it is," Lillie said, looking up at Tom, "a love potion."

"*Sì*. That is right." Anthony hooked his fingers beneath his suspenders and beamed at them like an avuncular guardian angel. "You two, I think you need something. One day you are talking, the next day you are not. It is too much for me to understand."

"Well, Anthony . . ." Tom took the bottle from Lillie and studied it. "I can't tell you how much we appreciate this. But you know something, Anthony?"

"*Sì*, what is it, signóre?"

Tom smiled over at Lillie. He leaned closer and brushed her lips with his. It was not so much a kiss as it was a gesture designed to gauge her reaction and the truth of all she'd told him.

Lillie smiled at the contact, and Tom felt his heart skip a beat. He kept his gaze fastened to Lillie's, more sure than ever that what he was about to tell Anthony was the truth, and more delighted than ever that it was. He tucked the bottle into his suit coat pocket. "I don't think we'll be needing any of this after all."

It was just for tonight.

Lillie tipped her head back, her eyes half-closed, and watched the spiral of colored lights and red, white, and blue bunting whirl past her like the dancing colors of a rainbow.

Hoping to keep the guilty voices inside her head at bay, she repeated her promise.

It was just for tonight.

Just for tonight she'd allow herself the delicious pleasure of gliding across the dance floor caught in Tom's arms. Just for tonight she would yield to the comfort of his company, the encouragement of his open, friendly smile, the excitement of his touch.

Just for tonight.

And tomorrow?

Tomorrow she would tell him his involvement with her was too dangerous to continue. She would remind him that the animosity between her and Elmore Montgomery was out in the open now, and tell him that Montgomery was an enemy who could prove deadly. Tomorrow she would explain about Hank.

That would be enough to convince Tom to leave her alone. And if he would not?

Opening her eyes, Lillie glanced at Tom. His face was flushed with the exertion of the waltz, washed with the yellows and oranges of the torches that flamed at each end of the dance floor.

Tom felt her eyes on him and looked down at her, and a smile touched his lips.

Lillie returned the smile even while her heart squeezed with the sting of regret.

Tomorrow, she decided, if he told her he would not—or could not—leave her be, she would announce she was going back to Cleveland, back to where she would no longer be either a temptation or a threat.

The dance ended and Tom slipped one arm around Lillie's waist and led her to the punch table. The gesture was so spontaneous, it was frightening. Nearly as frightening as how good it felt, and how natural, and how Lillie knew she was smiling back at the various townsfolk who saw the show of affection and nodded their approval.

Tom had just handed her a glass of punch and took one for himself when Anthony skidded across the dance floor and landed at their feet.

Tom gave him a glare of disapproval, a glare softened by a tiny smile and a look that said, though his entrance was not the most elegant, Anthony was certainly welcome to share the evening festivities.

The boy stood and brushed the legs of his trousers. "I see it work!" His dark eyes moved from Lillie to Tom, and he smiled.

Lillie swallowed a mouthful of punch. "What worked?" she asked.

"The *tonico* I give you, the tonic." Anthony nodded solemnly. "You are dancing. You are being friendly. Like lovers, yes? It was a good way to spend fifty cents, I think."

Tom laughed and ruffled one hand through Anthony's hair. "Love potions do not work," he told the boy, though it was apparent Anthony was far too pleased with himself to listen. "What works is when people respect each other, and admire each other, and—"

"And keep their hands off other people's property!"

How he'd come across the fairgrounds and the dance floor without them noticing, Lillie never knew. As if he'd materialized out of the night like a sinister wraith, Vincent Palusso suddenly stood toe-to-toe with Tom. He clamped one hand on Tom's wrist, wrenching it away from where it rested atop Anthony's head.

Tom's eyes sparked dark fire, his expression hardened. He brushed off Palusso's hand as if it were no more than a nuisance, like the annoying stick of a mosquito.

Neither man spoke, and something in the silence attracted the crowd's attention. About to launch into another waltz, the cornet band fell silent. Jonah Hatcher appeared from near the food table, brushed the last bits of chocolate cake crumbs from his hands, and stood at Tom's shoulder. Behind him Alex Campbell took his place, his keen eyes darting back and forth between the men, assessing the situation, sending Lillie a message both of encouragement and warning.

"Is there something we can do for you, Palusso?"

It took Lillie a moment to realize it was Tom who had spoken. His voice held a note of silky defiance and an edge f contempt.

Palusso did not answer. He met Tom's unwavering look for a minute before he turned his gaze to Lillie. His shoulders swayed as he did, and his eyes rolled back in his head when they met the light of the torch that flickered at Lillie's back.

It was only then she realized Palusso was drunk.

Instinctively Lillie laid one hand on Anthony's shoulder and pulled him into the shelter of her arms.

"No!" Palusso tugged Anthony away, one hand closing around his arm until the boy winced in pain. "He is not your boy." Palusso's upper lip curled. "He does not belong to any of you." He threw the challenge at the crowd along with a growl of resentment. "You keep your hands off my boy," he told Lillie. "He does not belong to you."

"Nor does he belong to you!" Lillie could not help herself. Though she suspected there was nothing to be gained from challenging a man who was obviously intoxicated and just as obviously irrational, the sight of Anthony's face, pale and frightened, caused her blood to surge through her veins like fire.

"He doesn't belong to anyone," she said, trading looks with Palusso. "He is his own person."

Palusso laughed, the sound blunted by the sultry night air. "And you," he stabbed one finger in Lillie's direction. "You do not know enough to mind your own business." He turned to Tom and winked. The gesture was meant as one of manly camaraderie. From Palusso it seemed more a parody of itself, a display more salacious than congenial.

Teetering slightly, one hand out to steady himself, Palusso leaned toward Tom. "You have not taught her this yet, Reilly? Perhaps you are not man enough to handle a woman such as this. This kind of woman"—he let his gaze slip from the top of Lillie's head to her waist and back again—"she need a strong man, a firm man. You must teach her to keep her nose out of my business even if you cannot teach her to stop from asking the questions about Boston and about your brother, Danny."

Tom's expression changed from ice to fire, and he took a step toward Palusso, his hands curled into fists at his sides.

He was stopped by Jonah.

Keeping one hand on Tom's arm to restrain him, the burly blacksmith stepped forward.

"We're peaceful people," Jonah told Palusso, though the look in his eyes was anything but friendly. "If you've come to join the celebration, Palusso, you're welcome. If you can behave yourself and keep your tongue in check where there are women and children present. If not—" Jonah poked his chin toward the other side of town. "If not, you'd better take yourself home."

"And my boy with me." Still holding Anthony in an iron grip, Palusso stepped back.

"Anthony—" Lillie made to follow them, one hand out in entreaty. Her hand clutched at nothing but the empty air left behind at Anthony's departure. Tom scooped it into his and held it tight at his side.

"You won't accomplish anything," Tom said. "Not this way. Perhaps we can find a judge who will listen when when we tell him Vincent Palusso isn't fit—"

"Not fit!" Palusso spat the words back at Tom, spinning to face him so quickly, he nearly knocked Anthony off his feet. "You tell me I am not fit? A man like this, he tells me I am not fit?" He cast a glance at the crowd. "Ask Reilly how fit he is. Ask him about Boston and how money can be won and lost in the sporting games there. Ask him about his brother and how a man can be murdered when his family abandons—"

"You low-down snake in the grass. I ought to—"

Before any of them realized what was happening, Alex Campbell sprang forward and administered a right upper-cut to Palusso's jaw. Palusso went down, more dazed than hurt, the last words of his biting accusation muffled by the blood that spurted from between his lips.

"Dag bust it!" Campbell hopped around on one foot, shaking his right hand. "I think it's broken." His face contorted with pain, he dragged himself to the punch table and leaned back against it.

Immediately the minister's five daughters were around him like bees around a spring bouquet; Suzannah brought ice, Mary dabbed Campbell's brow with a cool cloth, Annabelle loosened his tie, and Deborah and Margaret clucked sympathetic words into Campbell's ears.

It was an amazing show of compassion, Lillie thought. Especially when, for a moment, Campbell realized none of the girls was watching and gave Lillie a knowing smile and a very broad wink.

There was little time to puzzle through his odd behavior, and Lillie didn't even try. She turned her attention back to Palusso, who was shaking away all attempts to help him to his feet. He staggered upright and spat a stream of blood onto the ground.

It was only then he realized Anthony was gone.

Palusso's eyes narrowed and he looked around. His gaze landed on Lillie. "Where is he?"

Lillie honestly did not know. In the excitement of Campbell's attack she had not seen Anthony leave. She wasn't about to let Palusso know it.

"He's somewhere where he'll be safe," she said, lying so smoothly it surprised even her. "Somewhere where you won't harm him."

Palusso grumbled something in Italian, something that made Tom take two steps toward him.

"Go home," Tom said, his voice so quiet it could barely be heard above the hiss of the burning torches. "Sleep it off."

Palusso didn't stir for a long while, long enough so that when he did turn to go, he made the action seem like his own idea rather than Tom's. He stopped before he was across the dance floor and turned back to Lillie.

"You will be sorry," he said, his voice suddenly as cold and sober as the look he directed her way. "You will be very sorry you cross Vincent Palusso."

With that, Palusso stalked to the other side of the dance floor and was swallowed by the dark.

Lillie pressed one hand to her heart and closed her eyes, trying to will her emotions into some semblance of order. When she opened them again, Tom was regarding her with a look halfway between respect and exasperation.

"Have you always been this foolish," he asked, "or is it something the clean, fresh air of Wellington has brought out in you?"

She bristled at the criticism and met his scathing look straight on.

"If standing up to Palusso is foolish—"

"It is."

"Then, yes, I've always been foolish."

"Hell." Tom mumbled the word and ran one hand through his hair. "The man's dangerous, Lillie. I've told you that before. If you think you can—"

"I think I can take a walk and look for Anthony." Lillie pulled her shoulders back and, picking up her skirts, headed across the park.

"No need." Jonah called after her. "The boys are already lookin' for him. Nathan and his friends. They know his hidin' places. When they find him, they'll bring him back to my place for the night."

Lillie nodded her thanks. "Then it looks as if I can go home."

"Not by yourself." Tom was at her side in an instant. "I'll walk you home."

Still bristling from the sting of his criticism, Lillie shrugged off Tom's assistance. "I don't need a bodyguard," she assured him, her words clipped by her clenched teeth. "I can find my way home quite well by myself."

"Yes. And so can Vincent Palusso. And Elmore Montgomery, for that matter. Or do I need to remind you that you've made two enemies today?"

He didn't need to remind her. Lillie felt the disquiet pressing against her shoulders and the weight of concern tightening around her temples. Without another word she accepted Tom's arm and they walked side by side heading toward home.

They were halfway there when the fireworks started.

Tom would have been just as happy to ignore them. He couldn't remember a time when he'd been this out-of-sorts, this angry. Angry at Palusso for interfering with what had been a nearly perfect evening. Angry at Lillie for jeopardizing her own safety. Angry at himself for not doing more to help Anthony, and for not understanding why Alex Campbell had stepped in to silence Palusso, and for not rushing across the dance floor himself, when he had the chance, and knocking some sense into Palusso's head.

It was time to go home and get to bed, time to put it all out of his mind, at least for tonight.

But at the sound of the first rocket screeching into the sky, Lillie pulled to a stop in the middle of Prospect Street. She looked over her shoulder, back toward the fairgrounds, as wistful as a child.

Tom felt his anger ease with the first dreamy smile that lit Lillie's face, disappear with the second. "It's not too late to go back and watch the fireworks," he suggested.

As if his invitation had pulled her back from the simple pleasure of the display, back to the reality of Palusso's threats, Montgomery's warnings, and worries about Anthony, the smile fled Lillie's face. She shook off Tom's offer. "I can see them from the front porch of the house," she assured him, and she continued to walk toward home.

Most of the townsfolk must have been at the fairgrounds. The streets were deserted, the quiet punctuated only by the screech and pop of each rocket as it shot into the air and exploded in colored bursts, like fiery spiderwebs above their heads.

The gaudy light show in the sky was no match for the spectacle taking place all around them, a sight that seemed to capture Lillie's attention at the same time it caught Tom's. The first of the season's fireflies were out, blinking at them all along the way.

"They're like stars, fallen from the sky." Her gaze following its flight, Lillie scooped one of the insects out of the air and held it in the palm of her hand. She watched it for a moment, the worried expression on her face lit with the phantom glow of the firefly's light, before she lifted her hand and watched the little bug rise back up into the air.

When they arrived at her house, Lillie pointed toward the sky above the fairgrounds. "We can still see from here." Lillie sighed and, gathering her skirts, sat on the highest step of the front porch. Without another word she watched the show in the night sky.

There was not as much eloquence as there was anguish in her silence, an anguish Tom found nearly as unbearable as the troubled expression that shadowed her face.

While Lillie watched an especially spectacular yellow firework that burst into shooting stars, Tom took her hand. "We'll try to do something," he said, his words peppered by a background of hisses and pops. "I promise, we'll try to do something for Anthony."

"Can we?" Lillie turned to him, her face lit by the light of a red rocket. "Is there anything anyone can do to help a boy whose father is—"

"There must be." Tom squeezed her hand, realizing for the first time that his words were more than idle assurances designed to cheer Lillie. He meant every word of it. The conviction rang in his voice. "We can talk to Mayor Palmer in the morning. Or maybe Reverend Johnson. Surely a minister would know where a child could find safe haven."

The expression starting small and growing in brilliance with each word Tom spoke, Lillie smiled until her look was as radiant as the rocket that rose above their heads and exploded into a blinding flash of white, glittering light. She leaned forward and placed a kiss on Tom's cheek.

"I would like that," she said. Her voice was low and choked with emotion. She smiled into his eyes. "I would like that very much."

The kiss was so sudden and so unaffected that Tom could do little but smile at Lillie in return. When she turned to watch the rest of the fireworks show, he slipped his arm around her shoulders and pulled her to his side.

Lillie's eyes reflected the glowing colors that lit the night air, her face awash with blue one second, crimson the next, until the colors whirled before Tom's eyes like the dazzling bits of glass in a kaleidoscope. It was like being drunk, and Tom pulled his gaze away, his head already giddy, the thoughts stealing into his mind more impetuous than was prudent.

He should kiss her, thoroughly and soundly, the voices inside his head seemed to say. He should kiss her the way he'd been meaning to kiss her since the day she marched into his shop, her broken teapot in her hands. The suggestion resounded louder than the fireworks in Tom's ears. Hoping to still it, he loosened his hold on Lillie, propped his elbows on the floor of the front porch, and leaned back, watching Lillie profiled in the flashing lights.

The green gown Lillie had worn earlier in the day was both sensible and practical, its simplicity perfectly suited to a woman who needed to spend her day hauling equipment and developing photographs. Her work finished, her equipment stored safely at home, Lillie had changed for the evening festivities into a white confection of a dress, the fabric so delicate, it sailed around her effortlessly with her every move, like a cloud or a wreath of mist.

In the glow of the dance floor torches, the dress was captivating, its short, lace-edged sleeves showing off Lillie's slender arms to best advantage, its low-cut bodice revealing just enough of her bosom to be tantalizing at the same time it was demure. Now, in the flush of the light of the rockets, she looked more than captivating. She was mesmerizing, her white dress absorbing the colors and throwing them back into the night, like an opal that stored the sun's brilliance and dispersed it in a radiant display of color.

Lillie's dark hair was piled atop her head and Tom let his gaze wander to the tiny curls that had escaped from the upswept hairdo and clung to the nape of her neck. His gaze slid to her creamy shoulders and the intriguing line of her neck and spine, silhouetted beneath her skin.

He wondered how she'd taste.

The thought snuck up on Tom, nearly upsetting the fragile equilibrium he'd established only through sheer willpower and the deliberate attempt to keep himself at a distance.

That was all the Wellington rumor mill needed. The admonition was well taken, but it did little to silence the workings of his overactive imagination.

He wondered how she would taste, how it would feel to skim his lips over her neck and follow the line of her backbone down to her waist and up again.

"I said, the show's over." Lillie peered at Tom through the darkness, and he started at the sound of her voice and blinked at her like a nocturnal animal hypnotized by a light.

Not used to seeing him taken unawares, Lillie laughed. "I thought you'd fallen asleep."

"No." Tom let out a long, unsteady breath and hopped to his feet. He offered Lillie a hand to help her up.

She accepted it readily and stood smiling up at him.

Tom shifted from foot to foot. "Perhaps we should go to the back door," he said, glancing over his shoulder and the row of silent neighboring houses that lined the street.

"The back door." Lillie looked at him, puzzled, before she glanced at the front door, not four feet away. "Why would we want to go all the way around the back?" she asked. "We're right here." She made a move toward the door. "Come on."

Tom stopped her, one hand reaching for her arm to hold her in place, the other sliding around her waist.

"I think the back door," he said. "You see, Miss Valentine, I'm planning on kissing you good night. And if the neighbors see . . ."

It was like warm honey. Warm honey, the slow, delicious feeling traveling through her, invading every corner of her being. Lillie smiled, too content to keep the delicious feeling to herself. "Let them see," she said.

Still holding on to her arm, Tom took a step back. "What?" he asked with mock astonishment. "You're not going to protest? Isn't that one of the things you women are so good at doing? Why, sir!" He raised his voice in an amusing imitation of a woman's. "How can you even suggest such a shocking thing!"

"Don't be ridiculous." Lillie gave him a congenial poke in the ribs and, tossing a saucy look over her shoulder, pulled herself out of his grasp and headed to the front door. "I have every intention of letting you kiss me good night."

Tom's only response was a smile that perfectly matched hers. Following Lillie to the door, he slid both his arms around her and drew her near.

"Do you?" he asked, smiling down at her.

"I do," she assured him, and just to prove it, she slid her arms around his neck, tipped her head back, and raised her lips to his.

How such a simple pleasure could be at the same time so marvelous was beyond Lillie. She didn't stop to consider it. She merely enjoyed it. Enjoyed the feel of Tom, when he tightened his hold and held her close to him. Enjoyed the touch of him, when his hands flattened against her back and drew lazy circles along her ribs and up to her shoulders. Enjoyed the taste of him, when he deepened the kiss, parting her lips with his tongue to sample her sweetness.

It was enough to take her breath away, and Lillie linked her arms behind Tom's head, certain that if she didn't she would surely shoot into the night sky and explode, just another one of the holiday skyrockets.

"I promised myself this would be no more than a good-night kiss." Tom broke away long enough to look into her eyes, his breathing as jagged and irregular as hers.

"And that's all it's been." Lillie stepped back a pace and studied the silky darkness of Tom's eyes. He may have promised himself no more than a kiss, but it wasn't what he wanted. She could tell as much from the spark of desire that glowed in his eyes, the lingering smile that played around his mouth, the slow, hungry looks he slid from her face, to her breasts, to her hips.

It was not what she wanted, either.

Hoping she sounded more flirtatious than foolish, Lillie took a step toward the front door and rested her hand on the knob. "That's all it's been," she said again. "A good-night kiss. But that doesn't mean we can't finish it inside."

Tom accepted her invitation with a smile, pushing open the front door for her and ushering her in with a flourish.

The gentle playfulness in Tom's eyes bubbled through Lillie like the effervescence of champagne, and she laughed and, lifting her skirts, stepped into the house.

Her laughter died the moment she was over the threshold.

"Tom." There was something odd about the feel of the floor beneath her feet. Lillie grabbed for Tom's sleeve instinctively, hoping to balance herself on the strange, uneven surface, trying to calm the sudden thread of apprehension that caused the hair on the back of her neck to stand on end.

"Something's wrong." She darted a look around the darkened entryway, unable to place the peculiar, crunching noise she heard each time she moved.

It took her no more than a moment to grasp what had happened. The memories of Hank's hideous death came blasting back at her: the charred remains of what had once been Hank's studio, the ghastly smell of scorched wood and flesh, the horrifying sounds of the broken glass that grated beneath her feet.

"Tom!" She gripped his arm harder, panic building in her voice. "It's my glass-plate negatives. They've been smashed."

12

How long Tom was gone looking for a lamp, Lillie never knew. She stood in the center of the front hallway, her heart beating out the slow, painful minutes, her shoes grating against the bits of broken glass that covered the floor.

The parlor was to her left, and Lillie inched her way to the doorway and peered inside. There was little she could make out beyond what was nearest the window, but what she could see was covered with glass. Tabletops, carpets, even the cushions of the red velvet sofa; all covered with the remains of what had once been her glass-plate negatives.

The vandals had been thorough.

That one, coherent thought made its way through the swirl of shock and fright in Lillie's brain. They had been thorough. There was no other way there could be this much glass. They had been methodical, and thorough enough to find all the negatives. Not just those kept in the studio, but the ones stored in the basement as well. The negatives it had taken her years of arduous work to accumulate. Her negatives of the working children.

Lillie felt a rock of ice form in her stomach. Without waiting for either Tom or the lamp, she made her way toward the back of the house.

She was halfway there when she met Tom in the hallway. His face was lit by a halo of yellow light thrown from the kerosene lamp in his hand. In the glow Lillie could clearly see the anger etched in Tom's expression, the disbelief that caused his dark brows to dip over his eyes and turned his face as hard and gray as stone.

He intercepted Lillie before she got as far as the kitchen. One hand firmly on her upper arm, he pulled her back toward the front entryway. "Let's go. Let's get you—"

"No!" Lillie pulled away. "I need to see."

Tom followed her gaze with his own, back toward the kitchen and the tiny, locked room where she kept the photographs she hoped to present to the governor.

"It's all fine back there," Tom said, his words a little too hurried to be totally convincing. He snatched up Lillie's hand and blocked her way, herding her to the front door whether she would have it or not. "We'll get this mess cleaned up tomorrow, and then we'll—"

"I need to see my photographs."

Lillie's words resounded in the narrow hallway, echoing the demand.

Tom sighed, too exasperated to oppose her, or perhaps too certain it would do no good. Letting go of her hand, he moved aside so she could pass, and followed her, the lamp held out in front of him to light their way through the wreckage.

Even before she saw the smashed lock and the splintered remains of the door, Lillie knew what she would find. Pausing only long enough to lift her skirts so she could scramble over the shattered planks of wood, she went to stand in the center of the little room. She stared at the walls.

All was exactly as she'd left it, neat and tidy, not one frame out of position, not one askew. But her photographs were gone.

Lillie did not need to wait for Tom with the lamp to know where they were. She scuffed her shoes against the bare wood floor. Instead of the sounds of crunching glass, she heard a quieter, more terrifying sound, like the rasp of fallen leaves.

Tom came into the room and the lamp in his hand sent eerie shadows up the walls, its light glinting off the empty frames so that they winked back at Lillie like the vacant eye sockets of a skull. The floor was littered with scraps of paper; tiny, sad faces still distinguishable here and there, but most of the photographs torn too completely to tell who, or what, they were.

A shred of paper at Lillie's feet attracted her attention and she stooped to lift it to the light. It was a fragment of the photograph of her brother, Johnny. Lillie closed her hand around the scrap and held it to her heart.

"Lillie."

Only vaguely aware that Tom had set the lamp down and come up behind her, Lillie heard his voice in her ear, as soft as the touch of his hands where they closed around her shoulders.

"Lillie, come away." He urged her toward the door with a gentle tug.

"Certainly." Lillie cleared her throat and tucked the fragment of photograph into her pocket. She turned to the door. "Certainly I'll go," she assured Tom, her voice as firm as the look in her eye and the excruciating, steady pounding of her heart. "I'll go right to Elmore Montgomery. Elmore Montgomery, that son of a—"

"Lillie!" This time there was no delicacy in Tom's voice. He went to the doorway before Lillie could get there and stood blocking it. "I won't let you march over to Montgomery's. Not like this. Not in the middle of the night." Tom frowned. "Besides, how can you be so sure it was Montgomery? It could just as easily have been Palusso. There's nothing we can accomplish by—"

"I can let Montgomery know I won't take this without a fight." As sensible as Tom's reasoning was, Lillie dismissed his theory about Palusso out of turn. With each word she spoke, the outrage rose in her, and Lillie wrapped her fingers around themselves and held them tight, until her knuckles were white and aching. "I can let Montgomery know I won't stop. Does he think this can stop me?" Lillie spun around, taking in the devastation with one broad sweep of her arm.

"Does he?" she asked again, whirling to Tom and glaring her defiance. "If he thinks he can stop me, he's wrong. If he thinks . . . if he thinks . . ."

It was not the dreadful realization of all that had been lost, nor even the uncontrollable anger mounting in her that caused Lillie's words to stick in her throat. It was the look on Tom's face.

Another man may have shown sympathy, or pity, or even been patronizing.

Tom's expression was filled with understanding, an understanding so complete, it did what even the destruction of her life's work could not do. It brought tears to Lillie's eyes. When he opened his arms, Lillie rushed to him, and burying her face in his chest, she cried.

"My darling Lillie." His words no more than a whisper against the darkness, Tom wrapped his arms around Lillie and held her close, praying the embrace would be enough to help heal her anguish, yet fearing there was little he could do to blunt the pain of a loss so great.

Whispering soft consolation in her ear, stroking her with one hand to help ease the sobs that racked her, he waited for Lillie's crying to ease. When it did, Tom gently stood her upright and wiped the tears from her cheeks with his thumbs.

"You can't stay here tonight," he said. "We need to get you away. Somewhere safe." Tom paused, running through the possibilities that presented themselves. "Not the shop," he said, almost to himself. "You wouldn't be comfortable there." He looked down at her, gauging what was left of her strength. "Can you walk clear across town, do you think?"

Without waiting for Lillie to answer, Tom wrapped his arm around her shoulders, and taking a deep breath he hoped would fortify them both, he led her to the door. "You're coming home with me."

The heat was sweltering.

Too restless to keep still, too furious to even begin to cool down, Tom pulled off his collar and dropped it on the back steps as he descended them, heading toward the yard. A brisk walk across the lawn would do nothing to cool him off. He knew that much. But it might help dispel the anger seething inside him.

Making his way past the apple trees that flanked the garden path, Tom stretched his shoulders and undid the buttons along the front of his shirt. He cast a glance back toward the house and the darkened window of his bedroom.

Lillie should be asleep by now. Good.

Unable to help himself, Tom smiled slightly, remembering the scene when they arrived home: Lillie's spluttered protests when he insisted she take his bed for the night. The look on her face when he filled a tumbler with brandy and demanded she drink at least some of it.

"It was what she needed." He repeated the advice to himself in a whisper, the words he'd used to finally convince her to drink some of the liquor. It was what she needed to get some rest and regain her strength. It was what she needed so she could sleep, sleep and forget.

Poor, dear Lillie bundled away in his bed.

The memory of her shocked and frightened face did little to relieve Tom's anger. It did nothing to make him rescind his vow of revenge on whoever was responsible for the destruction of Lillie's negatives.

Poor, dear Lillie.

Tom felt the tightness in his neck and shoulders slacken at the same time his heart squeezed with affection and sympathy.

How lost and sad she'd looked when he pulled the blankets up around her and pressed a good-night kiss to her forehead. How much it hurt to leave her there, alone, when he wanted nothing more than to lay down at her side, and cradle her in his arms, and comfort her.

"Tom?"

As if his thoughts had caused her to materialize, Tom turned to find Lillie standing on the back porch. With the mellow light of a moon just past full caressing her every curve and curl, she looked more like a creature of his fancy than a woman of flesh and blood.

Her hair was loose, just as he'd pictured it so many times in his imagination; the soft, dark ringlets brushing her shoulders, tumbling down her back.

Her eyes were luminous. It was not the moonlight he saw reflected there, not the hint of starlight that glittered back at him. This fire came from within, a fire that called him to its flames and kindled inside him a twin spark.

Tom let go a long, uneven breath, the last of his anger incinerated in the fires of his imagination.

His reaction was just as he imagined it would be, too, from the dizzy feeling in his head, to the heat in his gut. Tom smiled to himself, pleased that reality could come so close to fantasy, and let his gaze wander even farther, down to where Lillie's white nightgown floated above the floorboards of the porch, brushing her bare toes.

He had imagined other parts of her unclad. Tom felt a tiny thread of guilt assail him at the thought, yet there was no denying it. He had lain in his bed—how many nights?—and thought of how long and slender Lillie's arms were and how her legs would be just as alluring. He had imagined the softness of her breasts, the silkiness of her thighs, the smoothness of her hips.

He had never pictured her bare toes.

Yet it all seemed to suit Lillie, somehow. The flowing gown, those pale, bare feet, the creamy skin of her face and arms, all gleaming in the moonlight, making her look more than ever the will-o'-the-wisp.

There was more to his imaginings, and Tom let his gaze wander along with his thoughts, up from the tips of Lillie's toes, past the fluid lines of the gown where it drifted over her legs and thighs, up past her waist.

There, his gaze stopped. Tom felt a frown crease his forehead.

In his imagination he could see it all: the swell of her breasts beneath the muslin nightgown, the small, hard roundness of her nipples outlined by the moonlight, the intriguing hollow at the base of her neck where each heartbeat pulsed against the mother-of-pearl perfection of her skin, marking the evidence of her excitement.

The reality was certainly different.

Tom shook his head, clearing away the fancies and concentrating, instead, on what was really before his eyes.

Instead of bare shoulders, instead of creamy breasts, he saw nothing but the old, pink quilt that usually lay, folded and unused, at the foot of his bed. Lillie had it wrapped around herself like a shawl, holding it close over her chest. Her hands, where they held the blanket to her body, were trembling.

It was all Tom needed to see. He crossed the yard as quickly as he could and climbed the back porch stairs, two steps at a time. "What is it?" Tom took Lillie's hands. They were cold, far too cold, and he chafed them between his own. "What's wrong?"

Lillie's gaze came up to meet Tom's, her eyes liquid amber in the moonlight. "This," she answered him simply with a look around the yard. "All this. It's wrong. It's—"

"Lillie." Something in the desperate intensity of her voice made Tom chuckle. He pulled her hands to his chest and folded his own over them. "You're not going to let yourself be concerned about scandal at a time like this, are you? There's nothing the rumor mill can say. Not this time. You're here because I need to keep you safe."

"You don't understand." Her voice as deadly calm as the look she gave Tom, Lillie pulled her hands free and moved to stand farther from him. She lay her palms flat against the porch rail and leaned forward, her expression hidden by the fall of hair that screened her face.

"It's not that I'm worried what the neighbors will say." She glanced around the picket-fenced yard. "From what I can see, you don't have any neighbors. And even if you did . . ." Lillie scooped the hair away from her face and tucked it behind her ears. She turned to Tom.

"I don't care what they say about us," she said, her gaze never leaving his. "I don't care what they know. I'm not ashamed to be seen with you or to have someone think we're intimate. I could never be ashamed of that."

It seemed to take hours for Tom to respond. Lillie watched him, waiting, her words hanging between them on the hot night air, as vivid as the fireflies that danced around their heads.

Tom's face went blank and he sucked in a sharp breath as if her admission had struck him squarely somewhere between his stomach and his heart. Then, slowly, his mouth tipped into a pleased and very satisfied grin.

He crossed the porch and with one, fluid movement, stripped the quilt from Lillie's shoulders and tossed it onto the floor. Before she could say another word, he took her in his arms and kissed her.

It was a kiss to get lost in.

Finding she had neither the strength nor the desire to fight the delicious rush of warmth that flooded through her at the touch of Tom's lips, Lillie tightened her arms around his neck and gave herself to the sensation.

It was a kiss to heal her soul, a kiss to chase away the nightmares that tormented her and exorcise the demons that haunted her, night and day.

All the demons except one.

Reluctantly Lillie pulled free of Tom's embrace, not breaking the sheltering circle of his arms, but moving far enough back to see his face.

"Tom." Her hands flat against his chest, she stopped him when he made to bend and take her lips with his again. "Tom. No. We need to talk."

Tom was not listening. He slid his gaze from Lillie's face to the front of her nightgown, revealed now that the quilt had been cast aside. With one finger he followed the square neckline of the gown, down her right shoulder, across her bosom, up to her left shoulder. A smile touched his lips when she made a small noise of surprise and delight, and he trailed his hand back to her breasts.

"I don't want to talk," Tom said, grazing his finger back and forth along the tops of her breasts. "I don't want to talk again for a very long time."

It was enough to make her lose what little self-control she had left, and Lillie closed her eyes, hoping to steel herself against the delicious sensation long enough to talk some sense into Tom.

"We have to talk." Her own words sounded far too breathy and disjointed to be convincing. Lillie swallowed them along with the contented sigh that escaped her when Tom's hand slipped inside the muslin gown to caress her bare breasts.

It was like drowning in pleasure.

In spite of her intentions Lillie tipped her head back and closed her eyes. It was like drowning in a pool of deep desire, and she wasn't sure she had the strength to fight it. How luscious it was, and how she longed to give herself to the sensation, to feel herself sink beneath the delicious waves of contentment and yearning that washed over her.

Already they were lapping around her, snatching the breath from her lungs, stealing the strength from her legs, robbing her of all perception except the feel of Tom's hands on her skin, the touch of his lips along her neck, the warm, moist stroke of his tongue where it made its way to the shadowy skin between her breasts.

It was like drowning in desire, and Lillie wrapped her arms tighter around Tom's neck, not sure if she was holding on to him to keep herself from going under, or hoping to take him down with her.

Somehow, the voice of reason made its way past the rushing noises inside Lillie's head. This wasn't fair to her. It wasn't fair to Tom. She owed him the truth and the chance to save himself. She owed him that, and more, before she could give herself to him.

"Tom." Fighting for breath, Lillie pushed against Tom's shoulders. "Tom. No. We can't."

Tom murmured an unintelligible response, his voice as dreamy as the fleeting smile he gave her.

"Tom." Lillie took his face between her hands and turned it up to hers. "We can't. I'm frightened."

Like water tossed on a fire, the spark went out of Tom's eyes. He stood straight, not as annoyed as Lillie thought he might be, but mystified, surely, and obviously troubled.

"Frightened?" With one hand Tom brushed the hair away from Lillie's cheek. The pleasure vanished from his face, and he frowned and looked into her eyes. "Not frightened of me?"

The question was enough to break her heart. Lillie stroked one hand along Tom's face and shook her head. "Not frightened of you. Never that," she whispered. "I'm frightened for you."

Tom's eyebrows rose and he gave her a one-sided, bewildered smile. "Damned if I can understand it. Why on earth should you be frightened for me?" A lock of hair had fallen over his forehead, and he pushed it back with an abrupt, impatient gesture. His hand froze there and he gave Lillie a penetrating look, a look suddenly as filled with awareness as it was with regret. Tom's smile vanished.

"I know you've been talking to Alex Campbell," he said. "If it's because of what happened in Boston . . . Boston's got nothing to do with you and me."

"I don't care what happened in Boston."

Lillie heard her words reverberate back from the painted ceiling of the porch. She drew in a sharp breath, as startled by the fact that she'd had the courage to utter the assertion as she was by the realization that it was absolutely true.

None of it mattered. The certainty of the declaration rang through Lillie's head and filled her heart until she was sure it would burst from both the exhilaration and the relief.

None of it mattered. Not what may or may not have happened back East or Alex Campbell's cryptic hints about it, not Vincent Palusso's veiled accusations or Tom's desperate attempts to keep his past a secret.

All that mattered was here and now; the integrity and decency that shone in Tom's eyes, the feel of his arms, strong and safe and tender around her, the certain knowledge that no matter what dark secrets rose to tear them apart, no power on heaven or earth could destroy the respect and love that had grown between them.

Lillie looked Tom in the eye. "I don't care what happened in Boston. All I care about is what happened in Cleveland."

Tom's brows settled, a dark line above his eyes. Without another word he grabbed for the quilt with one hand and for Lillie's arm with the other, and led her down the stairs and toward the back lawn.

Shaking the blanket out, he laid it on the grass, and tugged Lillie to sit down beside him. "Tell me what's troubling you," he said, his plea as mellow as the moonlight.

"It isn't easy to explain." Lillie looked down to where their hands were wound together. In the soft light it was difficult to tell where hers ended and his began. There was strength in his touch, and Lillie tightened her fingers in Tom's, drawing from it and giving back her own.

"It has to do with Hank, you see. You know that Hank was killed in a fire. What you don't know . . ." Lillie took a deep breath, not so much to calm herself as to give Tom the time to prepare for what she about to tell him. "What you don't know," she said, "is that Hank's death was my fault."

She expected Tom to be horrified. She expected him to be angry. Instead, he rejected the confession, rejected it instantly, with a small shake of his head and a gruff mumble of disbelief.

"What are you saying?" Tom spun around so that he was opposite Lillie, his knees touching hers. "You can't mean you—"

"No. Not directly." Too affected by it to endure the pain in Tom's eyes, she dismissed his worries before they had a chance to hurt him further. "Hank was more than my mentor. More than my friend. I loved him as much as I loved my own father. That's why, when the studio burned, I felt so guilty. If it hadn't been for me—"

"Now, wait a minute." Tom raised one hand to stop her. "You're talking in circles. You say it wasn't your fault and yet . . ." He stared at her, waiting for the details.

Now that it was time to explain, the words refused to come. Lillie bit her lower lip and looked up at the star-filled sky, hoping to find comfort there but finding, rather, only emptiness and the flickering reminder of Hank's fiery death.

In the months since the fire she had learned to bury her anger, to hide it safely away until it was lost to the urgency of her work, dulled by her concern for Anthony and all the other working children, forgotten in her affection for Tom. Now it came rushing back, more powerful and painful than ever. Lillie felt it twist inside her, winding round her composure and shattering it, wrenching from her the words that sliced the silence.

"It was my negatives."

For a moment Lillie was afraid Tom did not understand. She should have known better. He understood. She saw it after no more than an instant. He understood enough to take her hand, understood enough to be moved, enough to be angry. He narrowed his eyes. "You mean the fire—"

"Was started purposely. To destroy my negatives of the working children."

"Then you think—"

"I don't think it." Lillie ripped her hand from Tom's grasp. Her words were far more vehement than she intended, but she did not apologize or try to take them back. "I know it," she said. "That fire was bought and paid for. Hank's life was bought and paid for. By Elmore Montgomery."

Tom let out a long breath. "So that's why you're so sure Montgomery destroyed your negatives tonight. But what about the fire? How did the negatives survive the fire?"

"They weren't at the studio." Lillie pounded the faded quilt with her fist. "Dammit, don't you see? That's the worst of it. They weren't even at the studio. They were at my house."

Ignoring the tears of frustration and anger that sprang to her eyes, Lillie went on, her voice losing its edge of sharpness, her heart heavier with each word she spoke. "Hank insisted I keep them at my house. I didn't think a thing of it. Not at the time. It was only after the fire I realized he was setting himself up as a decoy. He was protecting me. Me and my negatives. It cost him his life."

"And you blame yourself?" Tom's question was as tender as the touch he pressed against her hand.

"Of course I blame myself." Lillie heard her own voice falter, the words filled with anguish. "If I hadn't been pigheaded . . . if I hadn't insisted on taking those pictures, Hank would still be alive. And where has it gotten me?" She laughed, the sound laced with hysteria and charged with self-contempt. "Montgomery's won. At least for now. And Hank . . . Hank died for nothing."

Lillie's words spiraled into the night and faded. Tom looked up, as if watching them vanish, and did not look back to her again until after they were gone, lost in the darkness and the clear night sky.

He leaned forward and, raising her hand to his lips, touched a kiss to her fingers. "I never knew Hank," he said, "but I'll never forget the photograph you showed me. That picture of the boys in the West Virginia coal mine. I don't think the man who took that picture would blame you for having the courage and the conviction to do what you know is right." Gently he cupped Lillie's face in his hand and kept her face level with his.

"He taught it to you, Lillie," Tom said. "It's Hank's intensity that runs through your veins and drives you. He showed you the children. And he knew you wouldn't turn away. I don't think he died for nothing."

His simple statement was like balm on an open wound. Lillie closed her eyes, savoring the warmth of Tom's words and the healing power of his touch. He understood about Hank, understood what drove her, what compelled her to pursue Montgomery and all the other taskmasters who built their opulent lives on the backs of the wretched working poor.

Still, it was not enough.

Lillie searched Tom's eyes, hoping to find there the understanding she heard ringing in his words. "But that's not all, don't you see? They hurt Hank. They hurt Hank because of me. Oh, God, Tom!" Her voice broke and she pressed her free hand to her lips to contain a sob. "I don't want them to hurt you, too!"

Tom slid forward and took Lillie into his arms. "Is that what you're afraid of?" He held her tight against him and stroked her hair.

"That's what I've always been afraid of," Lillie admitted. "That's why I pretended I didn't care for you. That's why I wanted you to leave town. I didn't want you hurt. I didn't want you involved."

Tom put her from him, his expression as reassuring as it was loving. "It's too late for that," he said. "I'm already involved.

I'm involved with your working children. I'm involved with your ambition to meet the governor. Hell, Lillie"—Tom smiled—"I'm involved with you. Heart and soul."

It was a mystery how the warmth of his smile could penetrate all the layers of her misery and wrap around her heart. A mystery Lillie did not stop to try and unravel. She merely accepted it. Accepted it as she did his embrace when he gathered her again into his arms and kissed her.

His kiss was as soft as the blanket where they sat, as warm as the night air, as comforting as the rhythmic song of the crickets chirping in the grass. Lillie closed her eyes and gave herself to the sweet sensation. The first kiss melted into a second, the second into a third, and Tom slid his hands up her arms to her shoulders and pressed her nearer.

Even that was not enough.

It was not enough when Tom's arms closed around her and he swirled his hands over her back, from the sensitive skin at the nape of her neck to her waist and up again. It was not enough when he deepened the kiss and nudged her lips open with his tongue. It was not enough when he splayed his fingers through her hair and smoothed it over her shoulder so he could bestow a line of kisses along her neck.

"Lillie, don't be afraid of what will happen if we're together." Tom's voice was suddenly as eager with desire as his touch. His hands laid a trail of fire along her collarbone and down to her breasts. "Don't ever be afraid of that. I'm not. The only thing that frightens me is what might happen if we're ever apart."

The last of Lillie's misgivings dissolved along with the final vestiges of her self-control. She twined her arms around Tom's neck and drew him nearer.

The kiss may have lasted a minute. It may have lasted an hour. Or a day. Time vanished and Lillie's misgivings vanished along with it. She found herself smiling, suddenly, foolishly. Smiling even as he kissed her.

Tom must have felt the smile on her lips. He laughed and pulled away and nuzzled his lips against Lillie's neck and shoulders. "You're not going to get skittish and start chattering again, are you?" He looked up at her, his eyes glittering, clearly saying he had not forgotten her nervousness when he'd ventured a kiss in her darkroom.

"No." Lillie tried to look offended and found it was impossible. It was impossible to feel anything but the joy that bubbled in her, softening the edges of her sorrow, banishing the misery of the past and paving the way for the bright promise of the future. She tossed her head. "I'm never nervous once I know exactly what it is I want."

"Is that so?" Tom wound a strand of Lillie's hair around his finger. He uncoiled the curl and stroked it against his hand. "And do you know what you want this time?"

"I think so." As soon as the words had left her mouth, Lillie shook her head, dismissing them. "No. I don't think so. I know so. I know exactly what I want."

She didn't wait for Tom to kiss her again. She kissed him, her action so quick and earnest it robbed him of his breath and nearly caused him to lose his balance. Tom righted himself, laughing, and hugged her, obviously as delighted to receive the kiss as Lillie was to give it.

"Oh, Miss Lillie Valentine." Still laughing, Tom sat back and let his gaze wander over her. "When you know what you want, it's not just wise to let you have your way, it's positively delightful."

"Very wise," Lillie agreed. She lowered her voice to a whisper and leaned closer, sharing the confidence. "And very delightful."

Delightful.

Tom turned the word over in his mind, examining it from every side, just as he was examining Lillie with his eyes.

Delightful. Lillie was that and more.

Tom slid his gaze from the dark mane of Lillie's hair to her shoulders. No more than twenty minutes ago he had imagined watching her heartbeat drumming against the hollow at the base of her throat, drumming its message of longing and desire. Now here it was, barely perceptible in the moonlight, yet there for him to see.

He pressed one finger to the pulsing skin, savoring the rhythm of her excitement.

Not three hours ago he had speculated about the taste of her, the feel and flavor of her bare skin beneath his lips and tongue.

Tom kissed Lillie's neck. "I promised myself we'd take this slow," he said, his voice breathless. He broke away and smiled when he realized Lillie was just as winded as he was. "I told myself we'd take our time."

"You did?" Lillie seemed more amused than surprised. She tipped her head to one side, her eyes alight with mischief. "I hadn't been aware this was something we've ever discussed doing. When, exactly, did you make that promise to yourself, Mr. Reilly?"

He had been caught, tricked into admitting how he'd imagined this scene over and over in his head. Tom accepted the culpability, but he refused to be embarrassed. It was about time Lillie knew how many nights he couldn't sleep and paced the floor, thinking of her. About time she learned the workings of his heart and the overworkings of an imagination that could be, at times, painfully graphic.

His hands strayed to the ribbon ties that cinched Lillie's nightgown up around her shoulders. "I promised myself," he said, running the ribbons through his fingers. "I promised myself when I lay in bed at night and thought about you. I promised myself when I pictured all this and what we'd say, and how we'd feel, and what we'd do."

Lillie darted him a look from beneath her lashes, a look that was incredibly seductive, whether she knew it or not. "And what else did you promise yourself?" she asked.

It was too much. Tom had promised himself a score of other things, yet now that the time was here, only one came to mind.

He had promised himself he would find out how she tasted.

Tom placed one hand on each of Lillie's shoulders. Completely disregarding the puzzled look she gave him, he nudged her until she spun around. He scooped her hair away from her neck and laid it over her shoulder while with his mouth he followed the line of her spine from the nape of her neck to where it disappeared beneath the square-cut neckline of the muslin gown.

She tasted marvelous.

For the second time tonight Tom congratulated himself on the accuracy of his imagination. She tasted as delectable as he supposed she would: flowery like her lilac cologne, salty with sweat, soft, and hot, and so incredibly feminine it took his breath away.

He nibbled his way back up her neck and, hooking one finger over each shoulder of her nightgown, pushed it down to her waist.

Her skin looked like alabaster. For a moment Tom did no more than sit back and enjoy the play of moonlight and shadow against the silky expanse of Lillie's bare back and arms. She sat perfectly still, as if sensing both his scrutiny and his approval, her arms braced at her sides, her hands flat against the faded quilt, her shoulders rising and falling to the tempo of her uneven breathing.

"Lillie." He brushed her name against the back of her neck along with a string of kisses. She tasted marvelous, and he sampled her again, learning the contours of her body, trailing a path from her neck to her waist.

With his tongue Tom traced the line of her backbone back up to her shoulders, whispering a small prayer of thanks as he did. A prayer of thanks. For the first time in a year.

Tom sat back for a moment, overcome by the realization of what he was doing, what he was thinking.

If it hadn't been for the scandal that drove him from Boston, he would never have had the good luck to land here in Wellington, and the even better luck of loving Lillie. If it hadn't been for all the terrible things that happened back home, he wouldn't be here now. He'd still be back East, all full of himself and his success, too dazzled by the wealth and splendor of high living to appreciate the small pleasures of life.

This was not one of them.

The irony of Tom's own thoughts struck him, and he smiled wide and whispered another prayer that Lillie could not see him. She'd think he was a simpleton, that was for certain, sitting here staring at her back, smiling like a loon.

Still, he couldn't seem to help himself and Tom kept on smiling. This was not one of life's simple pleasures. He glided one hand up Lillie's back to her shoulder and down under her arm.

This was more than a simple pleasure. This was life itself, and with every touch he could feel the hole in his heart closing, filling with Lillie's trust, healing with the power of her love.

Impatient for more, Tom shrugged out of his shirt and drew Lillie back to him, her skin soft and smooth against his chest. He slid his arms around her and stroked her nipples with his flattened palms.

Lillie was life itself, her spirit and intensity as electrifying as the feel of her skin beneath his fingers, the tempting sound of her jagged breathing, the flame that grew in his belly.

Tom rolled Lillie's nipples through his fingers. They were hard and round and full. Full of desire and urgency. Full of the need for him and the love and release he could give her. The thought was nearly as stirring as the feel of her bare skin, and Tom sucked in an unsteady breath. Promise or not, he wasn't sure if he could take his time, or even if he wanted to.

Lillie arched her back and wriggled her shoulders. Tom's fingers were rough and callused, yet his touch was so tender it made her ache for more. She sighed and leaned back, her head against Tom's shoulder. "Have you ever been drunk?" she asked him.

He had obviously not expected the question. Tom laughed, though he did not stop the gentle, kneading motion of his hands. "A time or two," he admitted. "Back in the days when I lived in Boston and I didn't realize there was more to life than carousing with my friends. Why do you ask?"

"Is this what it feels like?"

"This is much better," Tom said without hesitation. "It doesn't cost a thing." He smacked a kiss against her neck. "And it doesn't dull your senses." He placed another kiss on the slender ridge where her arm met her right shoulder. "And you never, never feel like the wrath of God the next morning."

Lillie purred her agreement and nestled closer. "I didn't know it would feel like this," she confessed, her voice dreamy.

Tom brushed her hair aside and proceeded to outline her ear with the tip of his tongue. "Like what?"

Reluctant to break the contact yet sensing, somehow, that what she had to tell him must be said face-to-face, Lillie sat up. She twirled around and took Tom's hands in hers, ignoring his look of pure delight as his gaze settled on her breasts and his bemused smile widened into a full-fledged grin.

"As if all my life I've been waiting for this moment," she said. She pressed his hands to her heart. "As if my body and my mind and my soul all want one thing for the very first time. As if there is no question you want the same thing. For all the same reasons."

"For all the right reasons." Tom leaned forward and captured her lips with his, forcing them apart with his tongue, his hands slipping from hers to caress her breasts.

Exhilarated by his touch, delighted by his kiss, Lillie moaned and brought her tongue to meet Tom's. She heard his answering groan, a sound that rumbled up from deep inside him. Moving closer, Lillie flattened her hands against his chest, savoring the vibration of his sigh, relishing the throb of his heart against her palms, the tempo in perfect time to her own wild pulse.

"Do you remember the day I took your picture?" Lillie swirled her hands through the mat of hair on Tom's chest. "I wanted to do this then, but I was too shy. Too terri-fied. I knew you'd feel just like this. Your muscles hard and your skin"—she slid her hands down to his waist and up again—"your skin burning as if there were fire inside you."

A single drop of perspiration trickled down Tom's neck. Lillie watched it slide over his heart and down the flat plane of his stomach before it disappeared into the waistband of his trousers. She followed the drop with her finger, trailing a delicate line over his chest, over his stomach, down to where the tiny droplet had vanished.

"Lillie."

191

She heard him say her name, his voice rough and urgent against her ear, his excitement more evident than ever when he moved against her hand.

One hand behind her back to brace her, Tom pressed Lillie onto the worn, pink quilt and traced his tongue down her neck to her breasts, teasing her nipples until she sighed with pleasure, teasing them more until she groaned with desire, her eyes half-closed, her fingers raking through his hair.

Tom sat up long enough to give her an approving smile. He whisked the fine sheen of perspiration from his forehead with the back of one hand. "It's not getting any cooler, is it?"

Lillie nodded. "Much hotter," she said.

Tom looked down to where her nightgown was still rumpled around her hips. "Then perhaps we should remove this?"

He didn't wait for her to answer. He didn't need an answer. Her rough breathing, the hunger in her eyes, the eager way she raised her hips to let him remove the gown, they were answer enough.

Raising himself to his knees, Tom straddled her body, one leg on either side of her hips. He slipped the nightgown down over her legs and set it aside, then sat back on his heels and simply stared.

Lillie's skin was luminous in the moonlight, every curve outlined by the glow. Her figure was stunning, as stunning as he thought it would be; her breasts, round and firm, her hips, slender and fine, her legs, lean and long.

In the ghostly light the dark curls between her legs seemed more shadow than substance. Tentatively Tom stretched out one hand and touched them, smiling at the texture, coarse yet silky, coiled tight like the keen thread of desire winding fire through his gut.

A jolt of anticipation quivered through Lillie. She took her lower lip between her teeth and braced herself, her body taut, every ounce of her being waiting.

Another touch and Lillie felt her muscles tighten even more. This time Tom allowed himself to linger, his fingers spreading through the glossy curls, probing ever so slightly to the slick and satiny delights that lay just beyond.

How the rest of her could relax so completely when it felt as if her insides were about to shatter into a million separate bits of pleasure and delight, Lillie did not know. She lay back against the quilt, her hands brushing over the whisper-soft fabric, moving in time to the gentle pressure of Tom's hand, moving faster, tightening, as the insistence of Tom's touch intensified.

He must have seen the quiver of anticipation that shuddered through her. Tom smiled up at her, his fingers still teasing, then hopped to his feet to peel off his trousers.

For just a moment Lillie was glad for the darkness. She was sure she was blushing, and the thought made her as nervous as it did irritated. There was certainly nothing to be embarrassed about. Not between her and Tom. And yet the sight of his body, hard, and muscular, and naked in the moonlight, made her feel more than ever like a stammering schoolgirl.

Tom laid down beside her. The look in his eyes told her he did not see her as a green, unsophisticated girl. In his eyes she was a beautiful woman. She could almost see the reflection, the mirrored image of her sparkling eyes, her parted lips, her smile, tempting, and tender, and inviting.

"You're beautiful." With one finger Tom traced a line from Lillie's collarbone to her waist. "You are the most exquisite, the most incredible woman!" He smiled down at her, affection glimmering in his eyes. It was a brief smile, a smile edged with desire so tangible, Lillie wondered how he could keep it reined.

After another moment he did not even try.

Tom brought his mouth down on Lillie's, his kiss as insistent as the unremitting pulse of desire that sharpened her senses and turned her blood to fire.

Recognizing her need, surrendering to his own, Tom moved over her, his body hard against her softness.

"I promised myself I'd take this slow," he said, his words as rough as his breathing. "I'm not sure I can. You'll let me know—"

"I'll let you know." Lillie smiled up at him and wrapped her arms around his neck.

As if deep inside her some primordial instinct had ingrained in her the motions of their silent lovers' dance, Lillie found herself moving in perfect counterpoint to the gentle rhythm Tom set. She heard herself groan, the feel of him inside her too exquisite to bear in silence. Through half-closed eyes she watched the fascinating motion of Tom's body against hers, his movements quickening as the rhythm of their lovemaking increased.

The tempo peaked in a flash of fire, a blaze of sensation that left Lillie trembling. Tom looked down at her and gave her a fleeting smile before he tensed and pushed harder against her. He threw his head back, his eyes closed, his face transformed by the glancing, soothing light, his expression as open and vulnerable as a child's.

The rhythm stilled, though the shudder of emotion that fluttered through Lillie did not. She wrapped her arms tighter around Tom's neck and returned the kiss he pressed to her lips.

The world was silent.

Her arms still around Tom, Lillie relaxed against the blanket and listened. Above the sounds of their own breaths mingling, their own hearts beating, there were no other noises. Even the crickets had finished their songs and gone to their beds for the night.

Lillie sighed. "It must be very late."

Still keeping her in the circle of his arms, Tom slid away to lay beside her. He skimmed his finger along the sensitive skin of her neck. "Very late," he agreed. "We'd better get inside."

But neither of them moved. The moment was far too delectable, the silence too absorbing, the feeling too mesmerizing.

Lillie simply enjoyed it. For another few minutes they lay in companionable silence, until an amusing thought pricked at Lillie's mind. She giggled and smiled at Tom, her voice faint and breathy, as giddy as the feeling inside her. "Am I still the most willful, stubborn, prying woman you've ever met?" she asked.

"Oh, yes!" Tom tried his hardest to look annoyed. He failed miserably. There was too much moonlight glinting in his eyes, too much playfulness and elation in his smile. He touched a kiss to the tip of Lillie's nose. "Willful," he said. "Stubborn." He kissed her forehead and lowered his voice to what was supposed to be a growl. "Prying." By the time he planted a kiss on her chin, Tom was laughing, too. He gathered Lillie into the circle of his arms and pulled her close against him. "And," he whispered, "I love you."

13

THERE WAS SOMETHING about knowing there had been strangers in the house that made the hair on the back of Lillie's neck stand on end and caused her insides to feel queasy.

She fought to push the sensation to the back of her mind, concentrating, instead, on cleaning the parlor rug. But with each whip of her beater against the Persian carpet, her anger intensified. The physical exertion of cleaning was not enough—not nearly enough—to alleviate her outrage.

As if to both prove her point and make a mockery of her labors, tiny shards of glass kept falling from the rug, no matter how hard or how long she beat it.

Lillie stepped back. She propped the beater against her hip and glared at the rug, ignoring the bright blue sky beyond it, the songs of the robins in the trees nearby, the gentle fall of Tom's boots on the gravel path that led from the house.

"If you kiss me, I'll scream."

Even before Tom had wrapped his arms around her waist and pulled her close, Lillie was fighting the embrace. She twisted away and turned to face him, her lips pulled into a sour frown, her eyes smarting from all the tears she'd tried to contain and could not. "I don't want to be kissed."

Tom threw both his hands into the air, his face the very picture of innocence. "I wasn't going to kiss you." He moved back a step. "I came out to see how you were doing."

"I'm doing awful, that's how I'm doing." Lillie pitched the rug beater onto the grass and stomped off to sit in the shade on the back porch. Sighing, she lowered herself onto the bottom step. Now that she was resting, she could feel her muscles screaming in protest against all the work she'd already done this morning. Her arms ached, and she stretched them over her head and leaned backward, trying to ease the kink in her neck and the stiffness in her back.

It didn't help her physically or mentally to realize she'd taken her anger out on Tom.

Glancing up, she looked at him. He was still standing where she'd left him, out in the middle of the lawn, looking a little lost in the wake of her abrupt departure.

A touch of embarrassment mingled with more than a bit of remorse and pricked Lillie's conscience. It was not Tom's fault. None of it was Tom's fault. It had been thoughtless of her to yell at him, foolish of her to reject the consolation he offered so generously.

Tom must have seen her watching him and taken it as a sign that even if she was not ready to repent, at least she was beginning to look remorseful. He came across the yard and dropped down on the step beside her, and Lillie looked away.

"I was saving my kisses for later." Tom's words were infinitely more gentle and patient than she deserved.

She turned back to him and took his hand. "I shouldn't have spoken to you that way. It's just that—"

"It's just that you're upset. And tired. And I'm the only one here you can scold. I understand." He raised his eyebrows and a roguish spark flickered in his dark eyes. "But don't make a habit of it. I don't intend to go through the rest of my life letting you take me to task. I—"

"But you don't deserve it." He was trying to be flip, trying to make her laugh. The thought made Lillie feel even worse. "I had no right to speak to you that way," she said. "I'm sorry." There was unbearable tenderness in Tom's eyes, unendurable affection in his touch, and Lillie fought back another onslaught of tears.

"There you go again." Tom slipped his arm around her and pulled her near, his voice soft, his face thoughtful and suddenly shaded with worry. "You're not having regrets, are you? About last night?"

Lillie sat up straight, her denial coming so quickly, she nearly tripped over her own words. "Last night? No! You can't mean . . . You didn't think . . . Oh, Tom. I'm sorry. I never meant for you to doubt I . . ." She dropped her head into her hands and tried to gather her wits about her. It was only when she was sure she could speak more sensibly that she dared to raise her eyes to his again.

"Last night is the one thing that's keeping me sane in all this." She cast a glance around the yard and the boxes they had already hauled outside, boxes filled with the remains of her glass-plate negatives. She smiled at Tom, a soft, adoring smile meant to convey her appreciation as well as her love. "No regrets about last night," she assured him. "No regrets about you. About us. If I didn't have you . . ." The thought was too distressing to continue and Lillie did not finish it. "I couldn't do it," she admitted. "Any of it. Not on my own. Not without you."

"Not without us." Tom pulled her to him again. "We'll get through this thing, Lillie. Together. We'll find a way." He tapped the tip of her nose with his index finger and smiled, his uneasiness borne away on the heels of her admission. "And I want you to know, I wasn't just trying to make you feel better. I really am saving my kisses for later." He leaned nearer, capturing her eyes with his own and holding them, his look delicate yet as thrilling as the gentle massage he'd begun on her shoulders. He lowered his voice and brushed her lips with his. "We'll have dinner at the American House tonight. And a long walk after. And after that we'll go to my house and—"

"Not the backyard again!" Lillie tried her best to look alarmed, but it was difficult to contain the smile she felt rising in her. "You may not have any neighbors, but word is bound to get out sooner or later. I wouldn't want an audience—"

"Good mornin'!"

Alex Campbell sauntered around the corner, resplendent in a brown and cream plaid suit that was just about as subtle as the knowing expression on his face. He gave them a broad, cheerful wink. "Hope I'm not interruptin' anything."

As if a cloud had scuttled past the sun and eclipsed its brilliance, Tom's features darkened. The tenderness Lillie had seen reflected in his eyes only moments ago was shrouded by a look both solemn and cautious. A look as suspicious as the one he tossed Alex Campbell's way. A look that caused a shiver to crawl up Lillie's spine.

Warding off the sudden chill, she hugged her arms tight around herself and squeezed her eyes shut.

It had been so easy to forget.

In all the wonder of last night, in all the hard work of this morning, it had been easy to forget the worries that dogged Tom's footsteps.

Opening her eyes again, Lillie looked over at Tom and her heart went out to him, anxious to help relieve his cares, desperate to try and soothe whatever troubles creased his brow and caused him to hold his back and shoulders so stiff and firm.

In the heat of last night's passion, in the contentment of the satisfaction that followed, in the exhaustion of this morning's cleaning, it had been easy to forget the specters that followed Tom night and day. Specters somehow embodied by Alex Campbell.

Tom stood and brushed the dust from the legs of his trousers. "Interrupting anything?" He gave Campbell a halfhearted shrug and looked around the yard before he chuckled, as if the decided lack of activity proved Campbell's question to be both presumptuous and unwarranted.

"Not a thing." Tom hooked his thumbs in the pockets of his trousers and leaned back on his heels, sizing up the reporter.

Campbell may have been easygoing, but he was not dull-witted. Lillie glanced his way. He must have seen the wariness in Tom's expression, just as she did, but Campbell did the one thing Lillie was not able to do. He ignored it.

Campbell hauled a lumpy bundle from his pocket. He took his time sorting through it, discarding sheets of paper, bits of string, and half-eaten pieces of rock candy and dropping them on the ground. When he finally made his way to the crumpled handkerchief at the center of the pile, he muttered a brief exclamation of triumph. He dusted his hands against his suit jacket and whisked the handkerchief across his forehead, scanning the cloudless sky.

"Gonna be another scorcher." Campbell crammed the square of cotton back in his pocket and smiled down at Lillie. "Just came by to see if everythin' was all right. After last night—"

"Miss Valentine is fine." Tom's words were as cool as his expression. "And whatever happened last night is none of your business."

Lillie hopped to her feet and wound one arm through Tom's, hoping to stop him before he said even more. Already, Campbell's eyes were alight, his nostrils flared with the scent of what was obviously too scandalous to be a newspaper story, but what was, nevertheless, surely grist for the town gossip mill.

"I believe Mr. Campbell was referring to our confrontation with Vincent Palusso last night," Lillie said, her words clipped by her clenched teeth and a forced and very strained smile. "We haven't had time to thank him formally for jumping in and—"

"And nearly getting his fool head knocked off." Tom pulled away from Lillie. Stuffing both hands in his pockets, he aimed a look at Campbell and shook his head with disgust. "You're lucky Palusso was drunk. If he'd been sober, he would have knocked you into next week."

"If he'd been sober, I wouldn't have gotten within twenty feet of him." Campbell shuddered at the thought. "Good Godfrey Daniel! Don't get any ideas about me bein' noble. I didn't wallop Palusso because he was disturbin' the festivities. I didn't even do it because he was all schnozzled up, though I should have. I did it for one reason and one alone. The man was about to go blabberin' about something he had no business talking about. And I'm not about to let a man go spreadin' half-truths and rumors." Campbell's face split with an enormous grin. "That's my job."

It may have been Campbell's open smile that disarmed Tom. It may have been the reminder that he really had helped Tom out, keeping Palusso from saying too much about Boston and Tom's past. Whatever the reason, Lillie saw some of Tom's resentment fade. He stuck one hand out to Campbell and gave him a begrudging smile.

"Whatever the reason, you jumped in at just the right time," Tom acknowledged, pumping Campbell's hand. "Thank you."

"No thanks necessary." Campbell could not control the blush that crept into his cheeks. "I got all the thanks I needed from the Reverend Johnson's girls. They are ministerin' angels, every one of them."

Lillie laughed. "And you?" she asked. "What are you?"

"I," Campbell said, "am insatiably curious." He craned his neck, looking into the nearest box of shattered negatives. "Had to see what everyone's buzzin' about."

"Buzzing?" Lillie gave Campbell a bewildered look.

"About all the cleanin' going on." Campbell nodded. "Word around town is that you two have been at it all mornin', buzzin' around like bees in a hive. Sweepin' and brushin'. Haulin' and packin'. Grace over at the bakery had it from Mildred at the dry goods shop. Anna, she heard it from Mr. Thrash, that old codger who lives up the street. There's a lot of idle chatter bein' exchanged this mornin'. Thought I'd better stop by and . . ." Campbell raised his shaggy eyebrows and looked at Lillie expectantly.

As if to shield her from the questions, Tom stepped between Lillie and Campbell. He answered before Lillie could. "You're bound to figure it out sooner or later. We may as well tell you. Miss Valentine has had some difficulty with her glass-plate negatives. We'd appreciate it, Campbell, if you wouldn't—"

"Elmore Montgomery!" Campbell let out a long whistle. "That son of a biscuit eater." His expression suddenly not as curious as it was concerned, he stepped around Tom and placed one hand on Lillie's arm. "You're all right, aren't you, Miss Valentine?" Campbell asked. "You weren't here when it happened? You weren't hurt?"

202

Lillie dismissed his anxiety with a small smile and a shake of her head. "I'm fine," she assured him. "Thanks to Tom." She looked past Campbell to Tom and held her hand out to him. Tom accepted it, winding his fingers through Lillie's, his face still solemn, but his touch filled with strength and all the emotion he could certainly hide from Campbell, but never from her.

Apparently convinced Lillie was in good hands and no longer needed what little comfort he could offer, Campbell stepped back. He had been genuinely concerned about her, Lillie was sure of that. But now, his anxiety relieved, the reporter was free to pursue her tantalizing story. His cheeks quivering with excitement, his eyes ablaze, Campbell asked, "When did it happen? Last night while we were at the social?"

His intuition was too perfect, his deduction too unerring. With a wave, Lillie invited Campbell to sit on the steps. She sat back down herself and pulled Tom down to sit beside her.

Campbell perched himself on the stair above Lillie's. "That's it, isn't it?" He didn't wait for an explanation, but merely assumed his instincts were, as usual, correct. "Happened while we were dancin' at the fairgrounds like fools. We should have seen it comin'." He looked down at Lillie, his mouth twisted into a rueful scowl. "We should have known after what happened to Hank Graham."

His pronouncement left Lillie speechless. She stared up at Campbell, confused and more than a little shaken by his unadorned statement. At her right she heard Tom suck in a sharp breath. His head shot up and he eyed Campbell carefully. "What do you know about Hank Graham?"

Campbell tapped the side of his nose with one finger. "Nose for news," he admitted, seeming neither proud nor pleased with the confession, but merely accepting it as fact. "Every reporter in Cleveland worth his salt suspected Montgomery was behind that fire. There were even one or two who tried to get the goods on him. Never could prove anythin'." Campbell held out both hands, palms up, the gesture as final as it was futile. "Expect we can't here, either." Obviously hoping they'd contradict him, Campbell waited for either Tom or Lillie to protest.

When neither of them did, he shrugged and looked to Lillie. "What are you gonna to do?" he asked.

Campbell's question had been fair enough, but Tom dismissed it with a grunt. "She's going to take new pictures, dammit. What else do you expect her to do?"

Lillie felt a rush of heat radiate from her heart to warm her, body and soul. She squeezed Tom's hand, offering her silent thanks for his support, and nodded her agreement. "I'll need to go back to Cleveland and retake the photographs. And someday"—she punctuated the word, her fist against her knee—"someday I'll get in to see the governor and show him what's going on behind the closed doors of the mills and the sweatshops and the factories in this state."

"Hm." With one hand Campbell rubbed his chin. "He's runnin' for president, you know? Governor Rutherford B. Hayes. Won the Republican nomination just last month. They say he doesn't have a snowball's chance in he—" Campbell cleared his throat and excused himself beneath his breath. "They say there's no chance he'll win," he amended the statement, "but it sure would be grand to get to the old boy while he's got the eyes of the entire nation watchin' him. What's your plan, Miss Valentine? When do you expect to see him?"

Lillie sighed, a familiar, gnawing despair eating away the edges of her aspirations. "I've written to Columbus more times than I care to recall," she explained, her voice sharp with the sting of the memory. "I get the same reply each time. The governor is a very busy man, they tell me. He simply doesn't have time to listen to some silly woman with half-baked ideas about what's wrong with our society." She shook her shoulders, dismissing the excuses, fighting the bitterness. "I'll find some other way."

Campbell was still deep in thought. He chewed at his lower lip a moment or two longer before his eyes opened wide. "Say, I know a fellow at the statehouse. Man by the name of Seamus McCleen. Not your everyday politician. Far too shady. Or maybe too honest." He laughed at his own shrewdness. "Anyway, ol' Seamus owes me a favor. Maybe he can pull a few strings."

"Would he?" The news sparkled through Lillie's veins like birdsong. She sat up and looked at Tom, smiling when she saw the mirrored excitement in his eyes. "Would he really? Would he help us, do you think?"

"I can't make any promises. But I could send a telegram. We—"

"Why?" Tom hopped from his seat on the stair and paced the length of the porch until he was standing nose to nose with Campbell, all the wariness back in his eyes, all the mistrust evident on his face. "Why are you so eager to help, Campbell? What do you want in return?"

Campbell leaned back and propped his elbows on the step above the one where he was sitting. "I would like to plead altruistic motives," he said. "But, unlike Miss Valentine here, I've got a mean streak a mile wide. You"—he looked down at Lillie—"you want to help the children. Pure and simple. Me? I'd like nothing better than to see Elmore Montgomery whirl from the nearest tree. And not just 'cause he takes advantage of all those poor kids who work in his mill." Campbell looked away, his face suddenly pale in spite of the heat of the noontime sun, his eyes clouded with some emotion too painful for him to reveal. He mumbled a curse, and for once did not excuse himself, before he blurted out his explanation. "Montgomery's tryin' his confoundest to buy the *Enterprise.*"

"What?" Lillie's voice overlapped with Tom's, and they stared at Campbell.

"I'm on my way to Cleveland today." Now that the announcement was out of his mouth, Campbell seemed more at ease. He cleared his throat again and looked down at his best suit as if that were explanation enough. "Got to see if I can talk some sense into those plague-goned bankers who own the newspaper."

"But don't you own the *Enterprise?*" Lillie was sure Tom was about to ask the same question. He had opened his mouth to speak. Now he snapped it shut and looked at Campbell, waiting for an answer.

"I do own the paper, at least for now. Three years ago, when I moved to Wellington, I took a loan to buy the *Enterprise.* I'm afraid I haven't been very regular about payin' it back.

The bank, they say they've sent me letters tellin' me I've got to be more reliable. Can't understand it." Campbell scratched his ear. "Can't find the doggone things in my office."

Lillie bit back the only reply she could offer. Alex Campbell couldn't find anything in his office, not even if his life, rather than just his livelihood, depended on it.

Campbell apparently had never considered the possibility. He shook his head. "They're tryin' to sell the *Enterprise* out from under me. And they say they've got a buyer. Elmore Montgomery."

"The folks in town will never stand for it." Lillie's voice rang across the yard. "The *Enterprise* is too important to them. They'd never let a man like Montgomery operate it."

In spite of his obvious distress Campbell could not avoid responding with the enthusiasm of any good reporter. His eyes lit with a mischievous gleam. "He'd never get away with it if you had the proof he's the kind of employer you know him to be."

Lillie corrected him. "If I had more pictures."

The objection meant nothing to Campbell. He picked a piece of fuzz from the leg of his trousers and flicked it into the air. "I know Montgomery's stayin' in town at least until the end of August," he said. "And I heard him talkin' last night. His foreman's stayin' on until the end of the week. There won't be anyone in authority up at the mill until then. Not anyone with the nerve to toss out a photographer who's good at pretendin' she has every right to be there."

Lillie sat up straight, her spirits rising with each word Campbell spoke. "This week?" she asked.

"That's right, Miss Valentine." Her enthusiasm was contagious. Campbell leaned forward, bright spots of color shining in his cheeks. "It might not be seemly for you to travel all that way unaccompanied, but may I remind you that I'm on my way to Cleveland this afternoon. If you'll—"

"Now, wait a minute!" Tom's objection cut through Campbell's smooth invitation like a knife through warm butter. "You just can't go running off to Cleveland because this man tells you—"

"I'd be going whether Alex told me about Montgomery's foreman or not," Lillie countered. "This is the perfect opportunity."

"Opportunity for what?" Tom had curbed his emotions long enough. Lillie could tell as much from the spark in his eyes as she could from the small note of skepticism that sharpened his voice and the quick, forceful movements of his hands cutting through the air, emphasizing each word he spoke. He was not as angry with her as he was perplexed, not as surprised that she would take advantage of an opportunity to replace her pictures as he was wary of who had offered her the chance. He turned his gaze from Lillie, still sitting on the porch, and aimed it full at Campbell. "What do you expect in return?"

"Not what you think." Alex Campbell stood up. "You think I'll take the opportunity of a long journey with Miss Valentine to ask her more questions. More questions about you."

Tom acknowledged the accuracy of Campbell's statement with one quick nod of his head. "The thought had crossed my mind."

Campbell waved away the problem. "I've tried that. It didn't work. Besides"—he descended the stairs and stood toe-to-toe with Tom—"you've got the wrong idea about me, Reilly. I've asked a lot of questions about you to a lot of people in this town. I always get the same answers. The people around here, they think a great deal of you. And they weren't shy about tellin' me why. Sure, they mentioned you've taken young Anthony Palusso under your wing. But they also told me about last winter when Jonah Hatcher and his family took sick and you helped them out, gettin' them the medicine they needed, keepin' up with the chores when they weren't strong enough. Then there's the base ball team. They mentioned that, too. How you taught the game to the boys." Campbell paused, letting Tom take in the information and all it implied. When he was sure it had, he looked at Lillie.

"Heard the same kind of thing from people all over town about Tom Reilly," Campbell said. "That's what made me change my mind. That's what made me decide to keep askin' more questions." He turned back to Tom. "Not to hurt you, but to help." Campbell smiled and, spinning around, headed into the garden and around to the front of the house. Before he got as far as the corner gate, he stopped and turned back to Tom and Lillie.

"Miss Valentine, I'll be at the railroad station waitin' for the two o'clock train. You can meet me there if you like. And Reilly, rest assured, I'm not tryin' to write an article that will ruin your reputation. Believe it or not, I'm trying to write one that will restore it."

Lillie watched Campbell go, her mind already ticking off the endless details that would need to be resolved before she could join him on the two o'clock train. What to pack, what equipment to take, where she would stay when she arrived in Cleveland. She ran through the possibilities. Even though she was preoccupied, she realized Campbell's parting words were cryptic, and that they had somehow cheered Tom and relieved him of at least some of his worry. She made a mental note to ask him to explain it all while she packed. Right now there wasn't time for anything else. She had just over two hours to get ready.

Lillie turned and hurdled up the porch stairs. Her hand was already on the studio door when she heard Tom's voice behind her.

"You're really going, aren't you?"

Tom had not moved from his spot at the base of the stairs. Lillie looked down at him. There was not disapproval in his eyes, only disappointment.

"You knew I would," she explained. "You knew I would go sometime. If you're worried about what Alex might try to find out—"

"No." Tom did not hesitate to discard the suggestion. "Not anymore. Don't ask me why, Lillie, but I actually believe the man. He wants to help." Tom ran one hand over the back of his neck. Though the *Enterprise* editor was long gone, Tom looked after him, as if staring at the empty space Campbell had recently occupied would help make sense of all he'd said. Finding no answers there, Tom looked back to Lillie. "But I am worried about you. What if Montgomery finds out?"

"It's only for a few days. What can Montgomery possibly find out in that time? Who would tell him?" In spite of her brave words the same worry was gnawing at Lillie's mind. She wasn't about to let Tom know it. Deciding it was safer, and wiser, to change the subject, she laughed and hoped the laugh didn't sound too forced. Lillie took two steps forward and gave Tom as coquettish a look as she could manage.

"You're disappointed about tonight, aren't you? That's it. You're thinking of yourself and how lonely it's going to be without that dinner at the American House, and that long walk home, and after that . . ."

Tom's head shot up. For a moment it looked as if he might deny her allegation. He gave up trying in an instant, admitting defeat with a small smile and a lift of his shoulders. He bounded up the stairs and took Lillie in his arms.

"Promise me there will be other nights." He whispered the words in her ear, his voice rough, his breathing ragged.

"There will be other nights for dinner at the American House," Lillie assured him, linking her arms around his neck.

"And other nights for long walks home?" Tom brushed his hands over her face as if memorizing the shape of her features, the feel of her skin.

"Lots of long walks." Lillie tried to brace herself against the surge of longing engendered by his touch. She could not. She could not do anything but murmur her approval of the kisses Tom scattered across her face and along her neck.

He straightened long enough to look into her eyes, and his voice dipped to a husky whisper. "And after?" he asked. "Lots of nights for what happens after?"

Lillie could not speak her agreement even though she wanted to. Tom's lips were on hers, his fingers working at the buttons along the front of her gown, his own need all the more evident when he finished unfastening the buttons and slid his hands to her backside, pressing her close against him.

Lillie pushed away long enough to cast a glance around the backyard, her gaze instinctively traveling between her neighbors on either side. "I think we'd better get into the house," she said.

It was the last thing she had a chance to say for a very long time.

"Five days was far too long for you to be away."

His body sleek with perspiration, his face beaming with satisfaction, Tom slid off Lillie and rolled over onto his side. Keeping one arm draped around her, he grazed his fingers along the ridge of her collarbone.

His touch was pleasing, but Lillie was far too ticklish to hold still. She giggled and rolled over. Plumping her pillow beneath her head, she nodded her agreement.

"Entirely too long," she said, her own breath still coming in short gasps, her body replete with contentment and warm with the afterglow of an entire afternoon spent making love. "Next time I go to Cleveland, you're coming with me." She did not speak the request as a question; she knew Tom would not object. "And if Alex Campbell really does get me an appointment with Governor Hayes, you'll come to Columbus with me, won't you, Tom?"

"Just try and make me stay here." Tom sat up and stretched his arms over his head. He pulled the blanket up around his waist and sat back against the headboard of Lillie's bed.

He could not have been chilly, not on an evening as close and uncomfortable as this. Lillie smiled to herself, somehow heartened by the thought that Tom could be as modest as he was passionate, as gentle as he was intense. For a few minutes she simply watched him, his profile outlined by the ever failing light. His eyes seemed darker than ever in the twilight, his face was smoothed of worry, his hair dipped over his forehead like a child's.

Lillie snuggled into the down pillow and remembered that, not quite four hours ago, Tom had met her at the train station, a bouquet of wildflowers in his hand. Every hair in place, his cuffs and collar pressed so stiff they looked as if they might crack, he had been wearing his best Sunday suit and a smile that turned Lillie's heart over inside her.

How strained and reserved his welcome was after their passionate goodbye five days ago. How odd and formal it seemed to shake his hand and how frustrating to receive Tom's equally awkward welcome when all Lillie wanted to do was kiss him.

She knew Tom felt the same. Knew it by the gleam in his eye, the impatient looks he gave her as they walked side by side through the station and out onto Kelley Street. She also knew the artifice was necessary. In addition to Alex Campbell, there were others at the train station waiting for family, bidding goodbye to friends. Far too many others for her to give Tom the kind of welcome she had dreamed of the entire time she'd spent in Cleveland.

That welcome had to wait.

Lillie's trip to Cleveland had been even more successful than she'd hoped; her access to Montgomery's mill as simple as Alex Campbell had promised it would be. But though she was relieved at the ease with which she'd obtained new photographs, Lillie was hardly complacent enough to believe that was the end of the matter.

Montgomery was sure to hear of her visit to the mill sooner or later, and when he did, Lillie would be prepared.

They stopped at Tom's house first and left some of her new glass-plate negatives there where she was sure Montgomery would never find them, then at Alex Campbell's office where they concealed another batch of plates beneath the biggest and most forbidding-looking stack of old newspapers they could find. It was only then they were able to bid Campbell good evening. Only then they were able to return to Lillie's.

They were barely inside the front door when the lowering clouds that had been hanging over the town all day burst and it began to rain.

They made love to the tempo of the raindrops, first in the parlor—the draperies discreetly closed against prying eyes, the painting of Flossie looking on in silent approval—and then upstairs in Lillie's brass bed.

Now the raindrops beat against the windows in perfect time to the pounding of Lillie's heart. She sighed, content, listening to the distant rumble of thunder, watching as the room lit, ever so slightly, from the flash of far-off lightning.

It was some time before she realized Tom was watching her carefully.

"What is it?" Suddenly self-conscious under his scrutiny, Lillie squirmed and tried to get under the blanket.

"Oh, no!" Tom yanked the blanket beyond her reach. "That's just how I like to see you." He let his gaze wander from the fall of Lillie's hair around her shoulders, down the slope of her back, to her bare behind. He leaned nearer and brushed the tips of his fingers over her skin, his hand following his gaze. "Just like Flossie." The thought seemed to amuse him, and Tom tipped his head back and laughed. "That's exactly who you look like," he told her. "Like Flossie in that painting downstairs."

As quickly as it came, the smile fled Tom's face. He drifted his fingers up and down along her backside, the movement unconscious, his expression faraway.

It was a marvelous sensation. Lillie nestled farther into the pillow, her eyes half-closed, a dreamy smile playing its way around her lips.

"You know what I'd like?" Tom's voice sounded as euphoric as Lillie felt.

"I can just imagine what you'd like!" Lillie laughed.

Her laughter brought Tom out of his daydream. He smiled in return and gave her another leisurely perusal. "Not this time," he admitted. He rolled his eyes. "We've been here all afternoon. I'm famished. It's time to get some dinner." He sat up and propped his elbows on his knees, his gaze still trained on Lillie.

"What I'd really like," he said, "is a photograph of you. A photograph of you just like this, stretched out on the bed, your hair down around your shoulders, your skin glistening in the light. Naked as the day you were born."

Lillie's surprise could not be more complete. She raised herself on her elbows, her pillow discreetly concealing her bare breasts. "You can't be serious." She waited for Tom to admit he was only teasing. He did not. From the spark in his eyes, the tension that suddenly tightened the muscles in his arms and neck, she knew he would not.

Lillie dropped back down on the bed. "It isn't seemly," she protested.

Tom would not be put off so easily. He leaned back. "Why? Why isn't it seemly? You look as modest as can be. That pillow's tucked around you so I can't see anything there." His lips twisted into a disappointed frown. "And your hair's covering just about all of your back. Now, here"—he patted her backside—"here we might have a problem. But if you added some palm plants like in Flossie's picture . . ." He raised his eyebrows, obviously hoping she'd give some thought to the suggestion. "I've seen less discreet pictures hanging in saloons." Though Lillie was sure he was earnest, Tom could not contain a smile. "Besides," he concluded, "I wouldn't hang it in my fix-it shop in a gold frame! It would be mine. Just for me."

The more he explained it, the more preposterous the idea seemed. Lillie groaned. "Why on earth would you want it?" she asked.

Tom cocked his head, considering the question. When he spoke, his voice was hushed below the sounds of the rain against the windows. "I think I'd like the picture because it would remind me of today," he said. He looked down at Lillie and smiled. "And every time I even started to take you for granted, I'd look at it and I'd remember what it was like when you were gone for five whole days and how I missed you so much I could taste it." Tom slid under the covers and, laying down on his side, wrapped one arm around Lillie's shoulders and pulled her near.

"And if we're ever parted again," he whispered, "I'd see you in that photograph and I'd remember the feel of your hair in my hand and the touch of your skin against mine and I'd know you'd come back to me. Or I'd come back to you. I'd see that picture and I'd know that nothing and no one could keep us apart. Not for long."

In spite of herself Lillie felt a smug little grin relieve her dour expression. It might be a ridiculous request, but it was certainly flattering. The thought caused a pleasant rush of warmth inside her. Lillie clicked her tongue and looked away, hiding her pleasure. "And where," she asked, "would you keep such a picture?"

"Right here." Taking one of her hands, Tom held it close to his heart. "Right here where it would warm me when I was all alone. And remind me that you'd always be there waiting for me."

There was no answer she could give him, and Lillie did not even try. Tom slid his hand from her wrist to her elbow, from her elbow to her shoulder, from her shoulder to her face. He tipped her face to his.

"You know," he said, "suddenly I'm not that hungry for dinner anymore."

14

"PRETTY SOON, MAYBE I won't have to be making any more pies for you. Maybe there will be someone else doing your cooking?" Sarah Hatcher's blue eyes danced in the evening light, her face aglow with merriment and the prospect of knowing a particularly tantalizing secret long before her neighbors got wind of it.

"You make the best pies in Lorain County." Disregarding the meaningful looks Sarah was giving him, Tom bent and breathed in the aroma of the fresh-baked blueberry pie in his hands. "You always will, Sarah. No one can top your baking." Tom made his move out the back door, hoping for a clean getaway down the garden path and the quickest possible escape.

Sarah would not be put off so easily. She wedged her foot firmly in the door so Tom was unable to close it and called in reinforcements. "Don't you think so, Jonah? Wouldn't it be nice if Tom had someone to do his cooking?" She tossed the question over her shoulder to her husband, who was just finishing up his dinner.

Jonah pushed back from the kitchen table, his chair scraping against the wooden floor. "I think there comes a time in every man's life when he realizes it's time to settle down." He joined his wife at the door, his plain face split with a grin, his eyes mirroring Sarah's playfulness as well as her curiosity. "And I think it would be remiss of any man not to tell his good friends what his matrimonial plans are. If"—he raised his eyebrows and pinned Tom with a look—"if, that is, he has any such plans."

"*If*"—Tom emphasized the word, just as Jonah had—"he had any such plans, he would certainly tell his friends. And they would promptly tell their friends, who would undoubtedly tell their friends. Pretty soon the entire township would know about it, long before the prospective bride had ever been asked. How would you like that?" He looked over at Sarah. "How would you like to find out a man wanted to marry you before he ever had the chance to ask?"

Recognizing defeat when she saw it, Sarah gave up the fight. "How do you think I knew Jonah was set on courting me?" she asked, laughing. "Heard it from my mother's second cousin twice removed, that's how."

Jonah's eyes widened until they were as big as saucers. "You did?" He looked down at his wife, his mouth open in a perfectly good imitation of surprise. "Why, that's exactly who told me you had your sights set on me! Do you mean, after all these years, we've finally come to realize neither one of us really wanted to marry the other?"

Sarah threw back her head and laughed, the easy camaraderie she shared with her husband evident in every line of her face. "You mean we aren't meant for each other?" She clapped one hand on Jonah's arm. "Whatever will we tell the children?"

Their merriment was infectious. Tom laughed, too. He could not help himself. He laughed, and a warm feeling filled his insides when he realized this was just the kind of comfortable companionship he was looking forward to with Lillie.

He was still laughing as he made his way around to the front of the Hatchers' house and down Taylor Street. He stepped over a puddle in the middle of the road, a reminder of last night's rain, and turned onto Main Street, headed for Lillie's.

Dinner would be on the table promptly at six, she'd assured him, and he didn't want to be late.

Tom smiled a greeting to every person he passed. What would they think, he wondered, if they'd seen him this morning? He pictured himself creeping out Lillie's back door long before the sun rose above the horizon, and his smile widened. What would the neighbors say if they knew Miss Valentine had a gentleman caller who not only came for the evening, but spent the night as well?

He shrugged the idea away without another thought. That was one secret that would remain a secret, Tom told himself. Even in this town.

There was no answer at Lillie's front door.

Tom looked back at his own face reflected in the door glass and frowned. He was about to knock again when he heard a peculiar sound coming from the backyard. He walked to the porch rail and leaned forward, listening. There it was again. And if he were a fanciful man, he would have sworn it was the sound of splashing.

Depositing the blueberry pie on the white wicker table that stood outside the parlor windows, Tom descended the stairs and rounded the house, heading toward the back garden.

The closer he got, the louder the sounds got, until there was no mistaking them. It was splashing, all right. Splashing, sprinkled with enough laughter to cause Tom to smile instinctively in return.

He stepped into the garden and stopped short.

Lillie was kneeling beside a large tub filled with soapy water with Anthony Palusso at her side. Together, they were trying their best to hang on to Tom the Dog. It wasn't working. The creature was covered with lather, wet as a fish, and mad as the proverbial wet hen. It was not a happy combination.

The more Lillie and Anthony struggled, the more restless the dog got. The more restless the dog got, the more he tried to shake the water from his coat. The more he tried to shake dry, the more Anthony ladled water over him, and the more Lillie and Anthony laughed.

Compared to this, the labors of Sisyphus were nothing. The poor man in the myth may have been sentenced to roll a boulder up a hill for all eternity, but Tom could guarantee, he had never faced anything as daunting as bathing a recalcitrant mutt.

Neither Lillie nor Anthony saw him, and Tom settled back against the fence and watched the burlesque being played out before him.

Lillie's gown was soaked with water, dotted with bubbles, and flecked with mud spots. Her hair looked as if a troop of wild bison had trampled through it. Half of it was down around her shoulders, the other half, stuck up into a roll at the back of her neck. The front of her hairdo had fared no better. It hung over Lillie's eyes in wet, soapy clumps. She pursed her lips and tried to blow a curl out of the way. Her attention was diverted for no more than a moment, but it was one moment too long.

Tom the Dog made a mad dash for dry land.

Lillie grabbed him around the middle. Her arms disappeared below the surface of the water, and she made a sound somewhere between a groan and a laugh and slumped forward, her head against the dog's wet fur. When she straightened again, Lillie's hair was in more of a shambles than ever, and her face was freckled with soap suds.

Anthony fared no better. Though his shoes and socks were off and his trousers were rolled above his ankles, his clothes were drenched. He didn't seem to mind. A cake of sturdy yellow soap in his hands, he fought with Tom's front end, trying, without much success, to scrub behind the dog's ears.

The scene was as close to utopia as Tom could imagine, and for a moment, he let himself pretend he came home from coaching the boys' base ball matches every evening and found something just like it. It was a minute or more before he felt something wrong gnawing at the back of his mind, and another minute before he realized what it was.

Anthony was not supposed to be here.

Tom stepped forward and cleared his throat.

Lillie's head came up and she smiled over the dog at Tom. She bounded to her feet, and the dog made his break for freedom. He was galloping across the back lawn with all the abandon of a prisoner loosed from his bonds by the time Lillie made her way to Tom.

Anthony took off after the dog, the bar of soap still in his hands, and Lillie watched them round the corner and head toward the front of the house leaving nothing behind them but a trail of water, suds, and giggles.

Lillie stood on tiptoe and planted a soapy kiss on Tom's cheek. "I had no idea it was six already." She wiped her hands against the skirt of her gown and headed into the house. "The soup's probably done and—" Halfway up the back porch stairs she turned to make sure Tom was following. He was not, and Lillie paused and looked down at him, sizing up everything from the solemn expression on his face to his rigid posture. "What's wrong?" she asked.

Tom shook off whatever was bothering him. He bounded up the stairs after Lillie. There was a towel on the topmost step, and he bent to pick it up and draped it across her shoulders. "There's nothing wrong." The inflection of Tom's voice belied his words. He held the back door for Lillie and allowed her to go inside ahead of him. "But I thought we'd agreed to stay away from Anthony. Both of us. After Palusso's threats, we agreed it was safer for the boy. At least for the time being."

Wanting to assuage Tom's worries, yet fearing to tell him too much, Lillie stalled for time. She washed her hands at the sink and dried them, lifted the lid of the soup pot, stirred the soup, and replaced the lid with care. She would need an explanation that would both satisfy Tom and ensure that he would ask no more questions.

The long silence was obviously too much for Tom to take. He paced the length of the kitchen and came to stand directly behind Lillie, his voice low, edged with annoyance. "We have Judge Baker looking into the possibilities of fosterage or some sort of guardianship. Lillie, I can't believe you'd jeopardize—"

"Vincent Palusso's gone." The words burst from Lillie before she could stop them. Telling the truth was far less painful than she imagined it would be, and she let out a long, unsteady breath. "He's been gone since Friday," she said, spinning to face Tom. "So Anthony says. Anthony's on his own. At least for a few days."

"Gone?" Tom considered the implications of her news. "But where—"

"I didn't think it would hurt to have Anthony here to eat dinner with us." Lillie ran one hand down the placket of Tom's shirt, her fingers idly outlining each button. She looked up at him. "Do you?"

Whatever questions may have been troubling Tom's mind vanished instantly. He shook his head and smiled. "I suppose not." The anxiety that had clouded his face cleared and he reached for Lillie's arms to draw her closer. His expression changed the instant his hands met the wet sleeves of her gown. "You're soaked." He sniffed the air experimentally. "And one of us smells like a wet dog. Maybe you should change before dinner?"

Without waiting for Tom to make the suggestion a second time, Lillie hurried through the kitchen and out into the hallway. She smiled to herself. Deliverance came from the strangest places. In this case, it came in the form of Tom the Dog, or at least in the wet and soapy souvenirs of his bath.

Lillie charged up the stairs, thanking whatever lucky stars governed the fates of lady photographers who preferred not to discuss the whereabouts of a certain young boy's father. She was already on the first landing when she heard Tom call after her.

"Where's Palusso gone?"

Lillie pretended she didn't hear.

"Bène!" Anthony sat back in his chair and patted his belly. "No one can cook like you, Signorina Lillie. Not even my mama." For just a second Anthony's lower lip quivered, and his eyes filled with tears. He banished the emotion and made sure no one else noticed it by topping off his comment with an immense burp. "I am very glad you ask me to come here tonight," he said, his melancholy expelled along with

the belch. "I am very glad my father, he is away."

Tom wiped his mouth and set his napkin down on the table. "Lillie says your father's been gone since Friday. Where did he go, Anthony?"

Before the question was out of Tom's mouth, Lillie was out of her chair. "Where did you say you put that blueberry pie?"

If he noticed anything odd in the hasty inquiry, Tom did not show it. He pointed idly toward the front porch. "Left it on the table out there," he said. He turned his attention back to Anthony. "How can he just go off and leave you like this?" Tom asked, his dark eyes filled with compassion, the kind of sympathy Anthony would never accept if it were expressed in words. "Where did you say he's gone?"

Before Lillie could even attempt to change the subject again, Anthony popped out of his chair and picked up his plate, headed to the sink. "He go with that man," he said over his shoulder. "You know, the one who has come to see him before."

Tom turned to Lillie for an explanation. "What's he talking about?"

Forcing a laugh, Lillie rolled her eyes. "Children! They do make up the funniest stories. Anthony, why don't you get the pie and—"

"Signorina!" Anthony deposited his dish in the sink with a bang and stomped across the kitchen, his fists against his slim hips, his angelic face screwed into an expression of utter disbelief. Instead of marching straight over to Lillie, he stopped in front of Tom. "She says children do not know what they are talking about? Women!" Anthony banged his forehead with the heel of one hand.

"How can she say this? I tell her about it before we give the dog his bath. I tell her it is the same man who came to see my father before. I even tell her what the man look like. I tell her he look just like you, Signóre Tom."

Lillie was certain time could not stand still—at least, that was what she had always been told. Yet for a long moment it seemed to stop, frozen like the silly smile she felt still clinging to her face; trapped like the tight breath caught in her lungs.

The kitchen clock continued to tick on the shelf above the stove, the cardinals continued to chirp their evening songs in the lilac bushes outside the window. Everything else came to a standstill.

Anthony stood near the table, his large, dark eyes filled with confusion, his shoulders thrown back in a childish display of outrage that was all the more excruciating because it was so ingenuous. He was waiting for her to apologize. Lillie could read the thought behind the hurt expression on his face. Anthony was waiting for her to apologize and expecting her to explain to Tom that he had been speaking the truth.

Lillie turned away, blocking the sight. It didn't help. Nothing could erase the sickening feeling of disloyalty and desertion that filled her or banish the fluttering tremor that had begun to ripple through her insides.

She turned and found Tom watching her carefully.

"You knew about this?" Tom's voice was low, his words simple, yet they caused a block of ice to form beneath Lillie's heart. Instinctively she took a step toward Tom, her hand out to him.

Either he didn't see the gesture, or he chose to ignore it. Tom turned his gaze on Anthony, and shaking off his surprise, he reached into his pocket. He came came up holding a shiny ten-cent piece. "I'll tell you what, Anthony. Why don't you go over to the Hatchers' and get Nathan? The two of you can stop at Baldwin's. I'm sure the store is closed by now, but knock on the back door. Someone's bound to be there working on the accounts. Get yourself a couple peppermint sticks."

"Peppermint sticks?" Anthony's eyes widened. "You are sure, Signóre Tom? You are sure we are allowed to buy something so wonderful? What about the blueberry pie?"

"The pie can wait." This time it was Lillie who spoke. Sensing what needed to be said was best said in private, she took Anthony by the shoulders and steered him toward the back door. "We'll have the pie tomorrow night."

"Sì, signorina." Anthony was not about to dispute his unexpected good fortune. He tossed the dime up into the air and watched it spin back down to his hand. When it did, he slapped it into his pocket. "*Grazie,* signóre." He smiled his gratitude, first at Tom, then at Lillie. "I will be back."

The back door had banged shut and Anthony's footsteps had faded before Lillie found the courage to look at Tom again.

He was still sitting in his chair, his hands clutched on the scrubbed wooden table. The confusion was gone from his face. In its place was a look as cold as a winter night. There was no bewilderment left in his eyes, only disapproval. No questioning, or indecision, or skepticism, only the chilling certainty that he had been betrayed, betrayed by the one woman he had trusted with his heart and his soul.

"You knew about this?"

The question reverberated across the kitchen and slammed into Lillie with all the force of a physical blow.

"I . . . I knew." She took two steps toward Tom, hoping the nearness would help close the sudden distance between them.

"You knew and you didn't tell me." This was not a question, but a statement of pure fact. A judgment. An accusation.

Lillie recoiled beneath the power of the words, but she refused to give ground. She planted her feet and met Tom's even gaze.

Her obstinacy was obviously something Tom had not anticipated. Challenged by the stubborn gleam in her eye, face-to-face with the unyielding set of her shoulders, Tom sprang from his chair so quickly, it tipped and crashed onto the floor. He did not bother to pick it up.

"Do you have any idea how important this is?" Tom asked, his eyes flashing fire like heat lightning, his fingers tightened around themselves. "Do you even realize what we're talking about here?"

It was not the cold edge in Tom's words that caused a sudden rush of anger to tear through Lillie's veins. It was the look in his eyes.

He was begging her to confess she had sinned on the side of caution, pleading with her to admit she had neglected to tell him Anthony's news, not because she wanted to hide the information from him, but because she did not recognize its

223

implications, or worse still, that she did not understand them.

It would have been far simpler to let him go on believing the lie, to bat her eyelashes and shrug her shoulders and perhaps top off the performance with a nervous, self-deprecating giggle. It would have been far simpler to act as if she didn't know, to pretend she didn't care.

It would be easy enough. One little lie would bring the sparkle back to Tom's eyes and convince him Lillie had tried to neither deceive nor mislead him. One small lie and they could go back to the way they had been before, with all thoughts of the past put safely to rest, far from where they could disturb the happiness of their days or destroy the rapture of their nights.

One little lie.

The thought streaked through Lillie's mind. It should have filled her with hope, should have lightened her heart. Instead, it left a hollow aching in its path, an anguish that spoke louder than the voices of temptation inside Lillie's head, a pain that told her if she lied to salvage the moment, she would certainly sacrifice the future.

Lillie sucked in a deep breath for courage and drew back her shoulders.

"I know very well what we're talking about," she said, her voice as cold and exact as Tom's, though her heart squeezed with regret inside her. "And if I didn't, I'd only need to fix my eyes on you to work it out. Look at you! Your fists are curled tight and your teeth are clenched. It has something to do with Vincent Palusso, doesn't it? All this has something to do with Vincent Palusso and why you followed him here to Wellington. It has something to do with why you trail after him in the middle of the night and ask questions about who he communicates with and who communicates with him. It has something to do with Boston."

Her words hit Tom like stones, each one making its mark in the strong shell he wrapped around himself to guard the secrets of his past. She saw him grimace and wished she could recall her words, but it was too late. Too late for anything but the truth.

Tom pulled himself up to his full height. If her words had injured him, they had also stoked his anger. He glared at her. "None of it is any of your business, Lillie. And you took it upon yourself to decide I shouldn't know about it. Who's life are we talking about here?"

"Mine! My life!" Lillie stabbed one finger at her chest, her voice raised to meet Tom's. "You're my life and we're talking about how much I love you. You can avoid every question I ask. You can brush me off and accuse me of prying into your private affairs, but it's my life, too, now." The words lodged behind the ball of emotion jammed into Lillie's throat. She cleared it away with a sound halfway between a cough and a sob and grabbed for the nearest chair. Locking her fingers around the spindles of the high back, Lillie steadied herself and forced her words to mask the chaos that churned through her body and turned her numb with panic.

"I've seen your face while you're sleeping," she said, her voice calmer now, her words edged with despair. "I've seen how it darkens with bad memories. I've seen how your brows drop over your eyes and how your mouth turns down with worry. And I get up in the middle of the night and I pace the floor because when that happens, I can't help but remember what Alex Campbell told me that first night he came to call. He said you'd leave." The words sounded a death knell in Lillie's ears. She squeezed her eyes shut and repeated them, an incantation designed to drive away the fears that plagued her.

"Alex said you'd leave because of something that happened in Boston. Something that involved Vincent Palusso. Don't you understand, Tom?" Lillie's eyes flew open, her head shot up, and she looked at Tom. "I don't care what happened in Boston. And I don't care who the man is that Anthony's seen. All I care about is you, and I won't"—she pounded her fists against the back of the chair—"I won't let any of this pull us apart. I'll fight it. Even if it means keeping things from you. I'll fight it every inch of the way."

While Lillie's anger vaporized into a haze of misery, Tom's only intensified. He took two steps forward, then pulled himself to a stop. "And what if I told you the man with Palusso could help?" he asked, his voice thick with exasperation. "What if I told you he's my brother and—"

"No!" There was malice in Tom's voice when he spoke the word *brother*, and instinctively Lillie fought against it. She warded off the hostility with a broad gesture of dismissal. "It couldn't be. Vincent Palusso says—"

"Palusso!" The criticism in Tom's eyes turned to resentment. Crossing the room in three strides, he grabbed for Lillie's arms and held her tight until she looked up at him and met his eyes. "What did he tell you?" When she did not respond, Tom tightened his hold. "What did he tell you, Lillie?"

Lillie shook off the grip. She sidestepped Tom and hurried to the other side of the room. It was only when the kitchen table was between them that she turned to face him again, the scene swimming through the veil of tears that filled her eyes. "Palusso said it was your fault," she said. "He said your brother was dead, and he said it was all your fault."

Tom tossed back his head and barked out a sound that was almost a laugh. He went to the back screen door and punched it open with one hand. Catching it as it came back to him, he tossed a look over his shoulder at Lillie. "You've missed the point after all, Lillie," he said. "That's exactly what they want you to think. It's exactly what everyone in Boston does think. But unless ghosts can walk and talk and spend their ill-gotten gains, I'm the one who's been right all along. This proves it, don't you see? Danny isn't dead."

"Danny isn't dead."

It wasn't the statement that sent a chill through Lillie. It was the way Tom said it. How odd, she thought, that such a simple collection of words could have so many implications.

Spoken with exhilaration, the sentence was a hosanna, a song of jubilation.

But Tom hadn't said the words with enthusiasm.

Spoken with disbelief, the words were charged with hopes and fears and longings, wishes desperately desired, fleeting dreams that might vanish if belief was ignored or faith abandoned.

But Tom hadn't said the words hopefully.

The way Tom spoke the words . . .

In spite of the heat, Lillie shivered.

The way Tom spoke the words caused a snake of fear to wind around her heart. She could still see him as clearly as that evening a week ago when he'd stomped out of her house, anger in his eyes, resentment in every taut muscle of his body, hatred and malice in his words: "Danny isn't dead."

"But Danny is your brother." Lillie whispered the words beneath her breath, images of her own brother Johnny's face drifting through her mind. "How can you hate your brother?"

The question echoed back at her, unanswered, in the darkness. Lillie reprimanded herself. She should have known better. She would probably get no more of an answer tonight than she'd gotten last night, or the night before. She would certainly not get a straight answer from Tom.

She sighed, remembering how she'd waited for him the evening after their argument, and how he hadn't come. She remembered the next day and how each time there was a knock at the door, she'd eagerly abandoned her darkroom and the new glass-plate negatives she took in Cleveland. But it was never Tom.

It was after the second night of waiting that Lillie decided he would not come, not as long as the secret that tangled his fate so completely with Vincent Palusso's still held him in its tight grip.

Only the truth could free Tom of the twisted web.

A roll of distant thunder startled Lillie from her musings, and she tipped her head from side to side, trying to alleviate the tightness in her neck and shoulders. Forty minutes of hunching behind a stack of packing crates in the loading dock of the Foundry Planing Mill had done little to better her mood, she noted with sour satisfaction. It had done nothing to improve her posture.

Lillie stretched and settled again into position, her back against the nearest wooden crate, her legs out in front of her. From this vantage point she could see not only part of the factory grounds, but the house and yard next door as well, the house that belonged to Vincent Palusso.

The place was quiet and dark except for the lights that burned in the front parlor and the one small lamp that shone through the window of the room just this side of the back steps. That was Anthony's room; Lillie knew as much from the stories he'd told her.

Anthony was the real reason she'd decided on her present plan. He had come back to the house the night of her argument with Tom, just as he promised he would. He stayed long enough to yawn and gaze at Lillie heavy-eyed, long enough to be invited to sleep on the sofa in the studio. He'd come to visit the next evening, too.

But the third and the fourth evening, there was no sign of Anthony. Lillie knew that could mean only one thing. Vincent Palusso had returned.

For once the township grapevine proved useful. Lillie knew Palusso was back, and she made sure everyone else in Wellington did, too. Two nights later, confident the rumor had spread far and fast, Lillie hid in the shadows of the foundry loading dock.

Tom did not disappoint her. Just past ten he appeared through the darkness of Johns Street, as quiet as a whisper. He stationed himself outside Palusso's house and simply waited.

Lillie waited, too, until nearly three in the morning. It was only then Tom gave up the long vigil. Only then he went home.

Lillie shifted positions and squinted into the blackness. If there was one thing she had learned about Tom Reilly, it was that he was neither a man who gave up easily nor one who could be put off by minor setbacks. He would return again tonight, she was certain of that. He would be back to continue the surveillance. He would be back to wait for Danny.

As if her thoughts had caused him to materialize, Lillie heard the crunch of boots in the street and saw a dark shape cross the yard and stand near the battered lean-to at the back of Palusso's house. In a sudden momentary flash of lightning, the identity of the shadow was unmistakable.

Lillie let her gaze drift over the shape, so dear and so familiar. She studied the breadth of Tom's shoulders and remembered the tenderness of his embrace. She watched him tilt his head back to scan the sky and found herself recalling the Fourth of July celebration, and Tom's profile outlined by the flush of fireworks.

The memory brought tears to Lillie's eyes. She banished them with a firm reproof and concentrated instead on Tom's movements as he paced before the dilapidated outbuilding, one fist silently slapping again and again into the palm of his other hand.

The watch continued until Lillie heard the bell in a nearby church tower chime eleven. At first she thought the sound had startled Tom. He stood straight, listening.

A second later Lillie knew why.

As the ring of the church bells died away, she heard another sound. The sound of whistling.

The person coming up the street from the direction of the railroad depot was obviously not concerned with secrecy. The piercing notes of his song floated into the night, the music all the more mysterious for the darkness, the melancholy tune hanging in the night air like moonlight.

It was a familiar melody, and Lillie found herself repeating the lyrics in her head. It took no more than a word or two for her to realize what the song was.

Lillie jumped to her feet. She navigated her way through the discarded crates and barrels that dotted the foundry yard, getting as close to Palusso's as she dared while still keeping to the shadows. Her view better than ever, she watched Tom walk to the front of the house and stop in the deeper shade of an oak tree.

He had recognized the song, too.

Lillie didn't have to get any nearer to know it. She knew Tom well enough to sense the tension that sat like a physical weight upon his shoulders, well enough to feel the emotions he held just barely in check.

There was little she could do beside wait and watch, and Lillie cursed herself. She wasn't sure what she had hoped to accomplish by spying on Tom. She wasn't sure what she would achieve, or if it would help, or how it might hurt.

She only knew she had to be here. Here where she could offer her silent support. Here where she could learn, finally, all she could about the past that tormented Tom and the secrets that threatened to destroy any hope they might have for the future.

The whistler drew nearer.

Lillie waited, helpless, listening to both the whistling and to her heart as it beat in perfect, painful time to the tune of "Danny Boy."

15

THERE WAS NO mistaking the stride, so loose and relaxed. No mistaking the jaunty tilt of the cap, the easy swing of the arms, the all-too-familiar tune of the song.

Tom planted his feet, resolving to stay put no matter how overpowering the temptation was to charge down the street and greet the whistler the way he deserved to be greeted. A gust of wind ruffled his hair and scattered the fat clouds gathering above his head. Tom paid it no mind. He smoothed his hair back into place and forced himself to stay in the shadows and watch the whistler approach.

The shadow took shape, and Tom cast his glance over the broad shoulders, so like his own, the long legs, the burly chest. The man was by far bulkier than Tom, his once enviable physique filled out and softened by drink that was too strong, and food that was too rich, and the absence of any activity more strenuous than making love to a woman.

Tom stepped forward just as the man was about to round the corner into Palusso's yard.

"Hello, Danny."

Danny Reilly pulled himself to a stop, the momentary flash of surprise on his face masked so quickly and effectively, Tom could only marvel at his uncanny ability at camouflage. Like a chameleon. Tom felt his mouth curve into an acerbic smile. Just like a chameleon.

Danny took one step forward and peered into the shadows. His mouth split with a tremendous grin. "Tommy! Little brother! I might have known I'd meet up with you sooner or later."

"You were obviously trying for later."

Tom's sarcasm was not lost on Danny. The smile fled his face and he frowned, his expression filled with the sting of Tom's insult.

"Is that any way to talk to a long-lost relative?" Danny moved another step closer and stuck out his right hand. "It's grand to see you again, Tommy."

Tom eyed his brother's extended hand as if it were a poisonous snake, coiled and ready to strike. He kept his own hands firmly at his sides. "Grand?" He tossed the word back at Danny. "If it's so grand, why haven't you been to see me before now? You've been to Wellington how many times in the past two months?"

Danny shrugged off the implied accusation with a nonchalant lift of his shoulders. "Haven't had time." He looked Tom up and down. "Country life seems to agree with you. I don't remember you being so tall. Must be all this fresh air, or maybe it's that business you're running. What is it? A repair shop?" Danny shook his head. "You always did like to tinker. But a fix-it shop? Really, Tommy, it's so delightfully provincial!"

His devil-may-care insouciance was nearly too much to take. Tom curled his hands into fists and took one step forward. "Flattery isn't one of your strong suits. It never was. You can stop now, Danny, and admit it, you're no happier to see me than I am to see you."

"What's this?" Danny's mouth dropped open. "Is that any way for a man to talk to his big brother?" He clicked his tongue. "I can't believe it. Not from you. You were always the one who worshipped me." Danny gave Tom a shrewd look and a one-sided smile that was so much like Tom's own, it made him wince.

"The one who followed me around like a puppy on the trail of its mother. Correct me if I'm wrong, Tommy, but you thought I was dead. Is this any way to welcome your brother back from the grave? Hell! I'm like Lazarus!" Danny raised his arms and his voice. "Back from the dead. You ought to be dancing with joy, and instead you're standing there looking as if someone just stole your woman, burned down your house, and rode off on your horse." Danny laughed and, stepping forward, clapped a hand to Tom's shoulder.

The forced camaraderie of the gesture was almost as difficult to ignore as the jaundiced gleam that shone in Danny's eyes.

He shouldn't have expected any more from Danny. Tom knew it. He had known it for years. Time and again he had depended on Danny, and Danny had let him down. Time and again he had trusted Danny, and Danny had made a mockery of that trust. Time and again he had rescued Danny from the perils of his own folly, the dangers of his drinking, the risks of his whoring, the results of his gambling. Time and again Danny had clapped him on the back and smiled his thanks, and gone right back to drinking and whoring and gambling.

It was too much. It had been too much for years. Back home in Boston, Danny had always been sheltered, first, and always, by their mother, then by a long succession of women—usually older women with plenty of money—who shielded Danny from the consequences of his indiscretions. Somehow, here in Wellington, it all seemed not only pathetic, but obscene.

In one quick movement Tom sidestepped his brother's hand. He glared at Danny, and the fragile composure he had forced himself to maintain snapped. Tom's words rang across the distance that divided them, echoing against the brick walls of the foundry mill next door.

"Is that all you can say?" Tom spoke above a rumble of thunder. "You've let the world think you were dead for an entire year. You've let our parents think you were dead. And that's all you can say?"

Danny shrugged and pasted on the kind of winsome smile that had melted so many matronly female hearts. "I'm sorry

233

about that, Tommy. I imagine Mother and Da were upset?"

"Upset?" Anger rose in Tom's throat and erupted along with the word he could not contain. "Dammit, Dan, they were more than upset. Do you have any idea what you've done to them?"

Danny's well-shaped mouth pinched with regret. "I really am sorry. If I would have had any other choice . . ."

This was too much to bear, and Tom did not even try. With a mumbled curse he spun away. He covered the distance between Palusso's house and the foundry in ten quick paces, then spun to stalk back to Danny again.

"That kind of nonsense may work on your women, Danny, but it won't work on me. Don't apologize, not when you don't mean a word of what you're saying, and for the love of Mike, don't whine. Let's set the record straight between us, once and for all. You were clever enough to fool those hoodlums you owed all that money to. You were cruel enough to fool our parents. But you didn't fool me, Danny. Not for more than a day or two. I knew you weren't dead."

"What's that?" Danny snickered, obviously hoping to make light of the accusation. But if Danny was anything, he was canny. He took a step back, and his wariness was evident in his voice. "You couldn't have known," he said. "Nobody knew." The arrogance that edged Danny's words evaporated, and he darted a look over his shoulder to Palusso's house. "Not unless . . ."

A flash of lightning slashed across the sky, and Tom realized Danny was not as good an actor as he pretended to be. With the darkness partially obscuring his face, it was easy to believe the carefree cheerfulness of Danny's words. But the streak of brilliance that lit the landscape illuminated Danny's face, too, clearly betraying the scowl that pulled his mouth down and the deep vee where his dark brows dipped over his eyes.

Danny was not nearly as unconcerned as he pretended to be. Tom didn't need a second flash of lightning to show him that much. Danny was hardly indifferent. And that made him all the more dangerous.

Danny's gaze darted from Palusso's house back to Tom, and this time he did not try to disguise his distaste. His voice was filled with suspicion, marked with conspicuous resentment. "Unless he told you. Has Palusso—"

"Palusso hasn't said a word." Tom cursed himself the moment the words left his mouth. There was something particularly agreeable about watching Danny squirm. He shouldn't have eased his misgivings so easily.

Regretting his recklessness, Tom regarded his brother with as much control as he could summon. Now that he'd begun, there was no turning back.

"You made sure of that." Tom added a tiny chuckle to the end of the statement, trusting it would go a long way toward making Danny think his information was more fact than educated fiction. "You held on to the money so Palusso had to depend on you for whatever you were willing to dole out. And you finally showed up when you thought it was safe, just to check on Palusso and give him some of his share of the money. Just to remind him to keep his mouth shut. Clever. But then, you've always been clever."

If Tom required any proof that he had latched on to the truth, he needed only to study Danny's reaction. Danny smiled, his teeth gleaming white in another burst of lightning, and regarded Tom with a look akin to a fox reconnoitering a henhouse. "Not clever enough to fool you." His words were underscored by the rumble of thunder. "How did you figure it out?"

Tom found himself laughing. A year of preparing for this day, a year of hiding his real identity, and lying about his past, and dodging the questions of everyone from Alex Campbell to Lillie Valentine had left him numb to all but the absurdity of the situation.

His laughter was punctuated by the lightning that had begun to flash with more regularity. It faded on another burst of wind and a single fat raindrop plopped to the ground at Tom's feet. "There was nothing to figure out," he admitted, his voice even. "For the first couple days I was so upset, I never bothered to look beyond the obvious. I really believed Palusso was the brains behind the whole scheme, just as you wanted me to. I really believed it when he told me you were dead. But it didn't take long. The fog in my head cleared a few days later.

"I didn't want to believe it at first. I fought it as long as I could. But the more I thought about it, the more it bothered me. The scheme had your stamp all over it. Good old Danny!" He looked at his brother, his eyes flashing with all the hostility he'd stored inside this past year. "Melodramatic as hell! It had to be your plan. No one else was crafty enough."

Tom forced himself to ignore another raindrop when it splattered on his shoulder, just as he pretended to disregard his brother's stance. Feet apart, shoulders back, Danny was preparing to deal with this little inconvenience the same way he dealt with every other bothersome issue in his life. If he could not talk his way out of the mess, he'd fight his way out.

And if that's what he wanted to do?

Tom didn't give the thought more than a moment of his time. It had surely been coming to this all along, and he wasn't about to back down from it. But not yet. Not now. Not before he'd heard Danny's admission of guilt. Not before he at least tried to solicit Danny's help.

The word Tom mumbled to himself surprised even him. He hadn't thought he remembered most of what he'd learned in the barrooms of Boston. But the metaphor was appropriate, and he accepted it as well deserved.

He was a silly ass.

He laundered the thought before he brought it out again. He was expecting help where he knew he would find none, looking for redemption at the hands of a man who was unredeemable.

But he had to try.

Tom squeezed his eyes closed, searching for some remembrance of the older brother who had been the model of his youth; the tall, handsome boy who had always been faster, always stronger, always more brilliant.

There were no good memories left, and even if there were, he was sure they would be eclipsed by other, more disturbing memories. The day their parents discovered Danny had been stealing the household money. The first time the police came to say they'd taken Danny into custody. The night the accountant from their father's shipping business had announced that a large portion of the receipts were missing. That was the night Danny tore out of the house in a fit of anger, leaving their mother crying inconsolably, pleading for his return.

Tom opened his eyes, welcoming the darkness. It was more comforting, somehow, than the emptiness that filled his insides when he tried to conjure up happy memories of Danny, more comforting than the hollowness he felt when he looked at his brother.

"I should have known from the day Palusso and his hired thugs visited me at the ballpark." Tom shook his head, just as amazed by his simplicity tonight as he had been one year ago.

"At first, when they asked me to purposely lose that game to St. Louis, I told them to go to the devil. But then they only promised me a portion of the gambling take. That was hardly enough to interest me. You know me, Danny. What is it you used to call me? The perfect fool? More interested in people than money. That's what you used to say. And you used to laugh, as if you couldn't understand it."

Danny snickered now, his memories of their days in Boston obviously far sweeter than Tom's. "You told them to go to the devil! You always were self-righteous, Tommy. I suppose I should thank you, though. If you hadn't said no the first time, I never would have thought to sweeten the pot."

"Sweeten it, indeed." The words nearly strangled in Tom's throat. He swallowed the disgust rising behind them and forced himself to continue, determined to hear the whole truth from his brother. "Palusso came back to me. And he told me you owed a great deal of money to a man named Gino Lenardi. He told me that if I didn't hippodrome that game to St. Louis, you'd be killed."

Danny acknowledged the truth of Tom's statement with a bob of his head. "Gino Lenardi is not a friendly fellow," he said. He wiped away a raindrop that landed on his cheek. "And

I did owe him money. A lot of money. Having you throw that game was one way of making sure he earned it back. With the money he made betting against Boston—"

"A team that hadn't lost all year."

"That's what made the plan so perfect." Danny closed his eyes for a moment, savoring the remembrance. "The Red Stockings hadn't lost. And no one expected them to. And, you know, I don't think anyone even caught on at first. The Red Stockings were the most honest club nine in base ball. And Tom Reilly"—Danny snorted—"Tom Reilly was the most honest man on the Red Stockings. When you bobbled those few balls and made sure St. Louis scored the winning aces . . ." Danny threw back his head and laughed. "Half the bookies on the East Coast lost their shirts."

"But Gino Lenardi made a great deal of money."

"And sent Vincent Palusso around to collect it for him." Danny pulled back his shoulders and puffed out his chest. "Lenardi may be powerful, but he's not nearly as smart as he thinks he is. Palusso and I had been acquaintances"—he gave the word a curious inflection—"for a good, long time. We'd already decided that as soon as Palusso collected the money, he'd leave town."

"But not until after he pretended to kill you anyway."

Danny did not reply; he merely smiled.

Tom leveled a look at him. "That was supposed to throw both me and Lenardi off the scent, am I right?" He shook away the memory. "And that body they found floating in the river? The clothes were yours. And the jewelry."

Whoever the man was, Danny dismissed him with a lift of one shoulder. He screwed up his face as if he were smelling something sour. "Some old drunk. He was dead when we found him, his face all bashed in like that. Honest, Tommy. You don't think—?"

"I think . . ." Tom could not finish the thought. It made him feel sick and queasy. He turned his face away. "I think you'd better tell me the rest."

Danny obliged, his voice raised against a roar of thunder that reverberated from the clouds directly above their heads.

"There's not much more to tell," he said, scanning the sky as if to determine just how long the storm would hold off. "As soon as Palusso got the money, we split it. Not fifty-fifty," he added quickly, in case Tom should get any wrong ideas about his benevolence.

"After all, I did all the thinking and planning. We split the money and sent you that telegram telling you I'd been killed. No one's the wiser. Lenardi's boys are on the lookout for Palusso, sure, but who the hell would ever think to look for him in a godforsaken place like this?" Danny cast a disparaging glance at their surroundings. "And Lenardi thinks I'm dead, so he won't come after me. Perfect!" Danny sighed, enjoying the moment. His contentment did not last long. The expression on his face sobered. "At least it was perfect, until you found out about it."

There was no mistaking the challenge that simmered just beneath the surface of Danny's indifference. Danny had never been a safe one to cross. Tom knew it, just as he knew that five years ago he might have run for cover, cowed by the look of malevolence that flashed in Danny's eyes, frightened by the barely suppressed strength that rippled through the muscles in his arms, terrified by the certain knowledge that Danny always got what he wanted. And tonight he wanted to be certain Tom would keep quiet.

Five years ago Tom might have run for cover. There was no pleasure in the thought, but he did not deny it. Five years ago he might have run. Ten years ago he certainly would have. But tonight?

Tonight Tom stood his ground and faced his brother.

"I traded my life for yours that day, Danny." He let his words slap against his brother along with another rush of wind. "It didn't take long for the newspapers to figure out what was going on. They never could prove anything, of course, but that didn't stop them. By the next day the story was all over Boston. Oh, there wasn't a word mentioned about you. I didn't think anyone would want to listen to excuses, so I never bothered to tell them why I betrayed the team. But they didn't fail to pick up the part of the story that was the juiciest. All about how Tom Reilly had double-crossed his own club nine. How he'd let down the cranks who sat in the seats and cheered the Red Stockings on. How he'd sold his honor and betrayed the entire city of Boston."

Tom forced the words past a ball of anger and emotion that had firmly lodged itself in his throat. He cleared it away with a cough and looked past Danny, past the tranquillity and happiness of the time he'd spent in Wellington, directly into the pain of last year.

"I left the team before they had the chance to demand my resignation. But when I tried to see the team owners . . . well, I might as well have been invisible. No one would see me. Not the team owners. Not Rebecca. Not our father." Tom moved his gaze to Danny, hoping to see some sort of reaction to the disclosure. There was none. He shook his head, not as amazed as he was disgusted.

"He wouldn't even let me in the house." Tom looked up at the trees, their leaves dancing in the wild wind, and tried to put the pain of the memory from his head. It didn't work and something inside him told him it never would. He would never forget. "Da didn't want to hear a word about why I hippodromed the game. He told me I was no better than my good-for-nothing older brother. No better than you, Danny. I think that's what hurt most, even more than when he sent me away before I had a chance to see Mother. Before I had a chance to attend what we thought was your funeral."

Sucking in a deep breath, Tom returned his gaze to Danny. "That's when I decided to follow Palusso's trail. That's when I decided you were part of the scheme. I decided to find you and take you back to Boston with me."

For the first time that evening genuine surprise showed on Danny's face. He opened his mouth, then shut it again. He grinned, then the grin faded. He took two quick steps toward Tom. "What the hell?"

Tom didn't move. He felt his expression harden, and even when the rain began in earnest, he paid it no mind. He stared at his brother through the steady downpour. "I want you to go back, Danny," he said. "I want you to come to the owners of

he ball club with me and tell them what happened. I want you
o buy back my life for me."

"You are a perfect fool!" A flash of lightning split the sky
bove the foundry long enough for Tom to see Danny spit on
he ground. "If Lenardi finds out, I might as well be dead,"
e said.

"And until he does, I'm dead."

Without answering, Danny spun around and stalked to
Palusso's house. His hand was already on the doorknob
when he turned to toss one final look at Tom. "You may
ave traded your life for mine, Tommy," he said. "But that
doesn't mean I have to be as big a fool as you."

He went inside, and the door of Palusso's house banged shut
behind him.

Tom did nothing more than stare at the closed door. It would
do no good to pound on it and demand that Danny come out.
It would do no good to force his way inside and drag Danny
out with him.

It would do no good.

Tom stood perfectly still, the rain cascading down his head,
stealing inside the collar of his shirt to soak his back, drenching
the legs of his trousers until they stuck to him like wet newspaper.

None of it would do any good.

Muttering one curse meant for Danny and another for himself, Tom hunched his shoulders against the rising wind and
turned to race home. He had gone no more than five steps
when he slammed into Lillie.

16

LILLIE WASN'T SURE what surprised her more, the unexpected force of Tom ramming into her or the infuriated fire in his eyes.

She had heard enough, seen enough, of Tom's interview with Danny to know what he was feeling. But nothing had prepared her for this.

Nothing had prepared her for the look on Tom's face when he came rocketing at her through the darkness. Nothing had prepared her for the firm set of his jaw, the thin, pitiless line of his mouth, the fury that transformed him, as real and just as dangerous as the storm that raged around them.

She had no more than a second to think about it. Tom grabbed her just before she fell flat into an ever-widening puddle, and she wrapped her arms around her ribs and bent at the waist, sucking in a deep breath to try and replace the one that had been knocked out of her.

It was not as easy to recover from the impact of the emotion that burned in Tom's eyes, and Lillie did not even attempt it. Her mouth open, her shoulders bowed, she gasped for breath and kept her face firmly turned toward the ground.

She needed time to brace herself against the intensity of his emotions, time to decide what she would say now that she had been discovered, time to prepare for Tom's response.

She heard him say something, the words barely discernible above the noise of the storm, saw Tom step back and reach his hands toward her, ready to help, and Lillie knew the time had come.

Standing upright, she scooped a wet lock of hair away from her face, not daring to narrow her eyes against the rain that stung them. If she did, Tom might think she was backing down, or worse still, he might suppose she was ashamed.

Lillie raised her chin and met Tom's steady gaze, grateful that the roaring thunder was masking the furious pounding of her heart.

As if it had been washed away by the pouring rain, the anger melted from Tom's expression. Left in its place was a look of utter bewilderment.

"No one but a maniac would be out on a night like this." Tom looked from Lillie back over his shoulder toward Palusso's house, then turned to let his gaze stray to the nooks and crannies that made the foundry mill yard such a marvelous place to hide. His face went ashen, and he turned his attention back to Lillie and glared at her.

"No one but a maniac, or a woman whose curiosity is far better developed than her common sense." The words tumbled from him. Angry at Lillie for lying in wait for him, angrier still at himself for being oblivious enough to be watched without knowing it, Tom lashed out at her. He grabbed for her shoulders and bent to look her in the eye. "Are you satisfied?"

Lillie stood her ground, her eyes mirroring the lightning flashing in the sky. "Satisfied you've never done anything to be ashamed of." She met Tom's look, her outrage as evident as his own. "Satisfied you did the only thing you thought you could do."

Tom wasn't listening. He mumbled an oath, then raised his voice, contending with the thunder, at war with the rhythm of the rain and the aching inside that told him without a doubt that his fate, and Lillie's, had been sealed. "Satisfied that you've done all you could to drive me away? That's what it's come to, don't you see?" The final words stuck in Tom's throat and fell dead against the curtain of rain that separated him from Lillie.

"I won't disgrace you, Lillie." Tom pulled away and turned to head toward home. Before he stepped into Johns Street, he looked over his shoulder at her one last time. "I won't dishonor the people of this town who took me in and gave me a life," he said. "I'll be gone by morning."

There must have been words to describe the pain that shot through Lillie, but after a moment she abandoned all hope of finding them. It was not words that would ease the anguish that squeezed the breath from her lungs and made her stomach feel like a stone inside her. It was not words that would save Tom, not words that would make him see how impossible it was for him to run from his past.

She called Tom's name, not expecting him to stop, but to serve as fair warning that she had every intention of following him, following him and doing everything in her power to prevent him from leaving.

They had gone no more than a few dozen feet when Lillie heard a door slam shut in a nearby house. She stopped long enough to squint into the rain, but it was impossible to see where the noise might have come from. The next moment a small, dark shape darted by her and pulled to a stop in the center of the street, directly between her and Tom.

It did not take Lillie long to realize who it was.

"Anthony?" She took two steps toward the boy, but he warned her off with a look and an abrupt wave of one hand. Anthony settled his shoulders and raised his voice.

"Signóre Tom!"

The boy's shout was pathetically small against the noise of the storm, but it did the one thing Lillie had been unable to do. It brought Tom to a stop.

Whirling around, he peered into the darkness. His gaze landed on Anthony, and his eyes narrowed. Charging back to the boy, he grabbed his arm and pulled him toward the house. "Has everyone in this town gone mad?"

Anthony planted his feet well apart in the muddy ruts at the center of the road and refused to move.

Acknowledging defeat, or perhaps just recognizing stubbornness when he saw it, Tom rolled his eyes and motioned toward the house. "Get inside, Anthony. It's dangerous out here. What on earth are you doing—"

Anthony did not wait to hear more. With a grunt he pulled out of Tom's grasp and fell back a few steps so that he was able to keep both Tom and Lillie in his line of vision.

Lillie stood mesmerized, watching the boy and the man square off, both of them standing as straight and tall as they could, both of them with heads raised in contempt of the rain, each eyeing the other.

Tom was already soaked, and Lillie did not give his condition more than another moment's notice. It was Anthony she was concerned about. He had come out without his coat, and now, as she watched, the rain soaked through his white cotton shirt completely, until she could clearly see his thin arms beneath it. A steady stream of water cascaded off Anthony's dark curls and rushed down his back, but the boy made no effort to shake it off. Lillie shivered, not so much from the cold and the rain, but from the look in Anthony's eyes, a look so like defiance, so close to hatred, it took her breath away.

Anthony propped his fists on his hips and scowled at Tom. "You lie to me."

Tom did not know what to say. He opened his mouth, but no words came from him. He took a step toward Anthony. "I don't know what you're talking about." All the anger was gone from Tom's voice, borne away on the wind, cleansed by the rain. Where once his face had shown both fury and exasperation, now there was only confusion.

Whatever offense, real or imagined, had fueled Anthony's reckless departure from the house, it was not so easily placated. He tossed back his head and barked a scornful laugh. "You cannot fool me again, Signóre Tom. I know you lie to me. Did you forget? You tell me a man must have his honor."

This time there was no mistaking the meaning of Anthony's words. The sting of the criticism drained all the color from Tom's face. He recovered as quickly as he could and stooped to face Anthony eye-to-eye, his arms open to the boy. "Anthony, let me explain."

"No." The word was snatched by the wind and taken up to the trees. Anthony slapped Tom's hands aside. "I hear it all. From my window, I hear it all. You think I will not find out, but now I know the truth, signóre. I know you have no honor." Anthony's voice cracked and he fought back a sob. As if to distance himself from Tom and all he represented, the boy took a step back. He aimed a venomous look at the house, a look he turned on Tom. "You are no different from him. No better than my father."

Stunned by the fierceness of Anthony's condemnation, disturbed by the high color in his cheeks, the frantic tumble of his words, Lillie hurried to the boy's side. She wrapped one arm around Anthony's trembling shoulders. The other hand she offered to Tom.

For a long while she wasn't sure he noticed. Tom was rooted to the spot, still hunched in the mud, staring at the place where Anthony had been. His face was as ghostly as Anthony's was dark, his eyes so distant, Lillie was sure he was seeing neither the rain nor the brilliant streaks of lightning that stabbed the sky.

He was drowning.

The idea rose in Lillie along with a wave of terror that made her heart pound against her ribs.

Like a drowning man, Tom was nearly lost in water, her vision of him more and more blurred as the rain came down even harder. Like a drowning man, he was being washed away, carried off by the burden of Anthony's anger, by the guilt that weighed him down and dragged him under, by the destiny he felt had sealed his fate one year ago in Boston.

Lillie drove the notion from her mind. She would not allow him to give in, and she thrust her hand closer toward Tom.

He took it.

Like a man waking from a long and nightmare-filled sleep, he grasped her hand, never looking at her, but clinging to the lifeline she offered. His skin was cold, and Lillie wrapped her fingers tight around his hand and raised Tom to his feet.

He blinked and looked down at Anthony, his voice very quiet. "We'll go home, Anthony. We'll talk." Tom reached out one hand to brush the rain-soaked hair from the boy's forehead.

As if his touch were fire, Anthony winced. He tore himself from Lillie's grasp, his dark eyes bright and wild.

Before either Tom or Lillie could grab on to him, Anthony turned and ran into the heart of the storm. "No!" He screamed the word one last time, the sound like that of an animal hurt beyond imagining, and disappeared behind a sheet of steady rain. All that was left was a mournful sound twisting on the wind, the sound of Anthony crying.

Their fingers were still entwined.

Grateful to be out of the rain, if only for a minute, Lillie sank back against the door of Tom's fix-it shop and looked down to where her fingers were still wound through his.

Tom's skin was cold and wet, as cold and as wet as hers must certainly be. Lillie didn't care. There was warmth, still, in his touch. It did little to increase the temperature of Lillie's skin, and nothing to drive away the chill permeating her clothes. But it did warm her soul.

Tom must have shared the same thoughts. He looked down at their hands, and a tiny smile lightened his expression. He lifted his hand and Lillie's, his eyes searching hers, and pressed a kiss to her fingers. "Like two parts of a whole."

His tender expression lasted no longer than a heartbeat. Though the rain had slackened and the thunder sounded no more now than a distant, disturbing rumble, the wind had not diminished. A cold gust stirred the stillness of their shelter and Tom dropped Lillie's hand and cast an anxious glance up and down Mechanics Street.

"There's colder weather on the end of this storm." Lillie put words to Tom's worries. "Can you feel it?" She pulled her hand from Tom's and hugged her arms tight around herself. "If Anthony stays out too much longer . . ." It was impossible to finish the thought, and Lillie banished it to the back of her mind where it belonged.

"We'll find him. He can't have disappeared." Sighing, Tom leaned his back against the door. "He's got to be somewhere."

"But where?" Lillie was not easily given to panic, yet something in the dark and the rain, something in the wind, sent shivers of fright scurrying up her back and into her mind. Trying to keep her fears at bay, she forced a calm efficiency into her words. "We've tried the passenger depot and the train yard." She ticked the sites off on her fingers. "We've been to the town hall and the newspaper office and . . ." Frustrated, she spun around and stood on tiptoe to look over Tom's shoulder, her nose pressed against the glass of the shop door. "Are you sure he's not in there?"

"Locked tight." Tom rattled the doorknob again, though he'd already tried it not once, but twice. "Just like I left it when I went home this evening."

Lillie shook her head, not sure if the gesture was designed to get her brain working or simply as a reflection of her frustration. "We've got to think." She underscored the words by tapping her knuckles against her chin. "We've got to think like Anthony."

Tom rubbed his jaw with one hand and trailed his fingers through his hair. "It's a shame no one else is out tonight." He looked again at the deserted street. "At least we could ask for help, but—"

"But no one but a maniac is out on a night like this?" There was little satisfaction in Lillie's voice, nor did she try to pretend any. It didn't help when Tom did not contradict her.

Accepting the unspoken but well-earned reprimand in silence, Lillie turned her attention back to finding Anthony. "We've got to think like him." She repeated the words, her eyes drifting closed with the effort of concentration. A second later her eyes flew open, and she grabbed for Tom's hand and dragged him into the street.

He ran behind her to keep pace. "Where are we going?"

Lillie hauled Tom down Mechanics Street and turned onto Main, headed toward the outskirts of town. "To get Anthony," she said. "I know exactly where he is."

17

BY THE TIME Tom and Lillie got to Greenwood Cemetery, the rain had stopped.

It sat like diamonds along the wrought-iron fence surrounding the graveyard and fell from the trees in fat drops that splashed against the saturated ground like tears.

It did not take them long to locate Anthony.

Even if Lillie hadn't remembered her first photography assignment in Wellington and the newly dug grave beneath the tulip trees, she would have found the boy. The sounds of his crying floated on the rain-soaked air, strangely unnerving in the dark.

As Tom and Lillie neared, the sound of Anthony's crying grew stronger, until it echoed from stone to stone, as if each marker had its own melancholy voice.

Anthony was on the ground, half-hidden in the sullen shadows beneath the trees, his white shirt a phantom shape against the granite column that marked his mother's grave. His small arms were wrapped around the cold stone, his face pressed to the spot where his mother's name was carved.

Lillie paused a short way from the boy, one hand reverently on the nearest tombstone to steady herself, her heart shattering into smaller and smaller pieces with each sob.

Tom stopped next to her, his keen, dark gaze measuring the situation, and Lillie felt him wrap one arm around her shoulder. He pulled her near in a fleeting embrace. Just as quickly he loosened his hold, and without speaking a word, he waded into the standing water that had made a small island of the tulip trees, the headstone, and the child.

Lillie heard Tom murmur something, his voice so low, she could not understand the words. The sound was soothing, nonetheless, and when Tom bent to loosen Anthony's hold on the stone and scoop the boy into his arms, Anthony did not protest.

His crying stopped.

Fighting the mud that sucked at his boots and made each step treacherous, Tom came back to Lillie's side. Anthony was curled in his arms like a babe, his dark head against Tom's shoulder. His eyes were wide open, and Lillie whispered sweet comfort in his ear and brushed his hair away from his face. The boy's forehead was hot, his eyes expressionless, and Lillie shot a look over his head to Tom, pleading silently for speed.

Tom did not need to be told of the urgency. His face reflecting Lillie's concern, he settled Anthony in his arms and headed out of the cemetery.

Before they got as far as the gate, Anthony roused himself. He looked from Tom to Lillie, and some understanding must have made its way past his heartache. He reached for Lillie and took her hand in his at the same time he buried his face in Tom's shoulder and started to weep again.

He cried all the way back to Lillie's house.

"He's finally asleep."

Lillie's voice sounded infinitely weary, blessedly relieved. Tom turned from where he was examining a row of photographs hung up to dry in the darkroom to find her at the studio door.

She'd discarded her wet clothes as soon as Anthony was settled in the big brass bed upstairs. Now she stood nearly lost in the folds of a cream-colored nightgown with a high, lace-edged neckline and long, billowing sleeves.

There were smudges of fatigue and worry beneath Lillie's eyes, eyes that still reflected the pain of all she had heard, all she had seen, tonight.

Tom's first instinct was to hurry across the room and take her into his arms. He fought the impulse. There were fences to mend between them first, fences he feared had been too ruined to repair until Lillie had charged into the rain-soaked street and held out her hand to him.

It was Tom's turn to extend the hand of friendship, to offer the proof of his gratitude and the gift of his love before he pressed Lillie for any show of affection. It was Tom's turn to be patient, as patient as she had been with him, and to wait for her invitation before he assumed a love he had no right to expect, one that might no longer exist.

Forcing himself to stay put, desperately wishing he could read minds, Tom continued to study Lillie.

Her hair was pulled away from her face, twisted into a heavy braid that tumbled down her back. A few errant curls had escaped her attempts at taming them. They danced around Lillie's face with every little current of air, her skin luminous against the soft, dark halo.

"You look like an angel." Tom had not meant to speak the words aloud, yet they escaped before he could contain them.

Lillie did not reply. Settling herself, one hand against the doorjamb, she simply stared at Tom.

He may have been embarrassed by the silence. He may have just been anxious to talk. Even Tom wasn't sure of the reason, but he rambled on, too impatient to wait for Lillie to respond. "Maybe you are an angel."

Lillie declined the compliment with a small shake of her head. It wasn't that she didn't want to bask in the special warmth of Tom's admiration. It was just that she did not know what to say.

Her heart was too full, her mind so filled with words, they were warring with each other to see which would come out first. The stalemate left her speechless.

Hoping to calm the emotions that churned inside her like a soup pot left too long at the boil, Lillie did nothing but let her dark gaze drift from Tom's face to his bare chest.

He'd been as soaked as she when they arrived home with Anthony, and how he'd fought her when she insisted he strip off his clothes while she got Anthony bedded down!

The memory brought a passing smile to Lillie's face.

Always resourceful, Tom had used the only thing handy to cover himself, a blanket that he'd wound around his waist. His bare chest looked like marble in the ethereal light that crept in from the studio walls and changed the sky outside from black to indigo.

"I'm no angel." Lillie found her voice and used it to dissipate the spell cast by Tom's words and the look in his eyes. "You're the one who brought Anthony here. I couldn't have done it myself."

"I wasn't talking about Anthony." Carefully, as if she were indeed a heavenly being who would vanish if he moved too quickly, Tom took a step toward Lillie. "I was talking about myself," he said, his words as cautious as his movements. "You saved me, Lillie. From the bitterness, from the loneliness. You saved me with one touch of your hand."

How any feeling as sweet as the one squeezing her insides could arise in the middle of her worry over Anthony and her utter exhaustion, Lillie was not sure. She felt the warmth tangle around her heart and soften her expression.

Lillie tightened her hold on the doorjamb, as if the feel of the wood beneath her fingers could give her both the strength and the courage to tell Tom all that was in her heart. "You didn't need saving," she said. "You've spent a year hiding from what you thought was your dishonor. Don't you see, Tom? There was no disgrace in what you did. You did it for Danny."

"Danny!" The mention of his brother's name banished all the tenderness from Tom's face. He snorted his displeasure.

Lillie wasn't sure if the sound was meant for Tom himself or for Danny. It didn't matter. She could not be put off so easily, and she vowed once and for all to let Tom know it. Lillie stepped forward. "For Danny. For your brother. There's no shame in that, Tom. No shame in trying to redeem a man."

Tom snickered. "A man I knew was unredeemable?"

She could not help herself. Lillie smiled. She lowered her voice, forcing Tom to pay close attention. "That's just it, don't you see? He isn't unredeemable. You knew that last year. If you didn't, you wouldn't have tried to help him. You know it now. Otherwise, you wouldn't have offered him another chance."

Tom dashed one hand over his eyes, whether to banish his fatigue or the emotion clouding his reason, he did not know. He knew only one thing: He desperately wanted to believe Lillie.

He wanted to believe she saw beyond his own biased view of the problem, beyond even what he would admit to himself. He wanted to believe she understood the reasons behind what he did for Danny and loved him still, in spite of it all.

"Two parts of a whole, isn't that what you said?"

It was Tom who had wished he could read Lillie's mind, but it seemed she'd turned the tables on him. She repeated the words he'd spoken out in the rain, her face aglow with a smile that brightened her eyes and warmed Tom's heart. She took another step closer and, taking Tom's hands in hers, pressed them to her breast.

"You'll have to tell Anthony something in the morning," Lillie said. "You need to help him make sense of what you did. You're his hero, Tom, a sort of substitute father. Far better than the real father he's been saddled with. I think he'll understand if you explain the kind of connection brother has to brother. He needs you to admit that sometimes the love between those brothers endures, even though one of them tries his best to destroy it, even though one, or both, of them tries to pretend it doesn't."

Lillie smiled up at him, and Tom found himself smiling in return.

"An angel and a philosopher!" His smile widened. Tom slipped his hands inside the sleeves of Lillie's nightgown and his smile vanished. "And you're as cold as icicles!" He chafed his hands up and down her arms. "I lit a fire in the parlor while you were upstairs with Anthony," he said. "Why don't we . . . ?"

Without waiting for Lillie to respond, Tom led her into the front parlor.

Just as Tom had promised, there was a fire dancing in the grate. It cast flickering shadows against the red velvet furniture and embellished the large painting of Flossie with a red-orange flush that brought out the color of the girl's hair and made the turquoise highlights in her eyes sparkle.

Lillie made her way to the sofa and the fire that crackled across the hearth rug from it. Her hands out to the heat, she settled onto the soft cushions. Tom sat down next to her and drew her into the circle of his arm. Lillie leaned back, her head against Tom's bare shoulder.

In the delicate light of the studio, his skin had looked like marble. It felt like velvet, as warm and smooth as the sofa where they sat, and Lillie sighed and turned her head to rub her cheek against his arm, savoring the texture, enjoying the familiar intimacy, and wondering that only a few short hours ago she had all but convinced herself their chance at happiness was past.

Tears sprang to Lillie's eyes. She dashed them away with the back of her hand before Tom could see how foolish she was being.

It was too late. Either seeing or sensing her tears, Tom crooked one finger beneath Lillie's chin and turned her face up to his. He looked at her and smiled, his eyes softened by the same tenderness that vibrated in his voice. "Is that relief or regret sparkling in your eyes?"

"Relief." Lillie blinked away the hot tears. They trickled down her cheeks, but she did not move to brush them off. She looked at Tom, her voice filled with the desperate need for reassurance. "Everything will be fine now, don't you think?"

Tom did not answer. He didn't need to. There was a sudden look of uneasiness in his eyes, a look that pricked Lillie to attention. She sat up straight and turned in her seat to face him.

"There's more, isn't there?"

Tom neither confirmed nor contradicted the statement. He gave her a fleeting, awkward smile, a boyish, flustered look that only served to sharpen Lillie's curiosity.

She pulled her lips into the kind of stern, thin smile she remembered an especially feared teacher using often and always to good effect. It worked as well now as it had so many years before. Tom shifted in his seat.

"There might have been more." His voice sounded far more hopeful than it did confident. It faded beneath the sound of a popping log.

"But?" Lillie brushed off his arm when he attempted to wrap it around her again.

"But . . ." Tom shrugged. "But now that everything's going so well, it might be best if—"

"If you get it off your chest, once and for all." Lillie moved even farther from him until her back was against the armrest of the sofa. She crossed her arms over her chest, her backbone straight as an arrow, and pinned Tom with a look, refusing to back down, even when he tried his best to put her off by acting embarrassed.

"You're a master at this." Recognizing certain defeat when he saw it, Tom had the good grace to give up the fight. He rubbed the dark stubble on his chin with one hand, and a corner of his mouth screwed into a half-smile that told Lillie, without a doubt, he expected to catch hell for whatever he was about to say.

"Her name was Rebecca." The bland statement rushed from Tom along with a breath of air that was either a sigh of relief, or one of resignation. "She's the daughter of the man who owns the Red Stockings base ball team. A beautiful girl, in a frivolous sort of way. Always laughing. Always carefree. Nothing much in her head except who's holding the next party and what she can buy to wear to it. Not at all like you." Tom looked at Lillie, trying his best to change the subject with an enticing smile and an inviting little lift of his eyebrows.

It didn't work.

Biting on the inside of her mouth to keep herself from smiling, Lillie gave Tom as icy a glare as she could manage. It was enough to start him talking again.

"I was young." Tom crossed his legs and uncrossed them. He settled his hands at his sides, then draped them across the back of the sofa again. "I suppose I was impressed by her wealth, dazzled by her beauty. I thought that's what love was supposed to be about. We were engaged to be married."

This was something Lillie had not anticipated. She opened her mouth, hoping some droll response would roll off her tongue, and found there was nothing to say.

Tom took her silence as a good sign. Obviously trying to finish before Lillie could think of a response, he rushed through the rest of his explanation. "When the story of how I hippodromed the game broke, I was certain that the woman I loved would stand by my side, even though everyone else had deserted me." He laughed, the sound honed with the sharp edge of sarcasm. "That was a mistake! Without my prestige as one of the Red Stockings, I was nothing. And Rebecca wasn't shy about telling me as much."

"She left you to face the scandal alone?" There was so much amazement in Lillie's voice, so much disgust, she could not even begin to try and disguise it. While Tom sloughed off the whole thing as nothing more than an embarrassing annoyance, she took it to heart.

Sensitive to the pain Tom must have felt, feeling the indignity as surely as he must have done, Lillie pressed her hands to her heart, fighting to hold back her tears.

She was so lost in the emotion of the disclosure that it took a minute for the implication of Tom's confession to make its way through her anguish. When it did, Lillie's compassion evaporated along with the tears she'd almost been stupid enough to shed. She sat up and eyed Tom with disbelief.

"You thought I'd do the same. You didn't want me to know what happened in Boston because you thought if I found out, I'd reject you, too, tell you to leave." The thought was incomprehensible, so incomprehensible it filled Lillie with sudden anger. Where only a few minutes ago she had bit at her lip to suppress a smile, now she bit it in the hopes of containing the indignation that rose in her.

Lillie bounded from the sofa and, swinging around, stalked to the other side of the parlor. She stopped before the painting of Flossie and gave the girl a conspiratorial look, the kind of secret, exasperated glance women share with each other when they discuss how mulish men can be.

There was no sympathy to be found in Flossie's vacuous expression, and Lillie clicked her tongue in annoyance and spun around. She stomped back to Tom and planted herself firmly in front of him, poking one finger in his bare stomach to emphasize her point.

"Rebecca may have been a flibbertigibbet, but that certainly doesn't mean I am. Your taste in women has obviously improved over the past year, Tom Reilly, and if you can't remember that by yourself, then I'll just have to remind you." Ignoring the red mark her finger was making in Tom's belly, Lillie glared down at him.

"I'm not that shallow," she said. "I never have been. And if you think I'm the type of woman who would walk out on the man she loves just because she finds out he's not some paragon, well, then . . ." Lillie could not finish the thought. Her exasperation escaped along with a shriek. As frustrated with herself for displaying her annoyance as she was with Tom for causing it, Lillie stomped her foot and opened her mouth, prepared to renew the barrage.

She never had the chance.

Before another word could leave her mouth, Tom snatched her hand and pulled her onto his lap.

"I knew I shouldn't tell you." He laughed and slipped his hand up to Lillie's shoulder while he wrapped his other arm around her waist. "You're as bullheaded as the best of them, Lillie Valentine. Perhaps that's why I love you so much."

There was no use fighting any longer, just as there was no use resisting the engaging look in Tom's eyes or the agreeable surge of longing that warmed Lillie's insides and made her head feel light and giddy. She smiled in spite of herself.

"You mean you're ready to agree your taste in women has improved?"

Tom brushed a kiss to her lips. "My taste in women," he said, "has never been better." His voice as dreamy as the look in his eyes, he nudged Lillie off his lap and pressed her back onto the red velvet pillows. He smiled down at her. "You don't give a tinker's damn about any of it, do you?"

Lillie twined her arms around Tom's neck, her fingers linked together. "The past doesn't matter," she said. "All that matters is the future."

"Our future."

Tom brought his mouth down on Lillie's. His lips were as warm as she remembered them, as soothing as sunshine after a storm, as soft and as welcomed as the morning light inching its way through the windows.

But try as she might to give herself to the delicious sensation, Lillie could not help but remember Anthony. She broke away from Tom long enough to cast an anxious glance out to the hallway and the stairs beyond. "I don't want to get too comfortable," she said. "In case Anthony calls. I don't want to fall asleep."

Tom's smile widened into a full-fledged grin. He unfastened the bone button that held the neck of Lillie's nightgown closed and pressed a kiss to the base of her throat. "Don't worry." He whispered the words, his eyes shining with the evidence of his desire. "I have no intention of letting you fall asleep."

18

LILLIE WIPED HER hands against the white linen apron tied at her waist and sighed, content.

The day's two appointments for portrait sittings had come and gone. The dinner dishes were washed and put away. The evening air was crystal clear and as cool as mint, a gift from yesterday's storm, and the sun streamed through the studio windows, gold-plating everything in its path. Beyond the sparkling glass Anthony was out in the yard.

The boy had slept soundly and woken with nothing more to show for last night's harrowing adventure than a stuffy nose. As if to prove just how hale and hearty he was feeling, Anthony insisted on playing outside with Tom the Dog.

How the animal knew Anthony's whereabouts was as much a mystery as how he'd unfastened himself from the sturdy rope that kept him tied to the back of the Palusso house. Lillie wondered if his arrival had to do with instinct or if it was simply a case of one dog with a very efficient nose. Either way the animal had announced his presence at Lillie's back door bright and early this morning, and he was there to give Anthony a wet and waggy greeting even before Anthony's eyes were open.

Now Anthony and the dog were romping through Lillie's garden, leaving a wake of slightly trampled zinnias, slightly tousled roses, and more than slightly jumbled honeysuckle in their path. Between the two of them they were making enough noise to wake the dead.

Lillie smiled. It was a perfect evening.

"I can't imagine what you said to comfort him so."

Lillie hadn't realized she'd spoken the words aloud until Tom responded, his voice sounding distant and muffled where it came from the darkroom.

"You're the one who told me what to say to Anthony." Tom poked his head around the door and into the studio. "I explained it, just the way you told me to. How brothers need to stick up for brothers. How there's sometimes love to be found in the oddest places." A smile split Tom's face. "It worked like a charm!"

Lillie settled back, half sitting, half leaning against the big maroon sofa that dominated the studio. She tilted her head and watched Anthony lead the dog on a merry chase through her snap beans. "He'll be all right, won't he?"

There was a thoughtful look on Tom's face when he crossed the studio and came to stand next to her. He wrapped one arm around Lillie's waist. "He'll be all right." Tom bent to touch a quick kiss to the top of her head. "He's young. He'll rally back from this like he's rallied back from every other hard knock life has handed him. All he needed was a little sleep and a lot of love."

Lillie was not convinced. She fanned one hand in front of her face, trying to chase away the worries that clouded her mind as if they were pesky mosquitoes. "If it was up to us, we'd take care of that, wouldn't we? A little sleep, a lot of love. Decent meals, a clean, soft bed, a chance to go to school. But it isn't up to us. He'll have to go back soon. His father must be wondering where he is."

Tom looked out the windows, his gaze following the track Anthony had made through the flowerbeds. The crystalline color of the sky was mirrored in his dark eyes, but even the brilliant light was not enough to hide the shadow of concern Lillie saw reflected there. "It will keep for a few more hours," he assured her.

His attitude was not as encouraging as his words. Tom moved away, and Lillie was certain he was as worried as she, though he did not want to show it. His boots tapped out his frustration against the hardwood floor, from the door to the darkroom, from the darkroom to the windows, from the windows to the door again.

His hands behind his back, Tom spun from the door to face Lillie. "You don't actually think Vincent Palusso's out scouring the town looking for Anthony, do you?" He stopped just short of sounding sarcastic. Tom shook his head, baffled by it all, and pulled in a deep breath to calm the anger that simmered in his eyes.

"Anthony's a lot like those children in your photographs." He tipped his head toward the darkroom, where Lillie's new pictures from Cleveland were still hanging in orderly rows.

The inference was hardly comforting. "I know that." Lillie raised her shoulders, pushing the thought aside. "He has the same lean, desolate stare they do. Those eyes that look right through you. The ones that follow me in all my dreams as if to ask, why are you letting this happen to me?" She shivered. "He's just like them."

"That's not what I meant."

Hurrying across the room, Tom grabbed for Lillie's hand, tugged her out of her seat, and pulled her into the darkroom. There was a single kerosene lamp burning on one of the worktables. In its mellow light he directed her to look at the photographs.

Lillie did not need to look. She knew the images, knew every inch of every one. They had been engraved upon her heart, etched there by memory as they were etched on her glass-plate negatives by her chemicals.

She followed where Tom's finger pointed, nonetheless, followed it to the first photograph, the one that showed a child of no more than six or seven working as a bobbin boy at the Montgomery Woolen Mill. His shoes were off so he could better climb the slippery, dangerous machinery that fed the thread into the weaving machines. His eyes were wide, the vast assortment of machinery as fascinating for him as it was daunting. The second photograph Tom directed her to was another she'd had a chance to take on her last visit to Cleveland. It showed a long row of carrying-in boys, the children who hauled glass to the fiery furnaces of a bottle factory.

"Anthony's tough and stubborn." Tom thrust one finger at the picture of the bottle factory boys. "Like them. Haven't you realized it yet? That's what makes your photographs so special. I think you started out to show people how pitiful these children are. But look at their faces, Lillie! Look what you've found beyond the lens of your camera!" Tom glanced from picture to picture, his face lighting with hope.

"You've caught the despondency, yes, but look at their eyes. These kids are bullheaded and so full of confidence, no one would have the heart to tell them it's all for nothing. They wouldn't listen even if someone did. And that's good. That means they'll fight all the way. All of them. Some of them won't make their way out of the misery and the poverty. But some of them will. Anthony will be one of them." Her hand still caught up in his, Tom held it tight between both his own. He brought it to his lips and breathed the words onto her fingers. "I swear it, Lillie, swear it to you here and now."

Lillie scanned the rows of small, sad faces bent over looms and furnaces, the cheerless eyes focused on stitching fabric in sweatshops, and fashioning paper flowers in poorly lit workrooms, and crying the news on street corners. "And the rest of them?" she asked.

"The rest of them?" To her surprise, Tom laughed. He patted her hand and winked at her. "You'll take care of the rest of them. If Alex Campbell is true to his word and gets you an appointment to see Governor Hayes . . . why, Lillie Valentine, I think you'll melt that old Republican's heart!"

It seemed sacrilegious to smile while the working children looked over her shoulder like melancholy guardian angels, yet Lillie could not help herself. The picture Tom painted was all she had ever hoped for, and she dared to let herself believe it would come true.

Her hopeful smile lasted far longer than Tom's. He let go of Lillie's hand long enough to finger the border of the nearest photograph. "You're sure nothing's going to happen to these?" He cast a glance over his shoulder as if he suspected someone might be listening. "I'd hate to have Montgomery get wind of these new pictures."

"If he does, we're ready for him." Lillie picked up the lamp and led Tom out of the darkroom. "Alex Campbell has a complete set," she told him. "And I'm convinced even if Montgomery ransacked the *Enterprise* office, he couldn't find them. I doubt if even Alex can find half of what he's got squirreled away in that place! And you've got some of the negatives, too." Embarrassed at the thought of their recent disagreement and the resulting estrangement, Lillie felt her face redden. She set the lamp on the nearest table and bent to extinguish the flame. "I'll get those negatives in the morning," she said. "And start printing them as soon as I can. If what Alex says is true, there might be a chance to—"

The thought was cut short by the clatter of the front door banging shut.

Lillie jumped at the sound, then scolded herself for her foolishness. It was surely Anthony, and she readied what she would say when he came into the room, a carefully worded and, she hoped, self-controlled statement that included admonitions against using the front door, closing it too forcefully, and running through the house.

A flash of movement outside the studio windows caught Lillie's attention. Anthony was still playing in the garden.

More curious than ever, Lillie turned just as Tom did, both their gazes drawn to the door that led from the studio into the kitchen. They were just in time to see Danny Reilly rush into the room.

If he had not known Danny was in town, Tom never would have guessed this was the same man he'd confronted out in the rain last night.

Last night Danny's shoulders had been thrown back, his head held high. He was a man filled not so much with confidence as he was with arrogance, a man whose laugh was as biting as the chill wind that heralded the storm.

Today Danny's shoulders were rounded as if he carried the weight of some unnamed burden, and his movements were as quick and furtive as those of a frightened animal. Except for the two spots of high color that glowed in his cheeks like warning beacons, his face was as pale as fireplace ashes.

Danny pulled to a stop just inside the doorway and glanced around. His gaze landed on Tom, and some emotion close to relief swept across his face.

"Tommy! You've got to help me, Tommy!" His hands out in a gesture of either entreaty or protection, Danny hurried over to Tom and skidded to a stop in front of him. "He knows," Danny said, his voice rasping out the words. "He knows all about it."

It was hard not to be taken in by the theatrics of it all. Hard not to be fooled by the trembling hands, the bulging eyes, the thin ribbon of sweat that sat on Danny's top lip like a glistening mustache.

It was hard not to be moved, and Tom was certain that's just what Danny was depending on. What he hadn't counted on, apparently, was Tom's memory.

Tom had seen it all before. He instructed himself to keep that much in mind. Danny was a consummate actor, and years of dealing with him had inured Tom to this sort of drama.

Crossing his arms over his chest in a gesture designed to show just how uninterested he was in it all, Tom stepped back and looked from Danny to Lillie.

It seemed Lillie was no more taken in by Danny's spectacular entrance than Tom was. She stood at Tom's left, her hands clutched together at her waist, her eyes narrowed, silently measuring Danny Reilly. Finding him wanting, she shifted her gaze back to Tom.

Her support was unspoken, but no less encouraging because of it. Tom felt himself instinctively reacting to the reassurance that glimmered in Lillie's eyes. His jaw held as tight as his straining patience, Tom looked his brother up and down.

"This is the home of a lady," he said. "It's not polite to barge in as if you've no more manners than a lout. You know that, Danny. I was there when Mother taught it to us both."

Danny grumbled an oath. "I don't have time for niceties," he said, and as if that were unusual, he added, "Not today." He ran one hand through his already disheveled hair, pulling at the ends until they stood up like dark spikes. "I'm in trouble, Tommy. A heap of trouble. I need to talk to you." He gave Lillie a passing glance and moved on, the look dismissing her as inconsequential. "Alone," he said.

Her shoulders rigid with outrage, Lillie stepped forward, and Tom could only imagine the tongue-lashing Danny had in store. He stopped Lillie with one movement of his hand, not opposed to giving Danny his due, but eager to get on with whatever game Danny was playing, eager to get it over.

Tom tipped his head in Lillie's direction. "Miss Valentine knows all about it, Danny. All about you. There isn't anything you can say that she can't be a party to."

As if to protest, Danny drew in a deep breath. But instead of coming out in a huff of annoyance, it escaped more as a sigh. "Very well." He thrust out his hand. Clutched in his trembling fingers was a folded message, the paper already worn through from Danny's tight grip and the sweat that dampened his palms.

"I just received a telegram," Danny said. "A telegram from Vincent Palusso. He's gone. And he won't be coming back. At least, that's what he says. Headed for parts unknown with no intention of returning here. Ever. He took every red cent I had to finance his departure. Cleaned me out completely while I was asleep, the Ginney bastard."

Tom shifted from foot to foot, the slur making him uncomfortable and more than a bit irritated. He chose to ignore it, at least for now. Plastering an apathetic smile to his face, Tom snickered. "So you're down on your luck. That's a real shame, Danny. A real shame. What is it you're looking for, a shoulder to cry on?"

The mockery was lost on Danny. He waved away Tom's offer as if it were genuine. "That's not the worst of it, Tommy, not by a long shot." Danny gulped down a breath of air. He fixed his eyes on Tom. "He knows."

Tom shook his head and turned away. Enough was enough, and he'd had enough of Danny's nonsense. Before he'd gone no more than a step or two, Danny's hand was on his arm, his fingers digging into Tom's flesh with all the desperation of a drowning man holding on to the last bit of dry land in sight.

"Dammit. Will you listen to me? I'm telling you something important here. You can't just turn away. You won't. Not now. Lenardi knows, Tommy. Gino Lenardi knows I'm still alive. Palusso decided it was too dangerous, now that the truth about our little scheme was out. He covered his own tail, sure enough. Wired Lenardi and told him the whole thing. All about how it was my idea. All about how we took the money and split it between us. He'll find Palusso, of course." There was a grudging note of satisfaction in Danny's voice, a subtle undertone that dissolved as soon as he followed the thought to its logical conclusion.

"He'll find me," Danny said, his voice rising. "My life's not worth a hill of beans. No matter where I go or where I hide, he'll find me. He always finds the men he's looking for and . . . and . . ."

It was not the sobs that shattered Danny's voice that convinced Tom to turn to his brother, not the trembling of Danny's hand where it still gripped Tom's sleeve, or the fear Tom could feel pouring from his brother, pouring as if it were a torrent that would swallow Danny whole.

It was Anthony.

Sometime while they talked, Anthony had crept into the room. He stood in the far corner near the back door, his head tilted as if he was hearing something both very interesting and very surprising, his eyes wide with wonder and worry and expectation.

"Sometimes there's love between brothers even when one tries to destroy it, even when one, or both, of them tries to pretend it doesn't exist."

Lillie's words echoed through Tom's head.

He had told Anthony much the same thing this morning, laid it all out for him when Anthony awoke from his sleep, his eyes still dark with the disturbing memories of all he'd heard the night before.

Tom had explained the hold family members had on each other. He had told Anthony of the indelible mark they left on each other's lives, for good or for bad, a mark that could not be easily erased either by time or turmoil. He had made it clear that actions did, indeed, speak louder than words.

Tom's actions last summer had been a mistake, he did not deny that to Anthony or to himself. It was a mistake to hippodrome the base ball game, a mistake to run from the resulting scandal. But if actions did speak louder than words, Tom's actions last summer said one thing strong and clear: He cared for Danny, cared enough to risk his honor and his livelihood, cared enough to try and save Danny's life.

What had been true then was no less true now. It was, it seemed, the time for action.

With another glance at Anthony and a quick wink to let the boy know he was aware of his presence, Tom turned to face his brother. "How can I help?" he asked.

What was left of Danny's defenses crumbled. Wiping the tears from his eyes with one hand, he patted Tom's arm with the other.

"I knew you'd come through when I needed you, Tom. Knew you wouldn't turn your back. I've thought it through as well as I can. There's only one solution. You've got to give me some money. Now. You've got to help me get away from here."

"Not so fast!" Shrugging away from Danny's touch, Tom perched himself on the edge of the maroon sofa. He eyed his brother carefully, daring Danny to lie to him. "You said it wouldn't do any good to run. You said Lenardi would find you, no matter what."

Danny was long past the stage of listening to levelheaded reasoning. He swung his arms in a wide arc, scattering Tom's objections. "There doesn't seem to be any other solution, does there? If I wait here, he's sure to find me. He's got connections in Cleveland. I know that for a fact. It won't take more than a day or two for him to send someone around."

Tom shook his head. "The bridge is out not ten miles up the railroad line. Swamped by the storm. Jonah told me this morning. No one will get into town from up north for at least three or four days. No. That's not the problem. Not this time."

Danny mumbled a particularly foul oath. "So I won't go to Cleveland. I can still go south or west. Cincinnati. Chicago. There must be someplace—"

Tom raised his voice, cutting off his brother before he could say another word. "No. It's time to stop running, Danny. I think you know that as well as I do; otherwise you wouldn't be here. The problem now is to figure out how to keep you safe. Moving from town to town like a tramp won't do it, and there's no use living the rest of your life looking over your shoulder."

Tom rubbed one hand along his jaw. He wanted time to think through the predicament, and he wished Danny would stop sobbing long enough to do the same.

"The safest place is Boston."

Lillie's voice, quiet and thoughtful, split the silence. Tom looked at her, a question glimmering in his eyes.

"Boston." She said the word again as if it were self-explanatory. "Danny can go back to Boston with you. He can present himself to the authorities." She turned to Danny. "You're bound to be safer in jail than you are out on the streets, especially if what you say about this man, Lenardi, is true. And while you're there"—Lillie controlled the nearly overpowering urge to smile—"while you're there, you can go before the base ball team owners with Tom. Tell them exactly what happened last summer."

"It's not a bad plan, Danny." Tom rose from his seat and went to stand next to Lillie. He wrapped one arm around her shoulder, a gesture of his gratitude. "I'm willing to travel back East with you," he told his brother. "Willing to see Mother and Da and tell them all that happened. Willing to go to the police and do as much as I can to make sure they let you off easy. But I think Miss Valentine brings up a legitimate point. Now's your chance, Danny. The chance of your lifetime. I'm willing to help you, but you must help me in return."

"Yes, yes. I think you're right." Danny stalked back and forth in front of the studio windows, his upper teeth furiously working over his bottom lip. His answer was so quick, Lillie was sure he hadn't heard most of what was said. He fastened himself on the most important point—for him—and clung to it with all the ferocity of a predator that had brought its kill to ground.

"They couldn't hold me for much more than fraud, could they?" Danny asked as he swung back around. "They couldn't hold me too long. And by the time I came out, well, maybe we could pay off Gino Lenardi by then, make certain he gets back every penny he was expecting to make on this deal. That would keep him happy, wouldn't it? That would make everything all right again."

The hope that lit Danny's face was so self-centered, it was pathetic. Lillie refused to allow it.

"What about Tom?" she demanded. "What about helping Tom?"

Danny stopped his frantic pacing long enough to look at Lillie as if she were speaking some foreign tongue. "Help Tom?" He shifted his gaze to Tom. "Is that what you want? To clear your name and play base ball again?"

Tom chuckled. "You're getting it all mixed up, Danny. The last thing I want to do is play base ball again. But, yes, I'll admit it, I'd like the team owners to know what really happened last summer. I'd like the chance to explain why I did the things I did. But that won't clear my name. Nothing can do that. There's no denying the fact that I hippodromed that game." Briefly Tom glanced at Anthony. Satisfied the boy was paying attention, he went on.

"I made a mistake. And I've paid for that mistake for a whole year, dodging questions about myself, pretending I had no past, no family. Forgetting that I had a future." He drew Lillie closer in a fleeting hug.

"I want to come back to Wellington," Tom said. "I want to put it all behind me and go on with my life. I want to stay right here with the people I've come to respect." Tom looked down at Lillie and smiled. "And the people I've come to love."

Danny looked from Tom to Lillie. He didn't understand a word of what Tom was saying, that much was certain. There was no room in Danny Reilly's head for the notions of loyalty, or honor, or love.

Lillie felt a wave of pity for the man.

But if he did not understand anything else, Danny did know all about self-preservation. He clearly saw that there was only one way out of his predicament. And this was it.

Danny nodded, acceding to Tom's demands.

Lillie pressed Tom's hand and smiled. Convinced that whatever else the brothers had to say to each other should be said in private, she turned to leave the room. It was only then she saw Anthony.

Lillie felt the blood drain from her face. She did not know how long Anthony had been there or how much he'd heard. She did not know how he would react to the terrible news she had to share. She only knew one thing: Someone needed to tell the boy that his father was gone. He was gone, and he wasn't coming back.

Lillie looked over her shoulder at Tom. Reading the silent appeal in her eyes, he came to stand behind her. She took a step forward. "Anthony," she said, "I need to speak to you."

Anthony smiled affably. He scampered across the room and threw himself at Lillie, his arms around her waist.

It was a gesture of innocent affection, a display so simple and poignant, it brought tears to Lillie's eyes. She smoothed the hair from Anthony's forehead and tipped his head back, expecting to see tears in his eyes, too, expecting that he had heard of his father's desertion.

But Anthony was still smiling. "Is it not wonderful, signorina?"

Lillie returned the smile, hers a far weaker version of the one Anthony was beaming up at her. "You're talking about Tom going back to Boston with Danny. Yes, that is wonderful, Anthony. But there's more, I'm afraid. It's your father—"

"*Sì*, my father." Anthony let go of Lillie. He threw his head

272

back and crowed with delight. "He is gone, Signorina Lillie! Do you not know what this means?"

"Do you know what it means?" Lillie looked down at the boy. There was no confusion in Anthony's eyes, no hesitancy in his words.

He laughed and twirled around. "It means I can live here with you, Signorina Lillie!"

It was something Lillie had not had time to think of, and she found herself reacting to the knowledge with a broad smile of her own. "Perhaps." She tried to temper her excitement, but it was little use. "Perhaps you can, Anthony," she said, her insides warming with a feeling that was half satisfaction, half hope. "There will be some legalities, of course, but—"

Anthony tossed away her objections with a laugh. Casting a quick glance at both Tom and Danny, he leaned closer to Lillie, his voice as hushed as if he were inside a church. "Do you know what else it means?" Anthony's face lit with a joy so absolute, it seemed to radiate from him. "It means she heard me, Signorina Lillie."

More than a little confused, Lillie shook her head. Not wanting to dull the edges of Anthony's excitement, but more curious than ever, she gave the boy a skeptical look. "She? I don't know what you're talking about."

"Last night!" Anthony looked from Lillie to Tom and rolled his eyes as if only another man could understand the frustrations of trying to explain something so simple to a woman. "Last night. When I go to the graveyard. I pray to my mama. You understand now, yes, Signorina Lillie? This is exactly what I ask her for!"

19

"YOU KNOW THIS is driving me mad, don't you?"

Tom's words were no more than ragged whispers against Lillie's ear.

He snuggled closer to her, his right arm around her shoulders, his left hand drifting to the front of her gown. With one finger he drew lazy rings around each of the buttons that fastened the dress closed, his finger circling slowly from Lillie's neck to her waist.

Tom's murmured declaration and the gentle pressure of his touch tickled through Lillie, sending shivers of delight and sweet longing from her ear all the way to her heart. She wriggled in her seat on the front porch swing and sighed.

She knew only too well what Tom was talking about.

It was driving her mad, too: the long days of separation, each of them preparing for the trip to Boston tomorrow morning. The longer nights spent apart, she with Anthony, Tom at home with his brother, Danny.

It was enough to make anyone a little crazy.

Lillie smiled to herself. It was enough to make her feel just a bit mischievous.

Pulling out of the circle of Tom's arm, she gave him a look of utter bewilderment. "I can't imagine what you're talking about," she said.

Tom flung his head back and aimed an exasperated look at the porch ceiling. He groaned. "I mean this." He looked around as if something in the still night air would automatically answer Lillie's question.

"I mean Anthony here with you." Tom stabbed one finger at the house. "And Danny there with me." He looked over his shoulder in the direction of his own house across town. "I mean it's driving me mad not to be with you."

"Oh, that." Trying her best to keep from giving herself away, Lillie nodded. A smile threatened to displace the thoughtful look she forced to her face. She stifled it and nodded sagely. "You're not sorry Anthony's here with me, are you?" she asked.

Tom's apology came quickly. "Of course I'm not sorry." He sat up and took one of Lillie's hands in his. "You know I'm thrilled Anthony is with you. You know I'm doing everything I can to make sure he can stay with you. Forever. It's just that . . ."

"Yes?" Lillie tilted her head, waiting for more.

"It's just that he's always here." The words burst from Tom in a rush that reminded Lillie of the sound champagne made when the cork was popped. As if he'd kept his frustration bottled for four days, ever since Vincent Palusso left town, the words burst from him.

"Anthony's here at breakfast, so I can't do any more than stop by and give you a chaste good-morning kiss. He's here at lunch, so all I can do is poke my head in and say hello. He's here at dinner, and he wants to talk about what he did all day. He's here now." Though it was nearly eleven and Anthony had gone upstairs more than an hour ago, Tom looked at the house as if he expected to see the boy at the nearest window watching them.

"It's not even like that night we brought him home in the storm. That night I was certain he was sound asleep. He hasn't slept soundly for days, he's been so excited waiting for word that the railroad bridge is open again. And now that he knows we'll be leaving in the morning . . ." Tom's mouth thinned. "I just know he's wide awake up there. And all I can do is si

276

n the porch and hold your hand. Dammit, Lillie. It's just not
nough."

Lillie looked at Tom out of the corner of her eye. "But we
on't want to scandalize the child!"

"No." It was Tom's turn to sigh. The sound was so heartfelt,
Lillie almost felt sorry for him. She decided to appease him by
hanging the subject.

"And Danny?" she asked.

"Danny." The disappointment in Tom's eyes turned into
omething more like concern. "It's a funny thing about Dan-
y. He's always been so full of himself. Always so cocksure
nd strong. Now . . ." Tom looked off into the distance as
f he could see there the answers to the troubles that were
laguing him.

"Now Danny's just scared. Plain and simple. I've never
een a man more frightened. Every day when I get back
rom the shop, I expect to find him gone, run off with his
ail between his legs. But he's still there. For the first time
n his life he's got nowhere to run, nowhere to hide. And
e's clinging to me, Lillie, holding on as if I'm his only
ope."

"You are." Feeling guilty, and more than a little disap-
ointed that she'd baited Tom out of his mellow, romantic
nood, Lillie turned in her seat. She pressed a tender kiss to
is lips. "You're his protector," she whispered. "It's an odd
ort of role to find yourself in, isn't it?" Lillie smoothed a
ock of hair back from Tom's forehead. "But you're doing a
plendid job."

The delicate kiss combined with the gentle brush of Lillie's
and brought the smile back to Tom's face. Before she could
ettle into place again, he wrapped his arms around her and
ulled her nearer.

Tom raised his eyebrows in a passable imitation of a leer.
His eyes sparkled, as shimmery as the star-filled sky, and when
e spoke, his voice was low and nearly as sultry as the night
ir. "I don't suppose you'd consider taking a walk over to my
hop, would you?"

Lillie laughed, but she did not attempt to move away. She

didn't need to ask what Tom had in mind. "I can't imagine we'd be comfortable in the midst of all those hammers and nails."

"No." Tom gave up the fight with so much good grace, it made Lillie ache to take him up on his offer. "I don't suppose we would," he conceded.

"And we wouldn't want to leave Anthony alone."

"Right." Tom sat back, his face as dispirited as the tiny frown that thinned his lips.

Lillie could not bear to see him so crestfallen. Leaning forward, she outlined his lips with the tip of one finger. "We'll have time alone once we get to Boston, won't we?"

Tom's lips twitched into something that was almost a smile.

"We'll leave Anthony with someone reliable. Perhaps after you've talked to your parents, explained about what happened with Danny, perhaps they'll be anxious to spend some time with Anthony." Lillie lowered her voice, the delightful promise of the scheme somehow more delicious because it was a secret. "And we'll spend a whole day together."

"At one of those fancy hotels near Beacon Hill." Tom's smile widened even further, and he touched a kiss to Lillie's finger.

"And we're leaving tomorrow," Lillie reminded him. "First thing in the morning. So it won't be very long. Not more than three or four days at most. Will you really go mad before then?"

"Yes!" Tom growled the word with good-natured enthusiasm and snatched Lillie into his arms. He kissed her once to prove just how mad the wait was making him, and a second time to prove just how well worth it the wait would be.

They were still locked in each other's arms when they heard the sound of the porch stairs creaking.

Startled, Lillie sat back just as Alex Campbell bounded up the last of the stairs. He looked around, perhaps hearing the cheerful scrape of the swing as it rocked back and forth, perhaps hearing the rasp of Tom's rough breathing or the tiny, satisfied sounds of contentment that rose from Lillie even though Tom had moved away.

Campbell turned toward the noises and peered into the darkness. If the light had been better, Lillie swore she would have seen him blush. Obviously disconcerted by the compromising pose he'd found them in, Campbell moved from foot to foot. He cleared his throat and passed the large paper portfolio he was carrying from one hand to another. "Sorry to intrude."

Tom accepted the apology with a smile. "We were just saying good night," he said by way of explanation. "Busy day ahead tomorrow. Have to be up bright and early for the trip back East."

"That's just what I've come about. I wanted to give you this." Campbell set the paper portfolio down at his feet and, reaching into his pocket, pulled out an envelope. A smattering of crumbs clung to the white paper, and he whisked them away and handed the envelope to Lillie.

"Somethin' for you," he said with a deep bow that caused a stick of rock candy to fall out of his pocket. "A gift in appreciation for all you've done for me and all you're tryin' to do for those kids in the factories." He tapped the envelope with one finger. "An invitation to see Governor Hayes."

Lillie opened her mouth, astounded and so pleased she could do no more than smile.

"No need to thank me." Campbell did not wait for Lillie to regain her voice. "Only thing is, Miss Valentine," he said, "you have to be in the capital in three days' time."

"But—"

"I know." Campbell held out one hand to keep her objections at bay. "But the governor's presidential campaign is startin' to pick up speed. He won't be spendin' too much time in Columbus this summer. It may be the only chance you'll have to catch him."

Lillie looked down at the envelope. The paper was thick and expensive. She turned it over in her fingers.

This was what she had always wanted.

A voice inside her head reminded her of the fact, though she was sure it didn't need to. There was something about the envelope, something about the way it felt in her hands, the weight of it, the electrifying charge that seemed to radiate from it, that confirmed the fact: This was something she had wanted all her life. Now it was hers, here in her hands. Now, when she was scheduled to leave for Boston with Tom in the morning.

As if he could read the thoughts behind Lillie's distant expression, Tom slid one arm around her and drew her closer.

"Three days, huh?" He pointed to the envelope clutched in Lillie's fingers. "Looks like we'll have to postpone that visit to Beacon Hill."

Lillie turned to face Tom, her approval and excitement shining in her smile, his thoughtfulness warming her heart. "You don't mind?" she asked.

"Of course I mind." Instead of disapproval, there was a broad smile on Tom's face and a glimmer of admiration in his eyes. "But you can't let this chance pass by, not after you've worked so hard for it. And I'll be back in three weeks. Perhaps Alex can keep an eye on you until then?" He turned to the reporter.

The suggestion was innocent enough, but it made Campbell more uncomfortable than ever. Shifting his stance, he lifted the portfolio. "I'd like nothin' better than to oblige. But I can't. I brought these." He handed the portfolio to Lillie. Before she could ask it, he answered the question that was on the tip of her tongue. "They're your photographs. The extra copies you made of the pictures you took in Cleveland, the ones you had me hold for safekeepin'. I wanted to give them to you before I leave."

"Leave?" The announcement seemed so irrational, it took Lillie a moment to process it. She set the photographs on the floor next to the swing and turned her attention full on Campbell. "What do you mean, leave? Where are you going?"

"Denver." Though the single word sounded no more assured than the tremble of uncertainty that quivered in his voice, Campbell nodded and kept on nodding. "Denver." He repeated the word, as if trying to convince himself of the reality of it. "I've got a ticket on the train that leaves for Cincinnati in half an hour and—"

"Denver?" It was Tom's turn to be surprised. The swing still swayed back and forth, as smooth and easy as the elegant tempo of a waltz. He stopped it, the tip of his boot wedged against the floor to hold them in place, and stared at Campbell, waiting for the details.

Lillie waited, too, but in spite of her anticipation, the *Enterprise* editor didn't say a word. He moved from foot to foot in a nervous, awkward dance and pulled at his fingers.

Finally steadying himself with a deep breath, Campbell blurted out, "Jiminitly! You may as well know what's goin' on. The way gossip spreads in this town, it's bound to be common knowledge by mornin'." His shoulders slumped, he went to stand at the porch rail. Settling himself on it, Campbell looked from Tom to Lillie, as if trying to gauge what their reactions to his announcement would be. He swallowed hard and, leaning forward, lowered his voice. "It's the Reverend Johnson."

Lillie glanced over at Tom. It was comforting to see he looked just as confused as she felt.

"The Reverend Johnson?" she said. "What's he got to do with Denver?"

"Nothin'." Campbell brushed aside any connection the two might have. "That's just it. He's got nothin' to do with Denver. It's far away. So far away I hope he never has anything to do with Denver."

Though Lillie was just as bewildered as ever, the light was obviously dawning on Tom. He stood, stepped forward, and clapped Campbell on the back. "Which of the girls is it?" he asked.

"Which?" The word squeaked out of Campbell's throat. He looked at the toes of his boots. "I'm afraid it's all of them."

Lillie's jaw went slack.

Noticing Lillie's astonishment and trying to put her at ease, Campbell rushed on. "I know what you must be thinkin', Miss Valentine, and I want you to know it's not like that at all. It's just that . . . it's just that Miss Suzannah, she makes the best raspberry pie this side of the Mississippi. I swear she does. And I can't resist raspberry pie." Campbell's eyes went blank and cloudy as if he were reliving the taste of Suzannah Johnson's delicious pie.

With a sound halfway between a grunt and a moan, he pulled himself back to the present. "And then there's Miss Mary." Campbell sighed. "Sings like an angel, that girl does. And I can't seem to remember myself when I hear beautiful music."

Like the memory of the pie, the recollection of Mary's music filled Campbell's face with euphoria. His eyes glowed, and a smile played its way around his lips.

"Then there's Miss Annabelle." Still smiling, Campbell continued. "She's got the prettiest hair, don't you think? Like the color of a golden sunset. And the face of a goddess."

By this time Lillie was gaping at Campbell. Her astonishment was apparently not shared by Tom. He gave the reporter a knowing look, and Lillie could tell he was trying his darndest not to laugh.

"And Deborah and Margaret?" Tom asked.

"Miss Deborah is the best listener God ever put on this earth, and as sweet-tempered a woman as any man could ever want." Campbell put one hand in the air as if he were attesting to the girl's virtues before a judge.

"And Miss Margaret!" He rolled his eyes and groaned. There was no annoyance in the sound, only a kind of resignation, the sort of sound that made it clear he did not regret whatever abilities set Margaret Johnson apart from her sisters, not in the least. "Miss Margaret," he said, "has talents I'm sure her father never dreamed of!"

Remembering himself only after the confession was out of his mouth, Campbell had the courtesy to stammer. "It's a . . . a difficult situation," he said. "I'm sure you understand."

"More difficult now that the reverend's aware of it?" Lillie ventured the guess.

"You always were perceptive." Campbell acknowledged her speculation. "The Reverend Johnson, in his own inimitable way, has made it quite clear that it's time for me to choose." He sucked in a long breath and let it out slowly.

"I can't," he said. He looked to the heavens for an answer. Finding none there, Campbell shrugged and glanced up and down Grove Street. "I'll miss this town and just about all the people in it. I know I won't be nearly as happy in Colorado. But I will definitely be safer. You've heard of fire and brimstone preachers? I found out tonight that the Reverend Johnson is one of them. And he has a shotgun under his bed to prove it."

Lillie could not bear to see him so miserable. "It certainly is troublesome," she conceded. "But that's no reason to leave. Not so suddenly."

The sound of a train whistle pierced the night, and Campbell flinched. "There's my train." A wistful look in his eyes, he glanced in the general direction of the railroad station. His face screwed into the kind of expression that made it clear there was something else he needed to say, something that was more than a little distressing.

Pulling his gaze back to Tom and Lillie, Campbell shrugged. "If that's all it was, I suppose I could handle it. I could marry Miss Margaret." For a moment his eyes lit and he tipped his head back, considering the possibilities. "I could marry Miss Margaret and still enjoy Miss Suzannah's pie. I could marry Miss Margaret and still admire Miss Mary's music. I could . . . No." Campbell set his fantasies firmly aside.

"That's not all of it, you see. There's more I need to tell you, and I swear, there's never been a thing more difficult to say to two people. I should have come this afternoon. Should have come the moment I heard about it, but I just didn't have the heart." Campbell thumped his hand against the porch railing, beating out the rhythm of his uneasiness.

"The paper's been sold." Barely able to control his agitation, he sprang up and paced back and forth, his hands behind his back. "That scalawag, Montgomery, bought it out from under me, just as I was afraid he would. Came by this afternoon, as happy as a clam. Couldn't wait to tell me the news."

As disturbed by the thought that Alex was leaving as she was by the news that Elmore Montgomery now owned the *Enterprise,* Lillie rose from her seat and intercepted Campbell as he made another round from the stairs to the front door. She wrapped one arm through his to hold him in place. "That's unfortunate for you and for the town," she said. "But surely you could stay on long enough to think this through. You could avoid Reverend Johnson and—"

"No." Pulling to a stop, Campbell untangled himself from Lillie. "That's not the worst of it, I'm afraid. When Montgomery showed up this afternoon, he made it quite clear there would be a lot of changes at the *Enterprise*. He told me if I wanted to stay on—as editor, reporter, or even copyboy—I had to make sure this was distributed to every house in Wellington tomorrow morning." Campbell reached into his right-hand breast pocket and drew out a single, folded newspaper page. He smoothed it open and handed it to Tom.

Lillie peered over Tom's shoulder. In the dim light it was difficult to make out most of what the front page of tomorrow's *Enterprise* said. But it was impossible to miss the headline emblazoned across the top of the page in immense, bold letters.

"Local Man Driven from Boston in Gambling Scandal. Scoundrel Forced from Honorable Game."

She read the terrible words, her lips shaping them, though she could not hear her own voice over the dreadful rushing noises in her head. Lillie looked at Campbell, hoping to see something in his expression that would explain away this cruel joke, praying it was all no more than a mistake, a mistake that could be easily corrected, quickly rectified.

It was not a joke. Lillie only needed to see Campbell's face to know it. She had never seen anyone hold himself in such tight control, as if the slightest nudge, the briefest word, would cause him to break down.

Campbell hid his distress behind anger. "I told Montgomery I'd have nothin' to do with his campaign to libel you, Tom. That would hurt even more than being at the wrong end of Reverend Johnson's shotgun. And that's the real reason I'm leavin'. At least in Denver I'll be able to look myself in the mirror and not see a stinkin', low-down, good-for-nothin' rat staring back at me."

"Don't sacrifice your career for me." Tom's voice was hollow. He kept his gaze on the newspaper page. "It's all true."

Campbell puffed out his cheeks. "I know it. I've known all along. How many Tom Reillys can there be? And how many of them can have thick Boston accents and be crackerjack base ball players? But I suspected there was more to the scandal than those big newspapers back East ever got wind of. That's why I was tryin' to nose out the story. I knew what you did. I wanted to find out why. And now I know that, too. I know they threatened to kill your brother."

"Then explain it to Montgomery!" Too infuriated to keep silent, Lillie nearly screamed the words.

Campbell shook his head. "He already knows. Vincent Palusso stopped by before he left town and offered the entire story to Montgomery—for a price. Montgomery doesn't care about the whys of the thing. That no-good son of a bachelor has completely left out the part that explains Tom's actions and concentrated instead on every sordid little detail he could find."

Lillie turned away, disgusted and too upset to keep still. Going to the railing, she leaned against it and slapped it with her palms. "And when folks in town see that story tomorrow?" She knew the answer to her question, but she asked it anyway, hoping against hope that Alex would offer some reply she did not expect.

"You know these people as well as I do." Alex's voice sank with the weight of the information. "They don't take lightly to what they see as a breach of faith. They've come to know Tom, and to trust him. When word of this gets out, I'd be willin' to bet they won't stop to ask why Tom did what he did. All they'll know is that he sold out his team, sold out the city of Boston. They'll never forgive him, you know that as well as I do."

Though she knew Alex was speaking the truth, Lillie refused to accept it. She pounded on the railing one last time and spun to face Tom.

He was not nearly as worried as she, though she could tell he was certainly upset. Tom's shoulders were back, his feet

285

were planted apart. A tiny muscle jumped at the base of his jaw, evidence of his outrage.

But anger was not alarm, and for a moment Lillie wondered that he could be so composed in the face of Montgomery's malice. There was no sign of the kind of worry that darkened Tom's face when they searched through the storm for Anthony, no evidence of the concern that shadowed his eyes all those weeks ago when he found Montgomery in the developing tent with Lillie.

Sensing that both Lillie and Alex Campbell were waiting for his reaction, Tom took a deep breath. "What is it Montgomery wants?" he asked.

"You know that slimy snake in the grass well enough, don't you?" Campbell let out a long, shaky breath, obviously relieved Tom had figured out this much of Montgomery's scheme and he wouldn't need to explain it further. He looked over his shoulder at Lillie. "This is the worst part."

Something in Campbell's eyes warned Lillie he was not exaggerating. She went to stand next to Tom, certain she would need his support, both emotional and physical, to hear the rest.

Tom didn't say a word. He didn't need to. He took Lillie's hand, and she wound her fingers through his. Shoulder to shoulder, they waited to hear whatever else Alex Campbell had in store for them.

"Montgomery will give you the newspapers," Campbell said. "All of them. But in exchange . . ." He looked at Lillie, but only for a second. The rest of the announcement he made with his eyes squeezed closed. "Somehow, he found out about your last trip to Cleveland. In exchange for the newspapers he wants your photographs."

It was not surprise that snatched Lillie's voice as much as it was revulsion. She fought the wave of nausea that threatened to overwhelm her, fought it by letting her anger take hold.

"My photographs!"

The words hit her, as sharp as a blow, and Lillie recoiled, instinctively trying to shield herself from the pain. Too angry to just stand and talk, she tried to pull away from Tom.

He would not have it. He tightened his hold and kept her in
ace, and when she threw him a look, he fired another back
her, a look that told her to keep still and keep calm. A look
at told her everything would be all right.

Lillie's anger disintegrated, melted by the warmth of Tom's
ncern, and in its place another thought lodged itself in
r mind.

It was Tom's reputation that would be destroyed in the
orning, Tom's chance for a serene, quiet life, the kind of
e he longed for.

The key to Tom's happiness was here in Lillie's photo-
aphs, the key to his peace of mind and to their future. It
as a key that would either keep his secret locked away and
sure them a tranquil life, or open the door on Tom's past and
ndemn them to moving from one town to another, always
e step ahead of the truth.

"My photographs . . . The children . . ." Lillie fought to form
e words that would make sense of her disjointed thoughts.
was little use. Try as she might, she could not banish the
ctures that formed in her mind.

Sad faces. Tired eyes. Children who were far too small for
eir ages, far too used to making do with too little food
d too little sleep, children who never saw the light of day
cept when it filtered down to them through grimy factory
indows.

They were her children. All of them. Lillie knew it now, and
e realization ached inside, as real as if they'd grown there
nder her heart. They had always been hers, from the first day
ank Graham had taken her inside the factory walls, until now.
hey were her children. And she could not forsake them.

"The children . . ." Lillie forced the words past the painful
all of emotion in her throat. She looked at Tom through a
aze of tears. "I'm sorry, Tom. I can't. Not the photographs.
ot the children."

For a moment Lillie was certain the strain was playing havoc
ith her mind. She could swear Tom was smiling at her. She
ashed the tears from her eyes and looked up at him again.
e was still smiling.

Lillie shook her head, and Tom began to laugh, and for moment she wondered if the tension had been playing games with his wits, too.

But this was not a hysterical laugh. There was nothing honest happiness in Tom's eyes, nothing but joy in the sound that skipped down Grove Street and flew up to the stars.

Tom kept on laughing, even when he gathered Lillie into arms and lifted her into the air, and he was still laughing when he smacked a kiss to her lips. Just as suddenly he set her back on her feet.

Lillie was still not certain what was going on inside Tom head. She gave him the kind of look she'd always reserved for Anthony when he was doing something particularly unfathomable like bringing frogs to the dinner table or feeding Tom Dog half his breakfast. "You mean you don't mind?"

"Mind?" Tom's laugh settled into a spacious smile. you'd said anything else, you wouldn't be the woman I love He chuckled. "You see it the same way I do, don't you? You know it doesn't make any difference. None of it. It doesn't matter what people think, what people know. Not as long we have each other." He slid one arm around Lillie's waist and pulled her to his side. "No matter what happens, we'll together. That's all that matters."

Tears of relief cascaded down Lillie's cheeks. She fumbled in her pocket for a handkerchief and, finding none then swiped at her cheeks with the back of one hand. She leaned her head against Tom's shoulder. "And if we have to leave she asked.

"Then we'll leave." Tom's voice was so matter-of-fact, made Lillie smile. "We'll leave if we have to leave," he said again, this time to Alex Campbell. "That's the price we'll pay for Lillie showing her pictures. And I think we'll find the price well worth it."

Campbell ran a hand through his hair. "I can't help but admire your pluck, and I know you both mean what you said But I wonder, have you thought of Anthony?"

"Anthony?" The bewilderment in Lillie's voice spoke her answer. She had not considered Anthony in all this. She la

r hand over Tom's where it rested against her waist and
aited for Campbell to explain.

"I'm sure you see where this is leadin'." Campbell shifted
om foot to foot like a man walking barefoot down a gravel
ath on a hot summer day. "I'm sure you don't need me to
ll you they'll try to take him away from you."

"No!" Lillie would not listen. She propelled herself away
om Tom and stood with her back to both men, Campbell's
ords ringing through her head, each of them as ponderous
d conclusive as a death knell.

"The authorities will say I'm not fit to raise a child, is that
hat you're saying?"

She heard Tom's voice behind her.

"I'm saying there are no 'authorities,' " Campbell shot back,
s frustration evident in his voice. "There are no high-up-on-
-mountain types somewhere who will listen to both sides
f the argument and judge as objectively as they can. The
eople of this town are the ones who will make that decision.
he judge, the mayor, even Reverend Johnson. Those are the
eople you'll need to vouch for you. And when they learn the
uth . . ."

Campbell's words trailed off into the night.

He was right, of course. Lillie turned to tell him so just as
he front door opened and Anthony poked his head outside.

She sighed with annoyance. It was hardly the time to try
nd explain all that happened this evening, and Lillie knew,
ven if she tried, she would have neither the courage nor the
resence of mind to tell the boy all he needed to know. She
ook a step forward, determined to shoo him back inside and
ack to bed.

Anthony ignored her. Without waiting to be invited, he
tepped out onto the porch. "Signóre Tom? Signorina Lillie?"
nthony's voice was as artless as his expression. He looked
ke a cherub in his long, white nightshirt, an angel who'd just
oared down from the ceiling of an ornate church.

Except that cherubs were usually blond-haired and blue-
yed and had cheeks the color of new-picked cherries.

Lillie found herself smiling at the thought. This cherub was

olive-skinned, his eyes as dark as the night sky. One lock
ink-black hair curled over his forehead and he smoothed
back to reveal a brow creased with worry.

He looked from Lillie to Tom. "Sometimes it is a good thi
to listen to what people say when they do not know you a
listening," he said. "Tonight, I stand at the upstairs windo
and I hear you say to Signorina Lillie that you will visit
Beacon Hill hotel, and I do not understand what this mea
but I know it make you both very happy. And this, it mak
Anthony happy, too. But sometimes . . ." Anthony sucked
his lower lip.

"Sometimes I am sorry to hear what I hear, and I preter
I never hear it. I do that a lot when my father was still he
Tonight I hear something I am sorry for, but this time I cann
pretend I did not hear it. I hear what Signóre Campbell h
to say to you. I hear when he tell you to give wicked Signó
Montgomery the pictures of the children. I hear him say th
will take Anthony away from you if you do not."

Lillie could not bear to see the worry in Anthony's eye
She held her hand out for the boy, but he did not take it. H
jaw tightened, his lips thinned.

"When I live in Boston, my father send me to a factory
work. I spend every day there, except for Sunday. All day
wind the thread they use to sew shoes for the rich people.
come home very late at night, after the sun has gone dow
And I wake up very early in the morning, always very ear
so I can get to the factory before they close the gates."

"We know, Anthony." Tom's voice was very tender. I
bent on one knee and took Anthony's left hand.

"Yes, you know this." Anthony nodded. "And Signorir
Lillie, she know this, too. I tell you both this story. But yc
do not know about my mother. She would never want anyor
to know, so I have kept her secret for her. I think you need
know this now. I think you need to know so you know wh
to do about Signóre Montgomery. About all the other childre
who work in the factories."

Lillie came to stand at the other side of Anthony. She kne
on the porch floor, face to face with Tom, and took Anthony

ight hand. "What is it about your mother?" she asked.

Anthony's chest rose and fell. He pulled himself up taller. "Every morning, she does not think I see her. I am busy drinking a little water, eating some of the bread from the day before. I pretend I am too busy to notice, but I see her. Every morning when I leave for the factory, I know my mother is crying." He looked directly into Lillie's eyes, "Signorina Lillie, we cannot give Signóre Montgomery your pictures. We have to try and change this. It is time to stop making mothers cry for their children."

Even though there were tears in Lillie's eyes, she smiled at Anthony. "It seems," she said, "that both the men I love are very brave." She looked at Tom and he returned her smile. Taking her hand, he stood and pulled her up to her feet.

"There you have it," Tom said to Campbell.

Another blast of a train whistle pierced the night air, closer this time. Campbell pulled at the lobe of one ear and looked over his shoulder. "Sounds like I have just enough time to stop over at Montgomery's," he said, a note of exceptional satisfaction warming his voice. "Can I give him a message for you?"

"Yes." Tom laughed.

His exhilaration was contagious, and soon Lillie and Anthony were laughing, too.

"Yes!" Tom said again. He wadded the newspaper he was holding into a tight ball and tossed it into Campbell's waiting hands. "You can give him this," he said. "There's our answer!"

20

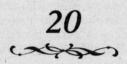

"I FOUND SOME late forget-me-nots in Miss Taylor's garden on my way here this morning." Tom brought his right hand out from behind his back. In it was a sprig of tiny blue flowers with cheerful yellow centers.

The flowers were considerably merrier than either of their moods, but Lillie pretended to be pleased by the sight of them, anyway. She forced a smile in return for the one she was certain Tom was pretending.

Both Lillie's and Anthony's suitcases were packed and waiting inside the back door. Tom maneuvered his way around them. "I didn't think she'd mind if I borrowed a few," he said. "She still owes me for that lamp of hers I fixed back in February." He offered the flowers to Lillie. "Will you . . .?"

"Wear them?"

This time the smile on Lillie's face was genuine. She was touched by the small, meaningful gift, so touched, she could feel her self-control begin to waver.

The last thing Tom needed this morning was a whimpering woman on his hands.

She reminded herself of the fact in no uncertain terms at the same time she bit her lower lip to contain a sob.

Tom didn't need to see how upset she was, or how the long sleepless night had taken its toll. She was still as determined to go through with all they'd decided last night. But this morning Lillie had to admit to herself, this morning she was scared afraid of what they'd find outside the door, nervous about the townfolks' reaction to Montgomery's newspaper story anxious, and so concerned for Tom, she could taste her fear.

Swallowing her anxiety along with her tears, Lillie stood still and allowed Tom to tuck the flowers into the lapel of her jacket. He fussed with them a moment or two, not, Lillie suspected, because they didn't look just right, but because he was stalling for time.

When he could delay no longer, he stepped back to admire both the flowers and Lillie.

"Of course I'll wear them." Lillie sniffed the flowers. There was little aroma, but she pretended she was enjoying the fragrance, just to make Tom feel good. "I'll wear them all the way to Columbus this afternoon."

Lillie glanced at the clock on the wall. There was still time before Tom's train to Boston arrived, fifteen minutes at least, and she knew he was not anxious to get to the station too early.

She swept the room with a glance, as if trying to determine if she'd left anything behind. Her gloves lay next to a large, brown envelope on a nearby table. She tucked the envelope under her arm, then picked up her gloves and tugged them on, carefully adjusting each finger before she went on to the next.

"Did you see Miss Taylor?" Her attention still on the gloves, Lillie ventured the question, unsure if she really wanted to hear the answer.

"No." Tom sounded more confused than upset, and Lillie looked up to find him shaking his head in wonder. "No sign of Miss Taylor, and you know what a Tartar she can be when it comes to her garden. No sign of Miss Taylor. No sign of anyone. I left Danny at the railroad station and didn't see another soul all the way here. No one on Main Street. No one up at the livery. Either everyone was whisked away during the night by a magic spell, or . . ."

"Or they read the *Enterprise* this morning, and they're going out of their way to avoid us?"

Tom ran one hand over the back of his neck and turned to stare out the studio windows. "I didn't sleep at all last night, thinking about it," he said. "It might be better, you know."

"If they were whisked away during the night?" Lillie could not resist the jest. She hoped it would bring a smile to Tom's face, but when he turned back to her, his dark brows were lower than ever over his eyes, and his mouth was pulled into a thin line.

"No. If they just avoided us. I think it might be better if they avoided us altogether. It would avert an ugly confrontation. I'm not sure I could keep my temper if there was a scene, and I don't think that's something you should be implicated in. I know it isn't something I want Anthony to see."

"Anthony is ready for anything!"

Anthony came around the corner, resplendent in brand-new tweed pants and a dazzling white shirt. He straightened his bow tie and smiled. It was the same arrogant smile his father had once turned on Lillie in the Morning Star Saloon, yet coming from Anthony, it did not repulse her as it had done that day.

On Anthony the smile was nothing short of exquisite. His teeth sparkled against his dark skin, and his eyes glowed with a confidence and determination Lillie had never seen in them before.

The boy struck a pose, his fists raised as if ready for a fight. "Anthony is ready for all of them," he said. "We will show them, *sì*, Signóre Tom? We will trounce them all if we have to."

"No one is going to trounce anyone else!" With one hand Tom ruffled the boy's hair. "We're going to the railroad station. That's all. My train for Boston arrives in just a few minutes. Yours to Columbus comes in later. We're going to the railroad station, and we're going to act like civilized human beings on the way there. No matter what anyone says or does."

"We will not fight them?" The fire went out in Anthony's eyes. He stuck his hands in his pockets. "We will not punch them if they say anything about you, Signóre Tom?"

"No." In spite of himself, Tom was smiling. Grateful to see the gloom lifted from his expression, Lillie offered a prayer of thanksgiving for the wonderful candidness of children.

"We will not punch them if they say anything about Anthony and call him bad names?" Anthony tried again.

Again, Tom shook his head. "No."

Anthony's face lit with sudden inspiration. "Ah, but we will have to punch them if they say anything about Signorina Lillie, yes?"

"No." Tom and Lillie answered in unison.

"No one's going to say anything about Lillie." Tom wrapped one arm around the boy's shoulders and led him to the door. He held his other hand out for Lillie.

Lillie took it and looked down at Anthony. "There are other ways to show courage besides fighting," she said "Sometimes it's far braver not to fight."

"Sì." Whether he understood or not, Anthony agreed. He scuffed his toes against the floor, obviously disappointed the morning would not be nearly as exciting as he'd hoped.

Lillie was the first to reach the door. Her hand on the knob, she straightened her shoulders and looked over Anthony's head at Tom. "Ready?" she asked.

He held the door so she could go out ahead of him. Once they were outside, he fell into step alongside her. "Ready," he said. "For anything."

Tom was right. There wasn't a soul around.

Lillie glanced up and down Main Street.

Though it was nearly ten in the morning and the town should have been teeming with both foot and wagon traffic, there wasn't a person to be seen.

The houses that lined the street were silent, their curtains shut tight. Union School, the town hall, the Methodist and Congregational churches that stood just this side of the American House Hotel, all of them were quiet, as if a magician's spell had, indeed, been cast during the night, a spell that had left Wellington intact but taken all its inhabitants.

Things were no different on Mechanics Street. Businesses that were usually bustling at this time of the day were closed as if it were a holiday.

But there was not so much an atmosphere of celebration in the air as there was a sense of conspiracy. The certain, troubling knowledge caused Lillie's footsteps to falter, and when a sudden breeze blew a copy of this morning's *Enterprise* across her path, the newspaper got tangled over Lillie's shoes. She kicked it aside, wishing she could discard her anger and resentment so easily.

Tom glanced over his shoulder, silently urging Lillie to keep up, and she adjusted the envelope that was tucked under her arm and continued on.

Turning from Mechanics Streets, they crossed the railroad yard, heading toward the depot. It was only then Lillie realized why the streets were so silent and deserted.

It seemed all of Wellington's citizens were gathered around the railroad station. They stood in a silent knot, blocking the entrance, so many people that they filled the platform out front and spilled into the street. Some of the younger and spryer folk had climbed the water tower, and as Tom, Lillie, and Anthony approached, one of them gave the cry, "Here they come!"

As one, the crowd turned, all eyes watching them.

Anthony was on Tom's left, and Tom settled his hand on the boy's shoulder. With his other hand he squeezed Lillie's and, with only the briefest of sidelong looks at her, led them into the heart of the crowd.

"Good morning." Lillie pasted a friendly smile to her face and tipped her head toward the people who lined Kelley Street. "Mr. Wadsworth, Miss Hamlin, good morning."

Though no one responded to her greeting, they did open a path, allowing Tom and Lillie to walk through. Lillie did not have to turn around to know the ranks were closing behind them. She could feel the press of the crowd at her back.

The closer they got to the station, the more familiar the faces became. Danny was already up on the platform, close to the station door, a look so like panic in his eyes, Lillie nearly felt sorry for him.

The Reverend and Mrs. Johnson stood silently as Tom and Lillie passed by, their five daughters at their sides. Suzannah looked as if she hadn't gotten a wink of sleep last night. Mary never lifted her gaze from the tips of her shoes. Annabelle stared straight ahead, her face devoid of all expression. Deborah stood wringing her hands. And Margaret?

Lillie craned her neck, searching for the youngest Johnson girl.

Margaret's face was buried in a huge, white handkerchief. She sniffed into it and looked up, her eyes swollen, the tip of her nose the color of a laundrywoman's hands.

J. S. DeWolf was next. He looked away as Lillie met his eyes, his mustaches twitching.

No one made a sound, and when a familiar noise broke the silence, Lillie started with alarm. It was just Tom the Dog, she realized after a moment. He was barking a greeting at Anthony, and Lillie scolded herself for being so skittish. Anthony had taken the animal to Nate Hatcher just after dinner last night so Nate could watch him until they returned. Now the dog bounded up to Anthony and gave him a wet kiss.

The two boys took the dog aside, and watching them, Lillie breathed a sigh of relief. Whatever else might happen this morning, at least Anthony's attention would be occupied.

The rest of the Hatcher family stood at the base of the stairs that led into the station. For some reason Jonah was wearing his Sunday best. He ran a finger around the inside of his collar and gave his wife, Sarah, a glance that said he was as ill at ease as he looked.

Lillie's display of bravado had been all very well and good for strangers and acquaintances, but she was sure she could not keep it up in the face of friends. She looked at the Hatcher family, and her smile slipped away. She held on tighter to Tom's hand.

"Good morning, Jonah." Tom stopped long enough to look Jonah Hatcher straight in the eye.

"Ain't much of a good morning." Jonah's voice echoed through the silence. He drew the piece of straw he was chewing out of his mouth and flicked it onto the ground. "Found out some pretty unpleasant things this morning," he said.

A few of the people around them nodded in agreement.

"And didn't like a bit of what we heard." The acknowledgment came from the back of the crowd. It was met with a murmur of assent.

Lillie moved closer to Tom at the same time Jonah climbed onto the first step of the depot stairs.

Jonah stood a head taller than most of the people in town even when he was standing on the ground. Up on the step he towered over them, commanding their attention. Jonah looked around and raised his voice. "We spent all morning meeting and talking," he said. "Talking about the things we learned this morning and what we wanted to do about them. This is a fine town full of fine and honest people. We decided it ain't fitting to have such a place tarnished with the presence of a sneaky, underhanded, no-good scoundrel."

Jonah's words hit Lillie like small, sharp stones. She glanced out of the corner of her eye and saw that Tom hadn't moved. He stood with his head as high as if he were leading a grand parade.

Anthony was another matter. Jonah's words had not failed to make their way past his preoccupation with the dog. He gestured toward the ground once, and certain that Tom the Dog had obeyed and was sitting, he curled his little hands into fists, stuck out his chin, and threw a defiant look at the people around them.

"We're as sorry as can be." Jonah was still talking, and Lillie pulled her gaze away from Anthony to watch him. The blacksmith shook his head and raised his hands in the air. The gesture might have been dramatic if Jonah's bow tie hadn't decided to come loose at the same moment. He squinted down his nose at his collar and mumbled something most of the crowd couldn't hear. He plucked the tie from his neck and tossed it down to Sarah. "Sorry . . ."

The incident caused Jonah to lose his train of thought as well as his tie. He looked up at the sky. He looked down at his shoes. He looked to the crowd for deliverance.

Someone on Lillie's right took pity on him. "Sorry we was foolish." The man supplied the next part of Jonah's speech in a stage whisper.

"That's right." Jonah coughed and started again. "We're sorry we was foolish enough to be taken in."

Another grumble of assent went through the crowd, a sound that reminded Lillie of the roll of thunder.

"Quit beatin' 'round the bush, Jonah!" Lillie recognized the voice of Mr. Hollenback, the town tailor. He stepped to the front of the crowd and raised his voice so that everyone could hear him. "We decided what to say this morning. Spit it out before this man's train gets here and he gets on it and goes away and never knows what we think."

"All right. All right." Jonah used both hands to silence the crowd. He looked around, and when he was sure he had everyone's attention, he looked down at Tom. "What we want to say to you is this. We don't want no dishonesty in this town, and we don't want people for neighbors who we can't feel neighborly toward. So—" Jonah drew in a deep breath, and his face cracked with an enormous smile.

"So we made it quite clear to Elmore Montgomery that he can put that big old house of his up for sale. We won't have his kind here, and we told him as much. Every one of us has agreed, we won't take his money in our businesses, his cook and his cleaning people have up and quit on him, and we all canceled our subscriptions to the *Enterprise* this morning!"

Jonah's announcement was met with a shout of approval that rang off the walls of the depot.

Lillie looked at Tom, too surprised and relieved to move or speak, too happy to do anything more than smile. Tom smiled, too, at Lillie, at Anthony, at the men of Wellington who were moving forward to clap him on the back and shake his hand.

Jonah cleared his throat with a loud "Ahem" and moved up another step. "Tom, Lillie"—he motioned toward them—"we want you to know Elmore Montgomery doesn't speak for the rest of us. He never did. We're sorry he treated you so shabby. We hope you ain't soured on the town and the people in it just 'cause one rotten apple was inside the barrel."

Tom looked around, his face a mirror of Lillie's, relief and happiness etched in every line of his face. "Are you telling us . . . ?"

"We're telling you we read Montgomery's tripe, and we don't care!" J. S. DeWolf was beaming from ear to ear. Another burst of applause and a few hearty "Huzzahs" greeted his comment.

Tom mounted the steps of the railroad station and looked at the crowd. "You don't care about my past?"

Jonah laughed. He thumped Tom on the back. "A man's past ain't nearly as important as his present." He offered Lillie a hand up and moved aside so she could stand next to Tom. "And not nearly as important as his future. We want you to know that we hope your future, and the future of your boy, is here with us in Wellington."

Lillie looked at the sea of wonderful, friendly faces around her and drew in a long, deep breath. Even Tom the Dog looked happy. He thumped his tail against the ground in approval of the commotion.

Tom slid one arm around Lillie's waist and smiled down at her. "Seems to me we've underestimated our neighbors," he said. He didn't have time to say anything else.

Sarah Hatcher ran up the steps and whispered into her husband's ear.

Jonah turned a decided shade of red. He set her aside with a gentle gesture, but Sarah would not be so easily put off. She folded her arms across her chest and tapped her toe against the wooden steps.

Jonah rolled his eyes and nodded. He called for the crowd to quiet down. "It's been brought to my attention that there's something else I need to ask these two fine people."

"Better say it before the train gets here!" DeWolf pointed down the tracks, where a long, white curl of smoke foretold the train's approach. A shrill whistle pierced the air.

Jonah settled one hand on Tom's shoulder, the other on Lillie's, and winked at his wife. "There's a rumor going about that when you get back from Boston, Tom, this town is going to see the grandest wedding that's been held around here for a very long time."

"I'm already planning the menu," DeWolf called up to them.

"A beautiful ceremony!" Reverend Johnson's eyes lit.

"And flowers from my garden," Miss Taylor stepped forward and piped in. Her gaze landed on the forget-me-nots in Lillie's lapel, and her mouth dropped open.

Before she had time to ask questions, Jonah leaned forward. He could barely keep himself from laughing. "What do you say? The story's all over town. Is it true?"

The train pulled into the station behind them, and Tom raised his voice to be heard over its roar. "Well?" He gave Lillie a smile as brilliant as the sun. "Is it true?"

Lillie felt her heart turn over inside her. She knew she was blushing like a girl. "Here." She shoved the envelope she was carrying into Tom's hands. "Here's your answer." She stopped him just as he was about to rip the envelope open. "No! Not here. Open it on the train. When you're alone."

Tom tried to read the meaning behind Lillie's coy answer. But what she wouldn't put into words was already in her eyes. Without a care to the fact that the entire population of Wellington was watching, he pulled her into his arms and kissed her.

She should have been embarrassed. The thought flickered through Lillie's mind, but only for a second. Shamelessly she twined her arms around Tom's neck and deepened the kiss, tasting rather than feeling the smile that tugged at his mouth.

A few of the more prudish ladies of the town—Miss Taylor among them—gasped with horror, and Lillie was certain she heard Margaret Johnson sob out loud, but the sounds were soon overpowered by a hearty ovation.

"All aboard!"

The conductor's voice broke through the pandemonium, and Tom reluctantly pulled away. He motioned to Anthony to come say goodbye, and the boy ran up the steps. Hoping to make him feel grown-up, Tom shook Anthony's hand, then, deciding to make himself feel better, he also gave him a quick hug and a hispered message to take care of Lillie.

With another wave at the crowd Tom motioned to Danny get on the train.

Danny shook his head, baffled by it all, and climbed aboard. om was about to follow suit. At the last moment he hurried ack to Lillie's side.

"Will you think about me every day we're apart?"

Lillie was feeling lightheaded and giddy. "No." She answered is question with a stifled laugh. Before Tom could say anying, she put one finger to his lips. "I will not think of you very day," she told him. "I will think of you every minute. that good enough?"

"Better and better." Tom looked as if he might kiss her gain. Another call from the conductor stopped him.

Just as he climbed onto the train, it gave a groan of protest nd began to move slowly from the station.

"Remember what I said last night?" Tom called to Lillie. By the time I get back here, I'll be a raving lunatic!"

Lillie laughed and waved. "And this raving lunatic," she romised, "will be right here waiting for you."

Danny fell asleep not twenty minutes into the trip, his head gainst the plush upholstery of their first-class compartment.

Tom sat back and sighed, grateful for the silence. He watched ie familiar scenery, from town to sprawling farmlands, roll by ast the window.

It was a few minutes before he remembered the envelope illie had given him at the station. Pulling it out of his pocket, 'om flipped it over, ran his finger under the flap, and tipped he contents into his hand.

A single item fell, face down, into his right hand, but he lidn't have to turn it over to know it was a cabinet card. The mall photographic portraits were wildly popular, and he'd een Lillie prepare dozens of them in the last few months. 'his one was mounted on the same heavy card stock she used o mount all her cabinet cards—Tom fingered the paper—and t had the same notice printed across the back in looping gold etters: "Valentine Photography Studio, Wellington, Ohio."

Tom flipped over the card. The photograph was, as usu mounted in the center. It was bordered in red, as were the cabinet card photos Lillie sold. This particular one, f whatever reason, had another added border, a band of shi gold that marched around the picture in neat, square lines un it came to the corners. There, it spiraled and curled in a patte as spirited as the last smile Lillie had given him as Tom's tra pulled out of the station.

Tom glanced at the picture mounted in the center of the ca and his bemused smile turned into one of amazement. It w a photograph of the painting of Flossie that hung in Lillie parlor, and for a moment he wondered why she would ha given it to him or what she had meant when she said the pictu was her answer to his marriage proposal.

Tom tipped the picture toward the light. Another, mo careful, look answered his questions.

It was not Flossie in the photograph, but Lillie. Lilli reclining on a plush sofa. Lillie, with her hair down arou her shoulders. Lillie, with her skin glistening in the light.

Tom's smile widened into one of utter delight.

The picture was small, not larger than six inches or so fro side to side, and on passing glance it might have been take for nothing more than a wonderfully engaging portrait.

Tom knew better.

Only Tom knew that Lillie's loose, flowing hair conceal her bare shoulders. Only Tom knew that the potted palms th had been artfully arranged around the sofa hid Lillie's nak backside.

"Naked as the day you were born!"

Tom spoke the words beneath his breath, remembering ho he'd asked Lillie for the picture as they lay together in her b brass bed.

"And where would you keep such a picture?"

He could still hear the incredulity in Lillie's voice, still s her expression, surprised, and overwhelmed, and just a litt flattered.

"Right here." Pressing his hand to his breast pocket, To repeated the answer he'd given her that rainy evening. "Rig

re next to my heart, where it will remind me that you'll
vays be waiting for me."

He looked at the photo once more.

Lillie was looking directly at the camera, her eyes sparkling
th mischief and the suggestion of a secret invitation meant
Tom alone.

Tom threw his head back and laughed out loud.

It was going to be a very long three weeks.

If you enjoyed this book, take advantage of this special offer. Subscribe now and...

Get a
Historical

No Obligation

FREE

Romance

(a $4.50 value)

Send in the Coupon Below

To get your FREE historical romance and start saving, fill out the coupon below and mail it today. As soon as we receive it we'll send you your FREE Book along with your first month's selections.

Mail To: **True Value Home Subscription Services, Inc. P.O. Box 5235**
120 Brighton Road, Clifton, New Jersey 07015-5235

YES! I want to start previewing the very best historical romances being published today. Send me my FREE book along with the first month's selections. I understand that I may look them over FREE for 10 days. If I'm not absolutely delighted I may return them and owe nothing. Otherwise I will pay the low price of just $4.00 each; a total $16.00 (at *least* an $18.00 value) and save at least $2.00. Then each month I will receive four brand new novels to preview as soon as they are published for the same low price. I can always return a shipment and I may cancel this subscription at any time with no obligation to buy even a single book. In any event the FREE book is mine to keep regardless.

Name		
Street Address		Apt. No.
City	State	Zip Code
Telephone		
Signature		

(if under 18 parent or guardian must sign)

901